The Brothers Grimm
101 Fairy Tales

Word Cloud Classics

The Brothers Grimm
101 Fairy Tales

Translation by Margaret Hunt

CANTERBURY CLASSICS
San Diego

All correspondence concerning the content of this book should be addressed to: Canterbury Classics
10350 Barnes Canyon Road, Suite 100
San Diego, CA 92121

Library of Congress Cataloging-in-Publication Data

Kinder-und Hausmärchen. English.
  The Brothers Grimm : 101 fairy tales / Jacob & Wilhelm Grimm.
    p. cm.
  ISBN 978-1-60710-557-2 -- ISBN 1-60710-557-8
1. Fairy tales--Germany. I. Grimm, Jacob, 1785-1863. II. Grimm, Wilhelm, 1786-1859.

GR166.K5312 2012
398.20943--dc23

2011052752

PRINTED IN CHINA

6 7 8 9 10 18 17 16 15 14

CONTENTS

1. THE FROG-KING,
OR IRON HENRY

In old times when wishing still helped one, there lived a king whose daughters were all beautiful, but the youngest was so beautiful that the sun itself, which has seen so much, was astonished whenever it shone in her face. Close by the King's castle lay a great dark forest, and under an old lime tree in the forest was a well, and when the day was very warm, the King's child went out into the forest and sat down by the side of the cool fountain, and when she was bored she took a golden ball, and threw it up on high and caught it, and this ball was her favorite plaything.

Now it so happened that on one occasion the princess's golden ball did not fall into the little hand which she was holding up for it, but on to the ground beyond, and rolled straight into the water. The King's daughter followed it with her eyes, but it vanished, and the well was deep, so deep that the bottom could not be seen. At this she began to cry, and cried louder and louder, and could not be comforted.

And as she thus lamented someone said to her, "What ails you, King's daughter? Your tears would melt a heart of stone."

She looked round to the side from where the voice came, and saw a frog stretching forth its thick, ugly head from the water. "Ah! Old water-splasher, is it you?" said she; "I am weeping for my golden ball, which has fallen into the well."

"Be quiet, and do not weep," answered the frog, "I can help you, but what will you give me if I bring your plaything up again?"

"Whatever you will have, dear frog," said she—"My clothes, my pearls and jewels, and even the golden crown which I am wearing."

The frog answered, "I do not care for your clothes, your pearls and jewels, or your golden crown, but if you will love me and let me be your companion and playmate, and sit by you at your little table, and eat off your little golden plate, and drink out of your little cup, and sleep in your little bed—if you will promise me this I will go down below, and bring you your golden ball up again."

"Oh yes," said she, "I promise you all you wish, if you will but bring me my ball back again." She, however, thought, "How the silly frog does talk! He lives in the water with the other frogs, and croaks, and can be no companion to any human being!"

But the frog when he had received this promise, put his head into the water and sank down, and in a short while came swimming up again with the ball in his mouth, and threw it on the grass. The King's daughter was delighted to see her pretty plaything once more, and picked it up, and ran away with it.

"Wait, wait," said the frog. "Take me with you. I can't run as you can."

But what did it avail him to scream his *croak, croak,* after her, as loudly as he could? She did not listen to it, but ran home and soon forgot the poor frog, who was forced to go back into his well again.

The next day when she had seated herself at table with the King and all the courtiers, and was eating from her little golden plate, something came creeping *splish splash, splish splash,* up the marble staircase, and when it had got to the top, it knocked at the door and cried, "Princess, youngest princess, open the door for me."

She ran to see who was outside, but when she opened the door, there sat the frog in front of it. Then she slammed the door, in great haste, sat down to dinner again, and was quite frightened. The King saw plainly that her heart was beating violently, and said, "My child, what are you so afraid of? Is there perchance a giant outside who wants to carry you away?"

"Ah, no," replied she. "It is no giant but a disgusting frog."

"What does a frog want with you?"

"Ah, dear father, yesterday as I was in the forest sitting by the well, playing, my golden ball fell into the water. And because I cried so, the frog brought it out again for me, and because he so insisted, I promised him he should be my companion, but I never thought he would be able to come out of his water! And now he is outside there, and wants to come in to me."

In the meantime it knocked a second time, and cried,

> "Princess! Youngest princess!
> Open the door for me!
> Do you not know what you said to me
> Yesterday by the cool waters of the fountain?
> Princess, youngest princess!
> Open the door for me!"

Then said the King, "That which you have promised you must perform. Go and let him in."

She went and opened the door, and the frog hopped in and followed her, step by step, to her chair. There he sat and cried, "Lift me up beside you." She delayed, until at last the King commanded her to do it. When the frog was once on the chair he wanted to be on the table, and when he was on the table he said, "Now, push your little golden plate nearer to me that we may eat together." She did this, but it was easy to see that she did not do it willingly. The frog enjoyed what he ate, but almost every mouthful she took choked her. At length he said, "I have eaten and am satisfied; now I am tired, carry me into your little room and make your little silken bed ready, and we will both lie down and go to sleep."

The King's daughter began to cry, for she was afraid of the cold frog which she did not like to touch, and which was now to sleep in her pretty, clean little bed. But the King grew angry and said, "He who helped you when you were in trouble ought not be despised by you afterwards."

So she took hold of the frog with two fingers, carried him upstairs, and put him in a corner. But when she was in bed he crept to her and said, "I am tired, I want to sleep as well as you, lift me up or I will tell your father."

Then she was terribly angry, and took him up and threw him with all her might against the wall. "Now, you will be quiet, odious frog," said she.

But when he fell down he was no frog but a King's son with beautiful kind eyes. And it came to pass that, with her father's consent, he became her dear companion and husband. He told her how he had been bewitched by a wicked witch, and how no one could have delivered him from the well but herself, and that tomorrow they would go together into his Kingdom. Then they went to sleep, and next morning when the sun awoke them, a carriage came driving up with eight white horses, which had white ostrich feathers on their heads, and were harnessed with golden chains, and behind stood the young King's servant Faithful Henry. Faithful Henry had been so unhappy when his master was changed into a frog, that he had caused three iron bands to be laid round his heart, lest it should burst with grief and sadness. The carriage was to conduct the young King into his Kingdom. Faithful Henry helped them both in, and placed himself behind again, and was full of joy because of this deliverance. And when they had driven a part of the way the King's son heard a cracking behind him as if something had broken. So he turned round and cried, "Henry, the carriage is breaking."

"No, master, it is not the carriage. It is a band from my heart, which was put there in my great pain when you were a frog and imprisoned in the well." Again and once again while they were on their way something cracked, and each time the King's son thought the carriage was breaking; but it was only the bands which were springing from the heart of faithful Henry because his master was set free and was happy.

2. CAT AND MOUSE IN PARTNERSHIP

A certain cat had made the acquaintance of a mouse, and had said so much to her about the great love and friendship she felt for her, that at length the mouse agreed that they should live and keep house together. "But we must make a provision for winter, or else we shall suffer from hunger," said the cat, "and you, little mouse, cannot venture everywhere, or you will be caught in a trap some day." The good advice was followed, and a pot of fat was bought, but they did not know where to put it. At length, after much consideration, the cat said, "I know no place where it will be better stored up than in the church, for no one dares take anything away from there. We will set it beneath the altar, and not touch it until we are really in need of it." So the pot was placed in safety, but it was not long before the cat had a great yearning for it, and said to the mouse, "I want to tell you something, little mouse; my cousin has brought a little son into the world, and has asked me to be godmother; he is white with brown spots, and I am to hold him over the font at the christening. Let me go out today, and you look after the house by yourself."

"Yes, yes," answered the mouse, "by all means go, and if you get anything very good, think of me, I should like a drop of sweet red christening wine, too."

All this, however, was untrue; the cat had no cousin, and had not been asked to be godmother. She went straight to the church, stole to the pot of fat, began to lick at it, and licked the top of the fat off. Then she took a walk upon the roofs of the town, looked out for opportunities, and then stretched herself in the sun, and licked her lips whenever she thought of the pot of fat, and not until it was evening did she return home.

"Well, here you are again," said the mouse, "no doubt you have had a merry day."

"All went off well," answered the cat.

"What name did they give the child?"

"Top off!" said the cat quite coolly.

"Top off!" cried the mouse, "that is a very odd and uncommon name, is it a usual one in your family?"

"What does it matter?" said the cat. "It is no worse than Crumb-stealer, as your god-children are called."

Before long the cat was seized by another fit of longing. She said to the mouse, "You must do me a favor, and once more manage the house for a day alone. I am again asked to be godmother, and, as the child has a white ring round its neck, I cannot refuse." The good mouse consented, but the cat crept behind the town walls to the church, and devoured half the pot of fat. "Nothing ever seems so good as what one keeps to oneself," said she, and was quite satisfied with her day's work.

When she went home the mouse inquired, "And what was this child christened?"

"Half-done," answered the cat.

"Half-done! What are you saying? I never heard the name in my life, I'll wager anything it is not in the calendar of saints!"

The cat's mouth soon began to water for some more licking. "All good things go in threes," said she, "I am asked to stand godmother again. The child is quite black, only it has white paws, but with that exception, it has not a single white hair on its whole body; this only happens once every few years, you will let me go, won't you?"

"Top-off! Half-done!" answered the mouse. "They are such odd names, they make me very thoughtful."

"You sit at home," said the cat, "in your dark-grey fur coat and long tail, and are filled with fancies, that's because you do not go out in the daytime." During the cat's absence the mouse cleaned the house, and put it in order but the greedy cat entirely emptied the pot of fat. "When everything is eaten up one has some peace," said she to herself, and well filled and fat she did not return home till night. The mouse at once asked what name had been given to the third child. "It will not please you more than the others," said the cat. "He is called All-gone."

"All-gone," cried the mouse, "that is the most suspicious name of all! I have never seen it in print. All-gone; what can that mean?" and she shook her head, curled herself up, and lay down to sleep.

From this time forth no one invited the cat to be godmother, but when the winter had come and there was no longer anything to be found outside, the mouse thought of their provision, and said, "Come cat, we will go to our pot of fat which we have stored up for ourselves—we shall enjoy that."

"Yes," answered the cat, "you will enjoy it as much as you would enjoy sticking that dainty tongue of yours out of the window." They set out on their way, but when they arrived, the pot of fat certainly was still in its place, but it was empty.

"Alas!" said the mouse. "Now I see what has happened, now it comes to light! You are a true friend! You have devoured all when you were standing godmother. First top off, then half done, then—"

"Will you hold your tongue," cried the cat, "one word more and I will eat you too."

"All gone" was already on the poor mouse's lips; scarcely had she spoken it before the cat sprang on her, seized her, and swallowed her down. And that is the way of the world.

3. OUR LADY'S CHILD

Near a great forest dwelt a woodcutter with his wife, who had an only child, a little girl three years old. They were so poor, however, that they no longer had daily bread, and did not know how to get food for her. One morning the woodcutter went out sorrowfully to his work in the forest, and while he was cutting wood, suddenly there stood before him a tall and beautiful woman with a crown of shining stars on her head, who said to him, "I am the Virgin Mary, mother of the child Jesus. You are poor and needy, bring your child to me, I will take her with me and be her mother, and care for her." The woodcutter obeyed, brought his child, and gave her to the Virgin Mary, who took her up to heaven with her. There the child fared well, ate sugar-cakes, and drank sweet milk, and her clothes were of gold, and the little angels played with her. And when she was fourteen years of age, the Virgin Mary called her one day and said, "Dear child, I am about to make a long journey, so take into your keeping the keys of the thirteen doors of heaven. Twelve of these you may open, and behold the glory which is within them, but the thirteenth, to which this little key belongs, is forbidden. Beware of opening it, or you will bring misery on yourself." The girl promised to be obedient, and when the Virgin Mary was gone, she began to examine the dwellings of the kingdom of heaven. Each day she opened one of them, until she had made the round of the twelve. In each of them sat one of the Apostles in the midst of a great light, and she rejoiced in all the magnificence and splendor, and the little angels who always accompanied her rejoiced with her. Then the forbidden door alone remained, and she felt a great desire to know what could be hidden behind it, and said to the angels, "I will not quite open it, and I will not go inside it, but I will unlock it so that we can just see a little through the opening."

"Oh no," said the little angels, "that would be a sin. The Virgin Mary has forbidden it, and it might easily cause you unhappiness."

Then she was silent, but the desire in her heart was not stilled, but gnawed there and tormented her, and let her have no rest. And once when the angels had all gone out, she thought, "Now I am quite alone, and I could peep in. If I do it, no one will ever know." She sought out the key, and when she had got it in her hand, she put it in the lock, and when she had put it in, she turned it round as well. Then the door sprang open, and she saw there the Trinity sitting in fire and splendor. She stayed there awhile, and looked at everything in amazement; then she touched the light a little with her finger, and her finger became quite golden. Immediately a great fear fell on her. She shut the door violently, and ran away. Her terror too would not quit her, let her do what she might, and her heart beat continually and would not be still; the gold too stayed on her finger, and would not go away, no matter how much she rubbed it and washed it.

It was not long before the Virgin Mary came back from her journey. She called the girl before her, and asked to have the keys of heaven back. When the maiden gave her the bunch, the Virgin looked into her eyes and said, "Have you not opened the thirteenth door also?"

"No," she replied.

Then she laid her hand on the girl's heart, and felt how it beat and beat, and saw right well that she had disobeyed her order and had opened the door. Then she said once again, "Are you certain that you have not done it?"

"Yes," said the girl, for the second time.

Then she perceived the finger which had become golden from touching the fire of heaven, and saw well that the child had sinned, and said for the third time "Have you not done it?"

"No," said the girl for the third time.

Then said the Virgin Mary, "You have not obeyed me, and besides that you have lied; you are no longer worthy to be in heaven."

Then the girl fell into a deep sleep, and when she awoke she lay on the earth below, and in the midst of a wilderness. She wanted to cry out, but she could bring forth no sound. She sprang up and wanted to run away, but wherever she turned herself, she was continually held back by thick hedges of thorns through which she could not break. In the desert in which she was imprisoned, there stood an old hollow tree, and this had to be her dwelling-place. Into this she crept when night came, and here she slept. Here, too, she found a shelter from storm and rain, but it was a miserable life, and bitterly did she weep when she remembered how happy she had been in heaven, and how the angels had played with her. Roots and wild berries were her only food, and for these she searched as far as she could go. In the autumn she picked up the fallen nuts and leaves, and carried them into the hole. The nuts were her food in winter, and when snow and ice came, she crept amongst the leaves like a poor little animal that she might not freeze. Before long her clothes were all torn, and one bit of them after another fell off her. As soon, however, as the sun shone warm again, she went out and sat in front of the tree, and her long hair covered her on all sides like a mantle. Thus she sat year after year, and felt the pain and the misery of the world.

One day, when the trees were once more clothed in fresh green, the King of the country was hunting in the forest, and followed a deer, and as it had fled into the thicket which shut in this part of the forest, he got off his horse, tore the bushes asunder, and cut himself a path with his sword. When he had at last forced his way through, he saw a wonderfully beautiful maiden sitting under the tree; and she sat there and was entirely covered with her golden hair down to her very feet. He stood still and looked at her full of surprise, then he spoke to her and said, "Who are you? Why are you sitting here in the wilderness?" But she gave no answer, for she could not open her mouth. The King continued, "Will you go with me to my castle?" Then she just nodded her head a little. The King took her in his arms, carried her to his horse, and rode home with her, and when he reached the royal castle he caused her to be dressed in beautiful garments, and gave her all things in abundance. Although she could not speak, she was still so beautiful and charming that he began to love her with all his heart, and it was not long before he married her.

After a year or so had passed, the Queen brought a son into the world. Thereupon the Virgin Mary appeared to her in the night when she lay in her bed alone, and said, "If you will tell the truth and confess that you did unlock the forbidden door, I will open your mouth and give you back your speech, but if you persevere in your sin, and deny obstinately, I will take your newborn child away with me."

Then the queen was permitted to answer, but she remained hard, and said, "No, I did not open the forbidden door;" and the Virgin Mary took the newborn child from her arms, and vanished with it. Next morning when the child was not to be found, it was whispered among the people that the Queen was a man-eater, and had killed her own child. She heard all this and could say nothing to the contrary, but the King would not believe it, for he loved her so much.

When a year had gone by the Queen again bore a son, and in the night the Virgin Mary again came to her, and said, "If you will confess that you opened the forbidden door, I will give you your child back and untie your tongue; but if you continue in sin and deny it, I will take away with me this new child also."

Then the Queen again said, "No, I did not open the forbidden door;" and the Virgin took the child out of her arms, and away with her to heaven. Next morning, when this child also had disappeared, the people declared quite loudly that the Queen had devoured it, and the King's councilors demanded that she should be brought to justice. The King, however, loved her so dearly that he would not believe it, and commanded the councilors under pain of death not to say any more about it.

The following year the Queen gave birth to a beautiful little daughter, and for the third time the Virgin Mary appeared to her in the night and said, "Follow me." She took the Queen by the hand and led her to heaven, and showed her there her two eldest children, who smiled at her, and were playing with the ball of the world. When the Queen rejoiced at this, the Virgin Mary said, "Is your heart not yet softened? If you will own that you opened the forbidden door, I will give you back your two little sons."

But for the third time the Queen answered, "No, I did not open the forbidden door." Then the Virgin let her sink down to earth once more, and took from her likewise her third child.

Next morning, when the loss was reported abroad, all the people cried loudly, "The Queen is a man-eater. She must be judged," and the King was no longer able to restrain his councilors.

Thereupon a trial was held, and as she could not answer, and defend herself, she was condemned to be burned alive. The wood was got together, and when she was fast bound to the stake, and the fire began to burn round about her, the hard ice of pride melted, her heart was moved by repentance, and she thought, "If I could but confess before my death that I opened the door." Then her voice came back to her, and she cried out loudly, "Yes, Mary, I did it;" and straight-away rain fell from the sky and extinguished the flames of fire, and a light broke forth above her, and the Virgin Mary descended with the two little sons by her side, and the newborn daughter in her arms.

She spoke kindly to her, and said, "He who repents his sin and acknowledges it, is forgiven." Then she gave her the three children, untied her tongue, and granted her happiness for her whole life.

4. THE STORY OF THE YOUTH
WHO WENT FORTH TO
LEARN WHAT FEAR WAS

A certain father had two sons, the elder of whom was smart and sensible, and could do everything, but the younger was stupid and could neither learn nor understand anything, and when people saw him they said, "There's a fellow who will give his father some trouble!"

When anything had to be done, it was always the elder who was forced to do it; but if his father asked him to fetch anything when it was late, or in the night-time, and the way led through the churchyard, or any other dismal place, he answered, "Oh, no, father, I'll not go there, it makes me shudder!" for he was afraid. Or when stories were told by the fire at night which made the flesh creep, the listeners sometimes said, "Oh, it makes us shudder!"

The younger sat in a corner and listened with the rest of them, and could not imagine what they could mean. "They are always saying 'it makes me shudder, it makes me shudder!' It does not make me shudder," thought he. "That, too, must be an art of which I understand nothing."

Now it came to pass that his father said to him one day, "Listen to me, you fellow in the corner there, you are growing tall and strong, and you too must learn something by which you can earn your living. Look how your brother works, but you do not even earn your salt."

"Well, father," he replied, "I am quite willing to learn something—indeed, if it could but be managed, I should like to learn how to shudder. I don't understand that at all yet."

The elder brother smiled when he heard that, and thought to himself, "Good God, what a blockhead that brother of mine is! He will never be good for anything as long as he lives. He who wants to be a sickle must bend himself early."

The father sighed, and answered him, "You shall soon learn what it is to shudder, but you will not earn your bread by that."

Soon after this the sexton came to the house on a visit, and the father bewailed his trouble, and told him how his younger son was so backward in every respect that he knew nothing and learned nothing. "Just think," said he, "when I asked him how he was going to earn his bread, he actually wanted to learn to shudder."

"If that be all," replied the sexton, "he can learn that with me. Send him to me, and I will soon polish him."

The father was glad to do it, for he thought, "It will train the boy a little." The sexton therefore took him into his house, and he had to ring the bell. After a day or two, the sexton awoke him at midnight, and bade him arise and go up into the church tower and ring the bell. "You shall soon learn what shuddering is," thought he, and secretly went there before him; and when the boy was at the top of the tower and turned round, and was just going to take hold of the bell rope, he saw a white figure standing on the stairs opposite the sounding hole.

"Who is there?" cried he, but the figure made no reply, and did not move or stir. "Give an answer," cried the boy, "or take yourself off, you have no business here at night."

The sexton, however, remained standing motionless that the boy might think he was a ghost. The boy cried a second time, "What do you want here?—Speak if you are an honest fellow, or I will throw you down the steps!" The sexton thought, "He can't intend to be as bad as his words," uttered no sound and stood as if he were made of stone. Then the boy called to him for the third time, and as that was also to no avail, he ran against him and pushed the ghost down the stairs, so that it fell down ten steps and remained lying there in a corner. Thereupon he rang the bell, went home, and without saying a word went to bed, and fell asleep.

The sexton's wife waited a long time for her husband, but he did not come back. At length she became uneasy, and wakened the boy, and asked, "Do you not know where my husband is? He climbed up the tower before you did."

"No, I don't know," replied the boy, "but someone was standing by the sounding hole on the other side of the steps, and as he would neither give an answer nor go away, I took him for a scoundrel, and threw him downstairs. Just go there and you will see if it was he. I should be sorry if it were." The woman ran away and found her husband, who was lying moaning in the corner, and had broken his leg.

She carried him down, and then with loud screams she hastened to the boy's father. "Your boy," cried she, "has been the cause of a great misfortune! He has thrown my husband down the steps and made him break his leg. Take the good-for-nothing fellow away from our house."

The father was terrified, and ran there and scolded the boy. "What wicked tricks are these?" said he, "The devil must have put this into your head."

"Father," he replied, "do listen to me. I am quite innocent. He was standing there by night like one who is intending to do some evil. I did not know who it was, and I warned him three times either to speak or to go away." "Ah," said the father, "I have nothing but unhappiness with you. Go out of my sight. I will see you no more."

"Yes, father, right willingly, wait only until it is day. Then I will go forth and learn how to shudder, and then I shall, at any rate, understand one art which will support me."

"Learn what you will," said the father, "It is all the same to me. Here are fifty talers for you. Take these and go into the wide world, and tell no one from where you come, and who is your father, for I have reason to be ashamed of you."

"Yes, father, it shall be as you will. If you desire nothing more than that, I can easily keep it in mind."

When day dawned, therefore, the boy put his fifty talers into his pocket, and went forth on the great highway, and continually said to himself, "If I could but shudder! If I could but shudder!"

Then a man approached who heard this conversation which the youth was holding with himself, and when they had walked a little farther to where they could see the gallows, the man said to him, "Look, there is the tree where seven men have married the ropemaker's daughter, and are now learning how to fly. Sit down below it, and wait till night comes, and you will soon learn how to shudder."

"If that is all that is wanted," answered the youth, "it is easily done; but if I learn how to shudder as fast as that, you shall have my fifty talers. Just come back to me early in the morning."

Then the youth went to the gallows, sat down below it, and waited till evening came. And as he was cold, he lighted himself a fire, but at midnight the wind blew so sharply that in spite of his fire, he could not get warm. And as the wind knocked the hanged men against each other, and they moved backwards and forwards, he thought to himself, "You shiver below by the fire, but how those up above must freeze and suffer!" And as he felt pity for them, he raised the ladder, and climbed up, unbound one of them after the other, and brought down all seven. Then he stirred the fire, blew it, and set them all round it to warm themselves. But they sat there and did not stir, and the fire caught their clothes. So he said, "Take care, or I will hang you up again." The dead men, however, did not hear, but were quite silent, and let their rags go on burning.

At this he grew angry, and said, "If you will not take care, I cannot help you, I will not be burnt with you," and he hung them up again each in his turn. Then he sat down by his fire and fell asleep, and the next morning the man came to him and wanted to have the fifty talers, and said, "Well, do you know how to shudder?"

"No," answered he, "how was I to get to know? Those fellows up there did not open their mouths, and were so stupid that they let the few old rags which they had on their bodies get burnt."

Then the man saw that he would not get the fifty talers that day, and went away saying, "One of this kind has never come my way before."

The youth likewise went his way, and once more began to mutter to himself, "Ah, if I could but shudder! Ah, if I could but shudder!"

A waggoner who was striding behind him heard that and asked, "Who are you?"

"I don't know," answered the youth.

Then the waggoner asked, "From where do you come?"

"I know not."

"Who is your father?"

"That I may not tell you."

"What is it that you are always muttering between your teeth?"

"Ah," replied the youth, "I do so wish I could shudder, but no one can teach me how to do it."

"Give up your foolish chatter," said the waggoner. "Come, go with me, I will see about a place for you."

The youth went with the waggoner, and in the evening they arrived at an inn where they wished to pass the night. Then at the entrance of the room the youth again said quite loudly, "If I could but shudder! If I could but shudder!"

The host who heard this laughed and said, "If that is your desire, there ought to be a good opportunity for you here."

"Ah, be silent," said the hostess, "so many inquisitive persons have already lost their lives, it would be a pity and a shame if such beautiful eyes as these should never see the daylight again."

But the youth said, "However difficult it may be, I will learn it and for this purpose I have journeyed forth." He let the host have no rest, until the latter told him that not far from there stood a haunted castle where anyone could very easily learn what shuddering was, if he would but sleep in it for three nights. The King had promised that he who would venture should have his daughter as wife, and she was the most beautiful maiden the sun shone on. Great treasures likewise lay in the castle which were guarded by evil spirits, and these treasures would then be freed, and would make a poor man rich enough. Already many men had gone into the castle, but as yet none had come out again. Then the youth went next morning to the King and said if he were allowed he would watch three nights in the haunted castle.

The King looked at him, and as the youth pleased him, he said, "You may ask for three things to take into the castle with you, but they must be things without life."

Then he answered, "Then I ask for a fire, a turning lathe, and a cuttingboard with the knife." The King had these things carried into the castle for him during the day. When night was drawing near, the youth went up and made himself a bright fire in one of the rooms, placed the cuttingboard and knife beside it, and seated himself by the turning-lathe. "Ah, if I could but shudder!" said he, "but I shall not learn it here either."

Towards midnight he was about to poke his fire, and as he was blowing it, something cried suddenly from one corner, "Au, miau! How cold we are!"

"You simpletons!" cried he, "What are you crying about? If you are cold, come and take a seat by the fire and warm yourselves."

And when he had said that, two great black cats came with one tremendous leap and sat down on each side of him, and looked savagely at him with their fiery eyes. After a short time, when they had warmed themselves, they said, "Comrade, shall we have a game at cards?"

"Why not?" he replied, "But just show me your paws." Then they stretched out their claws. "Oh," said he, "what long nails you have! Wait, I must first cut them for you." Thereupon he seized them by the throats, put them on the cuttingboard and screwed their feet fast. "I have looked at your fingers," said he, "and my fancy for card-playing has gone," and he struck them dead and threw them out into the water. But when he had made away with these two, and was about to sit down again by his fire, out from every hole and corner came black cats and black dogs with red-hot chains, and more and more of them came until he could no longer stir, and they yelled horribly, and got on his fire, pulled it to pieces, and tried to put it out. He watched them for a while quietly, but at last when they were going too far, he seized his cutting-knife, and cried, "Away with ye, vermin," and began to cut them down. Part of them ran away, but the others he killed, and threw out into the fish-pond.

When he came back he fanned the embers of his fire again and warmed himself. And as he thus sat, his eyes would keep open no longer, and he felt a desire to sleep. Then he looked round and saw a great bed in the corner. "That is the very thing for me," said he, and got into it. When he was just going to shut his eyes, however, the bed began to move of its own accord, and went over the whole of the castle.

"That's right," said he, "but go faster." Then the bed rolled on as if six horses were harnessed to it, up and down, over thresholds and steps, but suddenly hop, hop, it turned over upside down, and lay on him like a mountain. But he threw quilts and pillows up in the air, got out and said, "Now anyone who likes, may drive," and lay down by his fire, and slept till it was day.

In the morning the King came, and when he saw him lying there on the ground, he thought the evil spirits had killed him and he was dead. Then said he, "After all it is a pity—he is a handsome man."

The youth heard it, got up, and said, "It has not come to that yet." Then the King was astonished, but very glad, and asked how he had fared. "Very well indeed," answered he; "one night is past, the two others will get over likewise."

Then he went to the innkeeper, who opened his eyes very wide, and said, "I never expected to see you alive again! Have you learned how to shudder yet?"

"No," said he, "it is all in vain. If someone would but tell me."

The second night he again went up into the old castle, sat down by the fire, and once more began his old song, "If I could but shudder." When midnight came, an uproar and noise of tumbling about was heard; at first it was low, but it grew louder and louder. Then it was quiet for awhile, and at length with a loud scream, half a man came down the chimney and fell before him.

"Hollo!" cried he, "Another half belongs to this. This is too little!"

Then the uproar began again, there was a roaring and howling, and the other half fell down likewise.

"Wait," said the youth, "I will just blow up the fire a little for you." When he had done that and looked round again, the two pieces were joined together, and a frightful man was sitting in his place. "That is no part of our bargain," said the youth, "the bench is mine." The man wanted to push him away; the youth, however, would not allow that, but thrust him off with all his strength, and seated himself again in his own place. Then still more men fell down, one after the other; they brought nine dead men's legs and two skulls, and set them up and played at nine-pins with them. The youth also wanted to play and said, "Can I join you?"

"Yes, if you have any money."

"Money enough," replied he, "but your balls are not quite round." Then he took the skulls and put them in the lathe and turned them till they were round. "There, now, they will roll better!" said he. "Hurrah! Now it goes merrily!" He played with them and lost some of his money, but when it struck twelve, everything vanished from his sight. He lay down and quietly fell asleep.

Next morning the King came to inquire after him. "How has it fared with you this time?" asked he.

"I have been playing at nine-pins," he answered, "and have lost a couple of farthings."

"Have you not shuddered then?"

"Eh, what?" said he, "I have made merry. If I did but know what it was to shudder!"

The third night he sat down again on his bench and said quite sadly, "If I could but shudder." When it grew late, six tall men came in and brought a coffin. Then said he, "Ha, ha, that is certainly my little cousin, who died only a few days ago," and he beckoned with his finger, and cried, "Come, little cousin, come." They placed the coffin on the ground, but he went to it and took the lid off, and a dead man lay therein. He felt his face, but it was cold as ice. "Stop," said he, "I will warm you a little," and went to the fire and warmed his hand and laid it on the dead man's face, but he remained cold. Then he took him out, and sat down by the fire and laid him on his breast and rubbed his arms that the blood might circulate again. As this also did no good, he thought to himself, "When two people lie in bed together, they warm each other," and carried him to the bed, covered him over and lay down by him. After a short time the dead man became warm too, and began to move. Then said the youth, "See, little cousin, have I not warmed you?" The dead man, however, got up and cried, "Now I will strangle you."

"What!" said he, "Is that the way you thank me? You shall at once go into your coffin again," and he took him up, threw him into it, and shut the lid. Then came the six men and carried him away again. "I cannot manage to shudder," said he. "I shall never learn it here as long as I live."

Then a man entered who was taller than all others, and looked terrible. He was old, however, and had a long white beard. "You wretch," cried he, "you shall soon learn what it is to shudder, for you shall die."

"Not so fast," replied the youth.

"If I am to die, I shall have to have a say in it."

"I will soon seize you," said the fiend.

"Softly, softly, do not talk so big. I am as strong as you are, and perhaps even stronger."

"We shall see," said the old man. "If you are stronger, I will let you go—come, we will try." Then he led him by dark passages to a smith's forge, took an axe, and with one blow struck an anvil into the ground.

"I can do better than that," said the youth, and went to the other anvil. The old man placed himself near and wanted to look on, and his white beard hung down. Then the youth seized the axe, split the anvil with one blow, and struck the old man's beard in with it. "Now I have you," said the youth. "Now it is you who will have to die." Then he seized an iron bar and beat the old man till he moaned and entreated him to stop, and he would give him great riches. The youth drew out the axe and let him go.

The old man led him back into the castle, and in a cellar showed him three chests full of gold. "Of these," said he, "one part is for the poor, the other for the king, the third is yours."

In the meantime it struck twelve, and the spirit disappeared; the youth, therefore, was left in darkness. "I shall still be able to find my way out," said he, and felt about, found the way into the room, and slept there by his fire.

Next morning the King came and said, "Now you must have learned what shuddering is?"

"No," he answered; "what can it be? My dead cousin was here, and a bearded man came and showed me a great deal of money down below, but no one told me what it was to shudder."

"Then," said the King, "you have delivered the castle from enchantment, and shall marry my daughter."

"That is all very well," said he, "but still I do not know what it is to shudder."

Then the gold was brought up and the wedding celebrated; but however much the young king loved his wife, and however happy he was, he still said always, "If I could but shudder—if I could but shudder." And at last she was angry at this. Her waiting-maid said, "I will find a cure for him; he shall soon learn what it is to shudder." She went out to the stream which flowed through the garden, and had a whole bucketful of gudgeons brought to her. At night when the young king was sleeping, his wife was to draw the clothes off him and empty the bucketful of cold water with the gudgeons in it over him, so that the little fishes would sprawl about him. When this was done, he woke up and cried, "Oh, what makes me shudder so?—What makes me shudder so, dear wife? Ah! Now I know what it is to shudder!"

5. THE WOLF AND THE SEVEN LITTLE KIDS

There was once upon a time an old goat who had seven little kids, and loved them with all the love of a mother for her children. One day she wanted to go into the forest and fetch some food. So she called all seven to her and said, "Dear children, I have to go into the forest, be on your guard against the wolf; if he comes in, he will devour you all—skin, hair, and all. The wretch often disguises himself, but you will know him at once by his rough voice and his black feet."

The kids said, "Dear mother, we will take good care of ourselves; you may go away without any anxiety." Then the old one bleated, and went on her way with an easy mind.

It was not long before someone knocked at the door and called, "Open the door, dear children; your mother is here, and has brought something back with her for each of you."

But the little kids knew that it was the wolf, by the rough voice; "We will not open the door," cried they, "you are not our mother. She has a soft, pleasant voice, but your voice is rough; you are the wolf!"

Then the wolf went away to a shopkeeper and bought himself a great lump of chalk, ate this and made his voice soft with it. The he came back, knocked at the door of the house, and cried, "Open the door, dear children, your mother is here and has brought something back with her for each of you."

But the wolf had laid his black paws against the window, and the children saw them and cried, "We will not open the door, our mother has not black feet like you; you are the wolf."

Then the wolf ran to a baker and said, "I have hurt my feet, rub some dough over them for me." And when the baker had rubbed his feet over, he ran to the miller and said, "Strew some white meal over my feet for me." The miller thought to himself, "The wolf wants to deceive someone," and refused; but the wolf said, "If you will not do it, I will devour you." Then the miller was afraid, and made his paws white for him. Yes, that's how people are.

So now the wretch went for the third time to the door, knocked at it and said, "Open the door for me, children, your dear little mother has come home, and has brought everyone of you something back from the forest with her."

The little kids cried, "First show us your paws that we may know if you are our dear little mother." Then he put his paws in through the window, and when the kids saw that they were white, they believed that all he said was true, and opened the door. But who should come in but the wolf! They were terrified and wanted to hide themselves. One sprang under the table, the second into the bed, the third into the stove, the fourth into the kitchen, the fifth into the cupboard, the sixth under the washing-bowl, and the seventh into the clock-case. But the wolf found them, and used no great ceremony; one after the other he swallowed them down his throat. The youngest, who was in the clock-case, was the only one he did not find. When the wolf had satisfied his appetite he took himself off, laid himself down under a tree in the green meadow outside, and began to sleep.

Soon afterwards the old goat came home again from the forest. Ah! What a sight she saw there! The door stood wide open. The table, chairs, and benches were thrown down, the washing-bowl lay broken to pieces, and the quilts and pillows were pulled off the bed. She sought her children, but they were nowhere to be found. She called them one after another by name, but no one answered. At last, when she came to the youngest, a soft voice cried, "Dear mother, I am in the clock-case." She took the kid out, and it told her that the wolf had come and had eaten all the others. Then you may imagine how she wept over her poor children.

At length in her grief she went out, and the youngest kid ran with her. When they came to the meadow, there the wolf lay by the tree and snored so loud that the branches shook. She looked at him on every side and saw that something was moving and struggling in his gorged belly. "Ah, heavens," said she, "is it possible that my poor children whom he has swallowed down for his supper, can still be alive?" Then the kid had to run home and fetch scissors, and a needle and thread, and the goat cut open the monster's stomach, and hardly had she made one cut, than one little kid thrust its head out, and when she cut farther, all six sprang out one after another, and were all still alive, and had suffered no injury whatever, for in his greediness the monster had swallowed them down whole. What rejoicing there was! They embraced their dear mother, and jumped like a sailor at his wedding. The mother, however, said, "Now go and look for some big stones, and we will fill the wicked beast's stomach with them while he is still asleep." Then the seven kids dragged the stones there with all speed, and put as many of them into his stomach as they could get in; and the mother sewed him up again in the greatest haste, so that he was not aware of anything and never once stirred.

When the wolf at length had had his sleep out, he got on his legs, and as the stones in his stomach made him very thirsty, he wanted to go to a well to drink. But when he began to walk and move about, the stones in his stomach knocked against each other and rattled. Then cried he,

> "What rumbles and tumbles
> Against my poor bones?
> I thought 't was six kids,
> But it's naught but big stones."

And when he got to the well and stooped over the water and was just about to drink, the heavy stones made him fall in, and there was no help, but he had to drown miserably. When the seven kids saw that, they came running to the spot and cried aloud, "The wolf is dead! The wolf is dead!" and danced for joy round about the well with their mother.

6. FAITHFUL JOHN

There was once upon a time an old King who was ill, and thought to himself, "I am lying on what must be my deathbed." Then said he, "Tell Faithful John to come to me." Faithful John was his favorite servant, and was so called because he had for his whole life long been so true to him. Therefore when he came beside the bed, the King said to him, "Most faithful John, I feel my end approaching, and have no anxiety except about my son. He is still of tender age, and cannot always know how to guide himself. If you do not promise me to teach him everything that he ought to know, and to be his foster father, I cannot close my eyes in peace."

Then answered Faithful John, "I will not forsake him, and will serve him with fidelity, even if it should cost me my life."

At this, the old King said, "Now I die in comfort and peace." Then he added, "After my death, you shall show him the whole castle: all the chambers, halls, and vaults, and all the treasures which lie therein, but the last chamber in the long gallery, in which is the picture of the princess of the Golden Dwelling, you shall not show. If he sees that picture, he will fall violently in love with her, and will drop down in a swoon, and go through great danger for her sake; therefore you must preserve him from that." And when Faithful John had once more given his promise to the old King about this, the King said no more, but laid his head on his pillow, and died.

When the old King had been carried to his grave, Faithful John told the young King all that he had promised his father on his deathbed, and said, "This I will assuredly perform, and will be faithful to you as I have been faithful to him, even if it should cost me my life." When the mourning was over, Faithful John said to him, "It is now time that you should see your inheritance. I will show you your father's palace." Then he took him about everywhere, up and down, and let him see all the riches, and the magnificent apartments, only there was one room which he did not open, that in which hung the dangerous picture. The picture was, however, so placed that when the door was opened you looked straight on it, and it was so admirably painted that it seemed to breathe and live, and there was nothing more charming or more beautiful in the whole world.

The young King, however, plainly remarked that Faithful John always walked past this one door, and said, "Why do you never open this one for me?"

"There is something within it," he replied, "which would terrify you."

But the King answered, "I have seen all the palace, and I will know what is in this room also," and he went and tried to break open the door by force.

Then Faithful John held him back and said, "I promised your father before his death that you should not see that which is in this chamber, it might bring the greatest misfortune on you and on me."

"Ah, no," replied the young King, "if I do not go in, it will be my certain destruction. I should have no rest day or night until I had seen it with my own eyes. I shall not leave the place now until you have unlocked the door."

Then Faithful John saw that there was no help for it now, and with a heavy heart and many sighs, sought out the key from the great bunch. When he had opened the door, he went in first, and thought by standing before him he could hide the portrait so that the King should not see it in front of him, but to what avail? The King stood on tip-toe and saw it over his shoulder. And when he saw the portrait of the maiden, which was so magnificent and shone with gold and precious stones, he fell fainting to the ground. Faithful John took him up, carried him to his bed, and sorrowfully thought, "The misfortune has befallen us, Lord God, what will be the end of it?" Then he strengthened him with wine, until he came to himself again.

The first words the King said were, "Ah, the beautiful portrait! Whose is it?"

"That is the princess of the Golden Dwelling," answered Faithful John.

Then the King continued, "My love for her is so great, that if all the leaves on all the trees were tongues, they could not declare it. I will give my life to win her. You are my most faithful John, you must help me."

The faithful servant considered within himself for a long time how to set about the matter, for it was difficult even to obtain a sight of the King's daughter. At length he thought of a way, and said to the King, "Everything which she has about her is of gold—tables, chairs, dishes, glasses, bowls, and household furniture. Among your treasures are five tons of gold; let one of the goldsmiths of the Kingdom work these up into all manner of vessels and utensils, into all kinds of birds, wild beasts and strange animals, such as may please her, and we will go there with them and try our luck."

The King ordered all the goldsmiths to be brought to him, and they had to work night and day until at last the most splendid things were prepared. When everything was stowed on board a ship, Faithful John put on the clothing of a merchant, and the King was forced to do the same in order to make himself quite unrecognizable. Then they sailed across the sea, and sailed on until they came to the town where the princess of the Golden Dwelling resided.

Faithful John bade the King stay behind on the ship, and wait for him. "Perhaps I shall bring the princess with me," said he, "therefore see that everything is in order; have the golden vessels set out and the whole ship decorated." Then he gathered together in his apron all kinds of gold things, went on shore and walked straight to the royal palace. When he entered the courtyard of the palace, a beautiful girl was standing there by the well with two golden buckets in her hand, drawing water with them. And when she was just turning round to carry away the sparkling water she saw the stranger, and asked who he was. So he answered, "I am a merchant," and opened his apron, and let her look in.

Then she cried, "Oh, what beautiful gold things!" and put her pails down and looked at the golden wares one after the other. Then said the girl, "The princess must see these, she has such great pleasure in golden things that she will buy all you have." She took him by the hand and led him upstairs, for she was the waiting-maid.

When the King's daughter saw the wares, she was quite delighted and said, "They are so beautifully worked that I will buy them all from you."

But Faithful John said, "I am only the servant of a rich merchant. The things I have here are not to be compared with those my master has in his ship. They are the most beautiful and valuable things that have ever been made in gold." She wanted to have everything brought to her there, but he said, "There are so many of them that it would take a great many days to do that, and so many rooms would be required to exhibit them, that your house is not big enough."

Then her curiosity and longing were still more excited, until at last she said, "Take me to the ship, I will go there myself, and behold the treasures of your master."

On this Faithful John was quite delighted, and led her to the ship, and when the King saw her, he perceived that her beauty was even greater than the picture had represented it to be, and thought no other than that his heart would burst. Then she got into the ship, and the King led her within. Faithful John, however, remained behind with the pilot, and ordered the ship to be pushed off, saying, "Set all sails, till it fly like a bird in air."

Inside, however, the King showed her the golden vessels, everyone of them, and the wild beasts and strange animals. Many hours went by while she was seeing everything, and in her delight she did not observe that the ship was sailing away. After she had looked at the last piece, she thanked the merchant and wanted to go home, but when she came to the side of the ship, she saw that it was on the deep sea far from land, and hurrying onwards with all sails set. "Ah," cried she in her alarm, "I am betrayed! I am carried away and have fallen into the power of a merchant—I would rather die!"

The King, however, seized her hand, and said, "I am not a merchant. I am a king, and of no worse origin than you are, and if I have carried you away with subtlety, that has come to pass because of my exceeding great love for you. The first time that I looked on your portrait, I fell fainting to the ground." When the princess of the Golden Dwelling heard that, she was comforted, and her heart was inclined unto him, so that she willingly consented to be his wife.

It so happened, however, while they were sailing onwards over the deep sea, that Faithful John, who was sitting on the fore part of the vessel, making music, saw three ravens in the air, which came flying towards them. At this he stopped playing and listened to what they were saying to each other, for that he well understood. One cried, "Oh, there he is carrying home the princess of the Golden Dwelling."

"Yes," replied the second, "but he has not got her yet."

Said the third, "But he has got her, she is sitting beside him in the ship."

Then the first began again, and cried, "What good will that do him? When they reach land a chestnut horse will leap forward to meet him, and the prince will want to mount it, but if he does that, it will run away with him, and rise up into the air with him, and he will never see his maiden again."

Said the second, "But is there no escape?"

"Oh, yes, if anyone else gets on it swiftly, and takes out the pistol which must be in its holster, and shoots the horse dead with it, the young King is saved. But who knows that? And whoever does know it, and tells it to him, will be turned to stone from the toe to the knee."

Then said the second, "I know more than that; even if the horse is killed, the young King will still not keep his bride. When they go into the castle together, a wrought bridal garment will be lying there in a dish, and looking as if it were woven of gold and silver; it is, however, nothing but sulfur and pitch, and if he puts it on, it will burn him to the very bone and marrow."

Said the third, "Is there no escape at all?"

"Oh, yes," replied the second, "if anyone with gloves on seizes the garment and throws it into the fire and burns it, the young King will be saved. But what's the good in that? Whoever knows it and tells it to him, half his body will become stone from the knee to the heart."

Then said the third, "I know still more; even if the bridal garment be burnt, the young King will still not have his bride. After the wedding, when the dancing begins and the young queen is dancing, she will suddenly turn pale and fall down as if dead, and if someone does not lift her up and suck three drops of blood from her right breast and spit them out again, she will die. But if anyone who knows that were to declare it, he would become stone from the crown of his head to the sole of his foot."

When the ravens had spoken of this together, they flew onwards, and Faithful John had well understood everything, but from that time forth he became quiet and sad, for if he concealed what he had heard, his master would suffer, and if he revealed it to him, he himself must sacrifice his life. At length, however, he said to himself, "I will save my master, even if it brings destruction on myself."

When therefore they came to shore, all happened as had been foretold by the ravens, and a magnificent chestnut horse sprang forward. "Good," said the King, "he shall carry me to my palace," and was about to mount it when Faithful John got before him, jumped quickly on it, drew the pistol out of the holster, and shot the horse.

Then the other attendants of the King, who after all were not very fond of Faithful John, cried, "How shameful to kill the beautiful animal that was to have carried the King to his palace."

But the King said, "Hold your peace and leave him alone, he is my most faithful John. Who knows what good may come of his actions?" They went into the palace, and in the hall there stood a dish, and inside lay the bridal garment looking no otherwise than as if it were made of gold and silver. The young King went towards it and was about to take hold of it, but Faithful John pushed him away, seized it with gloves on, carried it quickly to the fire and burned it.

The other attendants again began to murmur, and said, "Behold, now he is even burning the King's bridal garment!"

But the young King said, "Who knows what good he may have done. Leave him alone, he is my most faithful John."

And now the wedding was solemnized: the dance began, and the bride also took part in it; then Faithful John was watchful and looked into her face, and suddenly she turned pale and fell to the ground, as if she were dead. At this he ran hastily to her, lifted her up and bore her into a chamber—then he laid her down, and knelt and sucked the three drops of blood from her right breast, and spat them out. Immediately she breathed again and recovered herself, but the young King had seen this, and being ignorant why Faithful John had done it, was angry and cried, "Throw him into a dungeon."

Next morning Faithful John was condemned, and led to the gallows, and when he stood up high, and was about to be executed, he said, "Everyone who has to die is permitted before his end to make one last speech; may I too claim the right?"

"Yes," answered the King, "it shall be granted."

Then said Faithful John, "I am unjustly condemned, and have always been true to you," and he related how he had hearkened to the conversation of the ravens when at sea, and how he had been obliged to do all these things in order to save his master.

Then cried the King, "Oh, my most faithful John. Pardon, pardon— bring him down." But as Faithful John spoke the last word he had fallen down lifeless and become a stone.

At this the King and the Queen suffered great anguish, and the King said, "Ah, how ill I have requited great fidelity!" and ordered the stone figure to be taken up and placed in his bedroom beside his bed. And as often as he looked at it he wept and said, "Ah, if I could bring you to life again, my most faithful John." Some time passed and the Queen bore twins, two sons who grew fast and were her delight. Once when the Queen was at church and the two children were sitting playing beside their father, the latter full of grief again looked at the stone figure, sighed and said, "Ah, if I could but bring you to life again, my most faithful John."

Then the stone began to speak and said, "You can bring me to life again *if* you will *sacrifice* what is dearest to you."

Then cried the King, "I will give everything I have in the world for you."

The stone continued, "If you will cut off the heads of your two children with your own hand, and sprinkle me with their blood, I shall be restored to life."

The King was terrified when he heard that he himself must kill his dearest children, but he thought of Faithful John's great fidelity, and how he had died for him, drew his sword, and with his own hand cut off the children's heads. And when he had smeared the stone with their blood, life returned to it, and Faithful John stood once more safe and healthy before him. He said to the King, "Your fidelity shall not go unrewarded," and took the heads of the children, put them on again, and rubbed the wounds with their blood, at which they became whole again immediately, and jumped about, and went on playing as if nothing had happened.

Then the King was full of joy, and when he saw the Queen coming he hid Faithful John and the two children in a great cupboard. When she entered, he said to her, "Have you been praying in the church?"

"Yes," answered she, "but I have constantly been thinking of Faithful John and what misfortune has befallen him through us."

Then said he, "Dear wife, we can give him his life again, but it will cost us our two little sons, whom we must sacrifice."

The Queen turned pale, and her heart was full of terror, but she said, "We owe it to him, for his great fidelity."

Then the King rejoiced that she thought as he had thought, and went and opened the cupboard, and brought forth Faithful John and the children, and said, "God be praised, he is saved, and we have our little sons again also," and told her how everything had occurred. Then they dwelt together in much happiness until their death.

7. THE GOOD BARGAIN

There was once a peasant who had driven his cow to the fair, and sold her for seven talers. On the way home he had to pass a pond, and already from afar he heard the frogs crying, "Aik, aik, aik, aik."

"Well," said he to himself, "they are talking without rhyme or reason, it is seven that I have received, not eight." When he got to the water, he cried to them, "Stupid animals that you are! Don't you know better than that? It is seven talers and not eight."

The frogs, however, stood to their "aik aik, aik, aik."

"Come, then, if you won't believe it, I can count it out to you." And he took his money out of his pocket and counted out the seven talers, always reckoning twenty-four groschen to a taler. The frogs, however, paid no attention to his reckoning, but still cried, "aik, aik, aik, aik."

"What," cried the peasant, quite angry, "since you are determined to know better than I, count it yourselves," and threw all the money into the water to them. He stood still and wanted to wait until they were done and had brought him his own again, but the frogs maintained their opinion and cried continually, "aik, aik, aik, aik," and besides that, did not throw the money out again. He still waited a long while until evening came and he was forced to go home. Then he abused the frogs and cried, "You water-splashers, you thick-heads, you goggle-eyes, you have great mouths and can screech till you hurt one's ears, but you cannot count seven talers! Do you think I'm going to stand here till you get done?" And with that he went away, but the frogs still cried, "aik, aik, aik, aik," after him till he went home quite angry.

After a while he bought another cow, which he killed, and he made the calculation that if he sold the meat well he might gain as much as the two cows were worth, and still have the hide in the bargain. When he got to the town with the meat, a great troop of dogs were gathered together in front of the gate, with a large greyhound at the head of them, which jumped at the meat, snuffed at it, and barked, "Wow, wow, wow."

As there was no stopping him, the peasant said to him, "Yes, yes, I know quite well that you are saying, 'wow, wow, wow,' because you want some of the meat; but I should fare badly if I were to give it to you."

The dog, however, answered nothing but "wow, wow."

"Will you promise not to devour it all then, and will you vouch for your companions?"

"Wow, wow, wow," said the dog.

"Well, if you insist on it, I will leave it for you. I know you well, and know who your master is, but this I tell you: I must have my money in three days or else it will go badly for you; you must bring it out to me." With that he unloaded the meat and turned back. The dogs fell upon it and loudly barked, "wow, wow."

The countryman, who heard them from afar, said to himself, "Now they all want some, but the big one is responsible to me for it."

When three days had passed, the countryman thought, "Tonight my money will be in my pocket," and was quite delighted. But no one would come and pay it. "There is no trusting anyone now," said he, and at last he lost patience, and went into the town to the butcher and demanded his money. The butcher thought it was a joke, but the peasant said, "Jesting apart, I will have my money! Did not the great dog bring you the meat of the slaughtered cow three days ago?" Then the butcher grew angry, snatched a broomstick and drove him out. "Wait a while," said the peasant, "there is still some justice in the world!" and went to the royal palace and begged for an audience. He was led before the King, who sat there with his daughter, and asked him what injury he had suffered. "Alas!" said he, "the frogs and the dogs have taken from me what is mine, and the butcher has paid me for it with the stick," and he related at full length all that had happened.

At this the King's daughter began to laugh heartily, and the King said to him, "I cannot give you justice in this, but you shall have my daughter to wed for it—in her whole life she has never yet laughed as she has just done at you, and I have promised her to the man who could make her laugh. You may thank God for your good fortune!"

"Oh," answered the peasant, "I will not have her. I have a wife already, and she is one too many for me; when I go home, it is just as bad as if I had a wife standing in every corner."

Then the King grew angry, and said, "You are a boor."

"Ah, lord King," replied the peasant, "what can you expect from a pig, but pork?"

"Stop," answered the King, "you shall have another reward. Be off now, but come back in three days, and then you shall have five hundred counted out in full."

When the peasant went out by the gate, the sentry said, "You have made the King's daughter laugh, so you will certainly receive something good."

"Yes, that is what I think," answered the peasant; "five hundred are to be counted out to me."

"Listen," said the soldier, "give me some of it. What can you do with all that money?"

"Because it is you," said the peasant, "you shall have two hundred; present yourself in three days' time before the King, and let it be paid to you."

A Jew, who was standing by and had heard the conversation, ran after the peasant, held him by the coat, and said, "Oh, wonder! What a lucky man you are! I will change it for you, I will change it for you into small coins. What would you do with the great talers?"

"Jew," said the countryman, "three hundred you can have; give it to me at once in coin. In three days from this, you will be paid for it by the King." The Jew was delighted with the profit, and brought the sum in bad groschen, three of which were worth two good ones. After three days had passed, according to the King's command, the peasant went before the King.

"Pull his coat off," said the latter, "and he shall have his five hundred."

"Ah!" said the peasant, "they no longer belong to me; I presented two hundred of them to the sentinel, and three hundred the Jew has changed for me, so by right nothing at all belongs to me."

In the meantime the soldier and the Jew entered and demanded what they were owed by the peasant, and this conduct angered the King. They received the blows strictly counted out. The soldier bore it patiently and knew already how it felt, but the Jew said sorrowfully, "Alas, alas, are these the hard talers?"

The King could not help laughing at the peasant, and once all his anger was gone, he said, "As you have already lost your reward before it came to you, I will give you something in the place of it. Go into my treasure chamber and get some money for yourself, as much as you will."

The peasant did not need to be told twice, and stuffed into his big pockets whatever would go in. Afterwards he went to an inn and counted out his money. The Jew had crept after him and heard how he muttered to himself, "That rogue of a King has cheated me after all. Why could he not have given me the money himself, and then I should have known what I had? How can I tell now if what I have had the luck to put in my pockets is right or not?"

"Good heavens!" said the Jew to himself, "that man is speaking disrespectfully of our lord the King. I will run and inform, and then I shall get a reward, and he will be punished as well."

When the King heard of the peasant's words he fell into a passion, and commanded the Jew to go and bring the offender to him. The Jew ran to the peasant, "You are to go at once to the lord King in the very clothes you have on."

"I know what's right better than that," answered the peasant, "I shall have a new coat made first. Do you think that a man with so much money in his pocket is to go there in his ragged old coat?"

The Jew, as he saw that the peasant would not stir without another coat, and as he feared that if the King's anger cooled, he himself would lose his reward, and the peasant his punishment, said, "I will out of pure friendship lend you a coat for the short time. What will people not do for love!" The peasant was contented with this, put the Jew's coat on, and went off with him.

The King reproached the countryman because of the evil speaking of which the Jew had informed him. "Ah," said the peasant, "what a Jew says is always false—no true word ever comes out of his mouth! That rascal there is capable of maintaining that I have his coat on."

"What is that?" shrieked the Jew. "Is the coat not mine? Have I not lent it to you out of pure friendship, in order that you might appear before the lord King?"

When the King heard that, he said, "The Jew has assuredly deceived one or the other of us, either myself or the peasant," and again he ordered something to be counted out to him in hard talers.

The peasant, however, went home in the good coat, with the good money in his pocket, and said to himself, "This time I have hit it!"

8. *THE WONDERFUL MUSICIAN*

There was once a wonderful musician, who went quite alone through a forest and thought of all manner of things, and when nothing was left for him to think about, he said to himself, "Time is beginning to pass heavily with me here in the forest, I will fetch a good companion for myself." Then he took his fiddle from his back, and played so that it echoed through the trees. It was not long before a wolf came trotting through the thicket towards him. "Ah, here is a wolf coming! I have no desire for him!" said the musician; but the wolf came nearer and said to him, "Ah, dear musician, how beautifully you do play. I should like to learn that, too."

"It is soon learned," the musician replied, "only you have to do all that I bid you."

"Oh, musician," said the wolf, "I will obey you as a scholar obeys his master." The musician had him follow, and when they had gone part of the way together, they came to an old oak tree which was hollow inside, and cleft in the middle.

"Look," said the musician, "if you will learn to fiddle, put your forepaws into this crevice." The wolf obeyed, but the musician quickly picked up a stone and with one blow wedged his two paws so fast that he was forced to stay there like a prisoner. "Stay there until I come back again," said the musician, and went his way.

After a while he again said to himself, "Time is beginning to pass heavily with me here in the forest, I will fetch another companion," and took his fiddle and again played in the forest. It was not long before a fox came creeping through the trees towards him. "Ah, there's a fox coming!" said the musician. "I have no desire for him."

The fox came up to him and said, "Oh, dear musician, how beautifully you do play! I should like to learn that too."

"That is soon learned," said the musician. "You have only to do everything that I bid you."

"Oh, musician," then said the fox, "I will obey you as a scholar obeys his master."

"Follow me," said the musician; and when they had walked part of the way, they came to a footpath, with high bushes on both sides of it.

There the musician stood still, and from one side bent a young hazel-bush down to the ground, and put his foot on the top of it, then he bent down a young tree from the other side as well, and said, "Now little fox, if you will learn something, give me your left front paw." The fox obeyed, and the musician fastened his paw to the left bough. "Little fox," said he, "now reach me your right paw," and he tied it to the right bough. When he had examined whether they were firm enough, he let go, and the bushes sprang up again, and jerked up the little fox, so that it hung struggling in the air. "Wait there till I come back again," said the musician, and went his way.

Again he said to himself, "Time is beginning to pass heavily with me here in the forest, I will fetch another companion," so he took his fiddle, and the sound echoed through the forest. Then a little hare came springing towards him. "Why, a hare is coming," said the musician, "I do not want him."

"Ah, dear musician," said the hare, "how beautifully you do fiddle; I too, should like to learn that."

"That is soon learned," said the musician, "you have only to do everything that I bid you."

"Oh, musician," replied the little hare, "I will obey you as a scholar obeys his master." They went a part of the way together until they came to an open space in the forest, where stood an aspen tree. The musician tied a long string round the little hare's neck, the other end of which he fastened to the tree.

"Now briskly, little hare, run twenty times round the tree!" cried the musician, and the little hare obeyed, and when it had run round twenty times, it had twisted the string twenty times round the trunk of the tree, and the little hare was caught, and let it pull and tug as it liked, it only made the string cut into its tender neck. "Wait there till I come back," said the musician, and went onwards.

The wolf, in the meantime, had pushed and pulled and bitten at the stone, and had worked so long that he had set his feet free and had drawn them once more out of the cleft. Full of anger and rage he hurried after the musician and wanted to tear him to pieces.

When the fox saw him running, he began to lament, and cried with all his might, "Brother wolf, come to my help, the musician has betrayed me!" The wolf drew down the little tree, bit the cord in two, and freed the fox, who went with him to take revenge on the musician.

They found the tied-up hare, whom likewise they released, and then they all sought the enemy together.

The musician had once more played his fiddle as he went on his way, and this time he had been more fortunate. The sound reached the ears of a poor woodcutter, who instantly, without a thought, gave up his work and came with his hatchet under his arm to listen to the music. "At last comes the right companion," said the musician, "for I was seeking a human being, and no wild beast." And he began and played so beautifully and delightfully that the poor man stood there as if bewitched, and his heart leaped with gladness. And as he thus stood, the wolf, the fox, and the hare came up, and he saw well that they had some evil design. So he raised his glittering axe and placed himself before the musician, as if to say, "Whoever wishes to touch him let him beware, for he will have to deal with me!" Then the beasts were terrified and ran back into the forest. The musician, however, played once more to the man out of gratitude, and then went onwards.

9. THE TWELVE BROTHERS

There were once upon a time a king and a queen who lived happily together and had twelve children, but they were all boys. Then said the King to his wife, "If the thirteenth child which you are about to bring into the world is a girl, the twelve boys shall die, in order that her possessions may be great, and that the kingdom may fall to her alone." He caused likewise twelve coffins to be made, which were already filled with shavings, and in each lay the little pillow for the dead, and he had them taken into a locked-up room, and then he gave the Queen the key of it, and bade her not to speak of this to anyone.

The mother, however, now sat and lamented all day long, until the youngest son, who was always with her, and whom she had named Benjamin, from the Bible, said to her, "Dear mother, why are you so sad?"

"Dearest child," she answered, "I may not tell you." But he let her have no rest until she went and unlocked the room, and showed him the twelve coffins ready filled with shavings. Then she said, "my dearest Benjamin, your father has had these coffins made for you and for your eleven brothers, for if I bring a little girl into the world, you are all to be killed and buried in them."

And as she wept while she was saying this, the son comforted her and said, "Weep not, dear mother, we will save ourselves, and go away."

But she said, "Go forth into the forest with your eleven brothers, and let one sit constantly on the highest tree which can be found, and keep watch, looking towards the tower here in the castle. If I give birth to a little son, I will put up a white flag, and then you may venture to come back, but if I bear a daughter, I will hoist a red flag, and then fly away as quickly as you are able, and may the good God protect you. And every night I will rise up and pray for you—in winter that you may be able to warm yourself at a fire, and in summer that you may not faint away in the heat."

After she had blessed her sons, they went forth into the forest. They each kept watch in turn, and sat on the highest oak and looked towards the tower. When eleven days had passed and the turn came to Benjamin, he saw that a flag was being raised. It was, however, not the white, but the blood-red flag which announced that they were all to die. When the brothers heard that, they were very angry and said, "Are we all to suffer death for the sake of a girl? We swear that we will avenge ourselves! Wherever we find a girl, her red blood shall flow."

Thereupon they went deeper into the forest, and in the midst of it, where it was the darkest, they found a little bewitched hut, which was standing empty. Then said they, "Here we will dwell, and you Benjamin, who are the youngest and weakest, you shall stay at home and keep house, we others will go out and get food." Then they went into the forest and shot hares, wild deer, birds and pigeons, and whatever there was to eat; this they took to Benjamin, who had to dress it for them in order that they might appease their hunger. They lived together ten years in the little hut, and the time did not appear long to them.

The little daughter which their mother the Queen had given birth to, was now grown up; she was good of heart, and fair of face, and had a golden star on her forehead. Once, when a big washing had been done, she saw twelve men's shirts among the things, and asked her mother, "To whom do these twelve shirts belong, for they are far too small for father?"

Then the Queen answered with a heavy heart, "Dear child, these belong to your twelve brothers."

Said the maiden, "Where are my twelve brothers, I have never yet heard of them?"

She replied, "God knows where they are, they are wandering about the world." Then she took the maiden and opened the chamber for her, and showed her the twelve coffins with the shavings, and pillows for the head. "These coffins," said she, "were destined for your brothers, but they went away secretly before you were born," and she related to her how everything had happened; then said the maiden, "Dear mother, weep not, I will go and seek my brothers."

So she took the twelve shirts and went forth, and straight into the great forest. She walked the whole day, and in the evening she came to the bewitched hut. Then she entered it and found a young boy, who asked, "Where do you come from, and where are you bound?" and was astonished that she was so beautiful, and wore royal garments, and had a star on her forehead.

And she answered, "I am a king's daughter, and am seeking my twelve brothers, and I will walk as far as the sky is blue until I find them." She likewise showed him the twelve shirts which belonged to them.

Then Benjamin saw that she was his sister, and said, "I am Benjamin, your youngest brother." And she began to weep for joy, and Benjamin wept also, and they kissed and embraced each other with the greatest love. But after this he said, "Dear sister, there is still one difficulty. We have agreed that every maiden whom we meet shall die, because we have been obliged to leave our kingdom on account of a girl."

Then said she, "I will willingly die, if by so doing I can save my twelve brothers."

"No," answered he, "you shall not die, seat yourself beneath this tub until our eleven brothers come, and then I will soon come to an agreement with them."

She did so, and when it was night the others came from hunting, and their dinner was ready. And as they were sitting at table, and eating, they asked, "What news is there?" Said Benjamin, "Don't you know anything?"

"No," they answered.

He continued, "You have been in the forest and I have stayed at home, and yet I know more than you do."

"Tell us then," they cried.

He answered, "But promise me that the first maiden who meets us shall not be killed."

"Yes," they all cried, "she shall have mercy, only do tell us."

Then said he, "Our sister is here," and he lifted up the tub, and the King's daughter came forth in her royal garments with the golden star on her forehead, and she was beautiful, delicate and fair. Then they were all rejoiced, and hugged, and kissed and loved her with all their hearts.

Now she stayed at home with Benjamin and helped him with the work. The eleven went into the forest and caught game, and deer, and birds, and wood-pigeons that they might have food, and the little sister and Benjamin took care to make it ready for them. She sought for the wood for cooking and herbs for vegetables, and put the pans on the fire so that the dinner was always ready when the eleven came. She likewise kept order in the little house, and put beautifully white clean coverings on the little beds, and the brothers were always contented and lived in great harmony with her.

Once on a time the two at home had prepared a beautiful meal, and when they were all together, they sat down and ate and drank and were full of gladness. There was, however, a little garden belonging to the bewitched house where there were twelve lily flowers, which are likewise called students. She wished to give her brothers pleasure, and plucked the twelve flowers, and thought she would present each brother with one while at dinner. But at the same moment that she plucked the flowers the twelve brothers were changed into twelve ravens, and flew away over the forest, and the house and garden vanished likewise. And now the poor maiden was alone in the wild forest, and when she looked around, an old woman was standing near her who said, "My child, what have you done? Why did you not leave the twelve white flowers growing? They were your brothers, who are now forevermore changed into ravens."

The maiden said, weeping, "Is there no way of saving them?"

"No," said the woman, "there is but one in the whole world, and that is so hard that you will not succeed at it, for you must be dumb for seven years, and may not speak or laugh, and if you speak one single word, and only an hour of the seven years is wanting, all is in vain, and your brothers will be killed by the one word."

Then said the maiden in her heart, "I know with certainty that I shall set my brothers free," and went and sought a high tree and she sat spinning, and she neither spoke nor laughed. Now it so happened that a king was hunting in the forest, who had a great greyhound which ran to the tree on which the maiden was sitting, and sprang about it, whining, and barking at her. Then the King came by and saw the beautiful King's daughter with the golden star on her brow, and was so charmed with her beauty that he called to ask her if she would be his wife. She made no answer, but nodded a little with her head. So he climbed up the tree himself, carried her down, placed her on his horse, and took her home. Then the wedding was solemnized with great magnificence and rejoicing, but the bride neither spoke nor smiled.

When they had lived happily together for a few years, the King's mother, who was a wicked woman, began to slander the young Queen, and said to the King, "This is a common beggar girl whom you have brought back with you. Who knows what impious tricks she practices secretly! Even if she is dumb, and not able to speak, she still might laugh for once; but those who do not laugh have bad consciences." At first the

King would not believe it, but the old woman urged this so long, and accused her of so many evil things, that at last the King let himself be persuaded and sentenced her to death.

And now a great fire was lighted in the courtyard in which she was to be burnt, and the King stood above at the window and looked on with tearful eyes, because he still loved her so much. And when she was bound fast to the stake, and the fire was licking at her clothes with its red tongue, the last instant of the seven years expired. Then a whirring sound was heard in the air, and twelve ravens came flying towards the place, and sank downwards, and when they touched the earth they were her twelve brothers, whom she had saved. They tore the fire asunder, extinguished the flames, set their dear sister free, and kissed and embraced her. And now as she dared to open her mouth and speak, she told the King why she had been dumb, and had never laughed. The King rejoiced when he heard that she was innocent, and they all lived in great unity until their death. The wicked stepmother was taken before the judge, and put into a barrel filled with boiling oil and venomous snakes, and died an evil death.

10. THE PACK OF RAGAMUFFINS

The cock once said to the hen, "It is now the time when our nuts are ripe, so let us go to the hill together and for once eat our fill before the squirrel takes them all away."

"Yes," replied the hen, "come, we will have some pleasure together."

Then they went away to the hill, and because it was a bright day they stayed till evening. Now I do not know whether it was that they had eaten till they were too fat, or whether they had become proud, but they would not go home on foot, and the cock had to build a little carriage of nut shells. When it was ready, the little hen seated herself in it and said to the cock, "You can just harness yourself to it."

"Ha, I like that!" said the cock, "I would rather go home on foot than let myself be harnessed to it; no, that is not our bargain. I do not mind being coachman and sitting on the box, but I will not drag it myself."

As they were thus disputing, a duck quacked at them, "You thieving folks, who told you to go to my nut-hill? Well, you shall suffer for it!" and ran with open beak at the cock.

But the cock also was not idle, and fell boldly on the duck, and at last wounded her so with his spurs that she begged for mercy, and willingly let herself be harnessed to the carriage as a punishment. The little cock now seated himself on the box and was coachman, and thereupon they went off in a gallop, with "Duck, go as fast as you can."

When they had driven a part of the way they met two foot-passengers, a pin and a needle. They cried, "Stop! Stop!" and said that it would soon be as dark as pitch, and then they could not go a step further, and that it was so dirty on the road, and asked if they could not get into the carriage for a while. They had been at the tailor's tavern by the gate, and had stayed too long over the beer. As they were thin and did not take up much room, the cock let them both get in, but they had to promise him and his little hen not to step on their feet. Late in the evening they came to an inn, and as they did not like to go further by night, and as the duck also was not strong on her feet, and fell from one side to the other, they went in. The host at first made many objections, his house was already full, and he thought they could not be very distinguished persons; but at last, as they made pleasant speeches, and told him that he should have the egg which the little hen has laid on the way, and should likewise keep the duck, which laid one every day, he at length said that they might stay the night. And now they had themselves well served, and they feasted and caroused. Early in the morning, when day was breaking, and everyone was asleep, the cock awoke the hen, brought the egg, pecked it open, and they ate it together, but they threw the shell on the hearth. Then they went to the needle which was still asleep, took it by the head and stuck it into the cushion of the landlord's chair, and put the pin in his towel, and at last without more ado they flew away over the heath. The duck, who liked to sleep in the open air and had stayed in the yard, heard them going away, made herself merry and found a stream, down which she swam, which was a much quicker way of traveling than being harnessed to a carriage.

The host did not get out of bed for two hours after this; he washed himself and wanted to dry himself, then the pin went over his face and made a red streak from one ear to the other. After this he went into the kitchen and wanted to light a pipe, but when he came to the hearth the eggshell darted into his eyes. "This morning everything attacks my head," said he, and angrily sat down on his grandfather's chair, but he quickly started up again and cried, "Woe is me," for the needle had pricked him still worse than the pin, and not in the head. Now he was thoroughly angry, and suspected the guests who had come so late the night before, and when he went and looked about for them, they were gone. Then he made a vow to take no more ragamuffins into his house, for they consume much, pay for nothing, and play mischievous tricks as thanks.

11. LITTLE BROTHER AND
LITTLE SISTER

Little brother took his little sister by the hand and said, "Since our mother died we have had no happiness; our stepmother beats us every day, and if we come near her she kicks us away with her foot. Our meals are the hard crusts of bread that are left over; and the little dog under the table is better off, for she often throws it a nice bit. May Heaven pity us. If our mother only knew! Come, we will go forth together into the wide world."

They walked the whole day over meadows, fields, and stony places; and when it rained the little sister said, "Heaven and our hearts are weeping together." In the evening they came to a large forest, and they were so weary with sorrow and hunger and the long walk, that they lay down in a hollow tree and fell asleep.

The next day when they awoke, the sun was already high in the sky, and shone down hot into the tree. Then the brother said, "Sister, I am thirsty; if I knew of a little brook I would go and just take a drink; I think I hear one running." The brother got up and took the little sister by the hand, and they set off to find the brook.

But the wicked stepmother was a witch, and had seen how the two children had gone away, and had crept after them stealthily, as witches do creep, and had bewitched all the brooks in the forest.

Now when they found a little brook leaping brightly over the stones, the brother was going to drink out of it, but the sister heard how it said as it ran, "Whoever drinks of me will become a tiger; whoever drinks of me will become a tiger." Then the sister cried, "Pray, dear brother, do not drink, or you will become a wild beast, and tear me to pieces."

The brother did not drink, although he was so thirsty, but said, "I will wait for the next spring."

When they came to the next brook the sister heard this also say, "Whoever drinks of me will become a wolf; whoever drinks of me will become a wolf." Then the sister cried out, "Pray, dear brother, do not drink, or you will become a wolf, and devour me."

The brother did not drink, and said, "I will wait until we come to the next spring, but then I must drink, say what you like; for my thirst is too great."

And when they came to the third brook the sister heard how it said as it ran, "Whoever drinks of me will become a deer; whoever drinks of me will become a deer." The sister said, "Oh, I pray you, dear brother, do not drink, or you will become a deer, and run away from me." But the brother had knelt down at once by the brook, and had bent down and drunk some of the water, and as soon as the first drops touched his lips he lay there a young deer.

And now the sister wept over her poor bewitched brother, and the little deer wept also, and sat sorrowfully near her. But at last the girl said, "Be quiet, dear little fawn, I will never, never leave you."

Then she untied her golden garter and put it round the fawn's neck, and she plucked reeds and wove them into a soft cord. With this she tied the little beast and led it on, and she walked deeper and deeper into the forest.

And when they had gone a very long way they came at last to a little house, and the girl looked in; and as it was empty, she thought, "We can stay here and live." Then she sought for leaves and moss to make a soft bed for the fawn; and every morning she went out and gathered roots and berries and nuts for herself, and brought tender grass for the fawn, who ate out of her hand, and was content and played round about her. In the evening, when the sister was tired, and had said her prayer, she laid her head upon the fawn's back: that was her pillow, and she slept softly on it. And if only the brother had had his human form it would have been a delightful life.

For some time they were alone like this in the wilderness. But it happened that the King of the country held a great hunt in the forest. Then the blasts of the horns, the barking of dogs, and the merry shouts of the huntsmen rang through the trees, and the fawn heard all, and was only too anxious to be there. "Oh," said he, to his sister, "let me be off to the hunt, I cannot bear it any longer," and he begged so much that at last she agreed.

"But," said she to him, "come back to me in the evening; I must shut my door for fear of the rough huntsmen, so knock and say, 'My little sister, let me in!' that I may know you; and if you do not say that, I shall not open the door." Then the young fawn sprang away; so happy was he and so merry in the open air.

The King and the huntsmen saw the pretty creature, and started after him, but they could not catch him, and when they thought that they surely had him, away he sprang through the bushes and could not be seen. When it was dark he ran to the cottage, knocked, and said, "My little sister, let me in." Then the door was opened for him, and he jumped in, and rested himself the whole night through upon his soft bed.

The next day the hunt went on afresh, and when the fawn again heard the bugle-horn, and the Ho! Ho! of the huntsmen, he had no peace, but said, "Sister, let me out, I must be off."

His sister opened the door for him, and said, "But you must be here again in the evening and say your password."

When the King and his huntsmen again saw the young fawn with the golden collar, they all chased him, but he was too quick and nimble for them. This went on for the whole day, but at last by the evening the huntsmen had surrounded him, and one of them wounded him a little in the foot, so that he limped and ran slowly. Then a hunter crept after him to the cottage and heard how he said, "My little sister, let me in," and saw that the door was opened for him, and was shut again at once. The hunter took notice of it all, and went to the King and told him what he had seen and heard. Then the King said, "Tomorrow we will hunt once more."

The little sister, however, was dreadfully frightened when she saw that her fawn was hurt. She washed the blood off him, laid herbs on the wound, and said, "Go to your bed, dear fawn, that you may get well again."

But the wound was so slight that the fawn, next morning, did not feel it any more. And when he again heard the sport outside, he said, "I cannot bear it, I must be there; they shall not find it so easy to catch me."

The sister cried, and said, "This time they will kill you, and here am I alone in the forest and forsaken by all the world. I will not let you out."

"Then you will have me die of grief," answered the fawn; "when I hear the bugle-horns I feel as if I must jump out of my skin." Then the sister could not do otherwise, but opened the door for him with a heavy heart, and the fawn, full of health and joy, bounded into the forest.

When the King saw him, he said to his huntsmen, "Now chase him all day long till nightfall, but take care that no one does him any harm."

As soon as the sun had set, the King said to the hunter, "Now come and show me the cottage in the wood;" and when he was at the door, he knocked and called out, "Dear little sister, let me in." Then the door

47

opened, and the King walked in, and there stood a maiden more lovely than any he had ever seen. The maiden was frightened when she saw, not her little fawn, but a man come in who wore a golden crown upon his head. But the King looked kindly at her, stretched out his hand, and said, "Will you go with me to my palace and be my dear wife?"

"Yes, indeed," answered the maiden, "but the little fawn must go with me, I cannot leave him."

The King said, "It shall stay with you as long as you live, and shall want nothing." Just then he came running in, and the sister again tied him with the cord of reeds, took it in her own hand, and went away with the King from the cottage.

The King took the lovely maiden upon his horse and carried her to his palace, where the wedding was held with great pomp. She was now the Queen, and they lived for a long time happily together; the fawn was tended and cherished, and ran about in the palace garden.

But the wicked stepmother, because of whom the children had gone out into the world, thought all the time that the sister had been torn to pieces by the wild beasts in the wood, and that the brother had been shot for a fawn by the huntsmen. Now when she heard that they were so happy, and so well off, envy and hatred rose in her heart and left her no peace, and she thought of nothing but how she could bring them again to misfortune. Her own daughter, who was ugly as night, and had only one eye, grumbled at her and said, "A Queen! That ought to have been my luck."

"Nevermind," answered the old woman, and comforted her by saying, "when the time comes I shall be ready."

As time went on, the Queen delivered a pretty little boy, and it happened when the King was out hunting. The old witch took the form of the chamber-maid, went into the room where the Queen lay, and said to her, "Come, the bath is ready; it will do you good, and give you fresh strength; make haste before it gets cold."

The daughter also was close by, so they carried the weakly Queen into the bathroom, and put her into the bath; then they shut the door and ran away. But in the bathroom they had made a fire of such deadly heat that the beautiful young Queen was soon suffocated.

When this was done the old woman took her daughter, put a nightcap on her head, and laid her in bed in place of the Queen. She gave her too the shape and the look of the Queen, only she could do nothing for the lost eye. But in order that the King might not see it, she was to lie on the side on which she had no eye.

In the evening when he came home and heard that he had a son he was heartily glad, and was going to the bed of his dear wife to see how she was. But the old woman quickly called out, "For your life leave the curtains closed; the Queen ought not to see the light yet, and must have rest." The King went away, and did not find out that a false Queen was lying in the bed.

But at midnight, when all slept, the nurse, who was sitting in the nursery by the cradle, and who was the only person awake, saw the door open and the true Queen walk in. The Queen took the child out of the cradle, laid it on her arm, and suckled it. Then she shook up its pillow, laid the child down again, and covered it with the little quilt. And she did not forget the fawn, but went into the corner where it lay, and stroked its back. Then she went quite silently out of the door again. The next morning the nurse asked the guards whether anyone had come into the palace during the night, but they answered, "No, we have seen no one."

She came thus many nights and never spoke a word. The nurse always saw her, but she did not dare to tell anyone about it.

When some time had passed in this manner, the Queen began to speak in the night, and said—

> "How fares my child, how fares my fawn?
> Twice shall I come, then never more."

The nurse did not answer, but when the Queen had gone again, went to the King and told him all. The King said, "Ah, heavens! What is this? Tomorrow night I will watch by the child." In the evening he went into the nursery, and at midnight the Queen again appeared and said—

> "How fares my child, how fares my fawn?
> Once will I come, then never more."

And she nursed the child as she did before she disappeared. The King dared not speak to her, but on the next night he watched again. Then she said—

> "How fares my child, how fares my fawn?
> This time I come, then never more."

Then the King could not restrain himself; he sprang towards her, and said, "You can be none other than my dear wife."

She answered, "Yes, I am your dear wife," and at the same moment she received life again, and by God's grace became fresh, rosy, and full of health.

Then she told the King the evil deed which the wicked witch and her daughter had been guilty of towards her. The King ordered both to be led before the judge, and judgment was delivered against them. The daughter was taken into the forest where she was torn to pieces by wild beasts, but the witch was cast into the fire and miserably burnt. And as soon as she was burnt the fawn changed his shape, and received his human form again, so the sister and brother lived happily together all their lives.

12. RAPUNZEL

There were once a man and a woman who had long in vain wished for a child. At length the woman hoped that God was about to grant her desire. These people had a little window at the back of their house from which a splendid garden could be seen, which was full of the most beautiful flowers and herbs. It was, however, surrounded by a high wall, and no one dared to go into it because it belonged to an enchantress named Dame Gothel, who had great power and was dreaded by all the world. One day the woman was standing by this window and looking down into the garden, when she saw a bed which was planted with the most beautiful rampion (rapunzel), and it looked so fresh and green that she longed for it, and had the greatest desire to eat some. This desire increased every day, and as she knew that she could not get any of it, she quite pined away, and looked pale and miserable. Then her husband was alarmed, and asked, "What ails you, dear wife?"

"Ah," she replied, "if I can't get some of the rampion, which is in the garden behind our house, I shall die."

The man, who loved her, thought, "Sooner than let your wife die, bring her some of the rampion yourself, let it cost you what it will." In the twilight of the evening, he clambered down over the wall into the garden of the enchantress, hastily clutched a handful of rampion, and took it to his wife. She at once made herself a salad of it, and ate it with much delight. She, however, liked it so much—so very much, that the next day she longed for it three times as much as before. If he was to have any rest, her husband must once more descend into the garden. In the gloom of evening, therefore, he let himself down again; but when he had clambered down the wall he was terribly afraid, for he saw the enchantress standing before him.

"How can you dare," said she with an angry look, "to descend into my garden and steal my rampion like a thief? You shall suffer for it!"

"Ah," answered he, "let mercy take the place of justice, I only made up my mind to do it out of necessity. My wife saw your rampion from the window, and felt such a longing for it that she would have died if she had not got some to eat."

Then the enchantress allowed her anger to be softened, and said to him, "If the case be as you say, I will allow you to take away with you as much rampion as you will, only I make one condition. You must give me the child which your wife will bring into the world; it shall be well treated, and I will care for it like a mother." The man in his terror consented to everything, and when the woman gave birth, the enchantress appeared at once, gave the child the name of Rapunzel, and took it away with her.

Rapunzel grew into the most beautiful child beneath the sun. When she was twelve years old, the enchantress shut her into a tower, which lay in a forest, and had neither stairs nor door, but quite at the top was a little window. When the enchantress wanted to go in, she placed herself beneath it and cried,

> "Rapunzel, Rapunzel,
> Let down your hair to me."

Rapunzel had magnificent long hair, fine as spun gold, and when she heard the voice of the enchantress she unfastened her braided tresses, wound them round one of the hooks of the window above, and then the hair fell twenty ells down, and the enchantress climbed up by it.

After a year or two, it came to pass that the King's son rode through the forest and went by the tower. Then he heard a song, which was so charming that he stood still and listened. This was Rapunzel, who in her solitude passed her time in letting her sweet voice resound. The King's son wanted to climb up to her, and looked for the door of the tower, but none was to be found. He rode home, but the singing had so deeply touched his heart, that every day he went out into the forest and listened to it. Once when he was thus standing behind a tree, he saw that an enchantress came there, and he heard how she cried,

> "Rapunzel, Rapunzel,
> Let down your hair."

Then Rapunzel let down the braids of her hair, and the enchantress climbed up to her. "If that is the ladder by which one mounts, I will at once try my fortune," said he, and the next day when it began to grow dark, he went to the tower and cried,

> "Rapunzel, Rapunzel,
> Let down your hair."

Immediately the hair fell down and the King's son climbed up.

At first Rapunzel was terribly frightened when a man such as her eyes had never yet beheld, came to her; but the King's son began to talk to her quite like a friend, and told her that his heart had been so stirred that it had let him have no rest, and he had been forced to see her. Then Rapunzel lost her fear, and when he asked her if she would take him for her husband, and she saw that he was young and handsome, she thought, "He will love me more than old Dame Gothel does;" and she said yes, and laid her hand in his. She said, "I will willingly go away with you, but I do not know how to get down. Bring with you a skein of silk every time that you come, and I will weave a ladder with it, and when that is ready I will descend, and you will take me on your horse." They agreed that until that time he should come to her every evening, for the old woman came by day. The enchantress remarked nothing of this, until once Rapunzel said to her, "Tell me, Dame Gothel, how it happens that you are so much heavier for me to draw up than the young King's son—he is with me in hardly a minute."

"Ah! You wicked child," cried the enchantress "What do I hear you say! I thought I had separated you from all the world, and yet you have deceived me." In her anger she clutched Rapunzel's beautiful tresses, wrapped them twice round her left hand, seized a pair of scissors with the right, and snip, snap, they were cut off, and the lovely braids lay on the ground. And she was so pitiless that she took poor Rapunzel into a desert where she had to live in great grief and misery.

On the same day that she cast out Rapunzel, the enchantress fastened the braids of hair which she had kept onto the hook of the window, and in the evening when the King's son came and cried,

> "Rapunzel, Rapunzel,
> Let down your hair,"

she let the hair down. The King's son ascended, but he did not find his dearest Rapunzel above, but the enchantress, who gazed at him with wicked and venomous looks.

"Aha!" she cried mockingly, "You would fetch your dearest, but the beautiful bird sits no longer singing in the nest; the cat has got it, and will scratch out your eyes as well. Rapunzel is lost to you; you will never see her more." The King's son was beside himself with pain, and in his despair he leapt down from the tower. He escaped with his life, but the thorns into which he fell pierced his eyes. Then he wandered quite blind about the forest, ate nothing but roots and berries, and did nothing but lament and weep over the loss of his dearest wife. Thus he roamed about in misery for some years, and at length came to the desert where Rapunzel, with the twins to which she had given birth, a boy and a girl, lived in wretchedness. He heard a voice, and it seemed so familiar to him that he went towards it, and when he approached, Rapunzel knew him and embraced him and wept. Two of her tears wetted his eyes and they grew clear again, and he could see with them as before. He led her to his Kingdom where he was joyfully received, and they lived for a long time afterwards, happy and contented.

13. THE THREE LITTLE MEN
IN THE WOOD

There was once a man whose wife died, and a woman whose husband died, and the man had a daughter, and the woman also had a daughter. The girls were acquainted with each other, and went out walking together, and afterwards came to the woman in her house. Then she said to the man's daughter, "Listen, tell your father that I would like to marry him, and then you shall wash yourself in milk every morning, and drink wine, but my own daughter shall wash herself in water and drink water."

The girl went home, and told her father what the woman had said. The man said, "What shall I do? Marriage is a joy and also a torment." At length as he could come to no decision, he pulled off his boot, and said, "Take this boot, it has a hole in the sole of it. Go with it up to the loft, hang it on the big nail, and then pour water into it. If it holds the water, then I will again take a wife, but if it runs through, I will not." The girl did as she was ordered, but the water drew the hole together, and the boot became full to the top. She informed her father how it had turned out. Then he himself went up, and when he saw that she was right, he went to the widow and wooed her, and the wedding was celebrated.

The next morning, when the two girls got up, there stood before the man's daughter milk for her to wash in and wine for her to drink, but before the woman's daughter stood water to wash herself with and water for drinking. On the second morning, stood milk for washing and wine for drinking before the man's daughter as well as water before the woman's daughter. And on the third morning stood water for washing and water for drinking before the man's daughter, and milk for washing and wine for drinking before the woman's daughter, and so it continued. The woman became bitterly unkind to her stepdaughter, and day by day did her best to treat her still worse. She was also envious because her stepdaughter was beautiful and lovable, and her own daughter ugly and repulsive.

Once, in winter, when everything was frozen as hard as a stone, and hill and vale lay covered with snow, the woman made a frock of paper, called her stepdaughter, and said, "Here, put on this dress and go out into the wood, and fetch me a little basketful of strawberries—I have a fancy for some."

"Good heavens!" said the girl, "No strawberries grow in winter! The ground is frozen, and besides the snow has covered everything. And why am I to go in this paper frock? It is so cold outside that one's very breath freezes! The wind will blow through the frock, and the thorns will tear it off my body."

"Will you contradict me again?" said the stepmother, "See that you go, and do not show your face again until you have the basketful of strawberries!" Then she gave her a little piece of hard bread, and said, "This will last you the day," and thought, "You will die of cold and hunger outside, and will never be seen again by me."

Then the maiden was obedient, and put on the paper frock, and went out with the basket. Far and wide there was nothing but snow, and not a green blade to be seen. When she got into the wood she saw a small house out of which peeped three elves. She wished them good day, and knocked modestly at the door. They cried, "Come in," and she entered the room and seated herself on the bench by the stove, where she began to warm herself and eat her breakfast. The elves said, "Give us, too, some of it."

"Willingly," she said, and divided her bit of bread in two and gave them the half.

They asked, "What are you doing in the forest in the winter time, in your thin dress?"

"Ah," she answered, "I am to look for a basketful of strawberries, and am not to go home until I can take them with me."

When she had eaten her bread, they gave her a broom and said, "Sweep away the snow at the back door with it." But when she was outside, the three little men said to each other, "What shall we give her as she is so good, and has shared her bread with us?" Then said the first, "My gift is, that she shall every day grow more beautiful." The second said, "My gift is, that gold pieces shall fall out of her mouth every time she speaks." The third said, "My gift is, that a king shall come and take her as wife."

The girl, however, did as the little men had bidden her, swept away the snow behind the little house with the broom, and what did she find but real ripe strawberries, which came up quite dark-red out of the snow! In her joy she hastily gathered her basket full, thanked the little men, shook hands with each of them, and ran home to take her stepmother what she had longed for so much. When she went in and said good evening, a piece of gold at once fell from her mouth. Thereupon she related what had happened to her in the wood, but with every word she spoke, gold pieces fell from her mouth, until very soon the whole room was covered with them.

"Now look at her arrogance," cried the stepsister, "to throw about gold in that way!" but she was secretly envious of it, and wanted to go into the forest also to seek strawberries.

The mother said, "No, my dear little daughter, it is too cold, you might die of cold." However, as her daughter let her have no peace, the mother at last yielded, made her a magnificent dress of fur, which she was obliged to put on, and gave her bread-and-butter and cake to take with her.

The girl went into the forest and straight up to the little house. The three little elves peeped out again, but she did not greet them, and without looking round at them and without speaking to them, she went awkwardly into the room, seated herself by the stove, and began to eat her bread-and-butter and cake. "Give us some of it," cried the little men; but she replied, "There is not enough for myself, so how can I give it away to other people?"

When she had finished eating, they said, "There is a broom for you, sweep all clean for us outside by the back door."

"Humph! Sweep for yourselves," she answered, "I am not your servant." When she saw that they were not going to give her anything, she went out by the door.

Then the little men said to each other, "What shall we give her as she is so naughty, and has a wicked envious heart, that will never let her do a good deed for anyone?"

The first said, "I grant that she may grow uglier every day."

The second said, "I grant that at every word she says, a toad shall spring out of her mouth."

The third said, "I grant that she may die a miserable death." The maiden looked for strawberries outside, but as she found none, she went angrily home. And when she opened her mouth, and was about to tell her mother what had happened to her in the wood, with every word she said, a toad sprang out of her mouth, so that everyone was seized with horror of her.

Then the stepmother was still more enraged, and thought of nothing but how to do every possible injury to the man's daughter, whose beauty, however, grew daily greater. At length she took a cauldron, set it on the fire, and boiled yarn in it. When it was boiled, she flung it on the poor girl's shoulder, and gave her an axe in order that she might go on the frozen river, cut a hole in the ice, and rinse the yarn. She was obedient, went and cut a hole in the ice; and while she was in the midst of her cutting, a splendid carriage came driving up, in which sat the King. The carriage stopped, and the King asked, "My child, who are you, and what are you doing here?"

"I am a poor girl, and I am rinsing yarn."

Then the King felt compassion, and when he saw that she was so very beautiful, he said to her, "Will you go away with me?"

"Ah, yes, with all my heart," she answered, for she was glad to get away from the mother and sister.

So she got into the carriage and drove away with the King, and when they arrived at his palace, the wedding was celebrated with great pomp, as the little men had granted to the maiden. When a year was over, the young Queen bore a son, and as the stepmother had heard of her great good fortune, she came with her daughter to the palace and pretended that she wanted to pay her a visit. Once, however, the King had gone out, and no one else was present, the wicked woman seized the Queen by the head, and her daughter seized her by the feet, and they lifted her out of the bed, and threw her out of the window into the stream which flowed by. Then the ugly daughter laid herself in the bed, and the old woman covered her up over her head. When the King came home again and wanted to speak to his wife, the old woman cried, "Hush, hush, that can't be now, she is lying in a violent perspiration; you must let her rest today." The King suspected no evil, and did not come back again till next morning; and as he talked with his wife and she answered him, with every word a toad leaped out, whereas formerly a piece of gold had fallen out. Then he asked what that could be, but the old woman said that she had got that from the violent perspiration, and would soon lose it again. During the night, however, the kitchen boy saw a duck come swimming up the gutter, and it said,

> "King, what are you doing?
> Are you awake, or slumbering?

And as he returned no answer, it said,

"And my guests, what about them?"

The kitchen boy said,

"They are sleeping soundly, too."

Then it asked again,

"What of my little baby mine?"

He answered,

"Asleep in her cradle."

Then she went upstairs in the form of the Queen, nursed the baby, shook up its little bed, covered it over, and then swam away again down the gutter in the shape of a duck. She came thus for two nights; on the third, she said to the kitchen boy, "Go and tell the King to take his sword and swing it three times over me on the threshold." Then the kitchen boy ran and told this to the King, who came with his sword and swung it thrice over the spirit, and at the third time, his wife stood before him strong, alive, and as healthy as she had been before. At this the King was full of great joy, but he kept the Queen hidden in a chamber until the Sunday when the baby was to be christened. And when it was christened he said, "What does a person deserve who drags another out of bed and throws him in the water?"

"The wretch deserves nothing better," answered the old woman, "than to be taken and put in a barrel stuck full of nails, and rolled downhill into the water."

"Then," said the King, "You have pronounced your own sentence;" and he ordered such a barrel to be brought, and the old woman to be put into it with her daughter, and then the top was hammered on, and the barrel rolled downhill until it went into the river.

14. THE THREE SPINNERS

There was once a girl who was idle and would not spin, and let her mother try as she might, she could not bring her to it. At last the mother was so overcome with anger and impatience, that she beat her, on which the girl began to weep loudly. Now at this very moment the Queen drove by, and when she heard the weeping she stopped her carriage, went into the house and asked the mother why she was beating her daughter so that the cries could be heard out on the road? Then the woman was ashamed to reveal the laziness of her daughter and said, "I cannot get her to quit spinning. She insists on spinning forever and ever, and I am poor, and cannot procure the flax."

Then answered the Queen, "There is nothing that I like better than the sound of spinning, and I am never happier than when the wheels are humming. Let me have your daughter with me in the palace. I have flax enough, and there she shall spin as much as she likes." The mother was heartily satisfied with this, and the Queen took the girl with her. When they had arrived at the palace, she led her up into three rooms which were filled from the bottom to the top with the finest flax. "Now spin me this flax," said she, "and when you have done it, you shall have my eldest son for a husband, even if you are poor. I do not care about that, for you are an industrious worker." The girl was secretly terrified, for she could not have spun the flax, no, not if she had lived till she was three hundred years old, and had sat at it every day from morning till night. When she was alone, she began to weep, and sat thus for three days without moving a finger. On the third day came the Queen, and when she saw that nothing had been spun yet, she was surprised; but the girl excused herself by saying that she had not been able to begin because of her great distress at leaving her mother's house. The queen was satisfied with this, but said when she was going away, "Tomorrow you must begin to work."

When the girl was alone again, she did not know what to do, and in her distress went to the window. Then she saw three women coming towards her, the first of whom had a broad flat foot, the second had such a great underlip that it hung down over her chin, and the third had a broad thumb. They remained standing before the window, looked up, and asked the girl what was amiss with her? She complained of her trouble, and then they offered her their help and said, "If you will invite us to the wedding, not be ashamed of us, and will call us your aunts, and likewise will place us at your table, we will spin up the flax for you, and that in a very short time."

"With all my heart," she replied, "come in and begin the work at once." Then she let in the three strange women, and cleared a place in the first room, where they seated themselves and began their spinning. The one drew the thread and trod the wheel, the other wetted the thread, the third twisted it, and struck the table with her finger, and as often as she struck it, a skein of thread fell to the ground that was spun in the finest manner possible. The girl concealed the three spinners from the Queen, and showed her whenever she came the great quantity of spun thread, until the latter could not praise her enough. When the first room was empty she went to the second, and at last to the third, and that too was quickly cleared.

Then the three women took leave and said to the girl, "Do not forget what you have promised us—it will make your fortune."

When the maiden showed the Queen the empty rooms, and the great heap of yarn, she gave orders for the wedding, and the bridegroom rejoiced that he was to have such a clever and industrious wife, and praised her mightily. "I have three aunts," said the girl, "and as they have been very kind to me, I should not like to forget them in my good fortune; allow me to invite them to the wedding, and let them sit with us at table."

The Queen and the bridegroom said, "Why should we not allow that?"

Therefore when the feast began, the three women entered in strange apparel, and the bride said, "Welcome, dear aunts."

"Ah," said the bridegroom, "how ever did you get such odious friends?" He went to the one with the broad flat foot, and said, "How do you come by such a broad foot?"

"By treading," she answered, "by treading."

Then the bridegroom went to the second, and said, "How do you come by your falling lip?"

"By licking," she answered, "by licking."

Then he asked the third, "How do you come by your broad thumb?"

"By twisting the thread," she answered, "by twisting the thread."

At this the King's son was alarmed and said, "Neither now nor ever shall my beautiful bride touch a spinning wheel." And thus she got rid of the hateful flax-spinning.

15. HANSEL AND GRETEL

Near a great forest dwelt a poor woodcutter with his wife and his two children. The boy was called Hansel and the girl Gretel. He had little to bite and to break, and when great scarcity fell on the land, he could no longer procure daily bread. Now when he thought over this at night in his bed, and tossed about in his anxiety, he groaned and said to his wife, "What is to become of us? How are we to feed our poor children, when we no longer have anything even for ourselves?"

"I'll tell you what, husband," answered the woman, "Early tomorrow morning we will take the children out into the forest where it is the thickest. There we will light a fire for them, and give each of them one piece of bread, and then we will go to our work and leave them alone. They will not find the way home again, and we shall be rid of them."

"No, wife," said the man, "I will not do that; how can I bear to leave my children alone in the forest?—the wild animals would soon come and tear them to pieces."

"O, you fool!" said she, "Then we must all four die of hunger. You may as well plane the planks for our coffins," and she left him no peace until he consented.

"But I feel very sorry for the poor children, all the same," said the man.

The two children had also not been able to sleep for hunger, and had heard what their stepmother had said to their father. Gretel wept bitter tears, and said to Hansel, "Now all is over for us."

"Hush, Gretel," said Hansel, "do not distress yourself, I will soon find a way to help us." And when the old folks had fallen asleep, he got up, put on his little coat, opened the door below, and crept outside. The moon shone brightly, and the white pebbles which lay in front of the house glittered like real silver pennies. Hansel stooped and put as many of them in the little pocket of his coat as he could possibly get in. Then he went back and said to Gretel, "Be comforted, dear little sister, and sleep in peace, God will not forsake us," and he lay down again in his bed.

When day dawned, but before the sun had risen, the woman came and awoke the two children, saying, "Get up, you sluggards! We are going into the forest to fetch wood." She gave each a little piece of bread, and said, "There is something for your dinner, but do not eat it up before then, for you will get nothing else." Gretel took the bread under her apron, as Hansel had the stones in his pocket. Then they all set out together on the way to the forest. When they had walked a short time, Hansel stood still and peeped back at the house, and did so again and again.

His father said, "Hansel, what are you looking at there and staying behind for? Mind yourself, and do not forget how to use your legs."

"Ah, father," said Hansel, "I am looking at my little white cat, which is sitting up on the roof, and wants to say goodbye to me."

The wife said, "Fool, that is not your little cat, that is the morning sun which is shining on the chimneys." Hansel, however, had not been looking back at the cat, but had been constantly throwing one of the white pebble-stones out of his pocket on the road.

When they had reached the middle of the forest, the father said, "Now, children, pile up some wood, and I will light a fire that you may not be cold." Hansel and Gretel gathered brushwood together, as high as a little hill.

The brushwood was lighted, and when the flames were burning very high, the woman said, "Now, children, lay yourselves down by the fire and rest. We will go into the forest and cut some wood. When we have done, we will come back and fetch you away."

Hansel and Gretel sat by the fire, and when noon came, each ate a little piece of bread, and as they heard the strokes of the wood-axe they believed that their father was near. It was not, however, the axe, it was a branch which he had fastened to a withered tree which the wind was blowing backwards and forwards. And as they had been sitting such a long time, their eyes shut with fatigue, and they fell fast asleep. When at last they awoke, it was already dark night. Gretel began to cry and said, "How are we to get out of the forest now?"

But Hansel comforted her and said, "Just wait a little, until the moon has risen, and then we will soon find the way." And when the full moon had risen, Hansel took his little sister by the hand, and followed the pebbles which shone like newly-coined silver pieces, and showed them the way.

They walked the whole night long, and by break of day came once more to their father's house. They knocked at the door, and when the woman opened it and saw that it was Hansel and Gretel, she said, "You naughty children, why have you slept so long in the forest? We thought you were never coming back at all!" The father, however, rejoiced, for it had cut him to the heart to leave them behind alone.

Not long afterwards, there was once more great scarcity in all parts, and the children heard their mother saying at night to their father, "Everything is eaten again, we have one half loaf left, and after that there is no more. The children must go. We will take them farther into the wood, so that they will not find their way out again; there is no other means of saving ourselves!"

The man's heart was heavy, and he thought, "It would be better for you to share the last mouthful with your children." The woman, however, would listen to nothing that he had to say, but scolded and reproached him. He who says A must say B, likewise, and as he had yielded the first time, he had to do so a second time also.

The children were, however, still awake and had heard the conversation. When the old folks were asleep, Hansel again got up, and wanted to go out and pick up pebbles as he had done before, but the woman had locked the door, and Hansel could not get out. Nevertheless he comforted his little sister, and said, "Do not cry, Gretel, go to sleep quietly, the good God will help us."

Early in the morning came the woman, and took the children out of their beds. Their bit of bread was given to them, but it was still smaller than the time before. On the way into the forest Hansel crumbled his in his pocket, and often stood still and threw a morsel on the ground.

"Hansel, why do you stop and look round?" said the father, "Go on."

"I am looking back at my little pigeon which is sitting on the roof, and wants to say goodbye to me," answered Hansel.

"Simpleton!" said the woman, "That is not your little pigeon, that is the morning sun that is shining on the chimney." Hansel, however, little by little, threw all the crumbs on the path.

The woman led the children still deeper into the forest, where they had never in their lives been before. Then a great fire was again made, and the mother said, "Just sit there, you children, and when you are tired you may sleep a little; we are going into the forest to cut wood, and in the evening when we are done, we will come and fetch you away."

When it was noon, Gretel shared her piece of bread with Hansel, who had scattered his by the way. Then they fell asleep and evening came and went, but no one came to the poor children. They did not awake until it was dark night, and Hansel comforted his little sister and said, "Just wait, Gretel, until the moon rises, and then we shall see the crumbs of bread which I have strewn about, they will show us our way home again." When the moon came they set out, but they found no crumbs, for the many thousands of birds which fly about in the woods and fields had picked them all up. Hansel said to Gretel, "We shall soon find the way," but they did not find it. They walked the whole night and all the next day, too, from morning till evening, but they did not get out of the forest, and were very hungry, for they had nothing to eat but two or three berries, which grew on the ground. And as they were so weary that their legs would carry them no longer, they lay down beneath a tree and fell asleep.

It was now three mornings since they had left their father's house. They began to walk again, but they always got deeper into the forest, and if help did not come soon, they would die of hunger and weariness. When it was midday, they saw a beautiful snow-white bird sitting on a bough, which sang so delightfully that they stood still and listened to it. And when it had finished its song, it spread its wings and flew away before them, and they followed it until they reached a little house, on the roof of which it alighted; and when they came quite up to the little house they saw that it was built of bread and covered with cakes, but that the windows were of clear sugar. "We will set to work on that," said Hansel, "and have a good meal. I will eat a bit of the roof, and you, Gretel, can eat some of the window, it will taste sweet." Hansel reached up above, and broke off a little of the roof to try how it tasted, and Gretel leaned against the window and nibbled at the panes. Then a soft voice cried from the room,

> "Nibble, nibble, gnaw,
> Who is nibbling at my little house?"

The children answered,

> "The wind, the wind,
> The heaven-born wind,"

and went on eating without disturbing themselves. Hansel, who thought the roof tasted very nice, tore down a great piece of it, and Gretel pushed out the whole of one round windowpane, sat down, and enjoyed herself with it. Suddenly the door opened, and a very, very old woman, who supported herself on crutches, came creeping out. Hansel and Gretel were so terribly frightened that they let fall what they had in their hands. The old woman, however, nodded her head, and said, "Oh, you dear children, who has brought you here? Do come in, and stay with me. No harm shall happen to you." She took them both by the hand, and led them into her little house. Then good food was set before them, milk and pancakes, with sugar, apples, and nuts. Afterwards two pretty little beds were covered with clean white linen, and Hansel and Gretel lay down in them, and thought they were in heaven.

The old woman had only pretended to be so kind; she was in reality a wicked witch, who lay in wait for children, and had only built the little house of bread in order to entice them there. When a child fell into her power, she killed it, cooked and ate it, and that was a feast day with her. Witches have red eyes, and cannot see far, but they have a keen scent like the beasts, and are aware when human beings draw near. When Hansel and Gretel came into her neighborhood, she laughed maliciously, and said mockingly, "I have them, they shall not escape me again!"

Early in the morning before the children were awake, she was already up, and when she saw both of them sleeping and looking so pretty, with their plump red cheeks, she muttered to herself, "That will be a dainty mouthful!"

Then she seized Hansel with her shriveled hand, carried him into a little stable, and shut him in with a grated door. He might scream as he liked, that was of no use. Then she went to Gretel, shook her till she awoke, and cried, "Get up, lazy thing, fetch some water, and cook something good for your brother, he is in the stable outside, and is to be made fat. When he is fat, I will eat him." Gretel began to weep bitterly, but it was all in vain; she was forced to do what the wicked witch ordered her.

And now the best food was cooked for poor Hansel, but Gretel got nothing but crab shells. Every morning the woman crept to the little stable, and cried, "Hansel, stretch out your finger that I may feel if you will soon be fat." Hansel, however, stretched out a little bone to her, and the old woman, who had dim eyes, could not see it, and thought it was Hansel's finger, and was astonished that there was no way of fattening him. When four weeks had gone by, and Hansel still stayed thin, she was seized with impatience and would not wait any longer.

"Now, Gretel," she cried to the girl, "be active, and bring some water. Let Hansel be fat or lean, tomorrow I will kill him, and cook him."

Ah, how the poor little sister did lament when she had to fetch the water, and how her tears did flow down over her cheeks! "Dear God, do help us," she cried. "If the wild beasts in the forest had devoured us, at least we should have died together."

"Just keep your noise to yourself," said the old woman, "all that won't help you at all."

Early in the morning, Gretel had to go out and hang up the cauldron with the water, and light the fire. "We will bake first," said the old woman. "I have already heated the oven, and kneaded the dough." She pushed poor Gretel out to the oven, from which flames of fire were already darting. "Creep in," said the witch, "and see if it is properly heated, so that we can shut the bread in." And once Gretel was inside, she intended to shut the oven and let her bake in it, and then she would eat her, too.

But Gretel saw what she had in her mind, and said, "I do not know how I am to do it; how do you get in?"

"Silly goose," said the old woman, "The door is big enough; just look, I can get in myself!" and she crept up and thrust her head into the oven. Then Gretel gave her a push that drove her far into it, and shut the iron door, and fastened the bolt. Oh! Then she began to howl quite horribly, but Gretel ran away, and the godless witch was miserably burnt to death.

Gretel, however, ran like lightning to Hansel, opened his little stable, and cried, "Hansel, we are saved! The old witch is dead!" Then Hansel sprang out like a bird from its cage when the door is opened for it. How they did rejoice and embrace each other, and dance about and kiss each other! And as they had no longer any need to fear her, they went into the witch's house, and in every corner there stood chests full of pearls and jewels.

"These are far better than pebbles!" said Hansel, and thrust into his pockets whatever could be got in, and Gretel said, "I, too, will take something home with me," and filled her pinafore full. "But now we will go away," said Hansel, "that we may get out of the witch's forest."

When they had walked for two hours, they came to a great body of water. "We cannot get over," said Hansel, "I see no foot-plank, and no bridge."

"And no boat crosses either," answered Gretel, "but a white duck is swimming there; if I ask her, she will help us over." Then she cried,

> "Little duck, little duck, do you see,
> Hansel and Gretel are waiting for you?
> There's never a plank, or bridge in sight,
> Take us across on your back so white."

The duck came to them, and Hansel seated himself on its back, and told his sister to sit by him. "No," replied Gretel, "that will be too heavy for the little duck; she shall take us across, one after the other." The good little duck did so, and when they were safely across and had walked for a short time, the forest seemed to be more and more familiar to them, and at length they saw from afar their father's house. Then they began to run, rushed into the parlor, and threw themselves into their father's arms. The man had not known one happy hour since he had left the children in the forest; the woman, however, was dead. Gretel emptied her pinafore until pearls and precious stones ran about the room, and Hansel threw one handful after another out of his pocket to add to them. Then all anxiety was at an end, and they lived together in perfect happiness. My tale is done, see the mouse run, whoever catches it, may make himself a big fur cap out of it.

16. THE THREE SNAKE-LEAVES

There was once on a time a poor man, who could no longer support his only son. Then said the son, "Dear father, things go so badly with us that I am a burden to you. I would rather go away and see how I can earn my bread." So the father gave him his blessing, and with great sorrow they parted. At this time the King of a mighty empire was at war, and the youth entered his service, and with him went out to fight. And when he came before the enemy, there was a battle, and great danger, and it rained shot until his comrades fell on all sides, and when the leader also was killed, those left were about to take flight, but the youth stepped forth, spoke boldly to them, and cried, "We will not let our fatherland be ruined!" Then the others followed him, and he pressed on and conquered the enemy. When the King heard that he owed the victory to him alone, he raised him above all the others, gave him great treasures, and made him the first in the Kingdom.

The King had a daughter who was very beautiful, but she was also very strange. She had made a vow to take no one as her lord and husband who did not promise to let himself be buried alive with her if she died first. "If he loves me with all his heart," said she, "of what use will life be to him afterwards?" On her side she would do the same, and if he died first, would go down to the grave with him. This strange oath had up to this time frightened away all wooers, but the youth became so charmed with her beauty that he cared for nothing, but asked her father for her.

"But do you know what you must promise?" said the King.

"I must be buried with her," he replied, "if I outlive her, but my love is so great that I do not mind the danger." Then the King consented, and the wedding was solemnized with great splendor.

They lived now for a while happy and contented with each other, and then it befell that the young Queen was attacked by a severe illness, and no physician could save her. And as she lay there dead, the young King remembered what he had been obliged to promise, and was horrified at having to lie down alive in the grave, but there was no escape. The King had placed sentries at all the gates, and it was not possible to avoid his fate. When the day came when the corpse was to be buried, he was taken down into the royal vault with it and then the door was shut and bolted.

Near the coffin stood a table on which were four candles, four loaves of bread, and four bottles of wine, and when this provision came to an end, he would have to die of hunger. And now he sat there full of pain and grief, ate every day only a little piece of bread, drank only a mouthful of wine, and nevertheless saw death daily drawing nearer. While he thus gazed before him, he saw a snake creep out of a corner of the vault and approach the dead body. And as he thought it came to gnaw at it, he drew his sword and said, "As long as I live, you shall not touch her," and hewed the snake in three pieces.

After a time a second snake crept out of the hole, and when it saw the other lying dead and cut in pieces, it went back, but soon came again with three green leaves in its mouth. Then it took the three pieces of the snake, laid them together, as they ought to go, and placed one of the leaves on each wound. Immediately the severed parts joined themselves together, the snake moved, and became alive again, and both of them hastened away together. The leaves were left lying on the ground, and a desire came into the mind of the unhappy man who had been watching all this, to know if the wondrous power of the leaves which had brought the snake to life again, could not likewise be of service to a human being. So he picked up the leaves and laid one of them on the mouth of his dead wife, and the two others on her eyes. And hardly had he done this than the blood stirred in her veins, rose into her pale face, and colored it again. Then she drew breath, opened her eyes, and said, "Ah, God, where am I?"

"You are with me, dear wife," he answered, and told her how everything had happened, and how he had brought her back to life again. Then he gave her some wine and bread, and when she had regained her strength, he raised her up and they went to the door and knocked, and called so loudly that the sentries heard it, and told the King. The King came down himself and opened the door, and there he found both strong and well, and rejoiced with them that now all sorrow was over.

The young King, however, took the three snake-leaves with him, gave them to a servant and said, "Keep them for me carefully, and carry them constantly about you; who knows in what trouble they may yet be of service to us!"

A change had, however, taken place in his wife; after she had been restored to life, it seemed as if all love for her husband had gone out of her heart. After some time, when he wanted to make a voyage over the sea, to visit his old father, and they had gone on board a ship, she forgot the great love and fidelity which he had shown her, and which had been the means of rescuing her from death, and conceived a wicked inclination for the skipper. And once when the young King lay there asleep, she called in the skipper and seized the sleeper by the head, and the skipper took him by the feet, and thus they threw him down into the sea. When the shameful deed was done, she said, "Now let us return home, and say that he died on the way. I will extol and praise you so to my father that he will marry me to you, and make you the heir to his crown." But the faithful servant who had seen all that they did, unseen by them, unfastened a little boat from the ship, got into it, sailed after his master, and let the traitors go on their way. He fished up the dead body, and by the help of the three snake-leaves which he carried about with him, and laid on the eyes and mouth, he fortunately brought the young King back to life.

They both rowed with all their strength day and night, and their little boat flew so swiftly that they reached the old King before the others did. He was astonished when he saw them come alone, and asked what had happened to them. When he learned the wickedness of his daughter he said, "I cannot believe that she has behaved so ill, but the truth will soon come to light," and bade both go into a secret chamber and keep themselves hidden from everyone. Soon afterwards the great ship came sailing in, and the godless woman appeared before her father with a troubled countenance. He said, "Why do you come back alone? Where is your husband?"

"Ah, dear father," she replied, "I come home again in great grief; during the voyage, my husband became suddenly ill and died, and if the good skipper had not given me his help, it would have gone badly for me. He was present at his death, and can tell you all." The King said, "I will make the dead alive again," and opened the chamber, and bade the two come out. When the woman saw her husband, she was thunderstruck, and fell on her knees and begged for mercy.

The King said, "There is no mercy. He was ready to die with you and restored you to life again, but you have murdered him in his sleep, and shall receive the reward that you deserve." Then she was placed with her accomplice in a ship which had been pierced with holes, and sent out to sea, where they soon sank amid the waves.

17. THE WHITE SNAKE

A long time ago there lived a king who was famed for his wisdom through all the land. Nothing was hidden from him, and it seemed as if news of the most secret things was brought to him through the air. But he had a strange custom; every day after dinner, when the table was cleared, and no one else was present, a trusty servant had to bring him one more dish. It was covered, however, and even the servant did not know what was in it, nor did anyone know, for the King never took off the cover to eat until he was quite alone.

This had gone on for a long time, when one day the servant, who took away the dish, was overcome with such curiosity that he could not help carrying the dish into his room. When he had carefully locked the door, he lifted up the cover, and saw a white snake lying on the dish. But when he saw it he could not deny himself the pleasure of tasting it, so he cut off a little bit and put it into his mouth. No sooner had it touched his tongue than he heard a strange whispering of little voices outside his window. He went and listened, and then noticed that it was the sparrows who were chattering together, and telling one another of all kinds of things which they had seen in the fields and woods. Eating the snake had given him power of understanding the language of animals.

Now it so happened that on this very day the Queen lost her most beautiful ring, and suspicion of having stolen it fell upon this trusty servant, who was allowed to go everywhere. The King ordered the man to be brought before him, and threatened with angry words that unless he could before the morrow point out the thief, he himself should be looked upon as guilty and executed. In vain he declared his innocence; he was dismissed with no better answer.

In his trouble and fear he went down into the courtyard and thought about how to help himself out of his trouble. Now some ducks were sitting together quietly by a brook and taking their rest; and, while they were making their feathers smooth with their bills, they were having a confidential conversation together. The servant stood by and listened. They were telling one another of all the places where they had been waddling about all the morning, and what good food they had found, and one said in a pitiful tone, "Something lies heavy in my stomach; as

I was eating in haste I swallowed a ring which lay under the Queen's window."

The servant at once seized her by the neck, carried her to the kitchen, and said to the cook, "Here is a fine duck; pray, kill her."

"Yes," said the cook, and weighed her in his hand; "she has spared no trouble to fatten herself, and has been waiting to be roasted long enough." So he cut off her head, and as she was being dressed for the spit, the Queen's ring was found inside her.

The servant could now easily prove his innocence; and the King, to make amends for the wrong, allowed him to ask a favor, and promised him the best place in the court that he could wish for. The servant refused everything, and only asked for a horse and some money for traveling, as he had a mind to see the world and go about a little.

When his request was granted he set out on his way, and one day came to a pond, where he saw three fishes caught in the reeds and gasping for water. Now, though it is said that fishes are mute, he heard them lamenting that they must perish so miserably, and, as he had a kind heart, he got off his horse and put the three prisoners back into the water. They quivered with delight, put out their heads, and cried to him, "We will remember you and repay you for saving us!"

He rode on, and after a while it seemed to him that he heard a voice in the sand at his feet. He listened, and heard an ant king complain, "Why cannot folks, with their clumsy beasts, keep off our bodies? That stupid horse, with his heavy hoofs, has been treading down my people without mercy!" So the servant turned on to a side path and the ant king cried out to him, "We will remember you—one good turn deserves another!"

The path led him into a wood, and here he saw two old ravens standing by their nest, and throwing out their young ones. "Out with you, you idle, good-for-nothing creatures!" cried they; "we cannot find food for you any longer; you are big enough, and can provide for yourselves."

But the poor young ravens lay upon the ground, flapping their wings, and crying, "Oh, what helpless chicks we are! We must shift for ourselves, and yet we cannot fly! What can we do, but lie here and starve?" So the good young fellow alighted and killed his horse with his sword, and gave it to them for food. Then they came hopping up to it, satisfied their hunger, and cried, "We will remember you—one good turn deserves another!"

And now he had to use his own legs, and when he had walked a long way, he came to a large city. There was a great noise and crowd in the streets, and a man rode up on horseback, crying aloud, "The King's daughter wants a husband; but whoever pursues her hand must perform a hard task, and if he does not succeed he will forfeit his life." Many had already made the attempt, but in vain; nevertheless when the youth saw the King's daughter he was so overcome by her great beauty that he forgot all danger, went before the King, and declared himself a suitor.

So he was led out to the sea, and a gold ring was thrown into it, in his sight; then the King ordered him to fetch this ring up from the bottom of the sea, and added, "If you come up again without it you will be thrown in again and again until you perish amid the waves." All the people grieved for the handsome youth; then they went away, leaving him alone by the sea.

He stood on the shore and considered what he should do, when suddenly he saw three fishes come swimming towards him, and they were the very fishes whose lives he had saved. The one in the middle held a mussel in its mouth, which it laid on the shore at the youth's feet, and when he had taken it up and opened it, there lay the gold ring in the shell. Full of joy he took it to the King, and expected that he would grant him the promised reward.

But when the proud princess perceived that he was not her equal in birth, she scorned him, and required him first to perform another task. She went down into the garden and strewed with her own hands ten sacks full of millet seed on the grass; then she said, "Tomorrow morning before sunrise these must be picked up, with not a single grain missing."

The youth sat down in the garden and considered how it might be possible to perform this task, but he could think of nothing, and there he sat sorrowfully awaiting the break of day, when he should be led to death. But as soon as the first rays of the sun shone into the garden he saw all the ten sacks standing side by side, quite full, and not a single grain was missing. The ant king had come in the night with thousands and thousands of ants, and the grateful creatures had by great industry picked up all the millet seed and gathered them into the sacks.

Presently the King's daughter herself came down into the garden, and was amazed to see that the young man had done the task she had given him. But she could not yet conquer her proud heart, and said,

"Although he has performed both the tasks, he shall not be my husband until he has brought me an apple from the Tree of Life."

The youth did not know where the Tree of Life stood, but he set out, and would have gone on forever, as long as his legs would carry him, though he had no hope of finding it. After he had wandered through three kingdoms, he came one evening to a wood, and lay down under a tree to sleep. But he heard a rustling in the branches, and a golden apple fell into his hand. At the same time three ravens flew down to him, perched themselves upon his knee, and said, "We are the three young ravens whom you saved from starving; when we had grown big, and heard that you were seeking the Golden Apple, we flew over the sea to the end of the world, where the Tree of Life stands, and have brought you the apple." The youth, full of joy, set out homewards, and took the Golden Apple to the King's beautiful daughter, who had no more excuses left to make. They cut the Apple of Life in two and ate it together; and then her heart became full of love for him, and they lived in undisturbed happiness to a great age.

18. THE STRAW, THE COAL, AND THE BEAN

In a village dwelt a poor old woman, who had gathered together a dish of beans and wanted to cook them. So she made a fire on her hearth, and so that it might burn quicker, she lighted it with a handful of straw. When she was emptying the beans into the pan, one dropped without her observing it, and lay on the ground beside a straw, and soon afterwards a burning coal from the fire leapt down to the two. Then the straw began and said, "Dear friends, from where do you come here?"

The coal replied, "I fortunately sprang out of the fire, and if I had not escaped by main force, my death would have been certain—I should have been burnt to ashes."

The bean said, "I too have escaped with a whole skin, but if the old woman had got me into the pan, I should have been made into broth without any mercy, like my comrades."

"And would a better fate have fallen to my lot?" said the straw. "The old woman has destroyed all my brethren in fire and smoke; she seized sixty of them at once, and took their lives. I luckily slipped through her fingers."

"But what are we to do now?" said the coal.

"I think," answered the bean, "that as we have so fortunately escaped death, we should keep together like good companions, and lest a new misfortune should overtake us here, we should go away together, to a foreign country."

The proposition pleased the two others, and they set out on their way in company. Soon, however, they came to a little brook, and as there was no bridge or foot-plank, they did not know how they were to get over it. The straw hit on a good idea, and said, "I will lay myself straight across, and then you can walk over on me as on a bridge." The straw therefore stretched itself from one bank to the other, and the coal, who was of an impetuous disposition, tripped quite boldly on to the newly-built bridge. But when she had reached the middle, and heard the water rushing beneath her, she was, after all, afraid, and stood still, and ventured no farther. The straw, however, began to burn, broke in two pieces, and fell into the stream. The coal slipped after her, hissed when she got into the water, and breathed her last. The bean, who had prudently stayed behind on the shore, could not but laugh at the event, was unable to stop, and laughed so heartily that she burst. It would have been all over for her, likewise, if, by good fortune, a tailor who was traveling in search of work, had not sat down to rest by the brook. As he had a compassionate heart he pulled out his needle and thread, and sewed her together. The bean thanked him most prettily, but as the tailor used black thread, all beans since then have a black seam.

19. THE FISHERMAN AND HIS WIFE

There was once upon a time a fisherman who lived with his wife in a miserable pigsty close by the sea, and every day he went out fishing. And once as he was sitting with his rod, looking at the clear water, his line suddenly went down, far down below, and when he drew it up again he brought out a large flounder. Then the flounder said to him, "Listen, you fisherman, I pray you, let me live, I am no flounder really, but an enchanted prince. What good will it do you to kill me? I should not be good to eat, put me in the water again, and let me go."

"Come," said the fisherman, "there is no need for so many words about it—a fish that can talk I should certainly let go, anyhow." With that he put him back again into the clear water, and the flounder went to the bottom, leaving a long streak of blood behind him. Then the fisherman got up and went home to his wife in the pigsty.

"Husband," said the woman, "have you caught nothing today?"

"No," said the man, "I did catch a flounder, who said he was an enchanted prince, so I let him go again."

"Did you not wish for anything first?" said the woman.

"No," said the man; "what should I wish for?"

"Ah," said the woman, "it is surely hard to have to live always in this dirty pigsty; you might have wished for a small cottage for us. Go back and call him. Tell him we want to have a small cottage, he will certainly give us that."

"Ah," said the man, "why should I go there again?"

"Why," said the woman, "you did catch him, and you let him go again; he is sure to do it. Go at once." The man still did not quite like to go, but did not like to oppose his wife, and went to the sea.

When he got there the sea was all green and yellow, and no longer so smooth; so he stood still and said,

> "Flounder, flounder in the sea,
> Come, I pray you, here to me;
> For my wife, good Isabel,
> Has sent me here against my will."

Then the flounder came swimming to him and said, "Well what does she want, then?"

"Ah," said the man, "I did catch you, and my wife says I really ought to have wished for something. She does not like to live in a wretched pigsty any longer. She would like to have a cottage."

"Go, then," said the flounder, "she has it already."

When the man went home, his wife was no longer in the pigsty, but instead of it there stood a small cottage, and she was sitting on a bench before the door. Then she took him by the hand and said to him, "Just come inside, look, now isn't this a great deal better?" So they went in, and there was a small porch, and a pretty little parlor and bedroom, and a kitchen and pantry, with the best of furniture, and fitted up with the most beautiful things made of tin and brass, whatever was wanted. And behind the cottage there was a small yard, with hens and ducks, and a little garden with flowers and fruit. "Look," said the wife, "is not that nice!"

"Yes," said the husband, "and so we must always think it. Now we will live quite contented."

"We will think about that," said the wife. With that they ate something and went to bed.

Everything went well for a week or a fortnight, and then the woman said, "Listen, husband, this cottage is far too small for us, and the garden and yard are little; the flounder might just as well have given us a larger house. I should like to live in a great stone castle; go to the flounder, and tell him to give us a castle."

"Ah, wife," said the man, "the cottage is quite good enough; why should we live in a castle?"

"What!" said the woman; "Just go there, the flounder can always do that."

"No, wife," said the man, "the flounder has just given us the cottage, I do not like to go back so soon, it might make him angry."

"Go," said the woman, "he can do it quite easily, and will be glad to do it; just you go to him."

The man's heart grew heavy, and he did not want to go. He said to himself, "It is not right," and yet he went. And when he came to the sea the water was quite purple and dark blue, and grey and thick, and no longer so green and yellow, but it was still quiet. And he stood there and said—

"Flounder, flounder in the sea,
Come, I pray you, here to me;
For my wife, good Isabel,
Has sent me here against my will."

"Well, what does she want, then?" said the flounder.

"Alas," said the man, half scared, "she wants to live in a great stone castle."

"Go to it, then, she is standing before the door," said the flounder.

Then the man went away, intending to go home, but when he got there, he found a great stone palace, and his wife was just standing on the steps going in, and she took him by the hand and said, "Come in." So he went in with her, and in the castle was a great hall paved with marble, and many servants, who flung the doors wide. And the walls were all bright with beautiful hangings, and in the rooms were chairs and tables of pure gold, and crystal chandeliers hung from the ceiling, and all the rooms and bed-rooms had carpets, and food and wine of the very best were standing on all the tables, so that they nearly broke down beneath it. Behind the house, too, there was a great courtyard, with stables for horses and cows, and the very best of carriages; there was a magnificent large garden, too, with the most beautiful flowers and fruit trees, and a park half a mile long, in which were stags, deer, and hares, and everything that could be desired. "Come," said the woman, "isn't that beautiful?"

"Yes, indeed," said the man, "now let it be; and we will live in this beautiful castle and be content."

"We will consider about that," said the woman, "and sleep upon it." Then they went to bed.

Next morning the wife awoke first, and it was just daybreak, and from her bed she saw the beautiful country lying before her. Her husband was still stretching himself, so she poked him in the side with her elbow, and said, "Get up, husband, and just peep out of the window. Look you, couldn't we be the King over all that land? Go to the flounder, we will be the King."

"Ah, wife," said the man, "why should we be King? I do not want to be King."

"Well," said the wife, "if you won't be King, I will; go to the flounder, for I will be King."

"Ah, wife," said the man, "why do you want to be King? I do not want to say that to him."

"Why not?" said the woman; "Go to him this instant; I must be King!"

So the man went, and was quite unhappy because his wife wished to be King. "It is not right; it is not right," thought he. He did not wish to go, but yet he went.

And when he came to the sea, it was quite dark-grey, and the water heaved up from below, and smelled putrid. Then he went and stood by it, and said,

> "Flounder, flounder in the sea,
> Come, I pray you, here to me;
> For my wife, good Isabel,
> Has sent me here against my will."

"Well, what does she want, then?" said the flounder.

"Alas," said the man, "she wants to be King."

"Go to her; she is King already."

So the man went, and when he came to the palace, the castle had become much larger, and had a great tower and magnificent ornaments, and the sentinel was standing before the door, and there were numbers of soldiers with kettle-drums and trumpets. And when he went inside the house, everything was of real marble and gold, with velvet covers and great golden tassels. Then the doors of the hall were opened, and there was the court in all its splendor, and his wife was sitting on a high throne of gold and diamonds, with a great crown of gold on her head, and a scepter of pure gold and jewels in her hand, and on both sides of her stood her maids-in-waiting in a row, each of them always one head shorter than the last.

Then he went and stood before her, and said, "Ah, wife, and now you are King."

"Yes," said the woman, "now I am King." So he stood and looked at her, and when he had looked at her thus for some time, he said, "And now that you are King, let all else be, now we will wish for nothing more."

"Nay, husband," said the woman, quite anxiously, "I find time passes very heavily, I can bear it no longer; go to the flounder—I am King, but I must be Emperor, too."

"Alas, wife, why do you wish to be Emperor?"

"Husband," said she, "go to the flounder. I will be Emperor."

"Alas, wife," said the man, "he cannot make you Emperor; I may not say that to the fish. There is only one Emperor in the land. An Emperor the flounder cannot make you! I assure you he cannot."

"What!" said the woman, "I am the King, and you are nothing but my husband; will you go this moment? Go at once! If he can make a King he can make an emperor. I will be Emperor; go instantly." So he was forced to go.

As the man went, however, he was troubled in mind, and thought to himself, "It will not end well; it will not end well! Emperor is too shameless! The flounder will at last be tired out."

With that he reached the sea, and the sea was quite black and thick, and began to boil up from below, so that it threw up bubbles, and such a sharp wind blew over it that it curdled, and the man was afraid. Then he went and stood by it, and said,

> "Flounder, flounder in the sea,
> Come, I pray you, here to me;
> For my wife, good Isabel,
> Has sent me here against my will."

"Well, what does she want, then?" said the flounder. "Alas, flounder," said he, "my wife wants to be Emperor."

"Go to her," said the flounder; "she is Emperor already."

So the man went, and when he got there the whole palace was made of polished marble with alabaster figures and golden ornaments, and soldiers were marching before the door blowing trumpets, and beating cymbals and drums; and in the house, barons, and counts, and dukes were going about as servants. Then they opened the doors to him, which were made of pure gold. And when he entered, there sat his wife on a throne, which was made of one piece of gold, and was at least two miles high; and she wore a great golden crown that was three yards high, and set with diamonds and carbuncles, and in one hand she had the scepter, and in the other the imperial orb; and on both sides of her stood the yeomen of the guard in two rows, each being smaller than the one before him, from the biggest giant, who was two miles high, to the very smallest dwarf, just as big as my little finger. And before it stood a number of princes and dukes.

Then the man went and stood among them, and said, "Wife, are you Emperor now?"

"Yes," said she, "now I am Emperor."

Then he stood and looked at her well, and when he had looked at her for some time, he said, "Ah, wife, be content, now that you are Emperor."

"Husband," said she, "why are you standing there? Now, I am Emperor, but I will be Pope too; go to the flounder."

"Alas, wife," said the man, "what will you not wish for? You cannot be Pope. There is but one in Christendom. He cannot make you Pope."

"Husband," said she, "I will be Pope; go immediately, I must be Pope this very day."

"No, wife," said the man, "I do not want to say that to him; that would not do, it is too much; the flounder can't make you Pope."

"Husband," said she, "what nonsense! If he can make an emperor he can make a pope. Go to him directly. I am Emperor, and you are nothing but my husband; will you go at once?"

Then he was afraid and went; but he was quite faint, and shivered and shook, and his knees and legs trembled. And a high wind blew over the land, and the clouds flew, and towards evening all grew dark, and the leaves fell from the trees, and the water rose and roared as if it were boiling, and splashed upon the shore. And in the distance he saw ships which were firing guns in distress, pitching and tossing on the waves. And yet in the midst of the sky there was still a small bit of blue, though on every side it was as red as in a heavy storm. So, full of despair, he went and stood in much fear and said,

> "Flounder, flounder in the sea,
> Come, I pray you, here to me;
> For my wife, good Isabel,
> Has sent me here against my will."

"Well, what does she want, then?" said the flounder.

"Alas," said the man, "she wants to be Pope."

"Go to her then," said the flounder; "she is Pope already."

So he went, and when he got there, he saw what seemed to be a large church surrounded by palaces. He pushed his way through the crowd. Inside, however, everything was lighted up with thousands and thousands of candles, and his wife clad in gold, and she was sitting on a much higher throne, and had three great golden crowns on, and round about her there was much ecclesiastical splendor; and on both sides of her was a row of candles the largest of which was as tall as the very tallest tower, down to the very smallest kitchen candle, and all the emperors and kings were on their knees before her, kissing her shoe. "Wife," said the man, and looked attentively at her, "are you now Pope?"

"Yes," said she, "I am Pope."

So he stood and looked at her, and it was just as if he was looking at the bright sun. When he had stood looking at her thus for a short time, he said, "Ah, wife, if you are Pope, do let well enough alone!" But she looked as stiff as a post, and did not move or show any signs of life. Then said he, "Wife, now that you are Pope, be satisfied, you cannot become anything greater now."

"I will consider about that," said the woman. At this they both went to bed, but she was not satisfied, and greediness let her have no sleep, for she was continually thinking what there was left for her to be.

The man slept well and soundly, for he had run about a great deal during the day; but the woman could not fall asleep at all, and flung herself from one side to the other the whole night through, thinking always what more was left for her to be, but unable to call to mind anything else. At length the sun began to rise, and when the woman saw the red of dawn, she sat up in bed and looked at it. And when, through the window, she saw the sun thus rising, she said, "Cannot I, too, order the sun and moon to rise?" "Husband," she said, poking him in the ribs with her elbow, "wake up! Go to the flounder, for I wish to be like God is."

The man was still half asleep, but he was so horrified that he fell out of bed. He thought he must have heard wrong, and rubbed his eyes, and said, "Alas, wife, what are you saying?"

"Husband," said she, "if I can't order the sun and moon to rise, and have to look on and see the sun and moon rising, I can't bear it. I shall not know what it is to have another happy hour, unless I can make them rise myself." Then she looked at him so terribly that a shudder ran over him, and said, "Go at once; I wish to be like God."

"Alas, wife," said the man, falling on his knees before her, "the flounder cannot do that; he can make an emperor and a pope; I beseech you, go on as you are, and be Pope."

Then she fell into a rage, and her hair flew wildly about her head, and she cried, "I will not endure this, I'll not bear it any longer; will you go?"

Then he put on his trousers and ran away like a madman. But outside a great storm was raging, and blowing so hard that he could scarcely keep his feet; houses and trees toppled over, the mountains trembled, rocks rolled into the sea, the sky was pitch black, and it thundered and lightened, and the sea came in with black waves as high as church-towers and mountains, and all with crests of white foam at the top. Then he cried, but could not hear his own words,

> "Flounder, flounder in the sea,
> Come, I pray you, here to me;
> For my wife, good Isabel,
> Has sent me here against my will."

"Well, what does she want, then?" said the flounder.

"Alas," said he, "she wants to be like God."

"Go to her, and you will find her back again in the dirty pigsty." And there they are living still at this very time.

20. THE VALIANT LITTLE TAILOR

One summer's morning a little tailor was sitting on his table by the window; he was in good spirits, and sewed with all his might. Then came a peasant woman down the street crying, "Good jams, cheap! Good jams, cheap!"

This rang pleasantly in the tailor's ears; he stretched his delicate head out of the window, and called, "Come up here, dear woman; here you will get rid of your goods." The woman came up the three steps to the tailor with her heavy basket, and he made her unpack all of the pots for him. He inspected all of them, lifted them up, put his nose to them, and at length said, "The jam seems to me to be good, so weigh me out three ounces, dear woman, and if it comes to a quarter of a pound I will not complain." The woman who had hoped to find a good sale, gave him what he desired, but went away quite angry and grumbling. "Now, God bless this jam," cried the little tailor, "and give me health and strength;" so he brought the bread out of the cupboard, cut himself a piece right across the loaf and spread the jam over it. "This won't taste bitter," said he, "but I will just finish the jacket before I take a bite." He laid the bread near him, sewed on, and in his joy, made bigger and bigger stitches. In the meantime the smell of the sweet jam ascended to the wall, where the flies were sitting in great numbers, that they were attracted and descended on it in hosts. "Ho! Who invited you?" said the little tailor, and drove the unbidden guests away. The flies, however, who understood no words, would not be turned away, but came back again in ever-increasing companies. The little tailor at last lost all patience, and got a bit of cloth from the hole under his worktable, and saying, "Wait, and I will give it to you," struck it mercilessly on them. When he drew it away and counted, there lay before him no fewer than seven, dead and with legs stretched out. "Are you a fellow of that sort?" said he, and could not help admiring his own bravery. "The whole town shall know of this!" And the little tailor hastened to cut himself a girdle, stitched it, and embroidered on it in large letters, "Seven at one stroke!" "What, the town!" he continued, "The whole world shall hear of it!" and his heart wagged with joy like a lamb's tail. The tailor put on the girdle, and resolved to go forth into the world, because he thought his workshop was too small for his valor. Before he went away, he sought about in the house to see if there was anything which he could take with him; however, he found nothing but old cheese, and that he put in his pocket. In front of the door he observed a bird which had caught itself in the thicket. It had to go into his pocket with the cheese. Now he took to the road boldly, and as he was light and nimble, he felt no fatigue. The road led him up a mountain, and when he had reached the highest point of it, there sat a powerful giant looking about him quite comfortably. The little tailor went bravely up, spoke to him, and said, "Good day, comrade, so you are sitting there overlooking the wide-spread world! I am just on my way there, and want to try my luck. Have you any inclination to go with me?"

The giant looked contemptuously at the tailor, and said, "You ragamuffin! You miserable creature!"

"Oh, indeed?" answered the little tailor, and unbuttoned his coat, and showed the giant the girdle, "There you may read what kind of a man I am!"

The giant read, "Seven at one stroke," and thought that they had been men whom the tailor had killed, and began to feel a little respect for the tiny fellow. Nevertheless, he wished to try him first, and took a stone in his hand and squeezed it together so that water dropped out of it. "Do that likewise," said the giant, "if you have strength?"

"Is that all?" said the tailor, "that is child's play with us!" and put his hand into his pocket, brought out the soft cheese, and pressed it until the liquid ran out of it. "Faith," said he, "that was good, wasn't it?"

The giant did not know what to say, and could not believe it of the little man. Then the giant picked up a stone and threw it so high that the eye could scarcely follow it. "Now, little mite of a man, do that likewise."

"Well thrown," said the tailor, "but after all the stone came down to earth again; I will throw you one which shall never come back at all." And he put his hand into his pocket, took out the bird, and threw it into the air. The bird, delighted with its liberty, rose, flew away and did not come back. "How does that shot please you, comrade?" asked the tailor.

"You can certainly throw," said the giant, "but now we will see if you are able to carry anything properly." He took the little tailor to a mighty oak tree which lay there felled on the ground, and said, "If you are strong enough, help me to carry the tree out of the forest."

"Readily," answered the little man; "you take the trunk on your shoulders, and I will raise up the branches and twigs; after all, they are the heaviest." The giant took the trunk on his shoulder, but the tailor seated himself on a branch, and the giant who could not look round, had to carry away the whole tree, and the little tailor to boot. The tailor was quite merry and happy, and whistled the song, "Three tailors rode forth from the gate," as if carrying the tree were child's play.

The giant, after he had dragged the heavy burden part of the way, could go no further, and cried, "Ho, I shall have to let the tree fall!"

The tailor sprang nimbly down, seized the tree with both arms as if he had been carrying it, and said to the giant, "You are such a great fellow, and yet cannot even carry the tree!"

They went on together, and as they passed a cherry tree, the giant laid hold of the top of the tree where the ripest fruit was hanging, bent it down, put it into the tailor's hand, and bade him eat. But the little tailor was much too weak to hold the tree, and when the giant let it go, it sprang back again, and the tailor was hurried into the air with it. When he had fallen down again without injury, the giant said, "What is this? Have you not strength enough to hold the weak twig?"

"There is no lack of strength," answered the little tailor. "Do you think that could be anything to a man who has struck down seven at one blow? I leapt over the tree because the huntsmen are shooting down there in the thicket. Jump as I did, if you can do it." The giant made the attempt, but could not get over the tree, and remained hanging in the branches, so that in this also the tailor kept the upper hand.

The giant said, "If you are such a valiant fellow, come with me into our cavern and spend the night with us." The little tailor was willing, and followed him. When they went into the cave, other giants were sitting there by the fire, and each of them had a roasted sheep in his hand and was eating it. The little tailor looked round and thought, "It is much more spacious here than in my workshop." The giant showed him a bed, and said he was to lie down in it and sleep. The bed, however, was too big for the little tailor; he did not lie down in it, but crept into a corner. When it was midnight, and the giant thought that the little tailor was lying in a sound sleep, he got up, took a great iron bar, cut through the bed with one blow, and thought he had given the runt his finishing stroke. With the earliest dawn the giants went into the forest, and had quite forgotten the little tailor, when all at once he walked up to them quite merrily and boldly. The giants were terrified, they were afraid that he would strike them all dead, and ran away in a great hurry.

The little tailor went onwards, always following his own pointed nose. After he had walked for a long time, he came to the courtyard of a royal palace, and as he felt weary, he lay down on the grass and fell asleep. While he lay there, the people came and inspected him on all sides, and read on his girdle, "Seven at one stroke." "Ah," said they, "Why is the great warrior here in the midst of peace? He must be a mighty lord." They went and announced him to the King, and gave it as their opinion that if war should break out, this would be a weighty and useful man who ought on no account to be allowed to depart. The counsel pleased the King, and he sent one of his courtiers to the little tailor to offer him military service when he awoke. The ambassador remained standing by the sleeper, waited until he stretched his limbs and opened his eyes, and then conveyed to him this proposal.

"For this very reason I have come here," the tailor replied, "I am ready to enter the King's service." He was therefore honorably received and a special dwelling was assigned him.

The soldiers, however, were set against the little tailor, and wished him a thousand miles away. "What is to be the end of this?" they said amongst themselves. "If we quarrel with him, and he strikes about him, seven of us will fall at every blow; not one of us can stand against him." They came therefore to a decision, went to the King, and begged for their dismissal. "We are not prepared," said they, "to stay with a man who kills seven at one stroke."

The King was sorry that for the sake of one he should lose all his faithful servants, wished that he had never set eyes on the tailor, and would willingly get rid of him again. But he did not venture to give him his dismissal, for he dreaded that he should strike him and all his people dead, and place himself on the royal throne. He thought about it for a long time, and at last found good counsel. He sent to the little tailor and had him informed that as he was such a great warrior, the King had one request to make to him. In a forest of his country lived two giants who caused great mischief with their robbing, murdering, ravaging, and burning, and no one could approach them without putting himself in danger of death. If the tailor conquered and killed these two giants, he would give him his only daughter to wed, and half of his kingdom as a dowry, likewise one hundred horsemen should go with him to assist him.

"That would indeed be a fine thing for a man like me!" thought the little tailor. "One is not offered a beautiful princess and half a kingdom every day of one's life!" "Oh, yes," he replied, "I will soon subdue the giants, and do not require the help of the hundred horsemen to do it; he who can hit seven with one blow has no need to be afraid of two."

The little tailor went forth, and the hundred horsemen followed him. When he came to the outskirts of the forest, he said to his followers, "Just stay waiting here, I alone will soon finish off the giants." Then he bounded into the forest and looked about right and left. After a while he perceived both giants. They lay sleeping under a tree, and snored so that the branches waved up and down. The little tailor, not idle, gathered two pocketfuls of stones, and with these climbed up the tree. When he was halfway up, he slipped down by a branch, until he sat just above the sleepers, and then let one stone after another fall on the breast of one of the giants. For a long time the giant felt nothing, but at last he awoke, pushed his comrade, and said, "Why are you knocking me?"

"You must be dreaming," said the other, "I am not knocking you." They laid themselves down to sleep again, and then the tailor threw a stone down on the second. "What is the meaning of this?" cried the other. "Why are you pelting me?"

"I am not pelting you," answered the first, growling. They disputed about it for a time, but as they were weary they let the matter rest, and their eyes closed once more. The little tailor began his game again, picked out the biggest stone, and threw it with all his might on the breast of the first giant. "That is too much!" cried he, and sprang up like a madman, and pushed his companion against the tree until it shook. The other paid him back in the same coin, and they got into such a rage that they tore up trees and belabored each other so long, that at last they both fell down dead on the ground at the same time. Then the little tailor leapt down.

"It is a lucky thing," said he, "that they did not tear up the tree on which I was sitting, or I should have had to spring on to another like a squirrel; but we tailors are nimble." He drew out his sword and gave each of them a couple of thrusts in the breast, and then went out to the horsemen and said, "The work is done; I have given both of them their finishing stroke, but it was hard work! They tore up trees in their sore need, and defended themselves with them, but all that is to no purpose when a man like myself comes, who can kill seven at one blow."

"But are you not wounded?" asked the horsemen.

"You need not concern yourself about that," answered the tailor, "They have not bent one hair of mine." The horsemen would not believe him, and rode into the forest; there they found the giants swimming in their blood, and all round about lay the torn-up trees.

The little tailor demanded of the King the promised reward; he, however, repented of his promise, and again thought of how he could get rid of the hero. "Before you receive my daughter, and the half of my kingdom," said he to him, "you must perform one more heroic deed. In the forest roams a unicorn which does great harm, and you must catch it first."

"I fear one unicorn still less than two giants. Seven at one blow, is my kind of affair." He took a rope and an axe with him, went forth into the forest, and again bade those who were sent with him to wait outside. He had to seek long. The unicorn soon came towards him, and rushed directly at the tailor, as if it would spear him on his horn without more ceremony. "Softly, softly; it can't be done as quickly as that," said he, and stood still and waited until the animal was quite close, and then sprang nimbly behind the tree. The unicorn ran against the tree with all its strength, and struck its horn so fast in the trunk that it had not enough strength to draw it out again, and thus it was caught. "Now, I have got him," said the tailor, and came out from behind the tree and put the rope round its neck, and then with his axe he hewed the horn out of the tree, and when all was ready he led the beast away and took it to the King.

The King still would not give him the promised reward, and made a third demand. Before the wedding the tailor was to catch him a wild boar that made great havoc in the forest, and the huntsmen should give him their help. "Willingly," said the tailor, "that is child's play!" He did not take the huntsmen with him into the forest, and they were well pleased that he did not, for the wild boar had several times received them in such a manner that they had no inclination to lie in wait for him. When the boar perceived the tailor, it ran at him with foaming mouth and whetted tusks, and was about to throw him to the ground, but the active hero sprang into a chapel which was near, and up to the window at once, and in one bound out again. The boar ran in after him, but the tailor ran round outside and shut the door behind it, and then the raging beast, which was much too heavy and awkward to leap out of the window, was caught. The little tailor called the huntsmen there that they might see the prisoner with their own eyes. The hero, went to the King, who was now, whether he liked it or not, obliged to keep his promise, and the King gave him his daughter and the half of his kingdom. Had he known that it was no warlike hero, but a little tailor who was standing before him, it would have made his heart even less happy than it was. The wedding was held with great magnificence and small joy, and out of a tailor a king was made.

After some time the young Queen heard her husband say in his dreams at night, "Boy, make me the doublet, and patch the pantaloons, or else I will rap the yard-measure over your ears." Then she discovered in what state of life the young lord had been born, and next morning complained of her wrongs to her father, and begged him to help her to get rid of her husband, who was nothing else but a tailor. The King comforted her and said, "Leave your bedroom door open this night, and my servants shall stand outside, and when he has fallen asleep shall go in, bind him, and take him on board a ship which shall carry him into the wide world." The woman was satisfied with this; but the King's amour-bearer, who had heard all, was friendly with the young lord, and informed him of the whole plot.

"I'll put a screw into that business," said the little tailor. At night he went to bed with his wife at the usual time, and when she thought that he had fallen asleep, she got up, opened the door, and then lay down again. The little tailor, who was only pretending to be asleep, began to cry out in a clear voice, "Boy, make me the doublet and patch me the pantaloons, or I will rap the yard-measure over your ears. I slayed seven at one blow. I killed two giants, I brought away one unicorn and caught a wild boar, and now I am expected to fear those who are standing outside the room." When these men heard the tailor speaking thus, they were overcome by a great dread, and ran as if the wild hunter were behind them, and none of them would venture anything further against him. So the little tailor was a king and remained one, to the end of his life.

21. CINDERELLA

The wife of a rich man fell sick, and as she felt that her end was drawing near, she called her only daughter to her bedside and said, "Dear child, be good and pious, and then the good God will always protect you, and I will look down on you from heaven and be near you." Then she closed her eyes and departed. Every day the maiden went out to her mother's grave, and wept, and she remained pious and good. When winter came the snow spread a white sheet over the grave, and when the spring sun had drawn it off again, the man had taken another wife.

The woman had brought two daughters into the house with her, who were beautiful and fair of face, but vile and black of heart. Now began a bad time for the poor stepchild. "Is the stupid goose to sit in the parlor with us?" said they. "He who wants to eat bread must earn it; out with the kitchen-wench." They took her pretty clothes away from her, put an old grey bed gown on her, and gave her wooden shoes. "Just look at the proud princess, how decked out she is!" they cried, and laughed, and led her into the kitchen. There she had to do hard work from morning till night, get up before daybreak, carry water, light fires, cook and wash. Besides this, the sisters did her every imaginable injury—they mocked her and emptied her peas and lentils into the ashes, so that she was forced to sit and pick them out again. In the evening when she had worked till she was weary she had no bed to go to, but had to sleep by the fireside in the ashes. And since on that account she always looked dusty and dirty, they called her Cinderella. It happened that the father was once going to the fair, and he asked his two stepdaughters what he should bring back for them.

"Beautiful dresses," said one.

"Pearls and jewels," said the second.

"And you, Cinderella," said he, "what will you have?"

"Father, break off for me the first branch which knocks against your hat on your way home." So he bought beautiful dresses, pearls and jewels for his two stepdaughters, and on his way home, as he was riding through a green thicket, a hazel twig brushed against him and knocked off his hat. Then he broke off the branch and took it with him. When he reached home he gave his stepdaughters the things which they had wished for, and to Cinderella he gave the branch from the hazel-bush. Cinderella thanked him, went to her mother's grave and planted the branch on it, and wept so much that the tears fell down on it and watered it. And it grew, however, and became a handsome tree. Thrice a day Cinderella went and sat beneath it, and wept and prayed, and a little white bird always came on the tree, and if Cinderella expressed a wish, the bird threw down to her what she had wished for.

It happened, however, that the King appointed a festival which was to last three days, and to which all the beautiful young girls in the country were invited, in order that his son might choose himself a bride. When the two stepsisters heard that they too were to appear among the number, they were delighted, called Cinderella and said, "Comb our hair for us, brush our shoes and fasten our buckles, for we are going to the festival at the King's palace." Cinderella obeyed, but wept, because she too would have liked to go with them to the dance, and begged her stepmother to allow her to do so.

"You go, Cinderella!" said she; "You are dusty and dirty and would go to the festival? You have no clothes and shoes, and yet would dance!" As, however, Cinderella went on asking, the stepmother at last said, "I have emptied a dish of lentils into the ashes for you, if you have picked them out again in two hours, you shall go with us."

The maiden went through the back door into the garden, and called, "You tame pigeons, you turtledoves, and all you birds beneath the sky, come and help me to pick

> "The good into the pot,
> The bad into the crop."

Then two white pigeons came in by the kitchen window, and afterwards the turtledoves, and at last all the birds beneath the sky, came whirring and crowding in, and alighted amongst the ashes. And the pigeons nodded with their heads and began pick, pick, pick, pick, and the rest began also pick, pick, pick, pick, and gathered all the good grains into the dish. Hardly had one hour passed before they had finished, and all flew out again. Then the girl took the dish to her stepmother, and was glad, and believed that now she would be allowed to go with them to the festival. But the stepmother said, "No,

Cinderella, you have no clothes and you cannot dance; you would only be laughed at." And as Cinderella wept at this, the stepmother said, "If you can pick two dishes of lentils out of the ashes for me in one hour, you shall go with us." And she thought to herself, "That she most certainly cannot do." When the stepmother had emptied the two dishes of lentils amongst the ashes, the maiden went through the back door into the garden and cried,

> "You tame pigeons,
> You turtledoves,
> And all you birds under heaven,
> Come and help me to pick
> The good into the pot,
> The bad into the crop."

Then two white pigeons came in by the kitchen window, and afterwards the turtledoves, and at length all the birds beneath the sky, came whirring and crowding in, and alighted amongst the ashes. And the doves nodded with their heads and began pick, pick, pick, pick, and the others began also pick, pick, pick, pick, and gathered all the good seeds into the dishes, and before half an hour was over they had already finished, and all flew out again. Then the maiden carried the dishes to the stepmother and was delighted, and believed that she might now go with them to the festival.

But the stepmother said, "All this will not help you; you can not go with us, for you have no clothes and cannot dance; we should be ashamed of you!" With this she turned her back on Cinderella, and hurried away with her two proud daughters.

As no one was now at home, Cinderella went to her mother's grave beneath the hazel tree, and cried,

> "Shiver and quiver, little tree,
> Silver and gold throw down over me."

Then the bird threw a gold and silver dress down to her, and slippers embroidered with silk and silver. She put on the dress with all speed, and went to the festival. Her stepsisters and the stepmother however did not know her, and thought she must be a foreign princess, for she looked so beautiful in the golden dress. They never once thought of

Cinderella, and believed that she was sitting at home in the dirt, picking lentils out of the ashes. The prince went to meet her, took her by the hand and danced with her. He would dance with no other maiden, and never let go of her hand, and if anyone else came to invite her, he said, "This is my partner."

She danced till it was evening, and then she wanted to go home. But the King's son said, "I will go with you and bear you company," for he wished to see to whom the beautiful maiden belonged. She escaped from him, however, and sprang into the pigeon-house. The King's son waited until her father came, and then he told him that the strange maiden had leapt into the pigeon-house.

The old man thought, "Can it be Cinderella?" and they had to bring him an axe and a pickaxe that he might hew the pigeon-house to pieces, but no one was inside it. And when they got home Cinderella lay in her dirty clothes among the ashes, and a dim little oillamp was burning on the mantlepiece, for Cinderella had jumped quickly down from the back of the pigeon-house and had run to the little hazel tree, and there she had taken off her beautiful clothes and laid them on the grave, and the bird had taken them away again, and then she had placed herself in the kitchen amongst the ashes in her grey gown.

Next day when the festival began afresh, and her parents and the stepsisters had gone once more, Cinderella went to the hazel tree and said—

> "Shiver and quiver, my little tree,
> Silver and gold throw down over me."

Then the bird threw down a much more beautiful dress than on the preceding day. And when Cinderella appeared at the festival in this dress, everyone was astonished at her beauty. The King's son had waited until she came, and instantly took her by the hand and danced with no one but her. When others came and invited her, he said, "She is my partner." When evening came she wished to leave, and the King's son followed her and wanted to see into which house she went. But she sprang away from him, and into the garden behind the house. There stood a beautiful tall tree on which hung the most magnificent pears. She clambered so nimbly between the branches like a squirrel that the King's son did not know where she had gone. He waited until her father came, and said to him, "The strange maiden has escaped from me, and

I believe she has climbed up the pear tree." The father thought, "Can it be Cinderella?" and had an axe brought and cut the tree down, but no one was on it. And when they got into the kitchen, Cinderella lay there amongst the ashes, as usual, for she had jumped down on the other side of the tree, had taken the beautiful dress to the bird on the little hazel tree, and put on her grey gown.

On the third day, when the parents and sisters had gone away, Cinderella went once more to her mother's grave and said to the little tree—

> "Shiver and quiver, my little tree,
> Silver and gold throw down over me."

And now the bird threw down to her a dress which was more splendid and magnificent than any she had yet had, and the slippers were golden. And when she went to the festival in the dress, no one knew how to speak for astonishment. The King's son danced with her only, and if anyone invited her to dance, he said, "She is my partner."

When evening came, Cinderella wished to leave, and the King's son was anxious to go with her, but she escaped from him so quickly that he could not follow her. The King's son had, however, used a stratagem, and had caused the whole staircase to be smeared with pitch, and there, when she ran down, had the maiden's left slipper which remained sticking. The King's son picked it up, and it was small and dainty, and all golden. Next morning, he brought it to the father, and said to him, "No one shall be my wife but she whose foot fits this golden slipper."

Then the two sisters were glad, for they had pretty feet. The eldest went with the shoe into her room and wanted to try it on, and her mother stood by. But she could not get her big toe into it, and the shoe was too small for her. Then her mother gave her a knife and said, "Cut the toe off; when you are Queen you will have no more need to go on foot." The maiden cut the toe off, forced the foot into the shoe, swallowed the pain, and went out to the King's son. Then he took her on his horse as his bride and rode away with her.

They were, however, obliged to pass the grave, and there, on the hazel tree, sat the two pigeons and cried,

"Turn and peep, turn and peep,
There's blood within the shoe,
The shoe it is too small for her,
The true bride waits for you."

Then he looked at her foot and saw how the blood was streaming from it. He turned his horse round and took the false bride home again, and said she was not the true one, and that the other sister was to put the shoe on. Then this one went into her chamber and got her toes safely into the shoe, but her heel was too large. So her mother gave her a knife and said, "Cut a bit off your heel; when you are Queen you will have no more need to go on foot." The maiden cut a bit off her heel, forced her foot into the shoe, swallowed the pain, and went out to the King's son.

He took her on his horse as his bride, and rode away with her, but when they passed by the hazel tree, two little pigeons sat on it and cried,

"Turn and peep, turn and peep,
There's blood within the shoe
The shoe it is too small for her,
The true bride waits for you."

He looked down at her foot and saw how the blood was running out of her shoe, and how it had stained her white stocking. Then he turned his horse and took the false bride home again. "This also is not the right one," said he. "Have you no other daughter?"

"No," said the man, "There is still a little stunted kitchen-wench which my late wife left behind, but she cannot possibly be the bride."

The King's son said he was to send her up to him; but the mother answered, "Oh, no, she is much too dirty, she cannot show herself!"

He absolutely insisted on it, and Cinderella had to be called. She first washed her hands and face clean, and then went and bowed down before the King's son, who gave her the golden shoe. Then she seated herself on a stool, drew her foot out of the heavy wooden shoe, and put it into the slipper, which fit like a glove. And when she rose up and the King's son looked at her face he recognized the beautiful maiden who had danced with him and cried, "That is the true bride!" The stepmother and the two sisters were terrified and became pale with rage; he, however, took Cinderella on his horse and rode away with her. As they passed by the hazel tree, the two white doves cried—

"Turn and peep, turn and peep,
 No blood is in the shoe,
 The shoe is not too small for her,
 The true bride rides with you,"

and when they had cried that, the two came flying down and placed themselves on Cinderella's shoulders, one on the right, the other on the left, and remained sitting there.

When the wedding with the King's son was celebrated, the two false sisters came and wanted to get into favor with Cinderella and share her good fortune. When the betrothed couple went to church, the elder was at the right side and the younger at the left, and the pigeons pecked out one eye of each of them. Afterwards as they came back, the elder was at the left, and the younger at the right, and then the pigeons pecked out the other eye of each. And thus, for their wickedness and falsehood, they were punished with blindness as long as they lived.

22. THE RIDDLE

There was once a King's son who was seized with a desire to travel about the world, and took no one with him but a faithful servant. One day he came to a great forest, and when darkness overtook him he could find no shelter, and knew not where to pass the night. Then he saw a girl who was going towards a small house, and when he came nearer, he saw that the maiden was young and beautiful. He spoke to her, and said, "Dear child, can I and my servant find shelter for the night in the little house?"

"Oh, yes," said the girl in a sad voice, "that you certainly can, but I do not advise you to venture it. Do not go in."

"Why not?" asked the King's son.

The maiden sighed and said, "My stepmother practices wicked arts; she is ill disposed toward strangers." Then he saw very well that he had come to the house of a witch, but as it was dark, and he could not go farther, and also was not afraid, he entered. The old woman was sitting in an armchair by the fire, and looked at the stranger with her red eyes.

"Good evening," growled she, and pretended to be quite friendly. "Take a seat and rest yourselves." She blew up the fire on which she was cooking something in a small pot. The daughter warned the two to be prudent, to eat nothing, and drink nothing, for the old woman brewed evil drinks. They slept quietly until early morning. When they were readying for their departure, and the King's son already seated on his horse, the old woman said, "Stop a moment, I will first hand you a parting draught." While she fetched it, the King's son rode away, and the servant who had to buckle his saddle tight, was the only one present when the wicked witch came with the drink. "Take that to your master," said she. But at that instant the glass broke and the poison spurted on the horse, and it was so strong that the animal immediately fell down dead. The servant ran after his master and told him what had happened, but would not leave his saddle behind him, and ran back to fetch it. When, however, he came to the dead horse a raven was already sitting on it devouring it.

"Who knows whether we shall find anything better today?" said the servant; so he killed the raven, and took it with him. And now they journeyed onwards into the forest the whole day, but could not get out of it. By nightfall they found an inn and entered it. The servant gave the raven to the innkeeper to make ready for supper. They had, however, stumbled on a den of murderers, and during the darkness twelve of these came, intending to kill the strangers and rob them. Before they set about this work, they sat down to supper, and the innkeeper and the witch sat down with them, and together they ate a dish of soup in which was cut up the flesh of the raven. Hardly, however, had they swallowed a couple of mouthfuls, before they all fell down dead, for the raven had passed on to them the poison from the horse-flesh. There was no one else left in the house but the innkeeper's daughter, who was honest, and had taken no part in their godless deeds. She opened all doors to the stranger and showed him the heaped-up treasures. But the King's son said she might keep everything, he would have none of it, and rode onwards with his servant.

After they had traveled about for a long time, they came to a town in which was a beautiful but proud princess, who had caused it to be proclaimed that whoever should set her a riddle which she could not guess, that man should be her husband; but if she guessed it, his head must be cut off. She had three days to guess it in, but was so clever that she always found the answer to the riddle given her, before the appointed time. Nine suitors had already perished in this manner, when the King's son arrived, and blinded by her great beauty, was willing to stake his life for it. Then he went to her and laid his riddle before her. "What is this?" said he, "One slew none, and yet slew twelve."

She did not know what that was, she thought and thought, but she could not find out, she opened her riddle books, but it was not in them—in short, her wisdom was at an end. As she did not know how to help herself, she ordered her maid to creep into the lord's sleeping-chamber, and listen to his dreams, and thought that he would perhaps speak in his sleep and discover the riddle. But the clever servant had placed himself in the bed instead of his master, and when the maid came there, he tore off from her the mantle in which she had wrapped herself, and chased her out with rods. The second night the King's daughter sent her maid-in-waiting, who was to see if she could succeed better in listening, but the servant took her mantle also away from her, and hunted her out with rods. Now the master believed himself safe for the third night, and lay down in his own bed. Then came the princess herself, and she had put on a misty-grey mantle, and she seated herself near him. And when she thought that he was asleep and dreaming, she spoke to him, and hoped that he would answer in his sleep, as many do, but he was awake, and understood and heard everything quite well. Then she asked, "One slew none, what is that?"

He replied, "A raven, which ate of a dead and poisoned horse, and died of it."

She inquired further, "And yet slew twelve, what is that?"

He answered, "That means twelve murderers, who ate the raven and died of it."

When she knew the answer to the riddle she wanted to steal away, but he held her mantle so fast that she was forced to leave it behind. Next morning, the King's daughter announced that she had guessed the riddle, and sent for the twelve judges and expounded it before them. But the youth begged for a hearing, and said, "She stole into my room in the night and questioned me, otherwise she could not have discovered it."

The judges said, "Bring us a proof of this."

Then the three mantles were brought by the servant, and when the judges saw the misty-grey one which the King's daughter usually wore, they said, "Let the mantle be embroidered with gold and silver, and then it will be your wedding mantle."

23. THE MOUSE, THE BIRD,
AND THE SAUSAGE

Once upon a time a mouse, a bird, and a sausage became companions, kept house together, lived well and happily with each other, and wonderfully increased their possessions. The bird's work was to fly every day into the forest and bring back wood. The mouse had to carry water, light the fire, and lay the table, but the sausage had to cook.

He who is too well off is always longing for something new. One day, therefore, the bird met with another bird on the way, to whom it related its excellent circumstances and boasted of them. The other bird, however, called it a poor simpleton for his hard work, but said that the two at home had good times. For when the mouse had made her fire and carried her water, she went into her little room to rest until they called her to lay the table. The sausage stayed by the pot, saw that the food was cooking well, and, when it was nearly time for dinner, it rolled itself once or twice through the broth or vegetables and then they were buttered, salted, and ready. When the bird came home and laid his burden down, they sat down to dinner, and after they had had their meal, they slept their fill till next morning, and that was a splendid life.

Next day the bird, prompted by the other bird, would go no more into the wood, saying that he had been servant long enough, and had been made a fool of by them, and that they must change about for once, and try to arrange it in another way. And, though the mouse and the sausage also begged most earnestly, the bird would have his way, and said it must be tried. They drew lots about it, and the lot fell on the sausage who was to carry wood, and the mouse became cook, and the bird was to fetch water.

What happened? The little sausage went out towards the wood, the little bird lighted the fire, the mouse stayed by the pot and waited alone until little sausage came home and brought wood for next day. But the little sausage stayed so long on the road that they both feared something was amiss, and the bird flew out a little way in the air to meet it. Not far off, however, it met a dog on the road who had fallen on the poor sausage as lawful booty, and had seized and swallowed it. The bird charged the dog with an act of barefaced robbery, but it was in vain to speak, for the dog said he had found forged letters on the sausage, a capital offense.

The bird sadly took up the wood, flew home, and related what he had seen and heard. They were much troubled, but agreed to do their best and remain together. The bird therefore laid the cloth, and the mouse prepared the food, and wanted to dress it, and to get into the pot as the sausage used to do, and roll and creep amongst the vegetables to mix them; but before she got into the midst of them she was stopped, and lost her skin and hair and life in the attempt.

When the bird came to carry up the dinner, no cook was there. In its distress the bird threw the wood here and there, called and searched, but no cook was to be found! Owing to his carelessness the wood caught fire, so that a conflagration ensued, the bird hastened to fetch water, and then the bucket dropped from his claws into the well, and he fell down with it, and could not recover himself, but had to drown there.

24. MOTHER HOLLE

There was once a widow who had two daughters—one of whom was pretty and industrious, while the other was ugly and idle. But she was much fonder of the ugly and idle one, because she was her own daughter; and the other, who was a stepdaughter, was obliged to do all the work, and be the Cinderella of the house. Every day the poor girl had to sit by a well, on the roadside, and spin and spin till her fingers bled.

Now it happened that one day the shuttle was marked with her blood, so she dipped it in the well, to wash the mark off; but it dropped out of her hand and fell to the bottom. She began to weep, and ran to her stepmother and told her of the mishap. But she scolded her sharply, and was so merciless as to say, "Since you have let the shuttle fall in, you must fetch it out again."

So the girl went back to the well, and did not know what to do; and in the sorrow of her heart she jumped into the well to get the shuttle. She lost her senses; and when she awoke and came to herself again, she was in a lovely meadow where the sun was shining and many thousands of flowers were growing.

Along this meadow she went, and at last came to a baker's oven full of bread, and the bread cried out, "Oh, take me out! Take me out! Or I shall burn; I have been baked a long time!" So she went up to it, and took out all the loaves one after another with the bread-shovel.

After that she went on till she came to a tree covered with apples, which called out to her, "Oh, shake me! Shake me! We apples are all ripe!" So she shook the tree till the apples fell like rain, and went on shaking till they were all down, and when she had gathered them into a heap, she went on her way.

At last she came to a little house, out of which an old woman peeped; but she had such large teeth that the girl was frightened, and was about to run away.

But the old woman called out to her, "What are you afraid of, dear child? Stay with me; if you will do all the work in the house properly, you shall be the better for it. Only you must take care to make my bed well, and shake it thoroughly till the feathers fly—for then it will snow on the earth. I am Mother Holle."

As the old woman spoke so kindly to her, the girl took courage and agreed to enter her service. She attended to everything to the satisfaction of her mistress, and always shook her bed so vigorously that the feathers flew about like snowflakes. So she had a pleasant life with her; never an angry word; and boiled or roast meat every day.

She stayed some time with Mother Holle, and then she became sad. At first she did not know what was the matter with her, but found at length that it was homesickness. Although she was many thousand times better off here than at home, still she had a longing to be there. At last she said to the old woman, "I have a longing for home; and however well off I am down here, I cannot stay any longer; I must go up again to my own people."

Mother Holle said, "I am pleased that you long for your home again, and as you have served me so truly, I myself will take you up again." Then she took her by the hand, and led her to a large door. The door was opened, and just as the maiden was standing beneath the doorway, a heavy shower of golden rain fell, and all the gold stuck to her, so that she was completely covered over with it.

"You shall have that because you have been so industrious," said Mother Holle, and at the same time she gave her back the shuttle which she had let fall into the well. Thereupon the door closed, and the maiden found herself up above upon the earth, not far from her mother's house.

And as she went into the yard the cock was standing by the well-side, and cried—

> "Cock-a-doodle-doo!
> Your golden girl's come back to you!"

So she went in to her mother, and as she arrived thus covered with gold, she was well received, both by her and her sister.

The girl told all that had happened to her; and as soon as the mother heard how she had come by so much wealth, she was very anxious to obtain the same good luck for the ugly and lazy daughter. She had to seat herself by the well and spin; and in order that her shuttle might be stained with blood, she stuck her hand into a thorn bush and pricked her finger. Then she threw her shuttle into the well, and jumped in after it.

She came, like the other, to the beautiful meadow and walked along the very same path. When she got to the oven the bread again cried,

"Oh, take me out! Take me out! Or I shall burn; I have been baked a long time!"

But the lazy thing answered, "As if I had any wish to make myself dirty!" and on she went.

Soon she came to the apple tree, which cried, "Oh, shake me! Shake me! We apples are all ripe!"

But she answered, "Wouldn't you like that! One of you might fall on my head," and so went on.

When she came to Mother Holle's house she was not afraid, for she had already heard of her big teeth, and she offered work to her immediately.

The first day she forced herself to work diligently, and obeyed Mother Holle when she told her to do anything, for she was thinking of all the gold that she would give her. But on the second day she began to be lazy, and on the third day still more so, and then she would not get up in the morning at all. Nor did she make Mother Holle's bed as she ought, and did not shake it so as to make the feathers fly up. Mother Holle was soon tired of this, and gave her notice to leave. The lazy girl was willing enough to go, and thought that now the golden rain would come. Mother Holle led her also to the great door; but while she was standing beneath it, instead of the gold a big kettleful of pitch was emptied over her. "That is the reward for your service," said Mother Holle, and shut the door.

So the lazy girl went home; but she was quite covered with pitch, and the cock by the well-side, as soon as he saw her, cried out—

> "Cock-a-doodle-doo!
> Your pitchy girl's come back to you!"

But the pitch stuck fast to her, and could not be got off as long as she lived.

25. THE SEVEN RAVENS

There was once a man who had seven sons, and still he had no daughter, however much he wished for one. At length his wife again gave him hope of a child, and when it came into the world it was a girl. The joy was great, but the child was sickly and small, and had to be privately baptized on account of its weakness. The father sent one of the boys in haste to the spring to fetch water for the baptism. The other six went with him, and as each of them wanted to be first to fill it, the jug fell into the well. There they stood and did not know what to do, and none of them dared to go home. As they still did not return, the father grew impatient, and said, "They have certainly forgotten it for some game, the wicked boys!" He became afraid that the girl would have to die without being baptized, and in his anger cried, "I wish the boys were all turned into ravens." Hardly was the word spoken before he heard a whirring of wings over his head in the air, looked up and saw seven coal-black ravens flying away. The parents could not recall the curse, and however sad they were at the loss of their seven sons, they still to some extent comforted themselves with their dear little daughter, who soon grew strong and every day became more beautiful.

For a long time she did not know that she had had brothers, for her parents were careful not to mention them before her, but one day she accidentally heard some people saying of herself, "that the girl was certainly beautiful, but that in reality she was to blame for the misfortune which had befallen her seven brothers." Then she was much troubled, and went to her father and mother and asked if it was true that she had had brothers, and what had become of them? The parents now dared keep the secret no longer, but said that what had befallen her brothers was the will of Heaven, and that her birth was not to blame. But the maiden took it to heart daily, and thought she must save her brothers. She had no rest or peace until she set out secretly, and went forth into the wide world to find her brothers and set them free, let it cost what it might. She took nothing with her but a little ring belonging to her parents as a keepsake, a loaf of bread against hunger, a little pitcher of water against thirst, and a little chair as a provision against weariness.

And now she went continually onwards, far, far to the very end of the world. Then she came to the sun, but it was too hot and terrible, and devoured little children. Hastily she ran away, and ran to the moon, but it was far too cold, and also awful and malicious, and when it saw the child, it said, "I smell, I smell the flesh of men."

At this she ran swiftly away, and came to the stars, which were kind and good to her, and each of them sat on its own particular little chair. But the morning star arose, and gave her the drumstick of a chicken, and said, "If you have not that drumstick you cannot open the glass mountain, and in the glass mountain are your brothers."

The maiden took the drumstick, wrapped it carefully in a cloth, and went onwards again until she came to the glass mountain. The door was shut, and she thought she would take out the drumstick; but when she undid the cloth, it was empty, and she had lost the good star's present. What was she now to do? She wished to rescue her brothers, and had no key to the glass mountain. The good sister took a knife, cut off one of her little fingers, put it in the door, and succeeded in opening it.

When she had gone inside, a little dwarf came to meet her, who said, "My child, what are you looking for?"

"I am looking for my brothers, the seven ravens," she replied.

The dwarf said, "The lord ravens are not at home, but if you will wait here until they come, step in." Thereupon the little dwarf carried the ravens' dinner in, on seven little plates, and in seven little glasses, and the little sister ate a morsel from each plate, and from each little glass she took a sip, but in the last little glass she dropped the ring which she had brought away with her.

Suddenly she heard a whirring of wings and a rushing through the air, and then the little dwarf said, "Now the lord ravens are flying home."

Then they came, and wanted to eat and drink, and looked for their little plates and glasses. Then said one after the other, "Who has eaten something from my plate? Who has drunk out of my little glass? It was a human mouth."

And when the seventh came to the bottom of the glass, the ring rolled against his mouth. Then he looked at it, and saw that it was a ring belonging to his father and mother, and said, "God grant that our sister may be here, and then we shall be free." When the maiden, who was standing behind the door watching, heard that wish, she came forth, and at this all the ravens were restored to their human form again. And they embraced and kissed each other, and went joyfully home.

26. LITTLE RED CAP

Once upon a time there was a dear little girl who was loved by everyone who looked at her, but most of all by her grandmother, and there was nothing that she would not have given to the child. Once she gave her a little cap of red velvet, which suited her so well that she would never wear anything else; so she was always called "Little Red Cap."

One day her mother said to her, "Come, Little Red Cap, here is a piece of cake and a bottle of wine; take them to your grandmother, she is ill and weak, and they will do her good. Set out before it gets hot, and when you are going, walk nicely and quietly and do not run off the path, or you may fall and break the bottle, and then your grandmother will get nothing; and when you go into her room, don't forget to say, 'Good morning,' and don't peep into every corner before you do it."

"I will take great care," said Little Red Cap to her mother, and gave her hand on it.

The grandmother lived out in the wood, half a league from the village, and just as Little Red Cap entered the wood, a wolf met her. Red Cap did not know what a wicked creature he was, and was not at all afraid of him.

"Good day, Little Red Cap," said he.

"Thank you kindly, wolf."

"Where do you go so early, Little Red Cap?"

"To my grandmother's."

"What have you got in your apron?"

"Cake and wine; yesterday was baking day, so poor sick grandmother is to have something good, to make her stronger."

"Where does your grandmother live, Little Red Cap?"

"A good quarter of a league farther on in the wood; her house stands under the three large oak trees, the nut trees are just below; you surely must know it," replied Little Red Cap.

The wolf thought to himself, "What a tender young creature! What a nice plump mouthful—she will be better to eat than the old woman. I must act craftily, so as to catch both." So he walked for a short time by the side of Little Red Cap, and then he said, "See Little Red Cap, how pretty the flowers are about here—why do you not look round? I believe, too, that you do not hear how sweetly the little birds are singing; you walk gravely along as if you were going to school, while everything else out here in the wood is merry."

Little Red Cap raised her eyes, and when she saw the sunbeams dancing here and there through the trees, and pretty flowers growing everywhere, she thought, "Suppose I take grandmother a fresh nosegay; that would please her too. It is so early in the day that I shall still get there in good time," and so she ran from the path into the wood to look for flowers. And whenever she had picked one, she fancied that she saw a still prettier one farther on, and ran after it, and so got deeper and deeper into the wood.

Meanwhile the wolf ran straight to the grandmother's house and knocked at the door.

"Who is there?"

"Little Red Cap," replied the wolf. "She is bringing cake and wine; open the door."

"Lift the latch," called out the grandmother, "I am too weak, and cannot get up."

The wolf lifted the latch, the door flew open, and without saying a word he went straight to the grandmother's bed, and devoured her. Then he put on her clothes, dressed himself in her cap, laid himself in bed and drew the curtains.

Little Red Cap, however, had been running about picking flowers, and when she had gathered so many that she could carry no more, she remembered her grandmother, and set out on the way to her.

She was surprised to find the cottage door standing open, and when she went into the room, she had such a strange feeling that she said to herself, "Oh dear! How uneasy I feel today, and at other times I like being with grandmother so much." She called out, "Good morning," but received no answer; so she went to the bed and drew back the curtains. There lay her grandmother with her cap pulled far over her face, and looking very strange.

"Oh! Grandmother," she said, "what big ears you have!"

"The better to hear you with, my child," was the reply.

"But, grandmother, what big eyes you have!" she said.

"The better to see you with, my dear."

"But, grandmother, what large hands you have!"

"The better to hug you with."

"Oh! But, grandmother, what a terrible big mouth you have!"

"The better to eat you with!"

And scarcely had the wolf said this, than with one bound he was out of bed and swallowed up Red Cap.

When the wolf had appeased his appetite, he lay down again in the bed, fell asleep and began to snore very loud. The hunter was just passing the house, and thought to himself, "How the old woman is snoring! I must just see if she wants anything." So he went into the room, and when he came to the bed, he saw that the wolf was lying in it. "Do I find you here, you old sinner!" said he. "I have long sought you!"

Then just as he was going to fire at him, it occurred to him that the wolf might have devoured the grandmother, and that she might still be saved, so he did not fire, but took a pair of scissors, and began to cut open the stomach of the sleeping wolf. When he had made two snips, he saw the little Red Cap shining, and then he made two snips more, and the little girl sprang out, crying, "Ah, how frightened I have been! How dark it was inside the wolf;" and after that the aged grandmother came out alive also, but scarcely able to breathe. Red Cap, however, quickly fetched great stones with which they filled the wolf's body, and when he awoke, he wanted to run away, but the stones were so heavy that he fell down at once, and fell dead.

Then all three were delighted. The hunter drew off the wolf's skin and went home with it; the grandmother ate the cake and drank the wine which Red Cap had brought, and revived, but Red Cap thought to herself, "As long as I live, I will never by myself leave the path, to run into the wood, when my mother has forbidden me to do so."

* * * * *

It is also related that once when Red Cap was again taking cakes to the old grandmother, another wolf spoke to her, and tried to entice her from the path. Red Cap, however, was on her guard, and went straight forward on her way, and told her grandmother that she had met the wolf, and that he had said "good morning" to her, but with such a wicked look in his eyes, that if they had not been on the public road she was certain he would have eaten her up. "Well," said the grandmother, "we will shut the door, that he may not come in."

Soon afterwards the wolf knocked, and cried, "Open the door, grandmother, I am little Red Cap, and am fetching you some cakes."

But they did not speak, or open the door, so the grey-beard stole twice or thrice round the house, and at last jumped on the roof, intending to wait until Red Cap went home in the evening, and then to steal after her and devour her in the darkness. But the grandmother saw what was in his thoughts. In front of the house was a great stone trough, so she said to the child, "Take the pail, Red Cap; I made some sausages yesterday, so carry the water in which I boiled them to the trough." Red Cap carried until the great trough was quite full. Then the smell of the sausages reached the wolf, and he sniffed and peeped down, and at last stretched out his neck so far that he could no longer keep his footing and began to slip, and slipped down from the roof straight into the great trough, and drowned. But Red Cap went joyously home, and never did anything to harm anyone.

27. THE BREMEN TOWN-MUSICIANS

Acertain man had a donkey, which had carried the sacks of corn to the mill tirelessly for many long years; but his strength was going, and he was growing more and more unfit for work. Then his master began to consider doing away with him; but the donkey, seeing that trouble was in the air, ran away and set out on the road to Bremen. "There," he thought, "I can surely join the town band." When he had walked some distance, he found a hound lying on the road, gasping like one who had run till he was tired. "Why are you gasping so, you big fellow?" asked the donkey.

"Ah," replied the hound, "as I am old, and daily grow weaker, and no longer can hunt, my master wanted to kill me, so I took to flight; but now how am I to earn my bread?"

"I tell you what," said the donkey, "I am going to Bremen, and shall be town-musician there; go with me and engage yourself also as a musician. I will play the lute, and you shall beat the kettledrum."

The hound agreed, and on they went.

Before long they came to a cat, sitting on the path, with a face like three rainy days. "Now then, old whiskers, what has gone askew with you?" asked the donkey.

"Who can be merry when his neck is in danger?" answered the cat. "Because I am now getting old, and my teeth are worn to stumps, and I prefer to sit by the fire and spin, rather than hunt about after mice, my mistress wanted to drown me, so I ran away. But now good advice is scarce. Where am I to go?"

"Go with us to Bremen. You understand night-serenading, you can be a town-musician."

The cat thought well of it, and went with them. After this the three fugitives came to a farmyard, where the cock was sitting upon the gate, crowing with all his might. "Your crow goes on and on," said the donkey. "What is the matter?"

"I have been foretelling fine weather, because it is the day on which Our Lady washes the Christ Child's little shirts, and wants to dry them," said the cock; "but guests are coming for Sunday, so the housewife has no pity, and has told the cook that she intends to eat me in the soup tomorrow, and this evening I am to have my head cut off. Now I am crowing at full pitch while I can."

"Ah, but red-comb," said the donkey, "you had better come away with us. We are going to Bremen; you can find something better than death everywhere; you have a good voice, and if we make music together it must have some quality!"

The cock agreed to this plan, and all four went on together. They could not, however, reach the city of Bremen in one day, and in the evening they came to a forest where they meant to pass the night. The donkey and the hound laid themselves down under a large tree, the cat settled itself in the branches, and the cock flew right to the top, where he was most safe. Before he went to sleep he looked round on all four sides, and thought he saw in the distance a little spark burning; so he called out to his companions that there must be a house not far off, for he saw a light. The donkey said, "If so, we had better get up and go on, for the shelter here is bad." The hound thought that a few bones with some meat on them would do him good, too.

So they made their way to the place where the light was, and soon saw it shine brighter and grow larger, until they came to a well-lighted robber's house. The donkey, as the biggest, went to the window and looked in.

"What do you see, my grey-horse?" asked the cock.

"What do I see?" answered the donkey; "a table covered with good things to eat and drink, and robbers sitting at it enjoying themselves."

"That would be the sort of thing for us," said the cock.

"Yes, yes; ah, how I wish we were there!" said the donkey.

Then the animals took counsel together how they should manage to drive away the robbers, and at last they thought of a plan. The donkey was to place himself with his forefeet upon the window ledge, the hound was to jump on the donkey's back, the cat was to climb upon the dog, and lastly the cock was to fly up and perch upon the head of the cat.

When this was done, at a given signal, they began to perform their music together: the donkey brayed, the hound barked, the cat mewed, and the cock crowed; then they burst through the window into the room, so that the glass clattered! At this horrible din, the robbers sprang up, thinking that a ghost had come in, and fled in a great fright out into the forest. The four companions now sat down at the table, well content with what was left, and ate as if they were going to fast for a month.

As soon as the four minstrels had done, they put out the light, and each sought for himself a sleeping-place according to his nature and to what suited him. The donkey laid himself down upon some straw in the yard, the hound behind the door, the cat upon the hearth near the warm ashes, and the cock perched himself upon a beam of the roof; and being tired from their long walk, they soon went to sleep.

When it was past midnight, and the robbers saw from afar that the light was no longer burning in their house, and all appeared quiet, the captain said, "We ought not to have let ourselves be frightened out of our wits," and ordered one of them to go and examine the house.

The messenger, finding all still, went into the kitchen to light a candle, and, taking the glistening fiery eyes of the cat for live coals, he held a match to them to light it. But the cat did not think it was funny, and flew in his face, spitting and scratching. He was dreadfully frightened, and ran to the back door, but the dog who lay there sprang up and bit his leg; and as he ran across the yard by the straw heap, the donkey gave him a smart kick with its hind foot. The cock, too, who had been awakened by the noise, and had become lively, cried down from the beam, "Cock-a-doodle-doo!"

Then the robber ran back as fast as he could to his captain, and said, "Ah, there is a horrible witch sitting in the house, who spat on me and scratched my face with her long claws; and by the door stands a man with a knife, who stabbed me in the leg; and in the yard there lies a black monster, who beat me with a wooden club; and above, upon the roof, sits the judge, who called out, 'Bring the rogue here to me!' so I got away as well as I could."

After this the robbers did not trust themselves in the house again; but it suited the four musicians of Bremen so well that they did not care to leave it any more. And the mouth of the man who last told this story is still warm.

28. THE SINGING BONE

In a certain country there was once great lamentation over a wild boar that ravaged the farmer's fields, killed the cattle, and ripped up people's bodies with his tusks. The King promised a large reward to anyone who would free the land from this plague; but the beast was so big and strong that no one dared to go near the forest in which it lived. At last the King gave notice that whoever should capture or kill the wild boar should have his only daughter as wife.

Now there lived in the country two brothers, sons of a poor man, who declared themselves willing to undertake the hazardous enterprise; the elder, who was crafty and shrewd, out of pride; the younger, who was innocent and simple, from a kind heart. The King said, "In order to be sure of finding the beast, you must go into the forest from opposite sides." So the elder went in on the west side, and the younger on the east.

When the younger had gone a short way, a little man stepped up to him. He held in his hand a black spear and said, "I give you this spear because your heart is pure and good; with this you can boldly attack the wild boar, and it will do you no harm."

He thanked the little man, shouldered the spear, and went on fearlessly.

Before long he saw the beast, which rushed at him; but he held the spear towards it, and in its blind fury it ran so swiftly against it that its heart was cut in two. Then he took the monster on his back and went homewards with it to the King.

As he came out at the other side of the wood, there stood at the entrance a house where people were making merry with wine and dancing. His elder brother had gone in here, and, thinking that after all the boar would not run away, was going to drink until he felt brave. But when he saw his young brother coming out of the wood laden with his booty, his envious, evil heart gave him no peace. He called out to him, "Come in, dear brother, rest and refresh yourself with a cup of wine."

The youth, who suspected no evil, went in and told him about the good little man who had given him the spear with which he had slain the boar.

The elder brother kept him there until the evening, and then they went away together, and when in the darkness they came to a bridge over a brook, the elder brother let the other go first; and when he was halfway across he gave him such a blow from behind that he fell down dead. He buried him beneath the bridge, took the boar, and carried it to the King, pretending that he had killed it; whereupon he obtained the King's daughter in marriage. And when his younger brother did not come back he said, "The boar must have killed him," and everyone believed it.

But as nothing remains hidden from God, this black deed was to come to light.

Years afterwards a shepherd was driving his herd across the bridge, and saw lying in the sand beneath, a snow-white little bone. He thought that it would make a good mouthpiece, so he clambered down, picked it up, and cut out of it a mouthpiece for his horn. But when he blew through it for the first time, to his great astonishment, the bone began of its own accord to sing:

> "Ah, friend, you blow upon my bone!
> Long have I lain beside the water;
> My brother slew me for the boar,
> And took for his wife the King's young daughter."

"What a wonderful horn!" said the shepherd; "It sings by itself; I must take it to my lord the King." And when he came with it to the King the horn again began to sing its little song. The King understood it all, and ordered the ground below the bridge to be dug up, and then the whole skeleton of the murdered man came to light. The wicked brother could not deny the deed, and was sewn up in a sack and drowned. But the bones of the murdered man were laid to rest in a beautiful tomb in the churchyard.

29. THE DEVIL WITH THE THREE GOLDEN HAIRS

There was once a poor woman who gave birth to a little son; and as he came into the world with a caul on, it was predicted that in his fourteenth year he would have the King's daughter for his wife. It happened that soon afterwards the King came into the village, and no one knew that he was the King, and when he asked the people what news there was, they answered, "A child has just been born with a caul on; whatever he undertakes in life will turn out well. It is prophesied, too, that in his fourteenth year he will have the King's daughter for his wife."

The King, who had a bad heart, and was angry about the prophecy, went to the parents, and, seeming quite friendly, said, "You poor people, let me have your child, and I will take care of it." At first they refused, but when the stranger offered them a large amount of gold for it, and they thought, "It is a luck child, and everything must turn out well for it," they at last consented, and gave him the child.

The King put it in a box and rode away with it until he came to a deep piece of water; then he threw the box into it and thought, "I have freed my daughter from her unlooked-for suitor."

The box, however, did not sink, but floated like a boat, and not a drop of water made its way into it. And it floated to within two miles of the King's chief city, where there was a mill, and it came to a standstill at the mill dam. A miller's boy, who by good luck was standing there, noticed it and pulled it out with a hook, thinking that he had found a great treasure, but when he opened it there lay a pretty boy inside, quite fresh and lively. He took him to the miller and his wife, and as they had no children they were glad, and said, "God has given him to us." They took great care of the foundling, and he grew up in all goodness.

It happened that once in a storm, the King went into the mill, and he asked the miller and his wife if the tall youth was their son. "No," answered they, "he's a foundling. Fourteen years ago he floated down to the mill dam in a box, and the mill boy pulled him out of the water."

Then the King knew that it was none other than the luck child which he had thrown into the water, and he said, "My good people, could not the youth take a letter to the Queen; I will give him two gold pieces as a reward?"

"Just as the King commands," answered they, and they told the boy to get ready.

Then the King wrote a letter to the Queen, in which he said, "As soon as the boy arrives with this letter, let him be killed and buried, and all must be done before I come home."

The boy set out with this letter; but he lost his way, and in the evening came to a large forest. In the darkness he saw a small light; he went towards it and reached a cottage. When he went in, an old woman was sitting by the fire quite alone. She started when she saw the boy, and said, "From where do you come, and where are you going?"

"I come from the mill," he answered, "and wish to go to the Queen, to whom I am taking a letter; but as I have lost my way in the forest I should like to stay here overnight."

"You poor boy," said the woman, "you have come into a den of thieves, and when they come home they will kill you."

"Let them come," said the boy, "I am not afraid; but I am so tired that I cannot go any farther," and he stretched himself upon a bench and fell asleep.

Soon afterwards the robbers came, and angrily asked what strange boy was lying there? "Ah," said the old woman, "it is an innocent child who has lost himself in the forest, and out of pity I have let him come in; he has to take a letter to the Queen." The robbers opened the letter and read it, and in it was written that as soon as he arrived the boy should be put to death. Then the hardhearted robbers felt pity, and their leader tore up the letter and wrote another, saying, that as soon as the boy came, he should be married at once to the King's daughter. Then they let him lie quietly on the bench until the next morning, and when he awoke they gave him the letter, and showed him the right way.

And the Queen, when she had received the letter and read it, did as was written in it, and had a splendid wedding feast prepared, and the King's daughter was married to the luck child, and as the youth was handsome and agreeable she lived with him in joy and contentment.

After some time the King returned to his palace and saw that the prophecy was fulfilled, and the luck child married to his daughter. "How has that come to pass?" said he; "I gave quite another order in my letter."

So the Queen gave him the letter, and said that he might see for himself what was written in it. The King read the letter and saw quite well that it had been exchanged for the other. He asked the youth what had become of the letter entrusted to him, and why he had brought another instead of it.

"I know nothing about it," answered he; "It must have been changed in the night, when I slept in the forest."

The King said in a passion, "You shall not have everything quite so much your own way; whoever marries my daughter must fetch me from Hell three golden hairs from the head of the Devil; bring me what I want, and you shall keep my daughter." In this way the King hoped to be rid of him forever. But the luck child answered, "I will fetch the golden hairs, I am not afraid of the Devil," thereupon he took leave of them and began his journey.

The road led him to a large town, where the watchman by the gates asked him what his trade was, and what he knew. "I know everything," answered the luck child.

"Then you can do us a favor," said the watchman, "if you will tell us why our marketplace's fountain which once flowed with wine has become dry, and no longer gives even water?"

"That you shall know," answered he, "Only wait until I come back."

Then he went farther and came to another town, and there also the gatekeeper asked him what was his trade, and what he knew. "I know everything," answered he.

"Then you can do us a favor and tell us why a tree in our town which once bore golden apples now does not even put forth leaves?"

"You shall know that," answered he, "Only wait until I come back."

Then he went on and came to a wide river over which he must go. The ferryman asked him what his trade was, and what he knew. "I know everything," answered he.

"Then you can do me a favor," said the ferryman, "and tell me why I must always be rowing backwards and forwards, and no one comes to relieve me?"

"You shall know that," answered he, "Only wait until I come back."

When he had crossed the water he found the entrance to Hell. It was black and sooty within, and the Devil was not at home, but his grandmother was sitting in a large armchair. "What do you want?" said she to him, but she did not look so very wicked.

"I should like to have three golden hairs from the Devil's head," answered he, "else I cannot keep my wife."

"That is a good deal to ask for," said she, "If the Devil comes home and finds you, it will cost you your life; but as I pity you, I will see if I cannot help you."

She changed him into an ant and said, "Creep into the folds of my dress, you will be safe there."

"Yes," answered he, "so far, so good; but there are three things besides that I want to know: why a fountain which once flowed with wine has become dry, and no longer gives even water; why a tree which once bore golden apples does not even put forth leaves; and why a ferryman must always be going backwards and forwards, and is never set free?"

"Those are difficult questions," answered she, "but only be silent and quiet and pay attention to what the Devil says when I pull out the three golden hairs."

As evening came, the Devil returned home. No sooner had he entered than he noticed that the air was not pure. "I smell man's flesh," said he, "All is not right here." Then he pried into every corner, and searched, but could not find anything.

His grandmother scolded him. "It has just been swept," said she, "and everything put in order, and now you are upsetting it again; you have always got man's flesh in your nose. Sit down and eat your supper."

When he had eaten and drunk he was tired, and laid his head in his grandmother's lap, and before long he was fast asleep, snoring and breathing heavily. Then the old woman took hold of a golden hair, pulled it out, and laid it down near her. "Oh!" cried the Devil, "What are you doing?"

"I have had a bad dream," answered the grandmother, "so I seized hold of your hair."

"What did you dream then?" said the Devil.

"I dreamed that a fountain in a marketplace from which wine once flowed was dried up, and not even water would flow out of it; what could be the cause of it?"

"Oh, ho! If they did but know it," answered the Devil, "There is a toad sitting under a stone in the well; if they killed it, the wine would flow again."

He went to sleep again and snored until the windows shook. Then she pulled the second hair out. "Ouch! What are you doing?" cried the Devil angrily.

"Do not get angry," said she, "I did it in a dream."

"What have you dreamt this time?" asked he.

"I dreamt that in a certain kingdom there stood an apple tree which had once borne golden apples, but now would not even bear leaves. What do you think was the reason?"

"Oh! If they did but know," answered the Devil. "A mouse is gnawing at the root; if they killed this they would have golden apples again, but if it gnaws much longer the tree will wither altogether. But leave me alone with your dreams; if you disturb me in my sleep again you will get a slap on the ear."

The grandmother spoke gently to him until he fell asleep again and snored. Then she took hold of the third golden hair and pulled it out. The Devil jumped up, roared out, and would have treated her ill if she had not quieted him once more and said, "Who can help bad dreams?"

"What was the dream, then?" asked he, and was quite curious. "I dreamt of a ferryman who complained that he must always ferry from one side to the other, and was never released. What is the cause of it?"

"Ah! The fool," answered the Devil, "When anyone comes and wants to go across he must put the oar in his hand, and the other man will have to ferry and he will be free." As the grandmother had plucked out the three golden hairs, and the three questions were answered, she let the old serpent alone, and he slept until daybreak.

When the Devil had gone out again the old woman took the ant out of the folds of her dress, and gave the luck child his human shape again. "There are the three golden hairs for you," said she. "What the Devil said to your three questions, I suppose you heard?"

"Yes," answered he, "I heard, and will take care to remember."

"You have what you want," said she, "and now you can go your way." He thanked the old woman for helping him in his need, and left hell well content that everything had turned out so fortunately.

When he came to the ferryman he was expected to give the promised answer. "Ferry me across first," said the luck child, "and then I will tell you how you can be set free," and when he reached the opposite shore he gave him the Devil's advice: "Next time anyone comes who wants to be ferried over, just put the oar in his hand."

He went on and came to the town where the unfruitful tree stood, and there too the watchman wanted an answer. So he told him what he had heard from the Devil: "Kill the mouse which is gnawing at its root, and it will again bear golden apples." Then the watchman thanked him, and gave him as a reward two asses laden with gold, which followed him.

At last he came to the town whose well was dry. He told the watchman what the Devil had said: "A toad is in the well beneath a stone; you must find it and kill it, and the well will again give wine in plenty." The watchman thanked him, and also gave him two asses laden with gold.

At last the luck child got home to his wife, who was heartily glad to see him again, and to hear how well he had prospered in everything. To the King he took what he had asked for, the Devil's three golden hairs, and when the King saw the four asses laden with gold he was quite content, and said, "Now all the conditions are fulfilled, and you can keep my daughter. But tell me, dear son-in-law, where did all that gold come from? This is tremendous wealth!"

"I was rowed across a river," answered he, "and got it there; the shore is made of gold instead of sand."

"Can I too fetch some of it?" said the King, and he was quite eager about it.

"As much as you like," answered he. "There is a ferryman on the river; let him ferry you over, and you can fill your sacks on the other side." The greedy King set out in all haste, and when he came to the river he beckoned to the ferryman to put him across. The ferryman came and bade him get in, and when they got to the other shore he put the oar in his hand and sprang out. But from this time forth the King had to ferry, as a punishment for his sins. Perhaps he is ferrying still? If he is, it is because no one has taken the oar from him.

30. *THE LOUSE AND THE FLEA*

A louse and a flea kept house together and were brewing beer in an eggshell. Then the little louse fell in and burnt herself. At this the little flea began to scream loudly. Then said the little door, "Little flea, why are you screaming?"

"Because the louse has burnt herself."

Then the little door began to creak. At this a little broom in the corner said, "Why are you creaking, little door?"

"Have I not reason to creak?

> "The little louse has burnt herself,
> The little flea is weeping."

So the little broom began to sweep frantically. Then a little cart passed by and said, "Why are you sweeping, little broom?"

"Have I not reason to sweep?

> "The little louse has burnt herself,
> The little flea is weeping,
> The little door is creaking."

So the little cart said, "Then I will run," and began to run wildly.

Then said the garbage heap by which it ran, "Why are you running so, little cart?"

"Have I not reason to run?

> "The little louse has burnt herself,
> The little flea is weeping,
> The little door is creaking,
> The little broom is sweeping."

The garbage heap said, "Then I will burn furiously," and began to burn in clear flames.

A little tree stood near the heap and said, "Garbage heap, why are you burning?"

"Have I not reason to burn?

> "The little louse has burnt herself,
> The little flea is weeping,
> The little door is creaking,
> The little broom is sweeping,
> The little cart is running."

The little tree said, "Then I will shake myself," and began to shake herself so that all her leaves fell off. A girl who came up with her water pitcher saw that, and said, "Little tree, why are you shaking yourself?"

"Have I not reason to shake myself?

> "The little louse has burnt herself,
> The little flea is weeping,
> The little door is creaking,
> The little broom is sweeping,
> The little cart is running,
> The little heap is burning."

At this the girl said, "Then I will break my little water pitcher," and she broke her little water pitcher.

Then said the little spring from which ran the water, "Girl, why are you breaking your water jug?"

"Have I not reason to break my water jug?

> "The little louse has burnt herself,
> The little flea is weeping,
> The little door is creaking,
> The little broom is sweeping,
> The little cart is running,
> The little heap is burning,
> The little tree is shaking itself."

"Oh, ho!" said the spring, "Then I will begin to flow," and began to flow violently. And in the water everything was drowned, the girl, the little tree, the little garbage heap, the little cart, the little broom, the little door, the little flea, the little louse, all together.

31. THE GIRL WITHOUT HANDS

A certain miller had little by little fallen into poverty, and had nothing left but his mill and a large apple tree behind it. Once when he had gone into the forest to fetch wood, an old man stepped up to him whom he had never seen before, and said, "Why do you plague yourself with cutting wood? I will make you rich, if you will promise me what is standing behind your mill."

"What can that be but my apple tree?" thought the miller, and said, "Yes," and gave a written promise to the stranger.

He, however, laughed mockingly and said, "When three years have passed, I will come and carry away what belongs to me," and then he went.

When the miller got home, his wife came to meet him and said, "Tell me, miller, from where comes this sudden wealth into our house? All at once every box and chest was filled; no one brought it in, and I know not how it happened."

He answered, "It comes from a stranger who met me in the forest, and promised me great treasure. I, in return, have promised him what stands behind the mill; we can very well give him the big apple tree for it."

"Ah, husband," said the terrified wife, "that must have been the devil! He did not mean the apple tree, but our daughter, who was standing behind the mill sweeping the yard."

The miller's daughter was a beautiful, God-fearing girl, and lived through the three years in piety and without sin. When therefore the time was over, and the day came when the Evil One was to fetch her, she washed herself clean, and made a circle round herself with chalk. The devil appeared quite early, but he could not come near her. Angrily, he said to the miller, "Take all water away from her, that she may no longer be able to wash herself, for otherwise I have no power over her." The miller was afraid, and did so.

The next morning the devil came again, but she had wept on her hands, and they were quite clean. Again he could not get near her, and furiously said to the miller, "Cut her hands off, or else I cannot get the better of her."

The miller was shocked and answered, "How could I cut off my own child's hands?"

Then the Evil One threatened him and said, "If you do not do it you are mine, and I will take you yourself."

The father became alarmed, and promised to obey him. So he went to the girl and said, "My child, if I do not cut off both your hands, the devil will carry me away, and in my terror I have promised to do it. Help me in my need, and forgive me the harm I do you."

She replied, "Dear father, do with me what you will, I am your child." Thereupon she laid down both her hands, and let them be cut off. The devil came for the third time, but she had wept so long and so much on the stumps, that after all they were quite clean. Then he had to give in, and had lost all right over her.

The miller said to her, "Because of you I have received such great wealth that I will keep you most delicately as long as you live."

But she replied, "Here I cannot stay, I will go forth, compassionate people will give me as much as I require." Thereupon she had her maimed arms bound to her back, and by sunrise she set out on her way, and walked the whole day until night fell. Then she came to a royal garden, and by the shimmering of the moon she saw that trees covered with beautiful fruits grew in it, but she could not enter, for there was much water round about it. And as she had walked the whole day and not eaten one mouthful, and hunger tormented her, she thought, "Ah, if I were but inside, then I might eat the fruit, else I must die of hunger!" Then she knelt down, called on God the Lord, and prayed. And suddenly an angel came towards her, who made a dam in the water, so that the moat became dry and she could walk through it. And now she went into the garden and the angel went with her. She saw a tree covered with beautiful pears, but they were all counted. Then she went to them, and to still her hunger, ate one with her mouth from the tree, but no more. The gardener was watching; but as the angel was standing by, he was afraid and thought the maiden was a spirit, and was silent, neither did he dare to cry out, or to speak to the spirit. When she had eaten the pear, she was satisfied, and went and concealed herself among the bushes. The King to whom the garden belonged, came down to it next morning, and counted, and saw that one of the pears was missing, and asked the gardener what had become of it, as it was not lying beneath the tree, but was gone.

Then answered the gardener, "Last night, a spirit came in, who had no hands, and ate off one of the pears with its mouth."

The King said, "How did the spirit get over the water, and where did it go after it had eaten the pear?"

The gardener answered, "Someone from heaven came in a snow-white garment and made a dam, and kept back the water, that the spirit might walk through the moat. And as it must have been an angel, I was afraid, and asked no questions, and did not cry out. When the spirit had eaten the pear, it went back again."

The King said, "If it is as you say, I will watch with you tonight."

When it grew dark the King came into the garden and brought a priest with him, who was to speak to the spirit. All three seated themselves beneath the tree and watched. At midnight the maiden came creeping out of the thicket, went to the tree, and again ate one pear off it with her mouth, and beside her stood the angel in white garments. Then the priest went out to them and said, "Come you from heaven or from earth? Are you a spirit, or a human being?"

She replied, "I am no spirit, but an unhappy mortal deserted by all but God."

The King said, "Though you are forsaken by all the world, I will not forsake you." He took her with him into his royal palace, and as she was so beautiful and good, he loved her with all his heart, had silver hands made for her, and took her for his wife.

After a year the King had to go to war, so he placed his young Queen in the care of his mother and said, "If she is brought to bed take care of her, nurse her well, and tell me of it at once in a letter." Then she gave birth to a fine boy. So the old mother made haste to write and announce the joyful news to him. But the messenger rested by a brook on the way, and as he was fatigued by the great distance, he fell asleep. Then came the Devil, who was always seeking to injure the good Queen, and exchanged the letter for another, in which was written that the Queen had brought a monster into the world. When the King read the letter he was shocked and much troubled, but he wrote in answer that they were to take great care of the Queen and nurse her well until his arrival. The messenger went back with the letter, but rested at the same place and again fell asleep. Then came the Devil once more, and put a different letter in his pocket, in which it was written that they were to put the Queen and her child to death. The old mother was terribly shocked when she received the letter, and could not believe it. She wrote back again to the King, but received no other answer, because each time the Devil substituted a false letter, and in the last letter it was also written that she was to preserve the Queen's tongue and eyes as a token that she had obeyed.

But the old mother wept to think such innocent blood was to be shed, and had a doe brought by night and cut out her tongue and eyes, and kept them. Then said she to the Queen, "I cannot have you killed as the King commands, but here you may stay no longer. Go forth into the wide world with your child, and never come here again." The poor woman tied her child on her back, and went away with eyes full of tears.

She came into a great wild forest, and then she fell on her knees and prayed to God, and the angel of the Lord appeared to her and led her to a little house on which was a sign with the words, "Here all dwell free." A snow-white maiden came out of the little house and said, "Welcome, Lady Queen," and led her inside. Then they unbound the little boy from her back, and held him to her breast that he might feed, and laid him in a beautifully-made little bed.

Then said the poor woman, "How do you know that I was a queen?"

The white maiden answered, "I am an angel sent by God, to watch over you and your child." The Queen stayed seven years in the little house, and was well cared for, and by God's grace, because of her piety, her hands which had been cut off, grew once more.

At last the King came home again from the war, and his first wish was to see his wife and the child. Then his aged mother began to weep and said, "You wicked man, why did you write to me that I was to take those two innocent lives?" and she showed him the two letters which the Evil One had forged, and then continued, "I did as you bade me," and she showed the tokens, the tongue and eyes. Then the King began to weep for his poor wife and his little son so much more bitterly than she was doing, that the aged mother had compassion on him and said, "Be at peace, she still lives; I secretly had a doe killed, and took these tokens from it; but I bound the child to your wife's back and bade her go forth into the wide world, and made her promise never to come back here again, because you were so angry with her."

Then spoke the King, "I will go as far as the sky is blue, and will neither eat nor drink until I have found again my dear wife and my child, if in the meantime they have not been killed, or died of hunger."

Thereupon the King traveled about for seven long years, and sought her in every cleft of the rocks and in every cave, but he did not find her, and thought she had died of want. During the whole of this time he neither ate nor drank, but God supported him. At length he came into a great forest, and found therein the little house whose sign was, "Here all dwell free." Then forth came the white maiden, took him by the hand, led him in, and said, "Welcome, Lord King," and asked him from where he came.

He answered, "I have traveled about for the space of seven years, and I seek my wife and her child, but cannot find them." The angel offered him meat and drink, but he did not take anything, and only wished to rest a little. Then he lay down to sleep, and put a handkerchief over his face.

Thereupon the angel went into the chamber where the Queen sat with her son, whom she usually called "Sorrowful," and said to her, "Go out with your child, your husband has come."

So she went to the place where he lay, and the handkerchief fell from his face. Then said she, "Sorrowful, pick up your father's handkerchief, and cover his face again." The child picked it up, and put it over his face again. The King in his sleep heard what passed, and had pleasure in letting the handkerchief fall once more.

But the child grew impatient, and said, "Dear mother, how can I cover my father's face when I have no father in this world? I have learnt to say the prayer, 'Our Father, which art in Heaven,' you have told me that my father was in Heaven, and was the good God, and how can I recognize a wild man like this? He is not my father." When the King heard that, he got up, and asked who they were.

Then said she, "I am your wife, and that is your son, Sorrowful."

And he saw her living hands, and said, "My wife had silver hands."

She answered, "The good God has caused my natural hands to grow again;" and the angel went into the inner room, and brought the silver hands, and showed them to him.

Then he knew for a certainty that it was his dear wife and his dear child, and he kissed them, and was glad, and said, "A heavy stone has fallen from off my heart." Then the angel of God gave them one meal with her, and after that they went home to the King's aged mother. There were great rejoicings everywhere, and the King and Queen were married again, and lived contentedly to their happy end.

32. CLEVER HANS

The mother of Hans said, "Where away, Hans?"
Hans answered, "To Gretel."

"Behave well, Hans."

"Oh, I'll behave well. Goodbye, mother."

"Goodbye, Hans."

Hans comes to Gretel. "Good day, Gretel."

"Good day, Hans. What do you bring that is good?"

"I bring nothing, I want to have something given to me." Gretel presents Hans with a needle. Hans says, "Goodbye, Gretel."

"Goodbye, Hans."

Hans takes the needle, sticks it into a hay cart, and follows the cart home. "Good evening, mother."

"Good evening, Hans. Where have you been?"

"With Gretel."

"What did you take her?"

"Took nothing; had something given to me."

"What did Gretel give you?"

"Gave me a needle."

"Where is the needle, Hans?"

"Stuck it in the hay cart."

"That was foolish, Hans. You should have stuck the needle in your sleeve."

"Never mind, I'll do better next time."

"Where away, Hans?"

"To Gretel, mother."

"Behave well, Hans."

"Oh, I'll behave well. Goodbye, mother."

"Goodbye, Hans."

Hans comes to Gretel. "Good day, Gretel."

"Good day, Hans. What do you bring that is good?"

"I bring nothing; I want to have something given to me." Gretel presents Hans with a knife. "Goodbye, Gretel."

"Goodbye Hans."

Hans takes the knife, sticks it in his sleeve, and goes home. "Good evening, mother."

"Good evening, Hans. Where have you been?"

"With Gretel."

"What did you take her?"

"Took her nothing, she gave me something."

"What did Gretel give you?"

"Gave me a knife."

"Where is the knife, Hans?"

"Stuck in my sleeve."

"That's foolish, Hans, you should have put the knife in your pocket."

"Never mind, will do better next time."

"Where away, Hans?"

"To Gretel, mother."

"Behave well, Hans."

"Oh, I'll behave well. Goodbye, mother."

"Goodbye, Hans."

Hans comes to Gretel. "Good day, Gretel."

"Good day, Hans. What good thing do you bring?"

"I bring nothing, I want something given to me." Gretel presents Hans with a young goat. "Goodbye, Gretel."

"Goodbye, Hans."

Hans takes the goat, ties its legs, and puts it in his pocket. When he gets home it is suffocated. "Good evening, mother."

"Good evening, Hans. Where have you been?"

"With Gretel."

"What did you take her?"

"Took nothing, she gave me something."

"What did Gretel give you?"

"She gave me a goat."

"Where is the goat, Hans?"

"Put it in my pocket."

"That was foolish, Hans, you should have put a rope round the goat's neck."

"Never mind, will do better next time."

"Where away, Hans?"

"To Gretel, mother."

"Behave well, Hans."

"Oh, I'll behave well. Goodbye, mother."

"Goodbye, Hans."

Hans comes to Gretel. "Good day, Gretel."

"Good day, Hans. What good thing do you bring?"

"I bring nothing, I want something given to me." Gretel presents Hans with a piece of bacon. "Goodbye, Gretel."

"Goodbye, Hans."

Hans takes the bacon, ties it to a rope, and drags it away behind him. The dogs come and devour the bacon. When he gets home, he has the rope in his hand, and there is no longer anything hanging to it. "Good evening, mother."

"Good evening, Hans."

"Where have you been?"

"With Gretel."

"What did you take her?"

"I took her nothing, she gave me something."

"What did Gretel give you?"

"Gave me a bit of bacon."

"Where is the bacon, Hans?"

"I tied it to a rope, brought it home, dogs took it."

"That was foolish, Hans, you should have carried the bacon on your head."

"Never mind, will do better next time."

"Where away, Hans?"

"To Gretel, mother."

"Behave well, Hans."

"I'll behave well. Goodbye, mother."

"Goodbye, Hans."

Hans comes to Gretel. "Good day, Gretel."

"Good day, Hans."

"What good thing do you bring?"

"I bring nothing, but would have something given." Gretel presents Hans with a calf. "Goodbye, Gretel."

"Goodbye, Hans."

Hans takes the calf, puts it on his head, and the calf kicks his face. "Good evening, mother."

"Good evening, Hans. Where have you been?"

"With Gretel."

"What did you take her?"

"I took nothing, but had something given me."

"What did Gretel give you?"

"A calf."

"Where is the calf, Hans?"

"I set it on my head and it kicked my face."

"That was foolish, Hans, you should have led the calf, and put it in the stall."

"Never mind, will do better next time."

"Where away, Hans?"

"To Gretel, mother."

"Behave well, Hans."

"I'll behave well. Goodbye, mother."

"Goodbye, Hans."

Hans comes to Gretel. "Good day, Gretel."

"Good day, Hans. What good thing do you bring?"

"I bring nothing, but would have something given."

Gretel says to Hans, "I will go with you."

Hans takes Gretel, ties her to a rope, leads her to the feed rack and binds her fast. Then Hans goes to his mother. "Good evening, mother."

"Good evening, Hans. Where have you been?"

"With Gretel."

"What did you take her?"

"I took her nothing."

"What did Gretel give you?"

"She gave me nothing, she came with me."

"Where have you left Gretel?"

"I led her by the rope, tied her to the rack, and scattered some grass for her."

"That was foolish, Hans, you should have cast friendly eyes on her."

"Never mind, will do better."

Hans went into the stable, cut out all the calves' and sheep's eyes, and threw them in Gretel's face. Then Gretel became angry, tore herself loose and ran away, and never became the bride of Hans.

33. THE THREE LANGUAGES

An aged count once lived in Switzerland, who had an only son, but he was stupid, and could learn nothing. Then said the father, "Listen, my son, I can get nothing into your head, let me try as I will. You must go from here, I will give you into the care of a celebrated master, who shall see what he can do with you." The youth was sent into a strange town, and remained a whole year with the master. At the end of this time, he came home again, and his father asked, "Now, my son, what have you learnt?"

"Father, I have learnt what the dogs say when they bark."

"Lord have mercy on us!" cried the father, "Is that all you have learnt? I will send you into another town, to another master." The youth was taken there, and stayed a year with this master likewise. When he came back the father again asked, "My son, what have you learnt?"

He answered, "Father, I have learnt what the birds say."

Then the father fell into a rage and said, "Oh, you lost man, you have spent precious time and learnt nothing; are you not ashamed to appear before my eyes? I will send you to a third master, but if you learn nothing this time also, I will no longer be your father." The youth remained a whole year with the third master also, and when he came home again, and his father inquired, "My son, what have you learnt?" he answered, "Dear father, I have this year learnt what the frogs croak."

Then the father fell into the most furious anger, sprang up, called his people over, and said, "This man is no longer my son, I cast him out, and command you to take him out into the forest, and kill him." They took him there, but when they should have killed him, they could not do it for pity, and let him go, and they cut the eyes and the tongue out of a deer that they might carry them to the old man as a token.

The youth wandered on, and after some time came to a fortress where he begged for a night's lodging. "Yes," said the lord of the castle, "if you will pass the night down there in the old tower, go there; but I warn you, it is at the peril of your life, for it is full of wild dogs, which bark and howl without stopping, and at certain hours a man has to be given to them, whom they at once devour." The whole district was in sorrow and dismay because of them, and yet no one could do anything to stop this.

The youth, however, was without fear, and said, "Just let me go down to the barking dogs, and give me something that I can throw to them; they will do nothing to harm me." Since he himself insisted, they gave him some food for the wild animals, and led him down to the tower. When he went inside, the dogs did not bark at him, but wagged their tails quite amicably around him, ate what he set before them, and did not hurt one hair on his head.

Next morning, to the astonishment of everyone, he came out again safe and unharmed, and said to the lord of the castle, "The dogs have revealed to me, in their own language, why they dwell there, and bring evil on the land. They are bewitched, and are obliged to watch over a great treasure which is below in the tower, and they can have no rest until it is taken away, and I have likewise learnt, from their discourse, how that is to be done." Then all who heard this rejoiced, and the lord of the castle said he would adopt him as a son if he accomplished it successfully. He went down again, and as he knew what he had to do, he did it thoroughly, and brought a chest full of gold out with him. The howling of the wild dogs was heard no more; they had disappeared, and the country was freed from the trouble.

After some time he took it into his head that he would travel to Rome. On the way he passed by a marsh, in which a number of frogs were sitting croaking. He listened to them, and when he became aware of what they were saying, he grew very thoughtful and sad. At last he arrived in Rome, where the Pope had just died, and there was great difficulty as to whom they should appoint as his successor. They at length agreed that the person chosen as pope should be distinguished by some divine and miraculous token. And just as that was decided on, the young count entered into the church, and suddenly two snow-white doves flew on his shoulders and remained sitting there. The ecclesiastics recognized that as a token from above, and asked him on the spot if he would be pope. He was undecided, and knew not if he were worthy of this, but the doves counseled him to do it, and at length he said yes. Then was he anointed and consecrated, and thus was fulfilled the prophecy he had heard from the frogs on his way, which had so disturbed him, that he was to be his Holiness the Pope. Then he had to sing a mass, and did not know one word of it, but the two doves sat continually on his shoulders, and said it all in his ear.

34. CLEVER ELSIE

There was once a man who had a daughter who was called Clever Elsie. And when she had grown up her father said, "We will get her married."

"Yes," said the mother; "if only anyone would come who would have her."

At length a man came from a distance and wooed her, who was called Hans; but he stipulated that Clever Elsie should be really wise. "Oh," said the father, "she's sharp enough," and the mother said, "Oh, she can see the wind coming up the street, and hear the flies coughing."

"Well," said Hans, "if she is not really wise, I won't have her."

When they were sitting at dinner and had eaten, the mother said, "Elsie, go into the cellar and fetch some beer." Then Clever Elsie took the pitcher from the wall, went into the cellar, and clapped the lid up and down as she went, to pass the time. When she was below she fetched herself a chair, and set it before the barrel so that she had no need to stoop, and did not hurt her back or do herself any unexpected injury. Then she placed the can before her, and turned the tap, and while the beer was running she would not let her eyes be idle, but looked up at the wall, and after much peering here and there, saw a pickaxe exactly above her, which the masons had accidentally left there.

Then Clever Elsie began to weep, and said, "If I get Hans, and we have a child, and he grows big, and we send him into the cellar here to draw beer, then the pickaxe will fall on his head and kill him." Then she sat and wept and screamed with all the strength of her body, over the misfortune which lay before her.

Those upstairs waited for the drink, but Clever Elsie still did not come. Then the woman said to the servant, "Just go down into the cellar and see where Elsie is." The maid went and found her sitting in front of the barrel, screaming loudly.

"Elsie, why do you weep" asked the maid.

"Ah," she answered, "have I not reason to weep? If I get Hans, and we have a child, and he grows big, and has to draw beer here, the pickaxe will perhaps fall on his head, and kill him."

Then said the maid, "What a clever Elsie we have!" and sat down beside her and began loudly to weep over the misfortune.

After a while, as the maid did not come back, those upstairs were thirsty for the beer, the man said to the boy, "Just go down into the cellar and see where Elsie and the girl are."

The boy went down, and there sat Clever Elsie and the girl both weeping together. Then he asked, "Why are you weeping?"

"Ah," said Elsie, "have I not reason to weep? If I get Hans, and we have a child, and he grows big, and has to draw beer here, the pickaxe will fall on his head and kill him."

Then said the boy, "What a clever Elsie we have!" and sat down by her, and likewise began to howl loudly.

Upstairs they waited for the boy, but as he still did not return, the man said to the woman, "Just go down into the cellar and see where Elsie is!"

The woman went down, and found all three in the midst of their lamentations, and inquired what was the cause; then Elsie told her that her future child was to be killed by the pickaxe, when it grew big and had to draw beer, and the pickaxe fell down. Then said the mother likewise, "What a clever Elsie we have!" and sat down and wept with them.

The man upstairs waited a short time, but as his wife did not come back and his thirst grew ever greater, he said, "I must go into the cellar myself and see where Elsie is." But when he got into the cellar, and they were all sitting together crying, and he heard the reason, and that Elsie's child was the cause, and that Elsie might perhaps bring one into the world some day, and that it might be killed by the pickaxe, if it should happen to be sitting beneath it, drawing beer just at the very time when it fell down, he cried, "Oh, what a clever Elsie!" and sat down, and likewise wept with them.

The bridegroom stayed upstairs alone for a long time; then as no one would come back he thought, "They must be waiting for me below; I too must go there and see what they are about." When he got down, five of them were sitting screaming and lamenting quite piteously, each outdoing the other. "What misfortune has happened then?" he asked.

"Ah, dear Hans," said Elsie, "if we marry each other and have a child, and he is big, and we perhaps send him here to draw something to drink, then the pickaxe which has been left up there might dash his brains out if it were to fall down, so have we not reason to weep?"

"Come," said Hans, "more understanding than that is not needed for my household, as you are such a clever Elsie, I will have you," and he seized her hand, took her upstairs with him, and married her.

After Hans had had her some time, he said, "Wife, I am going out to work and earn some money for us; go into the field and cut the corn that we may have some bread."

"Yes, dear Hans, I will do that." After Hans had gone away, she cooked herself some good broth and took it into the field with her. When she came to the field she said to herself, "What shall I do; shall I shear first, or shall I eat first? Oh, I will eat first." Then she emptied her basin of broth, and when she was fully satisfied, she once more said, "What shall I do? Shall I shear first, or shall I sleep first? I will sleep first." Then she lay down among the corn and fell asleep.

Hans had been at home for a long time, but Elsie did not come; then said he, "What a clever Elsie I have; she is so industrious that she does not even come home to eat." As evening came, however, she still stayed away, and Hans went out to see what she had cut, but nothing was cut, and she was lying among the corn asleep. Then Hans hastened home and brought a fowler's net with little bells and hung it round about her, and she still went on sleeping. Then he ran home, shut the door, and sat down in his chair and worked.

At length, when it was quite dark, Clever Elsie awoke and when she got up there was a jingling all round about her, and the bells rang at each step which she took. Then she was alarmed, and became uncertain whether she really was Clever Elsie or not, and said, "Is it I, or is it not I?" But she did not know the answer to this, and stood for a time in doubt; at length she thought, "I will go home and ask if it is me or not, they will be sure to know." She ran to the door of her own house, but it was shut; then she knocked at the window and cried, "Hans, is Elsie inside?"

"Yes," answered Hans, "she is inside."

At that she was terrified, and said, "Ah, heavens! Then it is not I," and went to another door; but when the people heard the jingling of the bells they would not open it, and she could get in nowhere. Then she ran out of the village, and no one has seen her since.

35. THE TAILOR IN HEAVEN

One very fine day it came to pass that the good God wished to enjoy himself in the heavenly garden, and took all the apostles and saints with him, so that no one stayed in heaven but Saint Peter. The Lord had commanded him to let no one in during his absence, so Peter stood by the door and kept watch. Before long someone knocked. Peter asked who was there, and what he wanted?

"I am a poor, honest tailor who prays for admission," replied a smooth voice.

"Honest indeed," said Peter, "like the thief on the gallows! You have been light-fingered and have stolen snippets of folks' clothes. You will not get into heaven. The Lord has forbidden me to let anyone in while he is out."

"Come, do be merciful," cried the tailor. "Little scraps which fall off the table of their own accord are not stolen, and are not worth speaking about. Look, I am lame, and have blisters on my feet from walking here, I cannot possibly turn back again. Let me in, and I will do all the rough work. I will carry the children, and wash their clothes, and wash and clean the benches on which they have been playing, and patch all their torn clothes." Saint Peter let himself be moved by pity, and opened the door of heaven just wide enough for the lame tailor to slip his lean body in. He was forced to sit down in a corner behind the door, and was to stay quietly and peaceably there, in order that the Lord, when he returned, might not observe him and be angry. The tailor obeyed, but once when Saint Peter went outside the door, he got up, and full of curiosity, went round about into every corner of heaven, and inspected the arrangement of every place. At length he came to a spot where many beautiful and delightful chairs were standing, and in the middle was a seat all of gold which was set with shining jewels. It was much higher than the other chairs, and a footstool of gold was before it. It was, however, the seat on which the Lord sat when he was at home, and from which he could see everything which happened on earth. The tailor stood still, and looked at the seat for a long time, for it pleased him better than all else. At last he could master his curiosity no longer, and climbed up and seated himself in the chair. Then he saw everything which was happening on earth, and observed an ugly old woman who was washing clothes by the side of a stream, secretly laying two veils on the side for herself. The sight of this made the tailor so angry that he laid hold of the golden footstool, and threw it down to earth through heaven, at the old thief. Since, however, he could not bring the stool back again, he slipped quietly out of the chair, seated himself in his place behind the door, and behaved as if he had never stirred from the spot.

When the Lord and master came back again with his heavenly companions, he did not see the tailor behind the door, but when he seated himself on his chair the footstool was missing. He asked Saint Peter what had become of the stool, but he did not know. Then he asked if he had let anyone come in. "I know of no one who has been here," answered Peter, "but a lame tailor, who is still sitting behind the door." Then the Lord had the tailor brought before him, and asked him if he had taken away the stool, and where he had put it?

"Oh, Lord," answered the tailor joyously, "I threw it in my anger down to earth at an old woman whom I saw stealing two veils while washing."

"Oh, you knave," said the Lord, "were I to judge as you judge, how do you think you could have escaped judgment so long? I should have no chairs, benches, seats, nay, not even fire tongs, for I would have thrown everything down at the sinners long ago. Now you can stay no longer in heaven, but must go outside the door again. Then go where you will. No one shall give punishment here, but I alone, the Lord."

Saint Peter was obliged to take the tailor out of heaven again, and as he had torn shoes, and feet covered with blisters, he took a stick in his hand, and went to Wait-a-bit, where the good soldiers sit and make merry.

36. THE WISHING TABLE, THE GOLD ASS, AND THE CUDGEL IN THE SACK

There was once upon a time a tailor who had three sons, and only one goat. But as the goat supported the whole of them with her milk, she was obliged to have good food, and to be taken every day to pasture. The sons, therefore, did this, in turn. Once the eldest took her to the churchyard, where the finest herbs were to be found, and let her eat and run about there. At night when it was time to go home he asked, "Goat, have you had enough?" The goat answered,

> "I have eaten so much,
> Not a leaf more I'll touch, meh! Meh!"

"Come home, then," said the youth, and took hold of the cord round her neck, led her into the stable and tied her up securely.

"Well," said the old tailor, "has the goat had as much food as she should?"

"Oh," answered the son, "she has eaten so much, not a leaf more she'll touch."

But the father wished to see for himself, and went down to the stable, stroked the dear animal and asked, "Goat, are you satisfied?" The goat answered,

> "Why should I be satisfied?
> Among the graves I leapt about,
> And found no food, so went without, meh! Meh!"

"What do I hear?" cried the tailor, and ran upstairs and said to the youth, "Hollo, you liar: you said the goat had had enough, and have let her hunger!" and in his anger he took the yard-measure from the wall, and drove him out with blows.

Next day it was the turn of the second son, who looked out for a place along the garden hedge, where nothing but good herbs grew, and the goat cleared them all off. At night when he wanted to go home, he asked, "Goat, are you satisfied?" The goat answered,

> "I have eaten so much,
> Not a leaf more I'll touch, meh! Meh!"

"Come home, then," said the youth, and led her home, and tied her up in the stable.

"Well," said the old tailor, "has the goat had as much food as she should?"

"Oh," answered the son, "she has eaten so much, not a leaf more she'll touch."

The tailor would not rely on this, but went down to the stable and said, "Goat, have you had enough?" The goat answered,

> "Why should I be satisfied?
> Among the graves I leapt about,
> And found no food, so went without, meh! Meh!"

"The godless wretch!" cried the tailor, "to let such a good animal hunger," and he ran up and drove the youth outside with the yard-measure.

Now came the turn of the third son, who wanted to do the thing well, and sought out some bushes with the finest leaves, and let the goat devour them. In the evening when he wanted to go home, he asked, "Goat, have you had enough?" The goat answered,

> "I have eaten so much,
> Not a leaf more I'll touch, meh! Meh!"

"Come home, then," said the youth, and led her into the stable, and tied her up.

"Well," said the old tailor, "has the goat had a proper amount of food?"

"She has eaten so much, not a leaf more she'll touch."

The tailor did not trust to that, but went down and asked, "Goat, have you had enough?" The wicked beast answered,

> "Why should I be satisfied?
> Among the graves I leapt about,
> And found no leaves, so went without, meh! Meh!"

"Oh, the brood of liars!" cried the tailor, "each as wicked and forgetful of his duty as the other! You shall no longer make a fool of me," and quite beside himself with anger, he ran upstairs and belabored the poor young fellow so vigorously with the yard-measure that he sprang out of the house.

The old tailor was now alone with his goat. Next morning he went down into the stable, caressed the goat and said, "Come, my dear little animal, I will take you to feed myself." He took her by the rope and led her to green hedges, and amongst milfoil, and whatever else goats like to eat. "There you may for once eat to your heart's content," said he to her, and let her browse till evening. Then he asked, "Goat, are you satisfied?" She replied,

> "I have eaten so much,
> Not a leaf more I'll touch, meh! Meh!"

"Come home, then," said the tailor, and led her into the stable, and tied her fast. When he was going away, he turned round again and said, "Well, are you satisfied for once?" But the goat did not behave the better to him, and cried,

> "Why should I be satisfied?
> Among the graves I leapt about,
> And found no leaves, so went without, meh! Meh!"

When the tailor heard that, he was shocked, and saw clearly that he had driven away his three sons without cause. "Wait, you ungrateful creature," cried he, "it is not enough to throw you out, I will mark you so that you will no more dare to show yourself amongst honest tailors." In great haste he ran upstairs, fetched his razor, lathered the goat's head, and shaved her as clean as the palm of his hand. And as the yard-measure would have been too good for her, he brought the horsewhip, and gave her such cuts with it that she ran away in violent haste.

When the tailor was thus left quite alone in his house he fell into great grief, and would gladly have had his sons back again, but no one knew where they had gone. The eldest had apprenticed himself to a carpenter, and learnt industriously and indefatigably, and when the time came for him to go traveling, his master presented him with a little table which had no particular appearance, and was made of common wood, but it had one good property; if anyone set it out, and said, "Little table, set yourself," the good little table was at once covered with a clean little cloth, and a plate was there, and a knife and fork beside it, and dishes with boiled meats and roasted meats, as many as there was room for, and a great glass of red wine shone so that it made the heart glad.

The young journeyman thought, "With this you have enough for your whole life," and went joyously about the world and never troubled himself at all whether an inn was good or bad, or if anything was to be found in it or not. When it suited him he did not enter an inn at all, but either on the plain, in a wood, a meadow, or wherever he fancied, he took his little table off his back, set it down before him, and said, "Set yourself," and then everything appeared that his heart desired. At length he took it into his head to go back to his father, whose anger would now be appeased, and who would now willingly receive him with his wishing table. It came to pass that on his way home one evening, he came to an inn which was filled with guests. They bade him welcome, and invited him to sit and eat with them, for otherwise he would have difficulty in getting anything. "No," answered the carpenter, "I will not take the few bites out of your mouths; rather than that, you shall be my guests." They laughed, and thought he was jesting with them; he, however, placed his wooden table in the middle of the room, and said, "Little table, set yourself." Instantly it was covered with food, so good that the host could never have procured it, and the smell of it ascended pleasantly to the nostrils of the guests. "Go ahead, dear friends," said the carpenter; and when the guests saw that he meant it, did not need to be asked twice, but drew near, pulled out their knives and attacked it valiantly. And what surprised them the most was that when a dish became empty, a full one instantly took its place of its own accord.

The innkeeper stood in one corner and watched the affair; he did not at all know what to say, but thought, "You could easily find a use for such a cook as that in your kitchen." The carpenter and his comrades made merry until late into the night; at length they lay down to sleep, and the young apprentice also went to bed, and set his magic table against the wall. The host's thoughts, however, let him have no rest; it occurred to him that there was a little old table in his storeroom which looked just like the apprentice's and he brought it out quite softly, and exchanged it for the wishing table. Next morning, the carpenter paid for his bed, took up his table, never thinking that he had got a false one, and went his way.

At midday he reached his father, who received him with great joy. "Well, my dear son, what have you learnt?" said he.

"Father, I have become a carpenter."

"A good trade," replied the old man, "but what have you brought back with you from your apprenticeship?"

"Father, the best thing which I have brought back with me is this little table."

The tailor inspected it on all sides and said, "You did not make a masterpiece when you made that; it is a bad old table."

"But it is a table which furnishes itself," replied the son. "When I set it out, and tell it to cover itself, the most beautiful dishes stand on it, and a wine also, which gladdens the heart. Just invite all our relations and friends, they shall refresh and enjoy themselves for once, for the table will give them all they require." When the company was assembled, he put his table in the middle of the room and said, "Little table, set yourself," but the little table did not stir itself, and remained just as bare as any other table which did not understand language. Then the poor apprentice became aware that his table had been changed, and was ashamed at having to stand there like a liar. The relations, however, mocked him, and were forced to go home without having eaten or drunk. The father brought out his patches again, and went on tailoring, but the son went to work with a master in the craft.

The second son had gone to a miller and had apprenticed himself to him. When his years were over, the master said, "As you have conducted yourself so well, I give you an ass of a peculiar kind, which neither draws a cart nor carries a sack."

"What use is he, then?" asked the young apprentice.

"He lets gold drop from his mouth," answered the miller. "If you set him on a cloth and say 'Bricklebrit,' the good animal will drop gold pieces for you."

"That is a fine thing," said the apprentice, and thanked the master, and went out into the world. When he had need of gold, he had only to say "Bricklebrit" to his ass, and it rained gold pieces, and he had nothing to do but pick them off the ground. Wherever he went, the best of everything was good enough for him, and the dearer the better, for he always had a full purse. When he had looked about the world for some time, he thought, "You must seek out your father; if you go to him with the gold ass he will forget his anger, and receive you well." It came to pass that he came to the same inn where his brother's table had been exchanged. He led his ass by the bridle, and the host was about to take the animal from him and tie him up, but the young apprentice said, "Don't trouble yourself, I will take my grey horse into the stable, and tie him up myself too, for I must know where he stands." This struck the host as odd, and he thought that a man who was forced to look after his ass himself, could not have much to spend; but when the stranger put his hand in his pocket and brought out two gold pieces, and said he was to buy something good for him, the host opened his eyes wide, and ran and sought out the best fare he could muster. After dinner the guest asked what he owed. The host did not see why he should not double the reckoning, and said the apprentice must give two more gold pieces. He felt in his pocket, but his gold was just at an end. "Wait an instant, sir host," said he, "I will go and fetch some money," but he took the tablecloth with him. The host could not imagine what this could mean, and being curious, stole after him, and as the guest bolted the stable door, he peeped through a hole left by a knot in the wood. The stranger spread out the cloth under the animal and cried, "Bricklebrit," and immediately the beast began to let gold pieces fall, so that it fairly rained down money on the ground.

"Eh, my word," said the host, "ducats are quickly coined there! A purse like that can't be wrong." The guest paid his score, and went to bed, but in the night the host stole down into the stable, led away the master of the mint, and tied up another ass in his place.

Early next morning the apprentice traveled away with his ass, and thought that he had his gold ass. At midday he reached his father, who rejoiced to see him again, and gladly took him in. "What have you made of yourself, my son?" asked the old man.

"A miller, dear father," he answered.

"What have you brought back with you from your travels?"

"Nothing else but an ass."

"There are asses enough here," said the father,

"I would rather have had a good goat."

"Yes," replied the son, "but it is no common ass, but a gold ass, when I say 'Bricklebrit,' the good beast opens its mouth and drops a whole sheetful of gold pieces. Just summon all our relations, and I will make them rich folks."

"That suits me well," said the tailor, "for then I shall have no need to torment myself any longer with the needle," and ran out himself and called the relations together.

As soon as they were assembled, the miller bade them make way, spread out his cloth, and brought the ass into the room. "Now watch," said he, and cried, "Bricklebrit," but no gold pieces fell, and it was clear that the animal knew nothing of the art, for every ass does not attain such perfection. Then the poor miller made a frown, saw that he was betrayed, and begged pardon of the relatives, who went home as poor as they came. There was no help for it, the old man had to take to his needle once more, and the youth hired himself to a miller.

The third brother had apprenticed himself to a turner, and as creating by lathe is skilled labor, he was the longest in learning. His brothers, however, told him in a letter how badly things had gone with them, and how the innkeeper had cheated them of their beautiful wishing gifts on the last evening before they reached home. When the turner had served his time, and had to set out on his travels, as he had conducted himself so well, his master presented him with a sack and said, "There is a cudgel in it."

"I can put on the sack," said he, "and it may be of good service to me, but why should the cudgel be in it? It only makes it heavy."

"I will tell you why," replied the master, "if anyone has done anything to injure you, do but say, 'Out of the sack, Cudgel!' and the cudgel will leap forth among the people, and play such a dance on their backs that they will not be able to stir or move for a week, and it will not leave off until you say, 'Into the sack, Cudgel!'"

The apprentice thanked him, and put the sack on his back, and when anyone came too near him, and wished to attack him, he said, "Out of the sack, Cudgel!" and instantly the cudgel sprang out, and beat the coat or jacket of one after the other right on their backs, and never stopped until it had stripped it off them, and it was done so quickly, that before anyone was aware, it was already his own turn. In the evening the young turner reached the inn where his brothers had been cheated. He laid his sack on the table before him, and began to talk of all the wonderful things which he had seen in the world. "Yes," said he, "people may easily find a table which will cover itself, a gold ass, and things of that kind—extremely good things which I by no means despise—but these are nothing in comparison with the treasure which I have won for myself, and am carrying about with me in my sack there."

The innkeeper pricked up his ears, "What in the world can that be?" thought he; "the sack must be filled with nothing but jewels; I ought to get them cheap too, for all good things go in threes."

When it was time for sleep, the guest stretched himself on the bench, and laid his sack beneath him for a pillow. When the innkeeper thought his guest was lying in a sound sleep, he went to him and pushed and pulled quite gently and carefully at the sack to see if he could possibly draw it away and lay another in its place. The turner had, however, been waiting for this for a long time, and now just as the innkeeper was about to give a hearty tug, he cried, "Out of the sack, Cudgel!" Instantly the little cudgel came forth, and fell on the innkeeper and gave him a sound thrashing.

The host cried for mercy; but the louder he cried, so much more heavily the cudgel beat the time on his back, until at length he fell to the ground exhausted. Then the turner said, "If you do not give back the table which covers itself, and the gold ass, the dance shall begin afresh."

"Oh, no," cried the host, quite humbly, "I will gladly produce everything, only make the accursed goblin creep back into the sack."

Then said the apprentice, "I will let mercy take the place of justice, but beware of getting into mischief again!" So he cried, "Into the sack, Cudgel!" and let him have rest.

Next morning the turner went home to his father with the wishing table, and the gold ass. The tailor rejoiced when he saw him once more, and asked him likewise what he had learned in foreign parts. "Dear father," said he, "I have become a turner."

"A skilled trade," said the father. "What have you brought back with you from your travels?"

"A precious thing, dear father," replied the son, "a cudgel in the sack."

"What!" cried the father, "A cudgel! That's worth your trouble, indeed! From every tree you can cut yourself one."

"But not one like this, dear father. If I say, 'Out of the sack, Cudgel!' the cudgel springs out and leads anyone who means ill with me a weary dance, and never stops until he lies on the ground and prays for fair weather. Look, with this cudgel I have got back the wishing table and the gold ass which the thievish innkeeper took away from my brothers. Now let them both be sent for, and invite all our kinsmen. I will give them food and drink, and will fill their pockets with gold too." The old tailor would not quite believe it, but nevertheless got the relatives together. Then the turner spread a cloth in the room and led in the gold ass, and said to his brother, "Now, dear brother, speak to him."

The miller said, "Bricklebrit," and instantly the gold pieces fell down on the cloth like a thundershower, and the ass did not stop until everyone of them had so much that he could carry no more. (I can see in your face that you also would like to be there.)

Then the turner brought the little table, and said, "Now dear brother, speak to it." And scarcely had the carpenter said, "Table, set yourself," than it was spread and amply covered with the most exquisite dishes. Then such a meal took place as the good tailor had never yet known in his house, and the whole party of kinsmen stayed together till far in the night, and were all merry and glad. The tailor locked away needle and thread, yard-measure and flatiron, in a cupboard, and lived with his three sons in joy and splendor.

* * * * *

(What, however, has become of the goat who was to blame for the tailor driving out his three sons? That I will tell you. She was ashamed that she had a bald head, and ran to a fox's hole and crept into it. When the fox came home, he was met by two great eyes shining out of the darkness, and was terrified and ran away. A bear met him, and as the fox looked quite disturbed, he said, "What is the matter with you, brother Fox, why do you look like that?"

"Ah," answered Redcoat, "a fierce beast is in my cave and stared at me with its fiery eyes."

"We will soon drive him out," said the bear, and went with him to the cave and looked in, but when he saw the fiery eyes, fear seized on him likewise; he would have nothing to do with the furious beast, and took to his heels.

The bee met him, and as she saw that he was ill at ease, she said, "Bear, you are really making a very pitiful face; what has become of all your gaiety?"

"It is all very well for you to talk," replied the bear, "a furious beast with staring eyes is in Redcoat's house, and we can't drive him out."

The bee said, "Bear, I pity you, I am a poor weak creature whom you would not turn aside to look at, but still, I believe, I can help you." She flew into the fox's cave, lighted on the goat's smoothly-shorn head, and stung her so violently, that she sprang up, crying "Meh, meh," and ran forth into the world as if mad, and to this hour no one knows where she has gone.)

37. THUMBLING

There was once a poor peasant who sat in the evening by the hearth and poked the fire, and his wife sat spinning. Then said he, "How sad it is that we have no children! With us all is so quiet, and in other houses it is noisy and lively."

"Yes," replied the wife, and sighed, "even if we had only one, and it were quite small, and only as big as a thumb, I should be quite satisfied, and we would still love it with all our hearts." Now it so happened that the woman fell ill, and after seven months gave birth to a child, that was perfect in all its limbs, but no longer than a thumb. Then said they, "It is as we wished it to be, and it shall be our dear child," and because of its size, they called it Thumbling. They fed it plenty of food, and the child did not grow taller, and remained as it had been at the first. Nevertheless it looked sensibly out of its eyes, and soon showed itself to be a wise and nimble creature, for everything it did turned out well.

One day the peasant was getting ready to go into the forest to cut wood, when he said as if to himself, "How I wish that there was anyone who would bring the cart to me!"

"Oh father," cried Thumbling, "I will soon bring the cart, rely on that; it shall be in the forest at the appointed time."

The man smiled and said, "How can that be done, you are far too small to lead the horse by the reins?"

"That's of no consequence, father, if my mother will only harness it, I shall sit in the horse's ear and call out to him how he is to go."

"Well," answered the man, "for once we will try it."

When the time came, the mother harnessed the horse, and placed Thumbling in its ear, and then the little creature cried, "Gee up, gee up!"

Then it went quite properly as if with its master, and the cart went the right way into the forest. It so happened that just as he was turning a corner, and the little one was crying, "Gee up," two strange men came towards him. "My word!" said one of them, "What is this? There is a cart coming, and a driver is calling to the horse and still he is not to be seen!"

"That can't be right," said the other, "we will follow the cart and see where it stops." The cart, however, drove right into the forest, and exactly to the place where the wood had been cut.

When Thumbling saw his father, he cried to him, "See, father, here I am with the cart; now take me down." The father got hold of the horse with his left hand and with the right took his little son out of the ear. Thumbling sat down quite merrily on a straw, but when the two strange men saw him, they did not know what to say for astonishment.

Then one of them took the other aside and said, "Listen, the little fellow would make our fortune if we exhibited him in a large town, for money. We will buy him." They went to the peasant and said, "Sell us the little man. He shall be well treated with us."

"No," replied the father, "he is the apple of my eye, and all the money in the world cannot buy him from me."

Thumbling, however, when he heard of the bargain, had crept up the folds of his father's coat, placed himself on his shoulder, and whispered in his ear, "Father do give me away, I will soon come back again." Then the father sold him to the two men for a handsome bit of money.

"Where will you sit?" they said to him.

"Oh just set me on the rim of your hat, and then I can walk backwards and forwards and look at the country, and still not fall down." They did as he wished, and when Thumbling had taken leave of his father, they went away with him. They walked until it was dusk, and then the little fellow said, "Do take me down, I want to come down." The man took his hat off, and put the little fellow on the ground by the wayside, and he leapt and crept about a little between the sods, and then he suddenly slipped into a mousehole which he had spied. "Good evening, gentlemen, just go home without me," he cried to them, and mocked them. They ran and stuck their sticks into the mousehole, but it was all lost labor. Thumbling crept still farther in, and as it soon became quite dark, they were forced to go home with their vexation and their empty purses.

When Thumbling saw that they were gone, he crept back out of the subterranean passage. "It is so dangerous to walk on the ground in the dark," said he, "how easily a neck or a leg is broken!" Fortunately he knocked against an empty snail shell. "Thank God!" said he. "In that, I can pass the night in safety," and got into it.

Not long afterwards, when he was just going to sleep, he heard two men go by, and one of them was saying, "How shall we contrive to get hold of the rich pastor's silver and gold?"

"I could tell you that," cried Thumbling, interrupting them.

"What was that?" said one of the thieves in fright, "I heard someone speaking."

They stood still listening, and Thumbling spoke again, and said, "Take me with you, and I'll help you."

"But where are you?"

"Just look on the ground, and observe from where my voice comes," he replied.

There the thieves at length found him, and lifted him up. "You little imp, how will you help us?" they said.

"A great deal," said he, "I will creep into the pastor's room through the iron bars, and will hand out to you whatever you want to have."

"Come then," they said, "and we will see what you can do."

When they got to the pastor's house, Thumbling crept into the room, but instantly cried out with all his might, "Do you want to have everything that is here?"

The thieves were alarmed, and said, "But do speak softly, so as not to waken anyone!"

Thumbling however, behaved as if he had not understood this, and cried again, "What do you want? Do you want to have everything that is here?"

The cook, who slept in the next room, heard this and sat up in bed, and listened. The thieves, however, had in their fright run some distance away, but at last they took courage, and thought, "The little rascal wants to mock us." They came back and whispered to him, "Come, be serious, and reach something out to us."

Then Thumbling again cried as loudly as he could, "I really will give you everything, just put your hands in." The maid, who was listening, heard this quite distinctly, and jumped out of bed and rushed to the door. The thieves took flight, and ran as if the Wild Huntsman were behind them, but as the maid could not see anything, she went to light a candle. When she came back with it, Thumbling, unperceived, fled to the barn, and the maid, after she had examined every corner and found nothing, lay down in her bed again, and believed that, after all, she had only been dreaming with open eyes and ears.

Thumbling had climbed up among the hay and found a beautiful place to sleep in; there he intended to rest until day, and then go home again to his parents. But he had other things to go through. Truly, there is much affliction and misery in this world! When day dawned, the maid arose from her bed to feed the cows. Her first walk was into the barn, where she laid hold of an armful of hay, and precisely that very one in which poor Thumbling was lying asleep. He, however, was sleeping so soundly that he was aware of nothing, and did not awake until he was in the mouth of the cow, who had picked him up with the hay. "Ah, heavens!" cried he, "How have I got into the mill?" but he soon discovered where he was. Then it was necessary to be careful not to let himself go between the teeth and be dismembered, but he was nevertheless forced to slip down into the stomach with the hay. "In this little room the windows are forgotten," said he, "and no sun shines in, neither will a candle be brought." His quarters were especially unpleasing to him, and the worst was, more and more hay was always coming in by the door, and the space grew less and less. Then at length in his anguish, he cried as loud as he could, "Bring me no more fodder, bring me no more fodder."

The maid was just milking the cow, and when she heard someone speaking, and saw no one, and perceived that it was the same voice that she had heard in the night, she was so terrified that she slipped off her stool, and spilled the milk. She ran in great haste to her master, and said, "Oh heavens, pastor, the cow has been speaking!"

"You are mad," replied the pastor; but he went himself to the barn to see what was there.

Hardly, however had he set his foot inside when Thumbling again cried, "Bring me no more fodder, bring me no more fodder." Then the pastor himself was alarmed, and thought that an evil spirit had gone into the cow, and ordered her to be killed. She was killed, but the stomach, in which Thumbling was, was thrown on the rubbish pile. Thumbling had great difficulty in working his way to the surface; however, he succeeded, but just as he was going to thrust his head out, a new misfortune occurred. A hungry wolf ran over, and swallowed the whole stomach in one gulp. Thumbling did not lose courage.

"Perhaps," thought he, "the wolf will listen to what I have got to say," and he called to him from his stomach, "Dear wolf, I know of a magnificent feast for you."

"Where is it?" said the wolf.

"In such and such a house; you must creep into it through the kitchen sink, and will find cakes, and bacon, and sausages, and as much of them as you can eat," and he described to him exactly his father's house. The wolf did not need to be told this twice, squeezed himself in at night through the sink, and ate to his heart's content in the larder. When he had eaten his fill, he wanted to go out again, but he had become so big that he could not go out by the same way. Thumbling had reckoned on this, and now began to make a violent noise in the wolf's body, and raged and screamed as loudly as he could.

"Will you be quiet," said the wolf, "you will wake up the people!"

"Nonsense," replied the little fellow, "you have eaten your fill, and I will make merry likewise," and began once more to scream with all his strength. At last his father and mother were aroused by it, and ran to the room and looked in through the opening in the door. When they saw that a wolf was inside, they ran away, and the husband fetched his axe, and the wife the scythe.

"Stay behind," said the man, when they entered the room. "When I have given him a blow, if he is not killed by it, you must cut him down and hew his body to pieces."

Then Thumbling heard his parents' voices and cried, "Dear father, I am here; I am in the wolf's body."

Said the father, full of joy, "Thank God, our dear child has found us again," and bade the woman take away her scythe, that Thumbling might not be hurt with it. After that he raised his arm, and struck the wolf such a blow on his head that he fell down dead, and then they got knives and scissors and cut his body open and drew the little fellow out. "Ah," said the father, "what sorrow we have gone through for your sake."

"Yes father, I have gone about the world a great deal. Thank heaven, I breathe fresh air again!"

"Where have you been, then?"

"Ah, father, I have been in a mouse's hole, in a cow's stomach, and then in a wolf's; now I will stay with you."

"And we will not sell you again, no, not for all the riches in the world," said his parents, and they embraced and kissed their dear Thumbling. They gave him food and drink, and had some new clothes made for him, for his own had been spoiled on his journey.

38. THE WEDDING OF MRS. FOX

FIRST STORY

There was once an old fox with nine tails, who believed that his wife was not faithful to him, and wished to test her. He stretched himself out under the bench, did not move a limb, and behaved as if he were stone dead. Mrs. Fox went up to her room, shut herself in, and her maid, Miss Cat, sat by the fire, and did the cooking. When it became known that the old fox was dead, wooers presented themselves. The maid heard someone standing at the door, knocking. She went and opened it, and it was a young fox, who said,

> "What may you be about, Miss Cat?
> Do you sleep or do you wake?"

She answered,

> "I am not sleeping, I am waking,
> Would you know what I am making?
> I am boiling warm beer with butter so nice,
> Will the gentleman enter and drink some likewise?"

"No, thank you, miss," said the fox. "What is Mrs. Fox doing?" The maid replied,

> "She sits all alone,
> And makes her moan,
> Weeping her little eyes quite red,
> Because old Mr. Fox is dead."

"Do just tell her, miss, that a young fox is here, who would like to woo her."
"Certainly, young sir."

> The cat goes up the stairs trip, trap,
> The door she knocks at tap, tap, tap,
> "Mistress Fox, are you inside?"

"Oh yes, my little cat," she cried.
"A wooer he stands at the door out there."
"Tell me what he is like, my dear?"

"But has he nine tails as beautiful as the late Mr. Fox?"
"Oh, no," answered the cat, "he has only one."
"Then I will not have him." Miss Cat went downstairs and sent the wooer away. Soon afterwards there was another knock, and another fox was at the door who wished to woo Mrs. Fox. He had two tails, but he did not fare better than the first. After this still more came, each with one tail more than the other, but they were all turned away, until at last one came who had nine tails, like old Mr. Fox. When the widow heard that, she said joyfully to the cat,

> "Now open the gates and doors all wide,
> And carry old Mr. Fox outside."

But just as the wedding was going to be solemnized, old Mr. Fox stirred under the bench, and cudgeled all the rabble, and drove them and Mrs. Fox out of the house.

SECOND STORY

When old Mr. Fox was dead, the wolf came as a wooer, and knocked at the door, and the cat who was servant to Mrs. Fox, opened it for him. The wolf greeted her, and said,

> "Good day, Mrs. Cat of Kehrewit,
> How comes it that alone you sit?
> What are you making that's good?"

The cat replied,

> "In milk I'm breaking bread so sweet,
> Will the gentleman please come in and eat?"

"No, thank you, Mrs. Cat," answered the wolf. "Is Mrs. Fox not at home?"
The cat said,

> "She sits upstairs in her room,
> Bewailing her sorrowful doom,
> Bewailing her trouble so sore,
> For old Mr. Fox is no more."

The wolf answered,

> "If she's in want of a husband now,
> Then will it please her to step below?
> The cat runs quickly up the stair,
> And lets her tail fly here and there,
> Until she comes to the parlor door.
> With her five gold rings at the door she knocks,
> "Are you within, good Mistress Fox?
> If you're in want of a husband now,
> Then will it please you to step below?"

Mrs. Fox asked, "Has the gentleman red stockings on, and has he a pointed mouth?"

"No," answered the cat.

"Then he won't do for me."

When the wolf was gone, came a dog, a stag, a hare, a bear, a lion, and all the beasts of the forest, one after the other. But one of the good points which old Mr. Fox had possessed, was always lacking, and the cat had continually to send the wooers away. At length came a young fox. Then Mrs. Fox said, "Has the gentleman red stockings on, and has he a little pointed mouth?"

"Yes," said the cat, "he has."

"Then let him come upstairs," said Mrs. Fox, and ordered the servant to prepare the wedding feast.

> "Sweep me the room as clean as you can,
> Up with the window, fling out my old man!
> For many a fine fat mouse he brought,
> Yet of his wife he never thought,
> But ate up everyone he caught."

Then the wedding was solemnized with young Mr. Fox, and there was much rejoicing and dancing; and if they have not left off, they are dancing still.

39. *THE ELVES*

FIRST STORY

A shoemaker, by no fault of his own, had become so poor that at last he had nothing left but leather for one pair of shoes. So in the evening, he cut out the shoes which he wished to begin to make the next morning, and as he had a good conscience, he lay down quietly in his bed, commended himself to God, and fell asleep. In the morning, after he had said his prayers, and was just going to sit down to work, the two shoes stood quite finished on his table. He was astounded, and knew not what to say to it. He took the shoes in his hands to observe them closer, and they were so neatly made that there was not one bad stitch in them, just as if they were intended as a masterpiece. Soon after, a buyer came in, and as the shoes pleased him so well, he paid more for them than was customary, and, with the money, the shoemaker was able to purchase leather for two pairs of shoes. He cut them out at night, and next morning was about to set to work with fresh courage; but he had no need to do so, for, when he got up, they were already made, and they found buyers who gave him money enough to buy leather for four pairs of shoes. The following morning, too, he found the four pairs made; and so it went on constantly, what he cut out in the evening was finished by the morning, so that he soon had his honest independence again, and at last became a wealthy man. Now it happened that one evening not long before Christmas, when the man had been cutting out, he said to his wife, before going to bed, "What do you think of staying up tonight to see who it is that lends us this helping hand?" The woman liked the idea, and lighted a candle, and then they hid themselves in a corner of the room, behind some clothes which were hanging up there, and watched. When it was midnight, two pretty little naked men came, sat down by the shoemaker's table, took all the work which was cut out before them and began to stitch, and sew, and hammer so skillfully and so quickly with their little fingers that the shoemaker could not turn away his eyes for astonishment. They did not stop until all was done, and stood finished on the table, and they ran quickly away.

Next morning the woman said, "The little men have made us rich, and we really must show that we are grateful for it. They run about so, and have nothing on, and must be cold. I'll tell you what I'll do: I will make them little shirts, and coats, and vests, and trousers, and knit both of them a pair of stockings, and you, too, make them two little pairs of shoes."

The man said, "I shall be very glad to do it," and one night, when everything was ready, they laid their presents all together on the table instead of the cut-out leather, and then concealed themselves to see how the little men would behave. At midnight they came bounding in, and wanted to get to work at once, but as they did not find any leather cut out, but only the pretty little articles of clothing, they were at first astonished, and then they showed intense delight. They dressed themselves rapidity, putting the pretty clothes on, and singing,

"Now we are boys so fine to see,
We should no longer cobblers be!"

Then they danced and skipped and leapt over chairs and benches. At last they danced out the door. From that time forth they came no more, but as long as the shoemaker lived all went well with him, and all his undertakings prospered.

SECOND STORY

There was once a poor servant girl, who was industrious and cleanly, and swept the house every day, and emptied her sweepings on the great heap in front of the door. One morning when she was just going back to her work, she found a letter on this heap, and as she could not read, she put her broom in the corner, and took the letter to her master and mistress. It was an invitation from the elves, who asked the girl to hold a child for them at its christening and be its godmother. The girl did not know what to do, but at length, after much persuasion, and as they told her that it was not right to refuse an invitation of this kind, she consented. Then three elves came and led her to a hollow mountain, where the little folks lived. Everything there was small, but more elegant and beautiful than can be described. The baby's mother lay in a bed of black ebony ornamented with pearls, the coverlids were embroidered with gold, the cradle was of ivory, the bath of gold. The girl stood as godmother, and then wanted to go home again, but the little elves begged her to stay three days with them. So she stayed, and passed the time in pleasure and gaiety, and the little folks did all they could to make her happy. At last she set out on her way home, after they filled her pockets quite full of money, and led her out of the mountain again. When she got home, she wanted to begin her work, and took the broom, which was still standing in the corner, in her hand and began to sweep. Then some strangers came out of the house, who asked her who she was, and what business she had there? And she had not, as she thought, been gone three days with the little men in the mountains, but seven years, and in the meantime her former masters had died.

THIRD STORY

A certain mother's child had been taken away out of its cradle by the elves, and a changeling with a large head and staring eyes, which would do nothing but eat and drink, laid in its place. In her trouble she went to her neighbor, and asked her advice. The neighbor said that she was to carry the changeling into the kitchen, set it down on the hearth, light a fire, and boil some water in two eggshells, which would make the changeling laugh, and if he laughed, that would be the end of him. The woman did everything that her neighbor bade her. When she put the eggshells with water on the fire, the imp said, "I am as old now as the Wester forest, but never yet have I seen anyone boil anything in an eggshell!" And he began to laugh at it. While he was laughing, suddenly came a host of little elves, who brought the right child, set it down on the hearth, and took the changeling away with them.

40. THE ROBBER BRIDEGROOM

There was once on a time a miller, who had a beautiful daughter, and as she grew up, he wished that she was provided for, and well married. He thought, "If any good suitor comes and asks for her, I will give her to him." Not long afterwards, a suitor came, who appeared to be very rich, and as the miller had no fault to find with him, he promised his daughter to him. The maiden, however, did not like him quite so much as a girl should like the man to whom she is engaged, and had no confidence in him. Whenever she saw, or thought of him, she felt a secret horror. Once he said to her, "You are my betrothed, and yet you have never once paid me a visit."

The maiden replied, "I know not where your house is."

Then said the bridegroom, "My house is out there in the dark forest." She tried to excuse herself and said she could not find the way there. The bridegroom said, "Next Sunday you must come out there to me; I have already invited the guests, and I will strew ashes so that you may find your way through the forest." When Sunday came, and the maiden had to set out on her way, she became very uneasy, she herself knew not exactly why, and to mark her way she filled both her pockets full of peas and lentils. Ashes were strewn at the entrance of the forest, and these she followed, but at every step she threw a couple of peas on the ground. She walked almost the whole day until she reached the middle of the forest, where it was the darkest, and there stood a solitary house, which she did not like, for it looked so dark and dismal. She went inside it, but no one was within, and the most absolute stillness reigned. Suddenly a voice cried,

> "Turn back, turn back, young maiden dear,
> 'Tis a murderer's house you enter here."

The maiden looked up, and saw that the voice came from a bird, which was hanging in a cage on the wall. Again it cried,

> "Turn back, turn back, young maiden dear,
> 'Tis a murderer's house you enter here."

Then the young maiden went on farther from one room to another, and walked through the whole house, but it was entirely empty and not one human being was to be found. At last she came to the cellar, and there sat an extremely aged woman, whose head shook constantly. "Can you not tell me," said the maiden, "if my betrothed lives here?"

"Alas, poor child," replied the old woman, "do you know where you have come? You are in a murderer's den. You think you are a bride soon to be married, but you will wed death at your wedding. Look, I have been forced to put a great kettle on there, with water in it, and when they have you in their power, they will cut you to pieces without mercy, will cook you, and eat you, for they are eaters of human flesh. If I do not have compassion on you, and save you, you are lost."

Thereupon the old woman led her behind a great barrel where she could not be seen. "Be as still as a mouse," said she, "do not make a sound, or move, or all will be over for you. At night, when the robbers are asleep, we will escape; I have long waited for an opportunity." Hardly was this done, than the godless crew came home. They dragged with them another young girl. They were drunk, and paid no heed to her screams and lamentations. They gave her wine to drink, three glasses full, one glass of white wine, one glass of red, and a glass of yellow, and with this her heart burst in two. Thereupon they tore off her delicate raiment, laid her on a table, cut her beautiful body in pieces and strewed salt on it. The poor bride behind the cask trembled and shook, for she saw right well what fate the robbers had destined for her. One of them noticed a gold ring on the little finger of the murdered girl, and as it would not come off at once, he took an axe and cut the finger off, but it sprang up in the air, away over the cask and fell straight into the bride's bosom. The robber took a candle and wanted to look for it, but could not find it. Then another of them said, "Have you looked behind the great barrel?"

But the old woman cried, "Come and get something to eat, and leave off looking till the morning, the finger won't run away from you."

Then the robbers said, "The old woman is right," and gave up their search, and sat down to eat, and the old woman poured a sleeping potion in their wine, so that they soon lay down in the cellar, and slept and snored. When the bride heard that, she came out from behind the barrel, and had to step over the sleepers, for they lay in rows on the ground, and great was her terror lest she should awaken one of them.

But God helped her, and she got safely over. The old woman went up with her, opened the doors, and they hurried out of the murderers' den with all the speed in their power. The wind had blown away the strewn ashes, but the peas and lentils had sprouted and grown up, and showed them the way in the moonlight. They walked the whole night, until in the morning they arrived at the mill, and then the maiden told her father everything exactly as it had happened.

When the day came when the wedding was to be celebrated, the bridegroom appeared, and the miller had invited all his relations and friends. As they sat at table, each was bidden to relate a story. The bride sat still, and said nothing. Then said the bridegroom to the bride, "Come, my darling, do you know nothing? Relate something to us like the rest."

She replied, "Then I will relate a dream. I was walking alone through a wood, and at last I came to a house, in which no living soul was, but on the wall there was a bird in a cage which cried,

> "Turn back, turn back, young maiden dear,
> 'Tis a murderer's house you enter here."

And this it cried once more. My darling, it was only a dream. Then I went through all the rooms, and they were all empty, and there was something so horrible about them! At last I went down into the cellar, and there sat a very, very old woman, whose head shook; I asked her, 'Does my bridegroom live in this house?'

She answered, 'Alas poor child, you have got into a murderer's den, your bridegroom does live here, but he will hew you in pieces, and kill you, and then he will cook you, and eat you.' My darling, it was only a dream. But the old woman hid me behind a great barrel, and, scarcely was I hidden, when the robbers came home, dragging a maiden with them, to whom they gave three kinds of wine to drink, white, red, and yellow, with which her heart broke in two. My darling, it was only a dream. Thereupon they pulled off her pretty clothes, and hewed her fair body in pieces on a table, and sprinkled them with salt. My darling, it was only a dream. And one of the robbers saw that there was still a ring on her little finger, and as it was hard to draw off, he took an axe and cut it off, but the finger sprang up in the air, and sprang behind the great barrel, and fell in my bosom. And there is the finger with the ring!" And with these words she drew it forth, and showed it to those present.

The robber, who had during this story become as pale as ashes, leapt up and wanted to escape, but the guests held him fast, and delivered him over to justice. Then he and his whole troop were executed for their infamous deeds.

41. MR. KORBES

There were once a cock and a hen who wanted to take a journey together. So the cock built a beautiful carriage, which had four red wheels, and harnessed four mice to it. The hen seated herself in it with the cock, and they drove away together. Not long afterwards they met a cat who said, "Where are you going?"

The cock replied, "We are going to the house of Mr. Korbes."

"Take me with you," said the cat.

The cock answered, "Most willingly, get up behind, lest you fall off in front. Take great care not to dirty my little red wheels. And you little wheels, roll on, and you little mice pipe out, as we go forth on our way to the house of Mr. Korbes."

After this came a millstone, then an egg, then a duck, then a pin, and at last a needle, who all seated themselves in the carriage, and drove with them. When, however, they reached the house of Mr. Korbes, Mr. Korbes was not there. The mice drew the carriage into the barn, the hen flew with the cock upon a perch. The cat sat down by the hearth, the duck on the sink. The egg rolled itself into a towel, the pin stuck itself into the chair cushion, the needle jumped onto the bed in the middle of the pillow, and the millstone laid itself over the door. Then Mr. Korbes came home, went to the hearth, and was about to light the fire, when the cat threw a quantity of ashes in his face. He ran into the kitchen in a great hurry to wash it off, and the duck splashed some water in his face. He wanted to dry it with the towel, but the egg rolled up against him, broke, and glued up his eyes. He wanted to rest, and sat down in the chair, and then the pin pricked him. He fell in a passion, and threw himself on his bed, but as soon as he laid his head on the pillow, the needle pricked him, so that he screamed aloud, and was just going to run out into the wide world in his rage, but when he came to the door, the millstone leapt down and struck him dead. Mr. Korbes must have been a very wicked man!

42. THE GODFATHER

A poor man had so many children that he had already asked everyone in the world to be godfather, and when still another child was born, no one else was left whom he could invite. He knew not what to do, and, in his perplexity, he lay down and fell asleep. Then he dreamed that he was to go outside the gate, and ask the first person who met him to be godfather. When he awoke, he was determined to obey his dream, and went outside the gate, and asked the first person who came up to him to be godfather. The stranger presented him with a little glass of water, and said, "This is a wonderful water, with it you can heal the sick, only you must see where Death is standing. If he is standing by the patient's head, give the patient some of the water and he will be healed, but if Death is standing by his feet, all trouble will be in vain, for the sick man must die." From this time forth, the man could always say whether a patient could be saved or not, and became famous for his skill, and earned a great deal of money. Once he was called in to the child of the King, and when he entered, he saw death standing by the child's head and cured it with the water, and he did the same a second time, but the third time Death was standing by its feet, and then he knew the child was meant to die.

Once the man thought he would visit the godfather, and tell him how he had succeeded with the water. But when he entered the house, it was such a strange establishment! On the first flight of stairs, the broom and shovel were disputing, and knocking each other about violently. He asked them, "Where does the godfather live?"

The broom replied, "One flight of stairs higher up."

When he came to the second flight, he saw a heap of dead fingers lying. He asked, "Where does the godfather live?"

One of the fingers replied, "One flight of stairs higher."

On the third flight lay a heap of dead skulls, which again directed him to the flight beyond. On the fourth flight, he saw fishes on the fire, which frizzled in the pans and baked themselves.

They, too, said, "One flight of stairs higher." And when he had ascended the fifth, he came to the door of a room and peeped through the keyhole, and there he saw the godfather who had a pair of long horns. When he opened the door and went in, the godfather got into bed in a great hurry and covered himself up.

Then said the man, "Sir godfather, what a strange household you have! When I came to your first flight of stairs, the shovel and broom were quarreling, and beating each other violently."

"How stupid you are!" said the godfather. "That was the boy and the maid talking to each other."

"But on the second flight I saw dead fingers lying."

"Oh, how silly you are! Those were some roots of scorzonera."

"On the third flight lay a heap of dead men's skulls."

"Foolish man, those were cabbages."

"On the fourth flight, I saw fishes in a pan, which were hissing and baking themselves." When he had said that, the fishes came and served themselves up. "And when I got to the fifth flight, I peeped through the keyhole of a door, and there, godfather, I saw you, and you had long, long horns."

"Oh, that is a lie!" The man became alarmed, and ran out, and if he had not, who knows what the godfather would have done to him.

43. FRAU TRUDE

There was once a little girl who was obstinate and inquisitive, and when her parents told her to do anything, she did not obey them, so how could she fare well? One day she said to her parents, "I have heard so much of Frau Trude, I will go to her some day. People say that everything about her does look so strange, and that there are such odd things in her house, that I have become quite curious!"

Her parents absolutely forbade her, and said, "Frau Trude is a bad woman, who does wicked things, and if you go to her; you are no longer our child."

But the maiden did not let herself be stopped by her parent's prohibition, and still went to Frau Trude. And when she got to her, Frau Trude said, "Why are you so pale?"

"Ah," she replied, and her whole body trembled, "I have been so terrified at what I have seen."

"What have you seen?"

"I saw a black man on your steps."

"That was a collier."

"Then I saw a green man."

"That was a hunter."

"After that I saw a blood-red man."

"That was a butcher."

"Ah, Frau Trude, I was terrified; I looked through the window and saw not you, but, as I verily believe, the devil himself with a head of fire."

"Oho!" said she, "Then you have seen the witch in her proper costume. I have been waiting for you, and wanting you a long time already; you shall give me some light." Then she changed the girl into a block of wood, and threw it into the fire. And when it was in full blaze she sat down close to it, and warmed herself by it, and said, "That shines bright for once."

44. GODFATHER DEATH

A poor man had twelve children and was forced to work night and day to provide them even with bread. When therefore the thirteenth came into the world, he knew not what to do in his trouble, but ran out into the great highway, and resolved to ask the first person whom he met to be godfather. The first to meet him was the good God who already knew what troubled him, and said to him, "Poor man, I pity you. I will hold your child at its christening, and will take charge of it and make it happy on earth."

The man said, "Who are you?"

"I am God."

"Then I do not desire to have you for a godfather," said the man, "You give to the rich, and leave the poor to hunger." Thus spoke the man, for he did not know how wisely God apportions riches and poverty. He turned therefore away from the Lord, and went farther.

Then the Devil came to him and said, "What do you seek? If you will take me as a godfather for your child, I will give him gold in plenty and all the joys of the world as well."

The man asked, "Who are you?"

"I am the Devil."

"Then I do not desire to have you for godfather," said the man, "You deceive men and lead them astray."

He went onwards, and then came Death striding up to him with withered legs, and said, "Take me as godfather."

The man asked, "Who are you?"

"I am Death, and I make all equal."

Then said the man, "You are the right one, you take the rich as well as the poor, without distinction; you shall be godfather."

Death answered, "I will make your child rich and famous, for he who has me for a friend can lack nothing."

The man said, "Next Sunday is the christening; be there at the right time." Death appeared as he had promised, and stood godfather quite in the usual way.

When the boy had grown up, his godfather one day appeared and bade him go with him. He led him forth into a forest, and showed him an herb which grew there, and said, "Now you shall receive your godfather's present. I make you a celebrated physician. When you are called to a patient, I will always appear to you. If I stand by the head of the sick man, you may say with confidence that you will make him well again, and if you give him this herb he will recover; but if I stand by the patient's feet, he is mine, and you must say that all remedies are in vain, and that no physician in the world could save him. But beware of using the herb against my will, or it might fare badly for you."

It was not long before the youth was the most famous physician in the whole world. People said of him: "He had only to look at the patient and he knew his condition at once, and if he would recover, or must die." From far and wide people came to him, sent for him when they had anyone ill, and gave him so much money that he soon became a rich man. Now it so happened that the King became ill, and the physician was summoned, and was to say if recovery were possible. But when he came to the bed, Death was standing by the feet of the sick man, and the herb did not grow which could save him. "If I could but cheat Death for once," thought the physician, "he is sure to be angry if I do, but, as I am his godson, he may shut one eye; I will risk it." He therefore took up the sick man, and laid him the other way, so that now Death was standing by his head. Then he gave the King some of the herb, and he recovered and grew healthy again.

But Death came to the physician, looking very black and angry, threatened him with his finger, and said, "You have overreached me; this time I will pardon it, as you are my godson; but if you venture it again, it will cost you your neck, for I will take *you* away with me."

Soon afterwards the King's daughter fell into a severe illness. She was his only child, and he wept day and night, so that he began to lose the sight of his eyes, and he made it known that whoever rescued her from death should be her husband and inherit the crown. When the physician came to the sick girl's bed, he saw Death by her feet. He ought to have remembered the warning given by his godfather, but he was so infatuated by the great beauty of the King's daughter, and the happiness of becoming her husband, that he flung all thought to the winds. He did not see that Death was casting angry glances on him, that he was raising his hand in the air, and threatening him with his withered fist. He raised up the sick girl, and placed her head where her feet had lain. Then he gave her some of the herb, and instantly her cheeks flushed red, and life stirred afresh in her.

When Death saw that for a second time he was defrauded of his own property, he walked up to the physician with long strides, and said, "All is over for you, and now the lot falls on you," and seized him so firmly with his ice-cold hand, that he could not resist, and led him into a cave below the earth. There he saw how thousands and thousands of candles were burning in countless rows, some large, others half-sized, others small. Every instant some were extinguished, and others again burnt up, so that the flames seemed to leap here and there in perpetual change. "See," said Death, "these are the lights of men's lives. The large ones belong to children, the half-sized ones to married people in their prime, the little ones belong to old people; but children and young folks likewise have often only a tiny candle."

"Show me the light of my life," said the physician, and he thought that it would be very tall.

Death pointed to a little end which was just threatening to go out, and said, "Look, it is there."

"Ah, dear godfather," said the horrified physician, "light a new one for me, do it for love of me, that I may enjoy my life, be King, and the husband of the King's beautiful daughter."

"I cannot," answered Death, "one must go out before a new one is lighted."

"Then place the old one on a new one, that will go on burning when the old one has come to an end," pleaded the physician. Death behaved as if he were going to fulfill his wish, and took hold of a tall new candle; but as he desired revenge, he purposely made a mistake in fixing it, and the little piece fell down and was extinguished. Immediately the physician fell on the ground, and now he himself was in the hands of Death.

45. THUMBLING'S TRAVELS

A certain tailor had a son, who happened to be small, and no bigger than a thumb, and on this account he was always called Thumbling. He had, however, some courage in him, and said to his father, "Father, I must and will go out into the world."

"That's right, my son," said the old man, and took a long darning needle and made a knob of sealing wax on it at the candle, "and there is a sword for you to take with you on the way." Then the little tailor wanted to have one more meal with them, and hopped into the kitchen to see what his mother had cooked for the last time. It was just dished up, and the dish stood on the hearth.

Then he said, "Mother, what is there to eat today?"

"See for yourself," said his mother.

So Thumbling jumped onto the hearth, and peeped into the dish, but as he stretched his neck in too far the steam from the food caught hold of him, and carried him up the chimney. He rode about in the air on the steam for a while, until at length he sank down to the ground again. Now the little tailor was outside in the wide world, and he traveled about, and went to work with a master in his craft, but the food was not good enough for him. "Mistress, if you give us no better food," said Thumbling, "I will go away, and early tomorrow morning I will write with chalk on the door of your house, 'Too many potatoes, too little meat! Farewell, Mr. Potato King.'"

"You wretched, grasshopper!" said the angry mistress, and seized a dishcloth, and was just going to strike him; but my little tailor crept nimbly under a thimble, peeped out from beneath it, and put his tongue out at the mistress. She took up the thimble, and wanted to get hold of him, but little Thumbling hopped into the cloth, and while the mistress was opening it out and looking for him, he got into a crevice in the table.

"Ho, ho, lady mistress," cried he, and thrust his head out, and when she began to strike him he leapt down into the drawer. At last, however, she caught him and drove him out of the house.

The little tailor journeyed on and came to a great forest, and there he fell in with a band of robbers who had a design to steal the King's treasure. When they saw the little tailor, they thought, "A little fellow like that can creep through a keyhole and serve as picklock to us."

"Hollo," cried one of them, "you giant Goliath, will you go to the treasure chamber with us? You can slip yourself in and throw out the money."

Thumbling reflected a while, and at length he said, "yes," and went with them to the treasure chamber. Then he looked at the doors above and below, to see if there was any crack in them. It was not long before he spied one which was broad enough to let him in. He was therefore about to get in at once, but one of the two sentries who stood before the door, observed him, and said to the other, "What an ugly spider is creeping there; I will kill it."

"Leave the poor creature alone," said the other; "it has done you no harm."

Then Thumbling got safely through the crevice into the treasure chamber, opened the window beneath which the robbers were standing, and threw out to them one taler after another. When the little tailor was in the full swing of his work, he heard the King coming to inspect his treasure chamber, and crept hastily into a hiding place.

The King noticed that several solid talers were missing, but could not conceive who could have stolen them, for locks and bolts were in good condition, and all seemed well guarded. Then he went away again, and said to the sentries, "Be on the watch, someone is after the money."

When Thumbling recommenced his labors, they heard the money moving, and a sound of *klink, klink, klink*. They ran swiftly in to seize the thief, but the little tailor, who heard them coming, was still swifter, and leapt into a corner and covered himself with a taler, so that nothing could be seen of him, and at the same time he mocked the sentries and cried, "Here I am!" The sentries ran over, but as they got there, he had already hopped into another corner under a taler, and was crying, "Ho, ho, here I am!" The watchmen sprang there in haste, but Thumbling had long ago got into a third corner, and was crying, "Ho, ho, here I am!" And thus he made fools of them, and drove them so long round about the treasure chamber that they were weary and went away. Then little by little he threw all the talers out, dispatching the last with all his might, then hopped nimbly upon it, and flew down with it through the window.

The robbers paid him great compliments. "You are a valiant hero," said they, "Will you be our captain?"

Thumbling, however, declined, and said he wanted to see the world first. They now divided the booty, but the little tailor only asked for a kreuzer because he could not carry more.

Then he once more buckled on his sword, bade the robbers goodbye, and took to the road. First, he went to work with some masters, but he had no liking for that, and at last he hired himself as servant in an inn. The maids, however, could not endure him, for he saw all they did secretly, without their seeing him, and he told their master and mistress what they had taken off the plates, and carried away out of the cellar, for themselves. Then said they, "Wait, and we will pay you off!" and arranged with each other to play a trick. Soon afterwards when one of the maids was mowing in the garden, and saw Thumbling jumping about and creeping up and down the plants, she mowed him up quickly with the grass, tied all in a great cloth, and secretly threw it to the cows. Now amongst them there was a great black one, who swallowed him down without hurting him. Down below, however, it did not please him, for it was quite dark, and there was no candle burning. When the cow was being milked he cried,

> "Strip, strap, strull,
> Will the pail soon be full?"

But the noise of the milking prevented his being understood. After this the master of the house came into the barn and said, "That cow shall be killed tomorrow."

Then Thumbling was so alarmed that he cried out in a clear voice, "Let me out first, for I am shut up inside her."

The master heard that quite well, but did not know from where the voice came. "Where are you?" asked he.

"In the black one," answered Thumbling, but the master did not understand what that meant, and went out.

Next morning the cow was killed. Happily Thumbling did not meet with one blow at the cutting up and chopping; he got among the sausage meat. And when the butcher came in and began his work, he cried out with all his might, "Don't chop too deep, don't chop too deep, I am amongst it." No one heard this because of the noise of the chopping knife. Now poor Thumbling was in trouble, but trouble sharpens the wits, and he sprang out so adroitly between the blows that none of them touched him, and he escaped with a whole skin. But still he could not get away, he could only let himself be thrust into a black pudding with the bits of bacon. His quarters there were rather confined, and besides that he was hung up in the chimney to be smoked, and there time did hang terribly heavy on his hands.

In winter he was taken down again, as the black pudding was to be served to a guest. When the hostess was cutting it in slices, he took care not to stretch out his head too far lest a bit of it should be cut off; at last he saw his opportunity, cleared a passage for himself, and jumped out.

The little tailor, however, would not stay any longer in a house where he fared so badly, so at once set out on his journey again. But his liberty did not last long. In the open country he met with a fox who snapped him up in a fit of absence. "Hollo, Mr. Fox," cried the little tailor, "it is I who am sticking in your throat, set me at liberty again."

"You are right," answered the fox. "You are next to nothing for me, but if you will promise me the fowls in your father's yard I will let you go."

"With all my heart," replied Thumbling. "You shall have all the cocks and hens, that I promise you."

Then the fox let him go, and even carried him home. When the father once more saw his dear son, he willingly gave the fox all the fowls which he had. "For this I likewise bring you a handsome bit of money," said Thumbling, and gave his father the kreuzer which he earned on his travels.

"But why did the fox get the poor chickens to eat?"

"Oh, you goose, *your* father would surely love his child far more than the fowls in the yard!"

46. FOWLER'S FOWL

There was once a wizard who used to take the form of a poor man, and went to houses and begged, and caught pretty girls. No one knew where he carried them, for they were never seen again. One day he appeared before the door of a man who had three pretty daughters; he looked like a poor weak beggar, and carried a basket on his back, as if he meant to collect charitable gifts in it. He begged for a little food, and when the eldest daughter came out and was just handing him a piece of bread, he barely touched her, and she was forced to jump into his basket. Then he hurried away with long strides, and carried her away into a dark forest to his house, which stood in the midst of it. Everything in the house was magnificent; he gave her whatever she could possibly desire, and said, "My darling, you will certainly be happy with me, for you have everything your heart can wish for." This lasted a few days, and then he said, "I must journey forth, and leave you alone for a short time; there are the keys of the house; you may go everywhere and look at everything except in one room, which this little key here opens, and I forbid you to go there on pain of death." He likewise gave her an egg and said, "Preserve the egg carefully for me, and carry it continually about with you, for a great misfortune would arise from the loss of it."

She took the keys and the egg, and promised to obey him in everything. When he was gone, she went all round the house from the bottom to the top, and examined everything. The rooms shone with silver and gold, and she thought she had never seen such great splendor. At length she came to the forbidden door; she wished to pass it by, but curiosity let her have no rest. She examined the key, it looked just like any other; she put it in the keyhole and turned it a little, and the door sprang open. But what did she see when she went in? A great bloody basin stood in the middle of the room, and therein lay human beings, dead and hewn to pieces, and nearby was a block of wood, and a gleaming axe lay upon it. She was so terribly alarmed that the egg which she held in her hand fell into the basin. She got it out and washed the blood off, but in vain, it appeared again in a moment. She washed and scrubbed, but she could not get it out.

It was not long before the man came back from his journey, and the first things which he asked for were the key and the egg. She gave them to him, but she trembled as she did so, and he saw at once by the red spots that she had been in the bloody chamber. "Since you have gone into the room against my will," said he, "you shall go back into it against your own. Your life is ended." He threw her down, dragged her there by her hair, cut her head off on the block, and hewed her in pieces so that her blood ran on the ground. Then he threw her into the basin with the rest.

"Now I will fetch myself the second," said the wizard, and again he went to the house in the shape of a poor man, and begged. Then the second daughter brought him a piece of bread; he caught her like the first, by simply touching her, and carried her away. She did not fare better than her sister. She allowed herself to be led away by her curiosity, opened the door of the bloody chamber, looked in, and had to atone for it with her life on the wizard's return. Then he went and brought the third sister, but she was clever and crafty. When he had given her the keys and the egg, and had left her, she first put the egg away with great care, and then she examined the house, and at last went into the forbidden room. Alas, what did she behold! Both her sisters lay there in the basin, cruelly murdered, and cut in pieces. But she began to gather their limbs together and put them in order, head, body, arms and legs. And when nothing further was wanting the limbs began to move and unite themselves together, and both the maidens opened their eyes and were once more alive. Then they rejoiced and kissed and caressed each other.

On his arrival, the man at once demanded the keys and the egg, and as he could perceive no trace of any blood on it, he said, "You have stood the test, you shall be my bride." Now he no longer had any power over her, and was forced to do whatever she desired.

"Oh, very well," said she, "you shall first take a basketful of gold to my father and mother, and carry it yourself on your back; in the meantime I will prepare for the wedding." Then she ran to her sisters, whom she had hidden in a little chamber, and said, "The moment has come when I can save you. The wretch shall carry you home again, but as soon as you are at home send help to me." She put both of them in a basket and covered them quite over with gold, so that nothing of them was to be seen, then she called in the wizard and said to him, "Now carry the basket away, but I shall look through my little window and watch to see if you stop on the way to stand or to rest."

The wizard raised the basket on his back and went away with it, but it weighed him down so heavily that the perspiration streamed from his face. Then he sat down and wanted to rest awhile, but immediately one of the girls in the basket cried, "I am looking through my little window, and I see that you are resting. Will you go on at once?"

He thought it was his bride who was calling that to him; and got up on his legs again. Once more he was going to sit down, but instantly she cried, "I am looking through my little window, and I see that you are resting. Will you go on directly?"

And whenever he stood still, she cried this, and then he was forced to go onwards, until at last, groaning and out of breath, he took the basket with the gold and the two maidens into their parents' house. At home, however, the bride prepared the marriage feast, and sent invitations to the friends of the wizard. Then she took a skull with grinning teeth, put some ornaments on it and a wreath of flowers, carried it upstairs to the attic window, and let it look out from there. When all was ready, she dipped into a barrel of honey, and then cut the featherbed open and rolled herself in it, until she looked like a wondrous bird, and no one could recognize her. Then she went out of the house, and on her way she met some of the wedding guests, who asked,

> "O, Fowler's fowl, how come you here?"
>   "I come from Fitz the Fowler's house quite near."
> "And what may the young bride be doing?"
>   "From cellar to garret she's swept all clean,
>   And now from the window she's peeping, I ween."

At last she met the bridegroom, who was coming slowly back. He, like the others, asked,

> "O, Fowler's fowl, how come you here?"
>   "I come from Fitz the Fowler's house quite near."
> "And what may the young bride be doing?"
>   "From cellar to garret she's swept all clean,
>   And now from the window she's peeping, I ween."

The bridegroom looked up, saw the decked-out skull, thought it was his bride, and nodded to her, greeting her kindly. But when he and his guests had all gone into the house, the brothers and kinsmen of the bride, who had been sent to rescue her, arrived. They locked all the doors of the house, that no one might escape, set fire to it, and the wizard and all his crew had to burn.

47. THE JUNIPER TREE

It is now long ago, at least two thousand years, since there was a rich man who had a beautiful and pious wife, and they loved each other dearly. They had, however, no children, though they wished for them very much, and the woman prayed for them day and night, but still they had none. Now there was a courtyard in front of their house in which was a juniper tree, and one day in winter the woman was standing beneath it, paring herself an apple, and while she was paring herself the apple she cut her finger, and the blood fell on the snow. "Ah," said the woman, and sighed heavily, and looked at the blood before her, and was most unhappy. "Ah, if I had but a child as red as blood and as white as snow!" And while she thus spoke, she became quite happy in her mind, and felt just as if that were going to happen.

Then she went into the house and a month went by and the snow was gone, and two months, and then everything was green, and three months, and then all the flowers came out of the earth, and four months, and then all the trees in the wood grew thicker, and the green branches were all closely entwined, and the birds sang until the wood resounded and the blossoms fell from the trees, then the fifth month passed away and she stood under the juniper-tree, which smelled so sweetly that her heart leapt, and she fell on her knees and was beside herself with joy, and when the sixth month was over the fruit was large and fine, and then she was quite still, and the seventh month she snatched at the juniper berries and ate them greedily, then she grew sick and sorrowful, then the eighth month passed, and she called her husband to her, and wept and said, "If I die then bury me beneath the juniper-tree." Then she was quite comforted and happy until the next month was over, and then she had a child as white as snow and as red as blood, and when she saw it she was so delighted that she died.

Then her husband buried her beneath the juniper-tree, and he began to weep sorely; after some time he was more at ease, and though he still wept he could bear it, and after some time longer he took another wife.

By the second wife he had a daughter named Marlinchen, but the first wife's child was a little son, and he was as red as blood and as white as snow. When the woman looked at her daughter she loved her very much, but then she looked at the little boy and it seemed to cut her to the heart, for the thought came into her mind that he would always stand in her way, and she was forever thinking how she could get all the fortune for her daughter, and the Evil One filled her mind with this till she quite hated the little boy, and slapped him here and cuffed him there, until the unhappy child was in continual terror, for when he came out of school he had no peace in any place.

One day the woman had gone upstairs to her room, and her little daughter went up too, and said, "Mother, give me an apple."

"Yes, my child," said the woman, and gave her a fine apple out of the chest, but the chest had a great heavy lid with a great sharp iron lock.

"Mother," said the little daughter, "is brother not to have one too?"

This made the woman angry, but she said, "Yes, when he comes out of school." And when she saw from the window that he was coming, it was just as if the Devil entered into her, and she snatched at the apple and took it away again from her daughter, and said, "You shall not have one before your brother." Then she threw the apple into the chest, and shut it. Then the little boy came in the door, and the Devil made her say to him kindly, "My son, will you have an apple?" and she looked wickedly at him.

"Mother," said the little boy, "how dreadful you look! Yes, give me an apple."

Then it seemed to her as if she were forced to say to him, "Come with me," and she opened the lid of the chest and said, "Take out an apple for yourself," and while the little boy was stooping inside, the Devil prompted her, and crash! She shut the lid down, and his head flew off and fell among the red apples. Then she was overwhelmed with terror, and thought, "If I could but make them think that it was not done by me!" So she went upstairs to her room to her chest of drawers, and took a white handkerchief out of the top drawer, and set the head on the neck again, and folded the handkerchief so that nothing could be seen, and she set him on a chair in front of the door, and put the apple in his hand.

After this Marlinchen came into the kitchen to her mother, who was standing by the fire with a pan of hot water before her which she was constantly stirring round. "Mother," said Marlinchen, "brother is sitting at the door, and he looks quite white and has an apple in his hand. I asked him to give me the apple, but he did not answer me, and I was quite frightened."

"Go back to him," said her mother, "and if he will not answer you, give him a box on the ear." So Marlinchen went to him and said, "Brother, give me the apple." But he was silent, and she gave him a box on the ear, on which his head fell down. Marlinchen was terrified, and began crying and screaming, and ran to her mother, and said, "Alas, mother, I have knocked my brother's head off!" and she wept and wept and could not be comforted.

"Marlinchen," said the mother, "what have you done? But be quiet and let no one know it; it cannot be helped now, we will make him into black puddings." Then the mother took the little boy and chopped him in pieces, put him into the pan and made him into black puddings; but Marlinchen stood by weeping and weeping, and all her tears fell into the pan and there was no need of any salt.

Then the father came home, and sat down to dinner and said, "But where is my son?" And the mother served up a great dish of black puddings, and Marlinchen wept and could not leave off. Then the father again said, "But where is my son?"

"Ah," said the mother, "he has gone across the country to his mother's great uncle; he will stay there awhile."

"And what is he going to do there? He did not even say goodbye to me."

"Oh, he wanted to go, and asked me if he might stay six weeks, he is well taken care of there."

"Ah," said the man, "I feel so unhappy. It's not right what he's done. He ought to have said goodbye to me." With that he began to eat and said, "Marlinchen, why are you crying? Your brother will certainly come back." Then he said, "Ah, wife, how delicious this food is, give me some more." And the more he ate the more he wanted to have, and he said, "Give me some more, you shall have none of it. It seems to me as if it were all mine." And he ate and ate and threw all the bones under the table, until he had finished the whole. But Marlinchen went away to her chest of drawers, and took her best silk handkerchief out of the bottom drawer, and got all the bones from beneath the table, and tied them up in her silk handkerchief, and carried them outside the door, weeping tears of blood. Then the juniper-tree began to stir itself, and the branches parted, and moved together again, just as if someone was rejoicing and clapping his hands. At the same time a mist seemed to arise from the tree, and in the centre of this mist it burned like a fire, and a beautiful bird flew out of the fire singing magnificently, and he flew high up in the air, and when he was gone, the juniper-tree was just as it had been before, and the handkerchief with the bones was no longer there. Marlinchen, however, was as gay and happy as if her brother were still alive. And she went merrily into the house, and sat down to dinner and ate.

But the bird flew away and lighted on a goldsmith's house, and began to sing,

> "My mother she killed me,
> My father he ate me,
> My sister, little Marlinchen,
> Gathered together all my bones,
> Tied them in a silken handkerchief,
> Laid them beneath the juniper-tree,
> Kywitt, kywitt, what a beautiful bird am I!"

The goldsmith was sitting in his workshop making a gold chain, when he heard the bird which was sitting singing on his roof, and very beautiful the song seemed to him. He stood up, but as he crossed the threshold he lost one of his slippers. But he walked right up the middle of the street with one shoe on and one sock; he had his apron on, and in one hand he had the gold chain and in the other his pincers, and the sun was shining brightly on the street. Then he went right over and stood still, and said to the bird, "Bird," said he then, "how beautifully you can sing! Sing me that piece again."

"No," said the bird, "I'll not sing it twice for nothing! Give me the golden chain, and then I will sing it again for you."

"There," said the goldsmith, "there is the golden chain for you, now sing me that song again." Then the bird came and took the golden chain in his right claw, and went and sat in front of the goldsmith, and sang,

> "My mother she killed me,
> My father he ate me,
> My sister, little Marlinchen,
> Gathered together all my bones,
> Tied them in a silken handkerchief,
> Laid them beneath the juniper-tree,
> Kywitt, kywitt, what a beautiful bird am I!"

Then the bird flew away to a shoemaker, and lighted on his roof and sang,

> "My mother she killed me,
> My father he ate me,
> My sister, little Marlinchen,
> Gathered together all my bones,
> Tied them in a silken handkerchief,
> Laid them beneath the juniper-tree,
> Kywitt, kywitt, what a beautiful bird am I!"

The shoemaker heard that and ran outside before even putting on a coat, and looked up at his roof, and was forced to hold his hand before his eyes lest the sun should blind him. "Bird," said he, "how beautifully you can sing!" Then he called in at his door, "Wife, just come outside, there is a bird, look at that bird, he can sing so well." Then he called his daughter and children, and apprentices, boys and girls, and they all came up the street and looked at the bird and saw how beautiful he was, and what fine red and green feathers he had, and how like real gold his neck was, and how his eyes shone like stars. "Bird," said the shoemaker, "now sing me that song again."

"Nay," said the bird, "I do not sing twice for nothing; you must give me something."

"Wife," said the man, "go to the garret, on the top shelf there stands a pair of red shoes, bring them down." Then the wife went and brought the shoes. "There, bird," said the man, "now sing me that piece again." Then the bird came and took the shoes in his left claw, and flew back on the roof, and sang,

> "My mother she killed me,
> My father he ate me,
> My sister, little Marlinchen,
> Gathered together all my bones,
> Tied them in a silken handkerchief,
> Laid them beneath the juniper-tree,
> Kywitt, kywitt, what a beautiful bird am I!"

And once he had sung it he flew away. In his right claw he had the chain and the shoes in his left, and he flew far away to a mill, and the mill went, *klipp klapp, klipp klapp, klipp klapp,* and in the mill sat twenty miller's men hewing a stone, and cutting, *hick hack, hick hack, hick hack*, and the mill went *klipp klapp, klipp klapp, klipp klapp*. Then the bird went and sat on a lime tree which stood in front of the mill, and sang,

> "My mother she killed me,"

then one of them stopped working,

> "My father he ate me,"

then two more stopped working and listened to that,

> "My sister, little Marlinchen,"

then four more stopped,

> "Gathered together all my bones,
> Tied them in a silken handkerchief,"

now eight only were hewing,

> "Laid them beneath,"

now only five,

> "The juniper-tree,"

and now only one,

> "Kywitt, kywitt, what a beautiful bird am I!"

Then the last stopped also, and heard the last words. "Bird," said he, "how beautifully you sing! Let me, too, hear that. Sing that once more for me."

"Nay," said the bird, "I will not sing twice for nothing. Give me the millstone, and then I will sing it again."

"Yes," said he, "if it belonged to only me, you should have it."

"Yes," said the others, "if he sings again he shall have it." Then the bird came down, and the twenty millers all set to work with a beam and raised the stone up. And the bird stuck his neck through the hole, and put the stone on as if it were a collar, and flew on to the tree again, and sang,

> "My mother she killed me,
> My father he ate me,
> My sister, little Marlinchen,
> Gathered together all my bones,
> Tied them in a silken handkerchief,
> Laid them beneath the juniper-tree,
> Kywitt, kywitt, what a beautiful bird am I!"

And when he was done singing, he spread his wings, and in his right claw he had the chain, and in his left the shoes, and round his neck the millstone, and he flew far away to his father's house.

In the room sat the father, the mother, and Marlinchen at dinner, and the father said, "How lighthearted I feel, how happy I am!"

"Nay," said the mother, "I feel so uneasy, just as if a heavy storm were coming."

Marlinchen, however, sat weeping and weeping, and then came the bird flying, and as it seated itself on the roof the father said, "Ah, I feel so truly happy, and the sun is shining so beautifully outside, I feel just as if I were about to see some old friend again."

"Nay," said the woman, "I feel so anxious, my teeth chatter, and I seem to have fire in my veins." And she tore her bodice open, but Marlinchen sat in a corner crying, and held her apron over her eyes and cried till it was quite wet. Then the bird sat on the juniper tree, and sang,

> "My mother she killed me,"

then the mother plugged her ears, and shut her eyes, and would not see or hear, but there was a roaring in her ears like the most violent storm, and her eyes burned and flashed like lightning,

> "My father he ate me."

"Ah, mother," says the man, "that is a beautiful bird! He sings so splendidly, and the sun shines so warm, and there is a smell just like cinnamon."

"My sister, little Marlinchen,"

then Marlinchen laid her head on her knees and wept without ceasing, but the man said, "I am going out, I must see the bird quite close."

"Oh, don't go," said the woman, "I feel as if the whole house were shaking and on fire." But the man went out and looked at the bird:

> "Gathered together all my bones,
>   Tied them in a silken handkerchief,
>   Laid them beneath the juniper tree,
>   Kywitt, kywitt, what a beautiful bird am I!"

On this the bird let the golden chain fall, and it fell exactly round the man's neck, and so exactly round that it fitted beautifully. Then he went in and said, "Just look what a fine bird that is, and what a handsome gold chain he has given me, and how pretty he is!" But the woman was terrified, and fell down on the floor in the room, and her cap fell off her head. Then sang the bird once more,

> "My mother she killed me."

"If only I were a thousand feet beneath the earth so as not to hear that!"

> "My father he ate me,"

then the woman fell down again as if dead.

> "My sister, little Marlinchen,"

"Ah," said Marlinchen, "I too will go out and see if the bird will give me anything," and she went out.

> "Gathered together all my bones,
>   Tied them in a silken handkerchief,"

then he threw down the shoes to her.

> "Laid them beneath the juniper-tree,
>   Kywitt, kywitt, what a beautiful bird am I!"

Then she was lighthearted and joyous, and she put on the new red shoes, and danced and leaped into the house. "Ah," said she, "I was so sad when I went out and now I am so lighthearted; that is a splendid bird, he has given me a pair of red shoes!"

"Well," said the woman, and sprang to her feet and her hair stood up like flames of fire, "I feel as if the world were coming to an end! I, too, will go out and see if my heart feels lighter." And as she went out the door, crash! the bird threw down the millstone on her head, and she was entirely crushed by it. The father and Marlinchen heard what had happened and went out, and smoke, flames, and fire were rising, and when that was over, there stood the little brother, and he took his father and Marlinchen by the hand, and all three were right glad, and they went into the house for dinner, and ate.

48. OLD SULTAN

A farmer once had a faithful dog called Sultan, who had grown old, and lost all his teeth, so that he could no longer hold anything tight. One day the farmer was standing with his wife before the door, and said, "Tomorrow I intend to shoot Old Sultan, he is no longer of any use."

His wife, who felt pity for the faithful beast, answered, "He has served us so long, and been so faithful, that we might well give him his keep."

"Eh! What?" said the man. "You are not very sharp. He has not a tooth left in his mouth, and not a thief is afraid of him; now he may be off. If he has served us, he has been well fed for it."

The poor dog, who was lying stretched out in the sun not far off, had heard everything, and was sorry that the morrow was to be his last day. He had a good friend, the wolf, and he crept out in the evening into the forest to him, and complained of the fate that awaited him. "Listen, friend," said the wolf, "be of good cheer, I will help you out of your trouble. I have thought of something. Tomorrow, early in the morning, your master is going with his wife to make hay, and they will take their little child with them, and no one will be left behind in the house. While at work they always lay the child under the hedge in the shade; you lay yourself there too, just as if you wished to guard it. Then I will come out of the wood, and carry off the child. You must rush swiftly after me, as if you would rescue it from me. I will let it fall, and you will take it back to its parents, who will think that you have saved it, and will be far too grateful to do you any harm; on the contrary, you will be in high favor, and they will never let you want for anything again."

The plan pleased the dog, and it was carried out just as it was arranged. The father screamed when he saw the wolf running across the field with his child, but when Old Sultan brought it back, then he was full of joy, and stroked him and said, "Not a hair of yours shall be hurt, you shall be well fed as long as you live." And to his wife he said, "Go home at once and make Old Sultan some soup that he will not have to chew, and bring the pillow from my bed, I will give him that to lie upon."

Hereforth Old Sultan was as well off as he could wish to be.

Soon afterwards the wolf visited him, and was pleased that everything had succeeded so well. "But now," said he, "you will just turn a blind eye if, when I have a chance, I carry off one of your master's fat sheep."

"Do not reckon upon that," answered the dog, "I will remain true to my master; I cannot agree to that."

The wolf, who thought that this could not be spoken in earnest, came creeping about in the night and was going to take away the sheep. But the farmer, to whom the faithful Sultan had told the wolf's plan, caught him and beat his hide soundly with the flail. The wolf had to flee, but he cried out to the dog, "Wait a bit, you scoundrel, you shall pay for this."

The next morning the wolf sent the boar to challenge the dog to come out into the forest so that they might settle the affair. Old Sultan could find no one to stand by him but a cat with only three legs, and as they went out together the poor cat limped along, and at the same time stretched out her tail into the air with pain.

The wolf and his friend were already on the spot appointed, but when they saw their enemy coming they thought that he was bringing a saber with him, for they mistook the outstretched tail of the cat for one. And when the poor beast hopped on its three legs, they could only think every time that it was picking up a stone to throw at them. So they were both afraid; the wild boar crept into the thicket and the wolf jumped up a tree.

The dog and the cat, when they came up, wondered that there was no one to be seen. The wild boar, however, had not been able to hide himself altogether; and one of his ears was still to be seen. While the cat was looking carefully about, the boar moved his ear; the cat, who thought it was a mouse moving there, jumped upon it and bit it hard. The boar made a fearful noise and ran away, crying out, "The guilty one is up in the tree." The dog and cat looked up and saw the wolf, who was ashamed of having shown himself so timid, and made friends with the dog again.

49. THE SIX SWANS

Once upon a time, a certain King was hunting in a great forest, and he chased a wild beast so eagerly that none of his attendants could follow him. When evening drew near he stopped and looked around him, and then he saw that he had lost his way. He sought a way out, but could find none. Then he perceived an aged woman with a head which nodded perpetually, who came towards him, but she was a witch. "Good woman," said he to her, "Can you not show me the way through the forest?"

"Oh, yes, Lord King," she answered, "that I certainly can, but on one condition, and if you do not fulfill that, you will never get out of the forest, and will die of hunger in it."

"What kind of condition is it?" asked the King.

"I have a daughter," said the old woman, "who is as beautiful as anyone in the world, and well deserves to be your wife, and if you will make her your Queen, I will show you the way out of the forest." In the anguish of his heart the King consented, and the old woman led him to her little hut, where her daughter was sitting by the fire. She received the King as if she had been expecting him, and he saw that she was very beautiful, but still she did not please him, and he could not look at her without secret horror. After he had taken the maiden up on his horse, the old woman showed him the way, and the King reached his royal palace again, where the wedding was celebrated.

The King had already been married once, and had by his first wife, seven children, six boys and a girl, whom he loved better than anything else in the world. As he now feared that the stepmother might not treat them well, and even do them some injury, he took them to a lonely castle which stood in the middle of a forest. It lay so concealed, and the way was so difficult to find that he himself would not have found it, if a wise woman had not given him a ball of yarn with wonderful properties. When he threw it down before him, it unrolled itself and showed him his path. The King, however, went so frequently away to his dear children that the Queen observed his absence; she was curious and wanted to know what he did when he was quite alone in the forest. She gave a great deal of money to his servants, and they betrayed the secret to her, and told her likewise of the ball which alone could point out the way. And now she knew no rest until she had learnt where the King kept the ball of yarn, and then she made little shirts of white silk, and as she had learnt the art of witchcraft from her mother, she sewed a charm inside them. And when the King had ridden off to hunt, she took the little shirts and went into the forest, and the ball showed her the way. The children, who saw from a distance that someone was approaching, thought that their dear father was coming to them, and full of joy, ran to meet him. Then she threw one of the little shirts over each of them, and no sooner had the shirts touched their bodies than they were changed into swans, and flew away over the forest. The Queen went home quite delighted, and thought she had got rid of her stepchildren, but the girl had not run out with her brothers, and the Queen knew nothing about her.

Next day the King went to visit his children, but he found no one but the little girl. "Where are your brothers?" asked the King.

"Alas, dear father," she answered, "they have gone away and left me alone!" and she told him that she had seen from her little window how her brothers had flown away over the forest in the shape of swans, and she showed him the feathers, which they had let fall in the courtyard, and which she had picked up. The King mourned, but he did not think that the Queen had done this wicked deed, and since he feared that the girl would also be stolen away from him, he wanted to take her away with him. But she was afraid of her stepmother, and begged the King to let her stay just this one night more in the forest castle.

The poor girl thought, "I can no longer stay here. I will go and seek my brothers." And when night came, she ran away, and went straight into the forest. She walked the whole night long, and next day also without stopping, until she could go no farther for weariness. Then she saw a forest hut, and went into it, and found a room with six little beds, but she did not venture to get into one of them, but crept under one, and lay down on the hard ground, intending to pass the night there. Just before sunset, however, she heard a rustling, and saw six swans come flying in at the window. They alighted on the ground and blew at each other, and blew all the feathers off, and their swan's skins stripped off like a shirt. Then the maiden looked at them and recognized her brothers, was glad and crept forth from beneath the bed.

The brothers were not less delighted to see their little sister, but their joy was of short duration. "Here can you not abide," they said to her. "This is a shelter for robbers, if they come home and find you, they will kill you."

"But can you not protect me?" asked the little sister.

"No," they replied, "only for one quarter of an hour each evening can we lay aside our swan's skins and have during that time our human form; after that, we are once more turned into swans."

The little sister wept and said, "Can you not be set free?"

"Alas, no," they answered, "the conditions are too hard! For six years you may neither speak nor laugh, and in that time you must sew together six little shirts of starflowers for us. And if one single word falls from your lips, all your work will be lost." And when the brothers had said this, the quarter of an hour was over, and they flew out of the window again as swans.

The maiden, however, firmly resolved to save her brothers, even if it should cost her her life. She left the hut, went into the middle of the forest, seated herself on a tree, and there passed the night. Next morning she went out and gathered starflowers and began to sew. She could not speak to anyone, and she had no inclination to laugh; she sat there and looked at nothing but her work. When she had already spent a long time there it came to pass that the King of the country was hunting in the forest, and his huntsmen came to the tree on which the maiden was sitting. They called to her and said, "Who are you?" But she made no answer. "Come down to us," said they. "We will not do you any harm." She only shook her head. As they pressed her further with questions she threw her golden necklace down to them, and thought this would satisfy them. They, however, did not cease, and then she threw her girdle down to them, and as this also was to no purpose, her garters, and by degrees everything that she had on that she could do without until she had nothing left but her shift. The huntsmen, however, did not let themselves be put off by that, but climbed the tree and fetched the maiden down and led her before the King.

The King asked, "Who are you? What are you doing on the tree?" But she did not answer. He put the question in every language that he knew, but she remained as mute as a fish. As she was so beautiful, the King's heart was touched, and he was smitten with a great love for her. He put his mantle on her, placed her before him on his horse, and carried her to his castle. Then he had her dressed in rich garments, and she shone in her beauty like bright daylight, but no word could be drawn from her. He placed her by his side at the able, and her modest bearing and courtesy pleased him so much that he said, "She is the one whom I wish to marry, and no other woman in the world." And after some days he united himself to her.

The King, however, had a wicked mother who was dissatisfied with this marriage and spoke ill of the young Queen. "Who knows," said she, "where she comes from? She is not worthy of a king!"

After a year had passed, when the Queen brought her first child into the world, the old woman took it away from her, and smeared her mouth with blood as she slept. Then she went to the King and accused the Queen of being a man-eater. The King would not believe it, and would not allow anyone to do her any injury. She, however, sat continually sewing at the shirts, and cared for nothing else. The next time, when she again bore a beautiful boy, the false stepmother used the same treachery, but the King could not bring himself to give credit to her words. He said, "She is too pious and good to do anything of that kind; if she were not dumb, and could defend herself, her innocence would come to light." But when the old woman stole away the newly-born child for the third time, and accused the Queen, who did not utter one word of defense, the King could do no otherwise than deliver her over to justice, and she was sentenced to suffer death by fire.

When the day came for the sentence to be executed, it was the last day of the six years during which she was not to speak or laugh, and she had delivered her dear brothers from the power of the enchantment. The six shirts were ready, only the left sleeve of the sixth was missing. When, therefore, she was led to the stake, she laid the shirts on her arm, and when she stood up high and the fire was just going to be lighted, she looked around and six swans came flying through the air towards her. Then she saw that she would be saved, and her heart leapt with joy. The swans swept towards her and sank down so that she could throw the shirts over them, and as they were touched by them, their swan's skins fell off, and her brothers stood in their own bodily form before her, and were vigorous and handsome. The youngest only lacked his left arm, and had in the place of it a swan's wing on his shoulder. They embraced and kissed each other, and the Queen went to the King, who was greatly moved, and she began to speak and said, "Dearest husband, now I may speak and declare to you that I am innocent, and falsely accused." And she told him of the treachery of the old woman who had taken away her three children and hidden them. Then to the great joy of the King they were brought there, and as a punishment, the wicked stepmother was bound to the stake, and burnt to ashes. But the King and the Queen with their six brothers lived many years in happiness and peace.

50. THE SLEEPING BEAUTY (BRIAR ROSE)

A long time ago there were a King and Queen who said every day, "Ah, if only we had a child!" but they never had one.

But it happened that once when the Queen was bathing, a frog crept out of the water onto the land, and said to her, "Your wish shall be fulfilled; before a year has gone by, you shall have a daughter."

What the frog had said came true, and the Queen had a little girl who was so pretty that the King could not contain himself for joy, and ordered a great feast. He invited not only his kindred, friends and acquaintance, but also the Wise Women, in order that they might be kind and well-disposed towards the child. There were thirteen of them in his kingdom, but, as he had only twelve golden plates for them to eat out of, one of them had to be left at home.

The feast was held with all manner of splendor and when it came to an end the Wise Women bestowed their magic gifts upon the baby: one gave virtue, another beauty, a third riches, and so on with everything in the world that one can wish for.

When eleven of them had made their promises, suddenly the thirteenth came in. She wished to avenge herself for not having been invited, and without greeting, or even looking at anyone, she cried with a loud voice, "The King's daughter shall in her fifteenth year prick herself with a spindle, and fall down dead." And, without saying a word more, she turned round and left the room.

They were all shocked; but the twelfth, whose good wish still remained unspoken, came forward, and as she could not undo the evil sentence, but only soften it, she said, "It shall not be death, but a deep sleep of a hundred years, into which the princess shall fall."

The King, who wished to keep his dear child from the misfortune, gave orders that every spindle in the whole kingdom should be burned. Meanwhile the gifts of the Wise Women came true for the young girl, for she was so beautiful, modest, good-natured, and wise, that everyone who saw her was bound to love her.

It happened that on the very day she turned fifteen years old, the King and Queen were not at home, and the maiden was left in the palace quite alone. So she went round into all sorts of places, looked into rooms and bedchambers just as she liked, and at last came to an old tower. She climbed up the narrow winding staircase, and reached a little door. A rusty key was in the lock, and when she turned it the door sprang open, and there in a little room sat an old woman with a spindle, busily spinning her flax.

"Good day, old dame," said the King's daughter; "what are you doing there?"

"I am spinning," said the old woman, and nodded her head. "What sort of thing is that, that rattles round so merrily?" said the girl, and she took the spindle and wanted to spin too. But scarcely had she touched the spindle when the magic decree was fulfilled, and she pricked her finger with it.

And, in the very moment when she felt the prick, she fell down upon the bed that stood there, and lay in a deep sleep. And this sleep extended over the whole palace; the King and Queen who had just come home, and had entered the great hall, began to go to sleep, and all of the court too. The horses, too, went to sleep in the stable, the dogs in the yard, the pigeons upon the roof, the flies on the wall; even the fire that was flaming on the hearth became quiet and slept, the roast meat left off frizzling, and the cook, who was just going to pull the hair of the kitchen boy, because he had forgotten something, let him go, and went to sleep. And the wind fell, and on the trees outside the castle not a leaf moved again.

But round about the castle there began to grow a hedge of thorns, which every year became higher, and at last grew close up round the castle and all over it, so that there was nothing of it to be seen, not even the flag upon the roof. But the story of the beautiful sleeping "Briar Rose," for so the princess was named, went about the country, so that from time to time kings' sons came and tried to get through the thorny hedge into the castle.

But they found it impossible, for the thorns held fast together, as if they had hands, and the youths were caught in them, could not get loose again, and died a miserable death.

After long, long years a King's son came again to that country, and heard an old man talking about the briar hedge, and that a castle was said to stand behind it in which a wonderfully beautiful princess, named Briar Rose, had been asleep for a hundred years; and that the King and

Queen and the whole court were asleep likewise. He had heard, too, from his grandfather, that many kings' sons had already come, and had tried to get through the thorny hedge, but they had remained sticking fast in it, and had died a pitiful death. Then the youth said, "I am not afraid, I will go and see the beautiful Briar Rose." The good old man tried to dissuade him, but he did not listen to his words.

But by this time the hundred years had just passed, and the day had come when Briar Rose was to awake again. When the King's son came near to the briar hedge, it was nothing but large and beautiful flowers, which parted from each other of their own accord, and let him pass unhurt, then they closed again behind him like a hedge. In the courtyard he saw the horses and the spotted hounds lying asleep; on the roof sat the pigeons with their heads under their wings. And when he entered the house, the flies were asleep upon the wall, the cook in the kitchen was still holding out his hand to seize the boy, and the maid was sitting by the black hen which she was going to pluck.

He went on farther, and in the great hall he saw the whole of the court lying asleep, and up by the throne lay the King and Queen.

Then he went on still farther, and all was so quiet that a breath could be heard, and at last he came to the tower, and opened the door into the little room where Briar Rose was sleeping. There she lay, so beautiful that he could not turn his eyes away; and he stooped down and gave her a kiss. But as soon as he kissed her, Briar Rose opened her eyes and awoke, and looked at him quite sweetly.

Then they went down together, and the King awoke, and the Queen, and the whole court, and looked at each other in great astonishment. And the horses in the courtyard stood up and shook themselves; the hounds jumped up and wagged their tails; the pigeons on the roof pulled out their heads from under their wings, looked round, and flew into the open country; the flies on the wall crept again; the fire in the kitchen burned up and flickered and cooked the meat; the roast began to turn and frizzle again, and the cook gave the boy such a box on the ear that he screamed, and the maid plucked the fowl ready for the spit.

And then the marriage of the King's son with Briar Rose was celebrated with all splendor, and they lived contented to the end of their days.

51. FUNDEVOGEL (FLEDGLING)

There was once a forester who went into the forest to hunt, and as he entered it he heard a sound of screaming as if a little child were there. He followed the sound, and at last came to a high tree, and at the top of this a little child was sitting, for the mother had fallen asleep under the tree with the child, and a bird of prey had seen it in her arms, had flown down, snatched it away, and set it up high on the tree.

The forester climbed up, brought the child down, and thought to himself, "You will take him home with you, and bring him up with your Lina." He took it home, therefore, and the two children grew up together. The one, however, which he had found on a tree was called Fundevogel, because a bird had carried it away. Fundevogel and Lina loved each other so dearly that when they did not see each other they were sad.

The forester had an old cook, who one evening took two pails and began to fetch water, and did not go once, but many times, out to the spring. Lina saw this and said, "Old Sanna, why are you fetching so much water?"

"If you will never repeat it to anyone, I will tell you why." So Lina said, no, she would never repeat it to anyone, and then the cook said, "Early tomorrow morning, when the forester is out hunting, I will heat the water, and when it is boiling in the kettle, I will throw in Fundevogel, and will boil him in it."

Early next morning the forester got up and went out hunting, and when he was gone the children were still in bed. Then Lina said to Fundevogel, "If you will never leave me, I too will never leave you."

Fundevogel said, "Neither now, nor ever will I leave you."

Then said Lina, "Then I will tell you. Last night, old Sanna carried so many buckets of water into the house that I asked her why she was doing that, and she said that if I would promise not to tell anyone she would tell me, and I said I would be sure not to tell anyone, and she said that early tomorrow morning when father was out hunting, she would set the kettle full of water, throw you into it and boil you; but we will get up quickly, dress ourselves, and go away together."

The two children therefore got up, dressed themselves quickly, and went away. When the water in the kettle was boiling, the cook went into the bedroom to fetch Fundevogel and throw him into it. But when she came in, and went to the beds, both the children were gone. Then she was terribly alarmed, and she said to herself, "What shall I say now when the forester comes home and sees that the children are gone? Quickly, they must be followed and brought back again."

Then the cook sent three servants after them, who were to run and overtake the children. The children, however, were sitting outside the forest, and when they saw from afar the three servants running, Lina said to Fundevogel, "Never leave me, and I will never leave you."

Fundevogel said, "Neither now, nor ever."

Then said Lina, "Do become a rosebush, and I will be the rose upon it."

When the three servants came to the forest, nothing was there but a rosebush and one rose on it, but the children were nowhere. Then said they, "There is nothing to be done here," and they went home and told the cook that they had seen nothing in the forest but a little rosebush with one rose on it.

Then the old cook scolded and said, "You simpletons, you should have cut the rosebush in two, broken off the rose and brought it home with you; go, and do it now." They had therefore to go out and look for the second time. The children, however, saw them coming from a distance.

Then Lina said, "Fundevogel, never leave me, and I will never leave you."

Fundevogel said, "Neither now, nor ever."

Said Lina, "Then you become a church, and I'll be the chandelier in it."

So when the three servants came, nothing was there but a church, with a chandelier in it. They said therefore to each other, "What can we do here, let us go home."

When they got home, the cook asked if they had not found them; so they said no, they had found nothing but a church, and that there was a chandelier in it. And the cook scolded them and said, "You fools! Why did you not pull the church to pieces, and bring the chandelier home with you?" And now the old cook herself got up, and went with the three servants in pursuit of the children. The children, however, saw from afar that the three servants were coming, and the cook waddling after them.

Then said Lina, "Fundevogel, never leave me, and I will never leave you."

Then said Fundevogel, "Neither now, nor ever."

Said Lina, "Be a fishpond, and I will be the duck upon it."

The cook, however, came up to them, and when she saw the pond she lay down by it, and was about to drink it up. But the duck swam quickly to her, seized her head in its beak and drew her into the water, and there the old witch had to drown. Then the children went home together, and were heartily delighted, and if they are not dead, they are living still.

52. KING THRUSHBEARD

A King had a daughter who was beautiful beyond all measure, but so proud and haughty that no suitor was good enough for her. She sent away one after the other, and ridiculed them as well.

Once the King made a great feast and invited there, from far and near, all the young men likely to marry. They were all marshaled in a row according to their rank and standing; first came the kings, then the grand-dukes, then the princes, the earls, the barons, and the gentry. Then the King's daughter was led through the ranks, but to everyone she had some objection to make; one was too fat, "A wine cask," she said. Another was too tall, "Long and thin has little in." The third was too short, "Short and thick is never quick." The fourth was too pale, "As pale as death." The fifth too red, "A fighting cock." The sixth was not straight enough, "A green log dried behind the stove."

So she had something to say against everyone, but she made herself especially merry over a good king who stood quite high up in the row, and whose chin had grown a little crooked. "Well," she cried and laughed, "he has a chin like a thrush's beak!" and from that time he got the name of King Thrushbeard.

But the old King, when he saw that his daughter did nothing but mock the people, and despised all the suitors who were gathered there, was very angry, and swore that she should have for her husband the very first beggar that came to his doors.

A few days afterwards a fiddler came and sang beneath the windows, trying to earn a small alms. When the King heard him he said, "Let him come up." So the fiddler came in, in his dirty, ragged clothes, and sang before the King and his daughter, and when he had ended he asked for a trifling gift. The King said, "Your song has pleased me so well that I will give you my daughter to wed."

The King's daughter shuddered, but the King said, "I have taken an oath to give you to the very first beggar, and I will keep it." All she could say was in vain; the priest was brought, and she had to let herself be wedded to the fiddler on the spot. When that was done the King said, "Now it is not proper for you, a beggar-woman, to stay any longer in my palace, you may just go away with your husband."

The beggar led her out by the hand, and she was obliged to walk away on foot with him. When they came to a large forest she asked, "To whom does that beautiful forest belong?" "It belongs to King Thrushbeard; if you had taken him, it would have been yours." "Ah, unhappy girl that I am, if I had but taken King Thrushbeard!"

Afterwards they came to a meadow, and she asked again, "To whom does this beautiful green meadow belong?"

"It belongs to King Thrushbeard; if you had taken him, it would have been yours."

"Ah, unhappy girl that I am, if I had but taken King Thrushbeard!"

Then they came to a large town, and she asked again, "To whom does this fine large town belong?"

"It belongs to King Thrushbeard; if you had taken him, it would have been yours."

"Ah, unhappy girl that I am, if I had but taken King Thrushbeard!"

"It does not please me," said the fiddler, "to hear you always wishing for another husband; am I not good enough for you?"

At last they came to a very little hut, and she said, "Oh goodness! What a small house; to whom does this miserable, shack belong?"

The fiddler answered, "That is my house and yours, where we shall live together."

She had to stoop in order to enter the low door. "Where are the servants?" said the King's daughter.

"What servants?" answered the beggar, "You must do yourself what you wish to have done. Just make a fire at once, and set on water to cook my supper, I am quite tired."

But the King's daughter knew nothing about lighting fires or cooking, and the beggar had to lend a hand to get anything fairly done. When they had finished their scanty meal they went to bed; but he forced her to get up quite early in the morning in order to look after the house.

For a few days they lived in this way, until they came to the end of all their provisions. Then the man said, "Wife, we cannot go on any longer eating and drinking here and earning nothing. You must weave baskets." He went out, cut some willows, and brought them home. Then she began to weave, but the tough willows wounded her delicate hands.

"I see that this will not do," said the man, "You had better spin, perhaps you can do that better." She sat down and tried to spin, but the hard thread soon cut her soft fingers so that the blood ran down. "See," said the man, "you are fit for no sort of work; I have made a bad bargain with you. Now I will try to make a business with pots and earthenware; you must sit in the marketplace and sell them."

"Alas," thought she, "if any of the people from my father's kingdom come to the market and see me sitting there, selling, how they will mock me!" But it was of no use, she had to yield unless she chose to die of hunger.

For the first time she succeeded, for the people were glad to buy the woman's wares because she was good-looking, and they paid her what she asked; many even gave her the money and left the pots with her as well. So they lived on what she had earned as long as it lasted, then the husband bought a new supply of crockery. With this she sat down at the corner of the marketplace, and set it out around her ready for sale. But suddenly there came a drunken hussar galloping along, and he rode right amongst the pots so that they were all broken into a thousand bits. She began to weep, and did now know what to do for fear. "Alas! what will happen to me?" cried she, "What will my husband say to this?"

She ran home and told him of the misfortune. "Who would seat herself at a corner of the marketplace with crockery?" said the man. "Stop crying, I see very well that you cannot do any ordinary work, so I have been to our King's palace and have asked whether they can find a place for a kitchen maid, and they have promised me to take you; in that way you will get your food for nothing."

The King's daughter was now a kitchen maid, and had to be at the cook's beck and call, and do the dirtiest work. In both her pockets she fastened a little jar, in which she took home her share of the scraps, and upon this they lived.

It happened that the wedding of the King's eldest son was to be celebrated, so the poor woman went up and placed herself by the door of the hall to watch. When all the candles were lit, and people, each more beautiful than the other, entered, and all was full of pomp and splendor, she thought of her fate with a sad heart, and cursed the pride and haughtiness which had humbled her and brought her to so great poverty.

The smell of the delicious dishes which were being taken in and out reached her, and now and then the servants threw her a few morsels of them: these she put in her jars to take home.

Suddenly the King's son entered, clothed in velvet and silk, with gold chains about his neck. And when he saw the beautiful woman standing by the door he seized her by the hand, and would have danced with her; but she refused and shrank with fear, for she saw that it was King Thrushbeard, her suitor whom she had driven away with scorn. Her struggles were of no avail, he pulled her into the hall; but the band to which her pockets were fastened broke, the pots fell down, the soup ran out, and the scraps were scattered all about. And when the people saw it, there arose general laughter and derision, and she was so ashamed that she would rather have been a thousand fathoms below the ground. She sprang to the door and would have run away, but on the stairs a man caught her and brought her back; and when she looked at him it was King Thrushbeard again.

He said to her kindly, "Do not be afraid, I am the fiddler who has been living with you in that wretched pigsty. For love of you I disguised myself so; and I also was the hussar who rode through your crockery. This was all done to humble your proud spirit, and to punish you for the insolence with which you mocked me."

Then she wept bitterly and said, "I have done great wrong, and am not worthy to be your wife."

But he said, "Be comforted, the evil days are past; now we will celebrate our wedding." Then the maids-in-waiting came and dressed her in the most splendid clothing, and her father and his whole court came and wished her happiness in her marriage with King Thrushbeard, and the joy now began in earnest. I wish you and I had been there too.

53. LITTLE SNOW WHITE

Once upon a time in the middle of winter, when the flakes of snow were falling like feathers from the sky, a queen sat at a window sewing, and the frame of the window was made of black ebony. And while she was sewing and looking out of the window at the snow, she pricked her finger with the needle, and three drops of blood fell upon the snow. And the red looked pretty upon the white snow, and she thought to herself, "If only I had a child as white as snow, as red as blood, and as black as the wood of the window frame."

Soon after that she had a little daughter, who was as white as snow, and as red as blood, and her hair was as black as ebony; and she was therefore called Little Snow White. And when the child was born, the Queen died.

After a year had passed the King took another wife. She was a beautiful woman, but proud and haughty, and she could not bear that anyone else should surpass her in beauty. She had a wonderful looking-glass, and when she stood in front of it and looked at herself in it, and said—

> "Looking-glass, Looking-glass, on the wall,
> Who in this land is the fairest of all?"

The looking-glass answered—

> "You, O Queen, are the fairest of all!"

Then she was satisfied, for she knew that the looking-glass spoke the truth.

But Snow White was growing up, and grew more and more beautiful; and when she was seven years old she was as beautiful as the day, and more beautiful than the Queen herself. And once when the Queen asked her looking-glass—

> "Looking-glass, Looking-glass, on the wall,
> Who in this land is the fairest of all?"

It answered—

"You are fairer than all who are here, Lady Queen."
But more beautiful still is Snow White, as I ween."

Then the Queen was shocked, and turned yellow and green with envy. From that time, whenever she looked at Snow White, her heart heaved in her breast, she hated the girl so much.

And envy and pride grew higher and higher in her heart like a weed, so that she had no peace day or night. She called a hunter, and said, "Take the child away into the forest; I will no longer have her in my sight. Kill her, and bring me back her heart as a token." The hunter obeyed, and took her away; but when he had drawn his knife, and was about to pierce Snow White's innocent heart, she began to weep, and said, "Ah dear hunter, spare me my life! I will run away into the wild forest, and never come home again."

And as she was so beautiful the hunter had pity on her and said, "Run away, then, you poor child." "The wild beasts will soon devour you," thought he, and yet it seemed as if a stone had been rolled from his heart since he no longer needed to kill her. And as a young boar just then came running by he stabbed it, and cut out its heart and took it to the Queen as proof that the child was dead. The cook had to salt this, and the wicked Queen ate it, and thought she had eaten the heart of Snow White.

But now the poor child was all alone in the great forest, and so terrified that she looked at every leaf of every tree, and did not know what to do. Then she began to run, and ran over sharp stones and through thorns, and the wild beasts ran past her, but did her no harm.

She ran as far as her feet would go until it was almost evening; then she saw a little cottage and went into it to rest. Everything in the cottage was small, but neater and cleaner than you can imagine. There was a table on which was a white cover, and seven little plates, and on each plate a little spoon; moreover, there were seven little knives and forks, and seven little mugs. Against the wall stood seven little beds side by side, and covered with snow-white bedspreads.

Little Snow White was so hungry and thirsty that she ate some vegetables and bread from each plate and drank a drop of wine out of each mug, for she did not wish to take all from only one. Then, as she was so tired, she laid herself down on each of the little beds, but none of them suited her; one was too long, another too short, but at last she found that the seventh one was right, and so she remained in it, said a prayer and went to sleep.

When it was quite dark the owners of the cottage came back; they were seven dwarfs who dug and delved in the mountains for ore. They lit their seven candles, and now that the cottage was lit they saw that someone had been there, foreverything was not in the same order in which they had left it.

The first said, "Who has been sitting on my chair?"

The second, "Who has been eating off my plate?"

The third, "Who has been taking some of my bread?"

The fourth, "Who has been eating my vegetables?"

The fifth, "Who has been using my fork?"

The sixth, "Who has been cutting with my knife?"

The seventh, "Who has been drinking out of my mug?"

Then the first looked round and saw that there was a little hole on his bed, and he said, "Who has been getting into my bed?" The others came up and each called out, "Somebody has been lying in my bed too." But the seventh when he looked at his bed saw little Snow White, who was lying asleep in it. And he called the others, who came running up, and they cried out with astonishment, and brought their seven little candles and let the light fall on little Snow White. "Oh, heavens! Oh, heavens!" cried they, "What a lovely child!" and they were so glad that they did not wake her up, but let her sleep in the bed. And the seventh dwarf slept with his companions, one hour with each, and so got through the night.

When it was morning little Snow White awoke, and was frightened when she saw the seven dwarfs. But they were friendly and asked her what her name was. "My name is Snow White," she answered.

"How have you come to our house?" said the dwarfs. Then she told them that her stepmother had wished to have her killed, but that the hunter had spared her life, and that she had run for the whole day, until at last she had found their dwelling. The dwarfs said, "If you will take care of our house, cook, make the beds, wash, sew, and knit, and if you will keep everything neat and clean, you can stay with us and you shall want for nothing."

"Yes," said Snow White, "with all my heart," and she stayed with them. She kept the house in order for them; in the mornings they went to the mountains and looked for copper and gold, in the evenings they came back, and then their supper had to be ready.

The girl was alone the whole day, so the good dwarfs warned her and said, "Beware of your stepmother, she will soon know that you are here; be sure to let no one come in."

But the Queen, believing that she had eaten Snow White's heart, was certain that she was again the first and most beautiful of all; and she went to her looking-glass and said—

"Looking-glass, Looking-glass, on the wall,
Who in this land is the fairest of all?"

And the glass answered—

"Oh, Queen, you are fairest of all I see,
But over the hills, where the seven dwarfs dwell,
Snow White is still alive and well,
And none is so fair as she."

Then she was astounded, for she knew that the looking-glass never spoke falsely, and she knew that the hunter had betrayed her, and that little Snow White was still alive.

And so she thought and thought again how she might kill her, for so long as she was not the fairest in the whole land, envy let her have no rest. And when she had at last thought of something to do, she painted her face, and dressed herself like an old peddler, and no one could have known her. In this disguise she went over the seven mountains to the seven dwarfs, and knocked at the door and cried, "Pretty things to sell, very cheap, very cheap."

Little Snow White looked out the window and called out, "Good day my good woman, what have you to sell?"

"Good things, pretty things," she answered; "laces of all colors," and she pulled out one which was woven of bright-colored silk.

"I may let the worthy old woman in," thought Snow White, and she unbolted the door and bought the pretty laces.

"Child," said the old woman, "what a fright you look; come, I will lace you properly for once." Snow White had no suspicion, but stood before her, and let herself be laced with the new laces. But the old woman laced so quickly and so tightly that Snow White lost her breath and fell down as if dead. "Now I am the most beautiful," said the Queen to herself, and ran away.

Not long afterwards, in the evening, the seven dwarfs came home, but were shocked that they saw their dear little Snow White lying on the ground, and that she neither stirred nor moved, and seemed to be dead. They lifted her up, and, as they saw that she was laced too tightly, they cut the laces; then she began to breathe a little, and after a while came to life again. When the dwarfs heard what had happened they said, "The old peddler was none other than the wicked Queen; take care and let no one come in when we are not with you."

But the wicked woman when she had reached home went in front of the glass and asked—

> "Looking-glass, Looking-glass, on the wall,
> Who in this land is the fairest of all?"

And it answered as before—

> "Oh, Queen, you are fairest of all I see,
> But over the hills, where the seven dwarfs dwell,
> Snow White is still alive and well,
> And none is so fair as she."

When she heard that, all her blood rushed to her heart with fear, for she saw plainly that little Snow White was again alive. "But now," she said, "I will think of something that shall put an end to you," and by the help of witchcraft, which she understood, she made a poisonous comb. Then she disguised herself and took the shape of another old woman.

So she went over the seven mountains to the seven dwarfs, knocked at the door, and cried, "Good things to sell, cheap, cheap!"

Little Snow White looked out and said, "Go away; I cannot let anyone come in."

"I suppose you can look," said the old woman, and pulled the poisonous comb out and held it up. It pleased the girl so well that she let herself be fooled, and opened the door. When they had struck a bargain the old woman said, "Now I will comb you properly for once." Poor little Snow White had no suspicion, and let the old woman do as she pleased, but hardly had she put the comb in her hair than the poison in it took effect, and the girl fell down senseless. "You paragon of beauty," said the wicked woman, "you are done for good," and she went away.

But fortunately it was almost evening, when the seven dwarfs came home. When they saw Snow White lying as if dead upon the ground they at once suspected the stepmother, and they looked and found the poisoned comb. Scarcely had they taken it out when Snow White came to, and told them what had happened. Then they warned her once more to be upon her guard and to open the door to no one.

The Queen, at home, went in front of the glass and said—

> "Looking-glass, Looking-glass, on the wall,
> Who in this land is the fairest of all?"

Then it answered as before—

> "Oh, Queen, you are fairest of all I see,
> But over the hills, where the seven dwarfs dwell,
> Snow White is still alive and well,
> And none is so fair as she."

When she heard the glass speak she trembled and shook with rage. "Snow White shall die," she cried, "even if it costs me my life!"

With that she went into a quite secret, lonely room, where no one ever came, and there she made a very poisonous apple. Outside it looked pretty, white with a red cheek, so that everyone who saw it longed for it; but whoever ate a piece of it must surely die.

When the apple was ready she painted her face, and dressed herself up as a country woman, and so she went over the seven mountains to the seven dwarfs. She knocked at the door. Snow White put her head out of the window and said, "I cannot let anyone in; the seven dwarfs have forbidden me."

"It is all the same to me," answered the woman, "I shall soon get rid of my apples. Here, I will give you one."

"No," said Snow White, "I dare not take anything."

"Are you afraid of poison?" said the old woman; "look, I will cut the apple in two pieces; you eat the red cheek, and I will eat the white."

The apple was so cunningly made that only the red cheek was poisoned. Snow White longed for the fine apple, and when she saw that the woman ate part of it she could resist no longer, and stretched out her hand and took the poisonous half. But hardly had she taken a bite than she fell down dead. Then the Queen looked at her with a dreadful look, and laughed aloud and said, "White as snow, red as blood, black as ebony wood! This time the dwarfs cannot wake you up again."

And when she asked the Looking-glass at home—

"Looking-glass, Looking-glass, on the wall,
Who in this land is the fairest of all?"

it answered at last—

"Oh, Queen, in this land you are fairest of all."

Then her envious heart had rest, so far as an envious heart can have rest.

The dwarfs, when they came home in the evening, found Snow White lying upon the ground; she breathed no longer and was dead. They lifted her up, looked to see whether they could find anything poisonous, unlaced her, combed her hair, washed her with water and wine, but it was all of no use; the poor child was dead, and remained dead. They laid her upon a bier, and all seven of them sat round it and wept for her, and wept three days long.

Then they were going to bury her, but she still looked as if she were alive, and still had her pretty red cheeks. They said, "We could not bury her in the dark ground," and they had a transparent coffin of glass made, so that she could be seen from all sides, and they laid her in it, and in golden letters wrote upon it her name, and that she was a king's daughter. Then they put the coffin out upon the mountain, and one of them always stayed by it and watched it. And birds came too, and wept for Snow White; first an owl, then a raven, and last a dove.

And now Snow White lay a long, long time in the coffin, and she did not change, but looked as if she were asleep; for she was as white as snow, as red as blood, and her hair was as black as ebony.

It happened, however, that a king's son came into the forest, and went to the dwarfs' house to spend the night. He saw the coffin on the mountain, and the beautiful Snow White inside it, and read what was written upon it in golden letters. Then he said to the dwarfs, "Let me have the coffin, I will give you whatever you want for it."

But the dwarfs answered, "We will not part with it for all the gold in the world."

Then he said, "Let me have it as a gift, for I cannot live without seeing Snow White. I will honor and prize her as my dearest possession." As he spoke in this way the good dwarfs took pity upon him, and gave him the coffin.

And now the King's son had it carried away by his servants on their shoulders. And it happened that they stumbled over a tree stump, and with the shock the poisonous piece of apple which Snow White had bitten off came out of her throat. And before long she opened her eyes, lifted up the lid of the coffin, sat up, and was once more alive. "Oh, heavens, where am I?" she cried.

The King's son, full of joy, said, "You are with me," and told her what had happened, and said, "I love you more than everything in the world; come with me to my father's palace, you shall be my wife."

And Snow White was willing, and went with him, and their wedding was held with great show and splendor. But Snow White's wicked stepmother was also invited to the feast. When she had dressed herself in beautiful clothes she went before the Looking-glass, and said—

> "Looking-glass, Looking-glass, on the wall,
> Who in this land is the fairest of all?"

The glass answered—

> "Oh, Queen, of all here the fairest is you,
> But the young Queen is fairer by far, it is true."

Then the wicked woman uttered a curse, and was so miserable, so utterly miserable, that she knew not what to do. At first she would not go to the wedding at all, but she had no peace, and must go to see the young Queen. And when she went in she knew Snow White; and she stood still with rage and fear, and could not stir. But iron slippers had already been put upon the fire, and they were brought in with tongs, and set before her. Then she was forced to put on the red-hot shoes, and dance until she dropped down dead.

54. THE KNAPSACK, THE HAT,
AND THE HORN

There were once three brothers who had fallen deeper and deeper into poverty, and at last their need was so great that they had to endure hunger, and had nothing to eat or drink. Then said they, "We cannot go on this way, we had better go into the world and seek our fortune." They therefore set out, and had already walked over many a long road and many a blade of grass, but had not yet met with good luck. One day they arrived in a great forest, and in the middle of it was a hill, and when they came nearer they saw that the hill was all silver.

Then spoke the eldest, "Now I have found the good luck I wished for, and I desire nothing more." He took as much of the silver as he could possibly carry, and then turned back and went home again.

But the two others said, "We want something more from good luck than mere silver," and did not touch it, but went onwards.

After they had walked for two days longer without stopping, they came to a hill which was all gold. The second brother stopped, thought to himself, and was undecided. "What shall I do?" said he, "Shall I take for myself so much of this gold that I have plenty for all the rest of my life, or shall I go farther?" At length he made a decision, and putting as much into his pockets as would go in, said farewell to his brother, and went home.

But the third said, "Silver and gold do not move me, I will not give up my chance of fortune, perhaps something even better will be given me."

He journeyed onwards, and when he had walked for three days, he got into a forest which was still larger than the one before, and never would come to an end, and as he found nothing to eat or to drink, he was exhausted. Then he climbed up a high tree to find out if up there he could see the end of the forest, but so far as his eye could see he saw nothing but the tops of trees. Then he began to descend the tree again, but hunger tormented him, and he thought to himself, "If I could but eat my fill once more!"

When he got down he saw with astonishment a table beneath the tree richly spread with food, the steam of which rose up to meet him. "This time," said he, "my wish has been fulfilled at the right moment." And without inquiring who had brought the food, or who had cooked it, he approached the table, and ate with enjoyment until he had appeased his hunger.

When he was done, he thought, "It would after all be a pity if the pretty little tablecloth were to be spoiled in the forest here," and folded it up tidily and put it in his pocket. Then he went onwards, and in the evening, when hunger arose again, he wanted to try out his little cloth, and spread it out and said, "I wish you to be covered with good cheer again," and scarcely had the wish crossed his lips than as many dishes with the most exquisite food on them stood on the table as there was room for. "Now I perceive," said he, "in what kitchen my cooking is done. You shall be dearer to me than the mountains of silver and gold." For he saw plainly that it was a wishing cloth. The cloth, however, was still not enough to enable him to return and sit quietly at home; he preferred to wander about the world and pursue his fortune farther.

One night he met, in a lonely wood, a dusty, black charcoal-burner, who was burning charcoal there, and had some potatoes by the fire that he was going to make into a meal. "Good evening, blackbird!" said the youth. "How do you get on in your solitude?"

"One day is like another," replied the charcoal-burner, "and every night potatoes! Have you a mind to have some, and will you be my guest?"

"Many thanks," replied the traveler, "I won't rob you of your supper; you did not reckon on a visitor, but if you will put up with what I have, you shall have an invitation."

"Who is to prepare it for you?" said the charcoal-burner. "I see that you have nothing with you, and there is no one within a two hours' walk who could give you anything."

"And yet there shall be a meal," answered the youth, "and better than any you have ever tasted." Thereupon he brought his cloth out of his knapsack, spread it on the ground, and said, "Little cloth, cover yourself," and instantly boiled meat and baked meat stood there, and as hot as if it had just come out of the kitchen.

The charcoal-burner stared, but did not require much pressing; he fell to, and thrust larger and larger mouthfuls into his black mouth. When they had eaten everything, the charcoal-burner smiled contentedly, and said, "Your tablecloth has my approval; it would be a fine thing for me in this forest, where no one ever cooks me anything good. I will propose an exchange to you; there in the corner hangs a soldier's knapsack, which is certainly old and shabby, but in it wonderful powers lie concealed; but, as I no longer use it, I will give it to you for the tablecloth."

"I must first know what these wonderful powers are," answered the youth.

"That I will tell you," replied the charcoal-burner; "every time you tap it with your hand, a corporal comes with six men armed from head to foot, and they do whatever you command them."

"So far as I am concerned," said the youth, "if nothing else can be done, we will exchange," and he gave the charcoal-burner the cloth, took the knapsack from the hook, put it on, and bade farewell.

When he had walked a while, he wished to make a trial of the magical powers of his knapsack and tapped it. Immediately the seven warriors stepped up to him, and the corporal said, "What does my lord and ruler wish for?"

"March with all speed to the charcoal-burner, and demand my wishing cloth back." They faced to the left, and it was not long before they brought what he required, and had taken it from the charcoal-burner without asking many questions. The young man bade them retire, went onwards, and hoped fortune would shine yet more brightly on him.

By sunset he came to another charcoal-burner, who was making his supper ready by the fire. "If you will eat some potatoes with salt, but with no dripping, come and sit down with me," said the sooty fellow.

"No, he replied, "this time you shall be my guest," and he spread out his cloth, which was instantly covered with the most beautiful dishes. They ate and drank together, and enjoyed themselves heartily.

After the meal was over, the charcoal-burner said, "Up there on that shelf lies a little old worn-out hat which has strange properties: when anyone puts it on, and turns it round on his head, the cannons go off as if twelve were fired all together, and they shoot down everything so that no one can withstand them. The hat is of no use to me, and I will willingly give it for your tablecloth."

"That suits me very well," he answered, took the hat, put it on, and left his tablecloth behind him. Hardly, however, had he walked away than he tapped on his knapsack, and his soldiers had to fetch the cloth back again. "One thing comes on the top of another," thought he, "and I feel as if my luck had not yet come to an end." Nor had his thoughts deceived him.

After he had walked on for the whole of one day, he came to a third charcoal-burner, who like the previous ones, invited him to potatoes without dripping. But he let him too dine with him from his wishing cloth, and the charcoal-burner liked it so well, that at last he offered him a horn for it, which had very different properties from those of the hat. When anyone blew it all the walls and fortifications fell down, and all towns and villages became ruins. He certainly gave the charcoal-burner the cloth for it, but he afterwards sent his soldiers to demand it back again, so that at length he had the knapsack, hat and horn, all three. "Now," said he, "I am a made man, and it is time for me to go home and see how my brothers are getting on."

When he reached home, his brothers had built themselves a handsome house with their silver and gold, and were living in prosperity. He went to see them, but as he came in a ragged coat, with his shabby hat on his head, and his old knapsack on his back, they would not acknowledge him as their brother. They mocked and said, "You claim that you are our brother who despised silver and gold, and craved for something still better for himself. He will come in his carriage in full splendor like a mighty king, not like a beggar," and they drove him out of doors. Then he fell into a rage, and tapped his knapsack until a hundred and fifty men stood before him armed from head to foot. He commanded them to surround his brothers' house, and two of them were to take hazel-rods with them, and beat the two insolent men until they knew who he was. A violent disturbance arose, people ran together, and wanted to lend the two some help in their need, but against the soldiers they could do nothing.

News of this at length came to the King, who was very angry, and ordered a captain to march out with his troop, and drive this disturber of the peace out of the town; but the man with the knapsack soon got a greater body of men together, who repulsed the captain and his men, so that they were forced to retire with bloody noses. The King said, "This vagabond is not brought to order yet," and next day sent a still larger troop against him, but they could do even less.

The youth set still more men against them, and in order to be done even sooner, he turned his hat twice round on his head, and heavy guns began to play, and the king's men were beaten and put to flight. "And now," said he, "I will not make peace until the King gives me his daughter for my wife, and I govern the whole kingdom in his name."

He caused this to be announced to the King, and the latter said to his daughter, "Necessity is a hard nut to crack, what remains for me but to do what he desires? If I want peace and to keep the crown on my head, I must give you away."

So the wedding was celebrated, but the King's daughter was vexed that her husband should be a common man, who wore a shabby hat, and put on an old knapsack. She wished much to get rid of him, and night and day studied how she could accomplish this. Then she thought to herself, "Is it possible that his wonderful powers lie in the knapsack?" and she dissembled and caressed him, and when his heart was softened, she said, "If you would but lay aside that ugly knapsack, it disfigures you so, that I can't help being ashamed of you."

"Dear child," said he, "this knapsack is my greatest treasure; as long as I have it, there is no power on earth that I am afraid of." And he revealed to her the wonderful virtue with which it was endowed. Then she threw herself in his arms as if she were going to kiss him, but dexterously took the knapsack off his shoulders, and ran away with it.

As soon as she was alone she tapped it, and commanded the warriors to seize their former master, and take him out of the royal palace. They obeyed, and the false wife sent still more men after him, who were to drive him quite out of the country. Then he would have been ruined if he had not had the little hat. But his hands were scarcely at liberty before he turned it twice. Immediately the cannon began to thunder, and struck down everything, and the King's daughter herself was forced to come and beg for mercy. As she entreated in such moving terms, and promised to change, he allowed himself to be persuaded and granted her peace. She behaved in a friendly manner to him, and acted as if she loved him very much, and after some time managed to so fool him, that he confided to her that even if someone got the knapsack into his power, he could do nothing against him so long as the old hat was still his. When she knew the secret, she waited until he was asleep, and then she took the hat away from him, and had it thrown out into the street. But the horn still remained to him, and in great anger he blew it with all his strength. Instantly all walls, fortifications, towns, and villages, toppled down, and crushed the King and his daughter to death. And had he not put down the horn and had blown just a little longer, everything would have been in ruins, and not one stone would have been left standing on another. Then no one opposed him any longer, and he made himself King of the whole country.

55. RUMPELSTILTSKIN

Once there was a miller who was poor, but who had a beautiful daughter. Now it happened that he had to go and speak to the King, and in order to make himself appear important he said to him, "I have a daughter who can spin straw into gold."

The King said to the miller, "That is an art which pleases me well; if your daughter is as clever as you say, bring her tomorrow to my palace, and I will try what she can do."

And when the girl was brought to him he took her into a room which was quite full of straw, gave her a spinning wheel and a reel, and said, "Now set to work, and if by tomorrow morning early you have not spun this straw into gold during the night, you must die." Thereupon he himself locked up the room, and left her in it alone. So there sat the poor miller's daughter, and for the life of her could not tell what to do; she had no idea how straw could be spun into gold, and she grew more and more miserable, until at last she began to weep.

But all at once the door opened, and in came a little man, and said, "Good evening, Mistress Miller; why are you crying so?"

"Alas!" answered the girl, "I have to spin straw into gold, and I do not know how to do it."

"What will you give me," said the manikin, "if I do it for you?"

"My necklace," said the girl. The little man took the necklace, seated himself in front of the wheel, and "whirr, whirr, whirr," three turns, and the reel was full; then he put another on, and whirr, whirr, whirr, three times round, and the second was full too. And so it went on until the morning, when all the straw was spun, and all the reels were full of gold.

By daybreak the King was already there, and when he saw the gold he was astonished and delighted, but his heart became only more greedy. He had the miller's daughter taken into another room full of straw, which was much larger, and commanded her to spin that also in one night if she valued her life. The girl knew not how to help herself, and was crying, when the door again opened, and the little man appeared, and said, "What will you give me if I spin that straw into gold for you?"

"The ring on my finger," answered the girl. The little man took the ring, again began to turn the wheel, and by morning had spun all the straw into glittering gold.

The King rejoiced beyond measure at the sight, but still he had not enough gold; and he had the miller's daughter taken into a still larger room full of straw, and said, "You must spin this, too, in the course of this night; but if you succeed, you shall be my wife." And he thought, "Even if she be a miller's daughter, I could not find a richer wife in the whole world."

When the girl was alone the manikin came again for the third time, and said, "What will you give me if I spin the straw for you this time also?"

"I have nothing left that I could give," answered the girl.

"Then promise me, if you should become Queen, your first child."

"Who knows whether that will ever happen?" thought the miller's daughter; and, not knowing how else to help herself in this strait, she promised the manikin what he wanted, and for that he once more span the straw into gold.

And when the King came in the morning, and found all as he had wished, he took her in marriage, and the pretty miller's daughter became a Queen.

A year after, she had a beautiful child, and she never gave a thought to the manikin. But suddenly he came into her room, and said, "Now give me what you promised."

The Queen was horror-struck, and offered the manikin all the riches of the kingdom if he would leave her the child. But the manikin said, "No, something that is living is dearer to me than all the treasures in the world." Then the Queen began to weep and cry, so that the manikin pitied her. "I will give you three days' time," said he, "if by that time you find out my name, then you shall keep your child."

So the Queen thought the whole night of all the names that she had ever heard, and she sent a messenger over the country to inquire, far and wide, for any other names that there might be. When the manikin came the next day, she began with Caspar, Melchior, Balthazar, and said all the names she knew, one after another; but to everyone the little man said, "That is not my name."

On the second day she had inquiries made in the neighborhood as to the names of the people there, and she repeated to the manikin the most uncommon and curious. "Perhaps your name is Shortribs, or Sheepshanks, or Laceleg?" but he always answered, "That is not my name."

On the third day the messenger came back again, and said, "I have not been able to find a single new name, but as I came to a high mountain at the end of the forest, where the fox and the hare bid each other good night, there I saw a little house, and before the house a fire was burning, and round about the fire quite a ridiculous little man was jumping: he hopped upon one leg, and shouted—

> "Today I bake, tomorrow brew,
> The next I'll have the young Queen's child.
> Ha! Glad am I that no one knew
> That Rumpelstiltskin I am styled."

You may think how glad the Queen was when she heard the name! And when soon afterwards the little man came in, and asked, "Now, Mistress Queen, what is my name?" at first she said, "Is your name Conrad?"

"No."

"Is your name Harry?"

"No."

"Perhaps your name is Rumpelstiltskin?"

"The devil has told you that! The devil has told you that!" cried the little man, and in his anger he plunged his right foot so deep into the earth that his whole leg went in; and then in rage he pulled at his left leg so hard with both hands that he tore himself in two.

56. SWEETHEART ROLAND

There was once on a time a woman who was a real witch and had two daughters, one ugly and wicked, and this one she loved because she was her own daughter, and one beautiful and good, and this one she hated, because she was her stepdaughter. The stepdaughter once had a pretty apron, which the other fancied so much that she became envious, and told her mother that she must and would have that apron. "Be quiet, my child," said the old woman, "and you shall have it. Your stepsister has long deserved death, tonight when she is asleep I will come and cut her head off. Only be careful that you are at the far side of the bed, and push her well to the front." It would have been all over with the poor girl if she had not just then been standing in a corner, and heard everything. All day long she dared not go out of doors, and when bedtime had come, the witch's daughter got into bed first, so as to lie at the far side, but when she was asleep, the other pushed her gently to the front, and took for herself the place at the back, close by the wall. In the night, the old woman came creeping in, she held an axe in her right hand, and felt with her left to see if anyone was lying on the outside, and then she grasped the axe with both hands, and cut her own child's head off.

When she had gone away, the girl got up and went to her sweetheart, who was called Roland, and knocked at his door. When he came out, she said to him, "Hear me, dearest Roland, we must fly in all haste; my stepmother wanted to kill me, but has struck her own child. When daylight comes, and she sees what she has done, we shall be lost."

"But," said Roland, "I counsel you first to take away her magic wand, or we cannot escape if she pursues us."

The maiden fetched the magic wand, and she took the dead girl's head and dropped three drops of blood on the ground, one in front of the bed, one in the kitchen, and one on the stairs. Then she hurried away with her lover. When the old witch got up next morning, she called her daughter, and wanted to give her the apron, but she did not come. Then the witch cried, "Where are you?"

"Here, on the stairs, I am sweeping," answered the first drop of blood.

The old woman went out, but saw no one on the stairs, and cried again, "Where are you?"

"Here in the kitchen, I am warming myself," cried the second drop of blood. She went into the kitchen, but found no one.

Then she cried again, "Where are you?"

"Ah, here in the bed, I am sleeping," cried the third drop of blood. She went into the room to the bed. What did she see there? Her own child, whose head she had cut off, bathed in her blood. The witch fell into a passion, sprang to the window, and as she could look forth quite far into the world, she perceived her stepdaughter hurrying away with her sweetheart Roland.

"That shall not serve you," cried she, "even if you have gone a long way off, you still shall not escape me." She put on her boots, in which she went an hour's walk with every step, and it was not long before she overtook them. The girl, however, when she saw the old woman striding towards her, used her magic wand to change her sweetheart Roland into a lake, and herself into a duck swimming in the middle of it. The witch placed herself on the shore, threw bread crumbs in, and took great pains to entice the duck; but the duck did not let herself be enticed, and the old woman had to go home at night as she had come. At this the girl and her sweetheart Roland resumed their natural shapes again, and they walked on the whole night until daybreak. Then the maiden changed herself into a beautiful flower which stood in the middle of a briar hedge, and her sweetheart Roland into a fiddler.

It was not long before the witch came striding up towards them, and said to the musician, "Dear musician, may I pluck that beautiful flower for myself?"

"Oh, yes," he replied, "I will play to you while you do it." As she was hastily creeping into the hedge and was just going to pluck the flower, for she well knew who the flower was, he began to play, and whether she would like it or not, she was forced to dance, for it was a magical dance. The quicker he played, the more violent springs she was forced to make, and the thorns tore her clothes from her body, and pricked her and wounded her till she bled, and as he did not stop, she had to dance till she lay dead on the ground.

When they were saved, Roland said, "Now I will go to my father and arrange for the wedding."

"Then in the meantime I will stay here and wait for you," said the girl, "and that no one may recognize me, I will change myself into a red milestone."

Then Roland went away, and the girl stood like a red milestone in the field and waited for her beloved. But when Roland got home, he fell into the snares of another, who prevailed on him so far that he forgot the maiden. The poor girl remained there a long time, but at length, as he did not return at all, she was sad, and changed herself into a flower, and thought, "Someone will surely come this way, and trample me down."

It happened, however, that a shepherd kept his sheep in the field, and saw the flower, and as it was so pretty, plucked it, took it with him, and laid it away in his chest. From that time forth, strange things happened in the shepherd's house. When he arose in the morning, all the work was already done, the room was swept, the table and benches cleaned, the fire on the hearth was lighted, and the water was fetched, and at noon, when he came home, the table was laid, and a good dinner served. He could not conceive how this came to pass, for he never saw a human being in his house, and no one could have concealed himself in it. He was certainly pleased with this good attendance, but still at last he was so afraid that he went to a wise woman and asked for her advice. The wise woman said, "There is some enchantment behind it, listen very early some morning if anything is moving in the room, and if you see anything, let it be what it may, throw a white cloth over it, and then the magic will be stopped."

The shepherd did as she bade him, and next morning just as day dawned, he saw the chest open, and the flower come out. Swiftly he sprang towards it, and threw a white cloth over it. Instantly the transformation came to an end, and a beautiful girl stood before him, who told him that she had been the flower, and that up to this time she had attended to his housekeeping. She told him her story, and since she pleased him he asked her if she would marry him, but she answered, "No," for she wanted to remain faithful to her sweetheart Roland, although he had deserted her. However, she promised not to go away, but to go on keeping house for the shepherd.

And now the time drew near when Roland's wedding was to be celebrated, and then, according to an old custom in the country, it was announced that all the girls were to be present at it, and sing in honor of the bridal pair. When the faithful maiden heard of this, she grew so sad that she thought her heart would break, and she would not go, but the other girls came and took her. When her turn came to sing, she stepped back, until at last she was the only one left, and then she could not refuse. But when she began her song, and it reached Roland's ears, he sprang up and cried, "I know the voice, that is the true bride, I will have no other!" Everything he had forgotten, and which had vanished from his mind, had suddenly come home again to his heart. Then the faithful maiden held her wedding with her sweetheart Roland, and grief came to an end and joy began.

57. *THE GOLDEN BIRD*

In olden times there was a king, who had behind his palace a beautiful garden in which there was a tree that bore golden apples. When the apples were getting ripe they were counted, but on the very next morning one was missing. This was told to the King, and he ordered that a watch should be kept every night beneath the tree.

The King had three sons, the eldest of whom he sent, as soon as night came on, into the garden; but when midnight came he could not keep himself from sleeping, and next morning again an apple was gone.

The following night the second son had to keep watch, it fared no better with him; as soon as twelve o'clock had struck he fell asleep, and in the morning an apple was gone.

Now it came to the turn of the third son to watch; and he was quite ready, but the King had not much trust in him, and thought that he would be of less use even than his brothers; but at last he let him go. The youth lay down beneath the tree, but kept awake, and did not let sleep master him. When it struck twelve, something rustled through the air, and in the moonlight he saw a bird coming whose feathers were all shining with gold. The bird alighted on the tree, and had just plucked off an apple, when the youth shot an arrow at him. The bird flew off, but the arrow had struck his plumage, and one of his golden feathers fell down. The youth picked it up, and the next morning took it to the King and told him what he had seen in the night. The King called his council together, and everyone declared that a feather like this was worth more than the whole kingdom. "If the feather is so precious," declared the King, "one alone will not do for me; I must and will have the whole bird!"

The eldest son set out; he trusted to his cleverness, and thought that he would easily find the Golden Bird. When he had gone some distance he saw a Fox sitting at the edge of a wood, so he cocked his gun and took aim at him. The Fox cried, "Do not shoot me! And in return I will give you some good counsel. You are on the way to the Golden Bird; and this evening you will come to a village in which stand two inns opposite to one another. One of them is lighted up brightly, and all goes on merrily within, but do not go into it; go rather into the other, even though it seems a bad one."

"How can such a silly beast give wise advice?" thought the King's son, and he pulled the trigger. But he missed the Fox, who stretched out his tail and ran quickly into the wood.

So he pursued his way, and by evening came to the village where the two inns were; in one they were singing and dancing; the other had a poor, miserable look. "I should be a fool, indeed," he thought, "if I were to go into the shabby tavern, and pass by the good one." So he went into the cheerful one, lived there in riot and revel, and forgot the bird and his father, and all good counsels.

When some time had passed, and the eldest son for month after month did not come back home, the second set out, wishing to find the Golden Bird. The Fox met him as he had met the eldest, and gave him the good advice of which he took no heed. He came to the two inns, and his brother was standing at the window of the one from which came the music, and called out to him. He could not resist, but went inside and lived only for pleasure.

Again some time passed, and then the King's youngest son wanted to set off and try his luck, but his father would not allow it. "It is of no use," said he, "he will find the Golden Bird no better than his brothers, and if a mishap were to befall him he knows not how to help himself; he is a little wanting at the best." But at last, as he had no peace, he let him go.

Again the Fox was sitting outside the wood, and begged for his life, and offered his good advice. The youth was good-natured, and said, "Be easy, little Fox, I will do you no harm."

"You shall not repent it," answered the Fox, "And that you may get on more quickly, get up behind on my tail." And scarcely had he seated himself when the Fox began to run, and away he went over stock and stone till his hair whistled in the wind. When they came to the village the youth got off; he followed the good advice, and without looking round turned into the little inn, where he spent the night quietly.

The next morning, as soon as he got into the open country, there sat the Fox already, and said, "I will tell you further what you have to do. Go on quite straight, and at last you will come to a castle, in front of which a whole regiment of soldiers is lying, but do not trouble yourself about them, for they will all be asleep and snoring. Go through the midst of them straight into the castle, and go through all the rooms, till at last you will come to a chamber where a Golden Bird is hanging in a wooden cage. Close by, there stands an empty gold cage for show, but beware of taking the bird out of the common cage and putting it into the fine one, or it may go badly for you." With these words the Fox again stretched out his tail, and the King's son seated himself upon it, and away he went over stock and stone till his hair whistled in the wind.

When he came to the castle he found everything as the Fox had said. The King's son went into the chamber where the Golden Bird was shut up in a wooden cage, while a golden one stood nearby; and the three golden apples lay about the room. "But," thought he, "it would be absurd if I were to leave the beautiful bird in the common and ugly cage," so he opened the door, laid hold of it, and put it into the golden cage. But at the same moment the bird uttered a shrill cry. The soldiers awoke, rushed in, and took him off to prison. The next morning he was taken before a court of justice, and as he confessed everything, was sentenced to death.

The King, however, said that he would grant him his life on one condition namely, if he brought him the Golden Horse which ran faster than the wind; and in that case he should receive, over and above, as a reward, the Golden Bird.

The King's son set off, but he sighed and was sorrowful, for how was he to find the Golden Horse? But all at once he saw his old friend the Fox sitting on the road. "Look," said the Fox, "this has happened because you did not give heed to me. However, be of good courage. I will give you my help, and tell you how to get to the Golden Horse. You must go straight on, and you will come to a castle, where in the stable stands the horse. The grooms will be lying in front of the stable; but they will be asleep and snoring, and you can quietly lead out the Golden Horse. But of one thing you must take heed; put on him the common saddle of wood and leather, and not the golden one, which hangs close by, else it will go badly for you." Then the Fox stretched out his tail, the King's son seated himself upon it, and away he went over stock and stone until his hair whistled in the wind.

Everything happened just as the Fox had said; the prince came to the stable in which the Golden Horse was standing, but just as he was going to put the common saddle upon him, he thought, "It will be a shame to such a beautiful beast, if I do not give him the good saddle which belongs to him by right." But scarcely had the golden saddle touched the horse than he began to neigh loudly. The grooms awoke, seized the youth, and threw him into prison. The next morning he was sentenced by the court to death; but the King promised to grant him his life, and the Golden Horse as well, if he could bring back the beautiful princess from the Golden Castle.

With a heavy heart the youth set out; yet luckily for him he soon found the trusty Fox. "I ought only to leave you to your bad luck," said the Fox, "but I pity you, and will help you once more out of your trouble. This road takes you straight to the Golden Castle, you will reach it by evening; and at night when everything is quiet the beautiful princess goes to the bathing-house to bathe. When she enters it, run up to her and give her a kiss, then she will follow you, and you can take her away with you; only do not allow her to take leave of her parents first, or it will go badly for you."

Then the Fox stretched out his tail, the King's son seated himself upon it, and away the Fox went, over stock and stone, till his hair whistled in the wind.

When he reached the Golden Castle it was just as the Fox had said. He waited until midnight, when everything lay in deep sleep, and the beautiful princess was going to the bathing-house. Then he sprang out and gave her a kiss. She said that she would like to go with him, but she asked him pitifully, and with tears, to allow her first to take leave of her parents. At first he withstood her prayer, but when she wept more and more, and fell at his feet, he at last gave in. But no sooner had the maiden reached the bedside of her father than he and all the rest in the castle awoke, and the youth was laid hold of and put into prison.

The next morning the King said to him, "Your life is forfeited, and you can only find mercy if you take away the hill which stands in front of my windows, and prevents my seeing beyond it; and you must finish it all within eight days. If you do that you shall have my daughter as your reward."

The King's son began, and dug and shoveled without leaving off, but when after seven days he saw how little he had done, and how all his work was as good as nothing, he fell into great sorrow and gave up all hope. But on the evening of the seventh day the Fox appeared and said, "You do not deserve that I should take any trouble for you; but just go away and lie down to sleep, and I will do the work for you."

The next morning when he awoke and looked out of the window the hill had gone. The youth ran, full of joy, to the King, and told him that the task was fulfilled, and whether he liked it or not, the King had to hold to his word and give him his daughter.

So the two set forth together, and it was not long before the trusty Fox came up with them. "You have certainly got what is best," said he, "but the Golden Horse also belongs to the maiden of the Golden Castle."

"How shall I get it?" asked the youth.

"That I will tell you," answered the Fox, "first take the beautiful maiden to the King who sent you to the Golden Castle. There will be unheard-of rejoicing; they will gladly give you the Golden Horse, and will bring it out to you. Mount it as soon as possible, and offer your hand to all in farewell; last of all to the beautiful maiden. And as soon as you have taken her hand swing her up onto the horse, and gallop away, and no one will be able to bring you back, for the horse runs faster than the wind."

All was carried out successfully, and the King's son carried off the beautiful princess on the Golden Horse.

The Fox did not remain behind, and he said to the youth, "Now I will help you to get the Golden Bird. When you come near the castle where the Golden Bird is to be found, let the maiden get down, and I will take her into my care. Then ride with the Golden Horse into the castleyard; there will be great rejoicing at the sight, and they will bring out the Golden Bird for you. As soon as you have the cage in your hand gallop back to us, and take the maiden away again."

When the plan had succeeded, and the King's son was about to ride home with his treasures, the Fox said, "Now you shall reward me for my help."

"What do you require for it?" asked the youth.

"When you get into the wood yonder, shoot me dead, and chop off my head and feet."

"That would be fine gratitude," said the King's son. "I cannot possibly do that for you."

The Fox said, "If you will not do it I must leave you, but before I go away I will give you a piece of good advice. Be careful about two things. Buy no gallows'-flesh, and do not sit at the edge of any well." And then he ran into the wood.

The youth thought, "That is a wonderful beast, he has strange whims; who is going to buy gallows'-flesh? and the desire to sit at the edge of a well has never yet seized me."

He rode on with the beautiful maiden, and his road took him again through the village in which his two brothers had remained. There was a great stir and noise, and, when he asked what was going on, he was told that two men were going to be hanged. As he came nearer to the place he saw that they were his brothers, who had been playing all kinds of wicked pranks, and had squandered all their wealth. He inquired whether they could not be set free. "If you will pay for them," answered the people, "but why should you waste your money on wicked men, and buy them free." He did not think twice about it, but paid for them, and when they were set free they all went on their way together.

They came to the wood where the Fox had first met them, and as it was cool and pleasant there, the two brothers said, "Let us rest a little by the well, and eat and drink." He agreed, and while they were talking he forgot himself, and sat down upon the edge of the well without thinking of any evil. But the two brothers threw him backwards into the well, took the maiden, the Horse, and the Bird, and went home to their father. "Here we bring you not only the Golden Bird," said they, "We have won the Golden Horse also, and the maiden from the Golden Castle." Then was there great joy; but the Horse would not eat, the Bird would not sing, and the maiden sat and wept.

But the youngest brother was not dead. By good fortune the well was dry, and he fell upon soft moss without being hurt, but he could not get out again. Even in this strait the faithful Fox did not leave him: it came and leapt down to him, and upbraided him for having forgotten its advice. "But yet I cannot give it up so," he said, "I will help you up again into daylight." He bade him grasp his tail and keep tight hold of it; and then he pulled him up.

"You are not out of all danger yet," said the Fox. "Your brothers were not sure of your death, and have surrounded the wood with watchers, who are to kill you if you let yourself be seen." But a poor man was sitting on the road, with whom the youth changed clothes, and in this way he got to the King's palace.

No one knew him, but the Bird began to sing, the Horse began to eat, and the beautiful maiden left off weeping. The King, astonished, asked, "What does this mean?"

Then the maiden said, "I do not know, but I have been so sorrowful and now I am so happy! I feel as if my true bridegroom has come."

She told him all that had happened, although the other brothers had threatened her with death if she were to betray anything.

The King commanded that all people who were in his castle should be brought before him; and amongst them came the youth in his ragged clothes; but the maiden knew him at once and fell upon his neck. The wicked brothers were seized and put to death, but he was married to the beautiful maiden and declared heir to the King.

But how did it fare with the poor Fox? Long afterwards the King's son was once again walking in the wood, when the Fox met him and said, "You have everything now that you can wish for, but there is never an end to my misery, and yet it is in your power to free me," and again he asked him with tears to shoot him dead and chop off his head and feet. So he did it, and scarcely was it done when the Fox was changed into a man, and was no other than the brother of the beautiful princess, who at last was freed from the magic charm which had been laid upon him. And now they never lacked in happiness as long as they lived.

58. THE DOG AND THE SPARROW

A sheep-dog had not a good master, but, on the contrary, one who let him suffer hunger. As he could stay no longer with him, he went quite sadly away. On the road he met a sparrow who said, "Brother dog, why are you so sad?"

The dog replied, "I am hungry, and have nothing to eat."

Then said the sparrow, "Dear brother, come into the town with me, and I will satisfy your hunger." So they went into the town together, and when they came in front of a butcher's shop the sparrow said to the dog, "Stay there, and I will pick a bit of meat down for you," and he alighted on the stall, looked about him to see that no one was observing him, and pecked and pulled and tore so long at a piece which lay on the edge, that it slipped down. Then the dog seized it, ran into a corner, and devoured it. The sparrow said, "Now come with me to another shop, and then I will get you one more piece that you may be satisfied."

When the dog had devoured the second piece as well, the sparrow asked, "Brother dog, have you now had enough?"

"Yes, I have had meat enough," he answered, "but I have had no bread yet."

Said the sparrow, "You shall have that also, come with me." Then he took him to a baker's shop, and pecked at a couple of little buns till they rolled down, and as the dog wanted still more, he led him to another stall, and again got bread for him. When that was consumed, the sparrow said, "Brother dog, have you now had enough?"

"Yes," he replied, "now we will walk awhile outside the town." Then they both went out onto the highway. It was, however, warm weather, and when they had walked a little way the dog said, "I am tired, and would like to sleep."

"Well, do sleep," answered the sparrow, "and in the meantime I will seat myself on a branch."

So the dog lay down on the road, and fell fast asleep. While he lay sleeping there, a waggoner came driving by, who had a cart with three horses, laden with two barrels of wine. The sparrow, however, saw that he was not going to turn aside, but was staying in the wheel track in which the dog was lying, so it cried, "Waggoner, don't do it, or I will make you poor."

The waggoner, however, growled to himself, "You will not make me poor," and cracked his whip and drove the cart over the dog, and the wheels killed him.

Then the sparrow cried, "You have run over my brother dog and killed him, it shall cost you your cart and horses."

"Cart and horses indeed!" said the waggoner. "What harm can you do me?" and drove onwards. Then the sparrow crept under the cover of the cart, and pecked so long at the bung-hole of one of the casks that he got the bung out, and then all the wine ran out without the driver noticing it. But once when he was looking behind him he saw that the cart was dripping, and looked at the barrels and saw that one of them was empty. "Unfortunate fellow that I am," cried he.

"Not unfortunate enough yet," said the sparrow, and flew onto the head of one of the horses and pecked his eyes out.

When the driver saw that, he drew out his axe and wanted to hit the sparrow, but the sparrow flew into the air, and he hit his horse on the head, and it fell down dead. "Oh, what an unfortunate man I am," cried he.

"Not unfortunate enough yet," said the sparrow, and when the driver drove on with the two horses, the sparrow again crept under the cover, and pecked the bung out of the second cask, so all the wine was spilled.

When the driver became aware of it, he again cried, "Oh, what an unfortunate man I am," but the sparrow replied, "Not unfortunate enough yet," and seated himself on the head of the second horse, and pecked his eyes out. The driver ran up to it and raised his axe to strike, but the sparrow flew into the air and the blow struck the horse, which fell.

"Oh, what an unfortunate man I am."

"Not unfortunate enough yet," said the sparrow, and lighted on the third horse's head, and pecked out his eyes. The driver, in his rage, struck at the sparrow without looking round, and did not hit him but killed his third horse likewise.

"Oh, what an unfortunate man I am," cried he.

"Not unfortunate enough yet," answered the sparrow. "Now will I make you unfortunate in your home," and flew away.

The driver had to leave the wagon standing, and full of anger and vexation went home. "Ah," said he to his wife, "what misfortunes I have had! My wine has run out, and the horses are all three dead!"

"Alas, husband," she answered, "what a malicious bird has come into the house! It has gathered together every bird there is in the world, and they have fallen on our corn up there, and are devouring it." Then he went upstairs, and thousands and thousands of birds were sitting in the loft and had eaten up all the corn, and the sparrow was sitting in the midst of them.

Then the driver cried, "Oh, what an unfortunate man I am."

"Not unfortunate enough yet!" answered the sparrow, "Waggoner, it shall cost you your life as well," and flew out.

Then the waggoner had lost all his property, and he went downstairs into the room, sat down behind the stove and was quite furious and bitter. But the sparrow sat outside in front of the window, and cried, "Waggoner, it shall cost you your life." Then the waggoner snatched the axe and threw it at the sparrow, but it only broke the window, and did not hit the bird. The sparrow now hopped in, placed itself on the stove and cried, "Waggoner, it shall cost you your life." The latter, quite mad and blind with rage, hacked the stove in two, and as the sparrow flew from one place to another, chopped all his household furniture, looking-glass, benches, table, and at last the walls of his house, and yet he could not hit the bird. At length, however, he caught it with his hand.

Then his wife said, "Shall I kill it?"

"No," cried he, "that would be too merciful. It shall die much more cruelly," and he took it and swallowed it whole.

The sparrow, however, began to flutter about in his body, and fluttered up again into the man's mouth; then it stretched out its head, and cried, "Waggoner, it shall still cost you your life."

The driver gave the axe to his wife, and said, "Wife, kill the bird in my mouth for me." The woman struck, but missed her blow, and hit the waggoner right on his head, so that he fell dead. But the sparrow flew up and away.

59. FREDERICK AND CATHERINE

There was once on a time a man who was called Frederick and a woman called Catherine, who had married each other and lived together as young married folks. One day Frederick said, "I will now go and plow, Catherine; when I come back, there must be some roast meat on the table for hunger, and a fresh draught for thirst."

"Just go, Frederick," answered Catherine, "just go, I will have all ready for you." Therefore when dinnertime drew near she got a sausage out of the chimney, put it in the frying pan, added some butter to it, and set it on the fire. The sausage began to fry and to hiss, Catherine stood beside it and held the handle of the pan, and had her own thoughts as she was doing it.

Then it occurred to her, "While the sausage is getting done you could go into the cellar and draw beer." So she set the frying pan safely on the fire, took a can, and went down into the cellar to draw beer.

The beer ran into the can and Catherine watched it, and then she thought, "Oh, dear! The dog upstairs is not fastened up, it might get the sausage out of the pan. Well thought of." And in a trice she was up the cellar steps again, but the dog had the sausage in its mouth already, and trailed it away on the ground. But Catherine, who was not idle, set out after it, and chased it a long way into the field; the dog, however, was swifter than Catherine and did not let the sausage journey easily, but skipped over the furrows with it.

"What's gone is gone!" said Catherine, and turned round, and as she had run till she was weary, she now walked quietly and comfortably, and cooled herself. During this time the beer was still running out of the cask, for Catherine had not turned the tap. And when the can was full and there was no other place for it, it ran into the cellar and did not stop until the whole cask was empty. As soon as Catherine was on the steps she saw the mischance. "Good gracious!" she cried. "What shall I do now to stop Frederick knowing it!"

She thought for a while, and at last she remembered that up in the loft was still standing a sack of the finest wheat flour from the last fair, and she would fetch that down and strew it over the beer. "Yes," said she, "he who saves a thing when he ought, has it afterwards when he needs it," and she climbed up to the loft and carried the sack below, and threw it straight down on the can of beer, which she knocked over, and Frederick's draught swam also in the cellar. "It is all right," said Catherine, "where the one is the other ought to be also," and she strewed the meal over the whole cellar. When it was done she was heartily delighted with her work, and said, "How clean and wholesome it does look here!"

At midday Frederick came home: "Now, wife, what have you ready for me?"

"Ah, Freddy," she answered, "I was frying a sausage for you, but while I was drawing the beer to drink with it, the dog took it away out of the pan, and while I was running after the dog, all the beer ran out, and while I was drying up the beer with the flour, I knocked over the can as well, but be easy, the cellar is quite dry again."

Said Frederick, "Catherine, Catherine, you should not have done that! To let the sausage be carried off and the beer run out of the cask, and throw out all our flour too!"

"Indeed, Frederick, I did not know that, you should have told me."

The man thought, "If my wife is like this, I must look after things more." Now he had got together a good number of talkers which he changed into gold, and said to Catherine, "Look, these are counters for playing games; I will put them in a pot and bury them in the stable under the cow's manger, but mind you keep away from them, or it will be the worse for you."

Said she, "Oh, no, Frederick, I certainly will stay away." And when Frederick was gone some peddlers came into the village who had cheap earthen bowls and pots, and asked the young woman if there was nothing she wanted to bargain in exchange for them?

"Oh, dear people," said Catherine, "I have no money and can buy nothing, but if you have any use for yellow counters I will buy from you."

"Yellow counters, why not? But just let us see them."

"Then go into the stable and dig under the cow's manger, and you will find the yellow counters. I am not allowed to go there." The rogues went there, dug and found pure gold. Then they laid hold of it, ran away, and left their pots and bowls behind in the house. Catherine thought she must use her new things, and as she had no lack in the kitchen already without these, she knocked the bottom out of every pot, and set them all as ornaments on the fence which went round about the house.

When Frederick came and saw the new decorations, he said, "Catherine, what have you been doing?"

"I have bought them, Frederick, for the counters which were under the cow's manger. I did not go there myself, the peddlers had to dig them out for themselves."

"Ah, wife," said Frederick, "what have you done? Those were not counters, but pure gold, and all our wealth; you should not have done that."

"Indeed, Frederick," said she, "I did not know that, you should have forewarned me."

Catherine stood for a while and thought to herself; then she said, "Listen, Frederick, we will soon get the gold back again, we will run after the thieves."

"Come, then," said Frederick, "we will try it; but take with you some butter and cheese that we may have something to eat on the way."

"Yes, Frederick, I will take them." They set out, and as Frederick was the better walker, Catherine followed him. "It is to my advantage," thought she, "when we turn back I shall be a little way in advance." Then she came to a hill where there were deep ruts on both sides of the road.

"There one can see," said Catherine, "how they have torn and skinned and galled the poor earth, it will never be whole again as long as it lives," and in her heart's compassion she took her butter and smeared the ruts right and left, that they might not be so hurt by the wheels, and as she was thus bending down in her charity, one of the cheeses rolled out of her pocket down the hill. Said Catherine, "I have made my way once up here, I will not go down again; another may run and fetch it back." So she took another cheese and rolled it down. But the cheeses did not come back, so she let a third run down, thinking, "Perhaps they are waiting for company, and do not like to walk alone."

As all three stayed away she said, "I do not know what that can mean, but it may perhaps be that the third has not found the way, and has gone wrong, I will just send the fourth to call it." But the fourth did no better than the third. Then Catherine was angry, and threw down the fifth and sixth as well, and these were her last. She remained standing for some time watching for their coming, but when they still did not come, she said, "Oh, you are good folks to send in search of death, you stay a fine long time away! Do you think I will wait any longer for you? I shall go my way, you may run after me; you have younger legs than I."

Catherine went on and found Frederick, who was standing waiting for her because he wanted something to eat. "Now just let us have what you have brought with you," said he. She gave him the dry bread. "Where have you the butter and the cheeses?" asked the man.

"Ah, Freddy," said Catherine, "I smeared the cart-ruts with the butter and the cheeses will come soon; one ran away from me, so I sent the others after to call it."

Said Frederick, "You should not have done that, Catherine, to smear the butter on the road, and let the cheeses run down the hill!"

"Really, Frederick, you should have told me."

Then they ate the dry bread together, and Frederick said, "Catherine, did you make the house safe when you came away?"

"No, Frederick, you should have told me to do it before."

"Then go home again, and make the house safe before we go any farther, and bring with you something else to eat. I will wait here for you."

Catherine went back and thought, "Frederick wants something more to eat, he does not like butter and cheese, so I will take with me a handkerchief full of dried pears and a pitcher of vinegar for him." Then she bolted the upper half of the door fast, but unhinged the lower door, and took it on her back, believing that when she had placed the door in security the house must be well taken care of. Catherine took her time on the way, and thought, "Frederick will rest himself so much the longer."

When she had once reached him she said, "Here is the door for you, Frederick, and now you can take care of the house yourself."

"Oh, heavens," said he, "what a wise wife I have! She takes the under-door off the hinges that everything may run in, and bolts the upper one. It is now too late to go back home again, but since you have brought the door here, you shall just carry it farther."

"I will carry the door, Frederick, but the dried pears and the vinegar-jug will be too heavy for me; I will hang them on the door, it may carry them."

And now they went into the forest, and sought the rogues, but did not find them. At length as it grew dark they climbed into a tree and resolved to spend the night there. Scarcely, however, had they sat down at the top of it than the rascals came to carry away with them what does not want to go, and find things before they are lost. They sat down under the very tree in which Frederick and Catherine were sitting, lighted a fire, and were about to share their booty. Frederick got down on the other side and collected some stones together. Then he climbed up again with them, and wished to throw them at the thieves and kill them. The stones, however, did not hit them, and the knaves cried, "It will soon be morning, the wind is shaking down the fir-apples."

Catherine still had the door on her back, and as it pressed so heavily on her, she thought it was the fault of the dried pears, and said, "Frederick, I must throw the pears down."

"No, Catherine, not now," he replied, "they might betray us."

"Oh, but, Frederick, I must! They weigh me down far too much."

"Do it, then, and be hanged!"

Then the dried pears rolled down between the branches, and the rascals below said, "The leaves are falling."

A short time afterwards, as the door was still heavy, Catherine said, "Ah, Frederick, I must pour out the vinegar."

"No, Catherine, you must not, it might betray us."

"Ah, but, Frederick, I must, it weighs me down far too much."

"Then do it and be hanged!" So she emptied out the vinegar, and it besprinkled the robbers.

They said amongst themselves, "The dew is already falling."

At length Catherine thought, "Can it really be the door which weighs me down so?" and said, "Frederick, I must throw the door down."

"No, not now, Catherine, it might reveal us."

"Oh, but, Frederick, I must. It weighs me down far too much."

"Oh, no, Catherine, do hold it fast."

"Ah, Frederick, I am letting it fall!"

"Let it go, then, in the devil's name."

Then it fell down with a violent clatter, and the rascals below cried, "The devil is coming down the tree!" and they ran away and left everything behind them. Early next morning, when the two came down they found all their gold again, and carried it home.

When they were once more at home, Frederick said, "And now, Catherine, you, too, must be industrious and work."

"Yes, Frederick, I will soon do that, I will go into the field and cut corn."

When Catherine got into the field, she said to herself, "Shall I eat before I cut, or shall I sleep before I cut? Oh, I will eat first." Then Catherine ate and eating made her sleepy, and she began to cut, and half in a dream cut all her clothes to pieces, her apron, her gown, and her shift. When Catherine awoke again after a long sleep she was standing there half-naked, and said to herself, "Is it I, or is it not I? Alas, it is not I."

Soon night came, and Catherine ran into the village, knocked at her husband's window, and cried, "Frederick."

"What is the matter?"

"I should very much like to know if Catherine is in?"

"Yes, yes," replied Frederick, "she must be in and asleep."

Said she, "'Tis well, then I am certainly at home already," and ran away.

Outside Catherine found some vagabonds who were going to steal. Then she went to them and said, "I will help you to steal." The rascals thought that she knew of a good place and opportunity, and were glad. But Catherine went in front of the houses, and cried, "Good folks, have you anything? We want to steal."

The thieves thought to themselves, "That's a fine way of doing things," and wished themselves once more rid of Catherine. Then they said to her, "Outside the village the pastor has some turnips in the field. Go there and pull up some turnips for us." Catherine went to the ground, and began to pull them up, but was so idle that she did not gather them together.

Then a man came by, saw her, and stood still and thought that it was the devil who was thus rooting amongst the turnips. He ran away into the village to the pastor, and said, "Mr. Pastor, the devil is in your turnip-field, rooting up turnips."

"Ah, heavens," answered the pastor, "I have a lame foot, I cannot go out and drive him away."

Said the man, "Then I will carry you on my back," and he carried him out on his back. And when they came to the ground, Catherine arose and stood up her full height.

"Ah, the devil!" cried the pastor, and both hurried away, and in his great fright the pastor could run better with his lame foot than the man who had carried him on his back could do with his sound one.

60. THE TWO BROTHERS

There were once upon a time two brothers, one rich and the other poor. The rich one was a goldsmith and evil-hearted. The poor one supported himself by making brooms, and was good and honorable. The poor one had two children, who were twin brothers and as like each other as two drops of water. The two boys went backwards and forwards to the rich house, and often got some of the scraps to eat. It happened once when the poor man was going into the forest to fetch brush-wood, that he saw a bird which was quite golden and more beautiful than any he had ever chanced to meet with. He picked up a small stone, threw it at him, and was lucky enough to hit him, but only one golden feather fell down, and the bird flew away.

The man took the feather and carried it to his brother, who looked at it and said, "It is pure gold!" and gave him a great deal of money for it. Next day the man climbed into a birch tree, and was about to cut off a couple of branches when the same bird flew out, and when the man searched he found a nest, and an egg lay inside it, which was of gold. He took the egg home with him, and carried it to his brother, who again said, "It is pure gold," and gave him what it was worth. At last the goldsmith said, "I should indeed like to have the bird itself."

The poor man went into the forest for the third time, and again saw the golden bird sitting on the tree, so he took a stone and knocked it down and carried it to his brother, who gave him a great heap of gold for it. "Now I can get on," thought he, and went contentedly home.

The goldsmith was crafty and cunning, and knew very well what kind of a bird it was. He called his wife and said, "Roast me the gold bird, and take care that none of it is lost. I have a fancy to eat it all myself." The bird, however, was no common one, but of so wondrous a kind that whoever ate its heart and liver found every morning a piece of gold beneath his pillow. The woman made the bird ready, put it on the spit, and let it roast.

Now it happened that while it was on the fire, and the woman was forced to go out of the kitchen on account of some other work, the two children of the poor broom-maker ran in, stood by the spit and turned it round once or twice. And as at that very moment two little bits of the bird fell down into the dripping-tray, one of the boys said, "We will eat these two little bits; I am so hungry, and no one will ever miss them."

Then the two ate the pieces, but the woman came into the kitchen and saw that they were eating something and said, "What have you been eating?"

"Two little morsels which fell out of the bird," answered they.

"That must have been the heart and the liver," said the woman, quite frightened, and so that her husband might not miss them and be angry, she quickly killed a young cock, took out his heart and liver, and put them beside the golden bird. When it was ready, she carried it to the goldsmith, who consumed it all alone, and left none of it. Next morning, however, when he felt beneath his pillow, and expected to bring out the piece of gold, no more gold pieces were there than there had always been.

The two children did not know what a piece of good fortune had fallen to their lot. Next morning when they arose, something fell rattling to the ground, and when they picked it up there were two gold pieces! They took them to their father, who was astonished and said, "How can that have happened?"

When next morning they again found two, and so on daily, he went to his brother and told him the strange story. The goldsmith at once knew how it had come to pass, and that the children had eaten the heart and liver of the golden bird, and in order to avenge himself, and because he was envious and hard-hearted, he said to the father, "Your children are in league with the Evil One, do not take the gold, and do not suffer them to stay any longer in your house, for he has them in his power, and may ruin you likewise." The father feared the Evil One, and painful as it was to him, he nevertheless led the twins forth into the forest, and with a sad heart left them there.

And now the two children ran about the forest, and sought the way home again, but could not find it, and only lost themselves more and more. At length they met with a hunter, who asked, "To whom do you children belong?"

"We are the poor broom-maker's boys," they replied, and they told him that their father would not keep them any longer in the house because a piece of gold lay every morning under their pillows.

"Come," said the hunter, "that is not so very bad, if at the same time you keep honest, and are not idle." As the good man liked the children, and had none of his own, he took them home with him and said, "I will be your father, and bring you up till you are big." They learned huntership from him, and the piece of gold which each of them found when he awoke, was kept for them by him in case they should need it in the future.

When they were grown up, their foster father one day took them into the forest with him, and said, "Today you shall make your trial shot, so that I may release you from your apprenticeship, and make you hunters." They went with him to lie in wait and stayed there a long time, but no game appeared. The hunter, however, looked above him and saw a covey of wild geese flying in the form of a triangle, and said to one of them, "Shoot me down one from each corner." He did it, and thus accomplished his trial shot. Soon after another covey came flying by in the form of the figure two, and the hunter bade the other also bring down one from each corner, and his trial shot was likewise successful.

"Now," said the foster father, "I pronounce you out of your apprenticeship; you are skilled hunters."

Thereupon the two brothers went forth together into the forest, and took counsel with each other and planned something. And in the evening when they had sat down to supper, they said to their foster father, "We will not touch food, or take one mouthful, until you have granted us a request."

Said he, "What, then, is your request?"

They replied, "We have now finished learning, and we must prove ourselves in the world, so allow us to go away and travel."

Then spoke the old man joyfully, "You talk like brave hunters, that which you desire has been my wish; go forth, all will go well with you." Thereupon they ate and drank joyously together.

When the appointed day came, their foster father presented each of them with a good gun and a dog, and let each of them take as many of his saved-up gold pieces as he chose. Then he accompanied them a part of the way, and when taking leave, he gave them a bright knife, and said, "If ever you separate, stick this knife into a tree at the place where you part, and when one of you goes back, he will be able to see how his absent brother is faring, for the side of the knife which is turned in the direction that he went, will rust if he dies, but will remain bright as long as he is alive."

The two brothers went still farther onwards, and came to a forest which was so large that it was impossible for them to get out of it in one day. So they passed the night in it, and ate what they had put in their hunting-pouches, but they walked all the second day likewise, and still did not get out. As they had nothing to eat, one of them said, "We must shoot something for ourselves or we shall suffer from hunger," and loaded his gun, and looked about him. And when an old hare came running up towards them, he laid his gun on his shoulder, but the hare cried,

> "Dear hunters, do but let me live,
> Two little ones to you I'll give,"

and sprang instantly into the thicket, and brought two young ones. But the little creatures played so merrily, and were so pretty, that the hunters could not find it in their hearts to kill them. They therefore kept them with them, and the little hares followed on foot. Soon after this, a fox crept past; they were just going to shoot it, but the fox cried,

> "Dear hunters, do but let me live,
> Two little ones I'll also give."

He, too, brought two little foxes, and the hunters did not like to kill them either, but gave them to the hares for company, and they followed behind. It was not long before a wolf strode out of the thicket; the hunters made ready to shoot him, but the wolf cried,

> "Dear hunters, do but let me live,
> Two little ones I'll likewise give."

The hunters put the two wolves beside the other animals, and they followed behind. Then a bear came who wanted to trot about a little longer, and cried:

> "Dear hunters, do but let me live,
> Two little ones I, too, will give."

The two young bears were added to the others, and there were already eight of them. At length who came? A lion came, and tossed his mane. But the hunters did not let themselves be frightened and aimed at him likewise, but the lion also said,

"Dear hunters, do but let me live,
Two little ones I, too, will give."

And he brought his little ones to them, and now the hunters had two lions, two bears, two wolves, two foxes, and two hares, who followed them and served them. In the meantime their hunger was not appeased by this, and they said to the foxes, "Listen, cunning fellows, provide us with something to eat. You are crafty and deep."

They replied, "Not far from here lies a village, from which we have already brought many a fowl; we will show you the way there." So they went into the village, bought themselves something to eat, had some food given to their beasts, and then traveled onwards. The foxes, however, knew their way very well about the district and where the henhouses were, and were able to guide the hunters.

Now they traveled about for a while, but could find no suitable place where they could remain together, so they said, "There is nothing else to do, we must part." They divided the animals, so that each of them had a lion, a bear, a wolf, a fox, and a hare, then they took leave of each other, promised to love each other like brothers till their death, and stuck the knife which their foster father had given them, into a tree, after which one went east, and the other went west.

The younger, however, arrived with his beasts in a town which was all hung with black crape. He went into an inn, and asked the host if he could accommodate his animals. The innkeeper gave him a stable, where there was a hole in the wall, and the hare crept out and fetched himself the head of a cabbage, and the fox fetched himself a hen, and when he had devoured that got the cock as well, but the wolf, the bear, and the lion could not get out because they were too big. Then the innkeeper let them be taken to a place where a cow was just then lying on the grass, that they might eat till they were satisfied. And when the hunter had taken care of his animals, he asked the innkeeper why the town was thus hung with black crape? Said the host, "Because our King's only daughter is to die tomorrow."

The hunter inquired if she was "sick unto death?"

"No," answered the host, "she is vigorous and healthy, nevertheless she must die!"

"How is that?" asked the hunter.

"There is a high hill outside the town, where dwells a dragon who every year must have a pure virgin, or he will destroy the whole country, and now all the maidens have already been given to him, and there is no longer anyone left but the King's daughter, yet there is no mercy for her; she must be given up to him, and that is to be done tomorrow."

Said the hunter, "Why is the dragon not killed?"

"Ah," replied the host, "so many knights have tried it, but it has cost all of them their lives. The King has promised that he who conquers the dragon shall have his daughter as wife, and shall likewise govern the kingdom after his own death."

The hunter said nothing more to this, but next morning took his animals, and with them ascended the dragon's hill. A little church stood at the top of it, and on the altar three full cups were standing, with the inscription, "Whoever empties the cups will become the strongest man on earth, and will be able to wield the sword which is buried before the threshold of the door." The hunter did not drink, but went out and sought for the sword in the ground, but was unable to move it from its place. Then he went in and emptied the cups, and now he was strong enough to take up the sword, and his hand could quite easily wield it. When the hour came when the maiden was to be delivered over to the dragon, the King, the marshal, and courtiers accompanied her. From afar she saw the hunter on the dragon's hill, and thought it was the dragon standing there waiting for her, and did not want to go up to him, but at last, because otherwise the whole town would have been destroyed, she was forced to go the miserable journey. The King and courtiers returned home full of grief; the King's marshal, however, was to remain, and see all from a distance.

When the King's daughter got to the top of the hill, it was not the dragon which stood there, but the young hunter, who comforted her, and said he would save her, led her into the church, and locked her in. It was not long before the seven-headed dragon came there with loud roaring. When he perceived the hunter, he was astonished and said, "What business have you here on the hill?"

The hunter answered, "I want to fight with you."

Said the dragon, "Many knights have left their lives here, I shall soon have made an end of you too," and he breathed fire out of seven jaws. The fire was to have lighted the dry grass, and the hunter was to have been suffocated in the heat and smoke, but the animals came running up and trampled out the fire. Then the dragon rushed upon the hunter, but he swung his sword until it sang through the air, and struck off three of his heads. Then the dragon grew right furious, and rose up in the air, and spat out flames of fire over the hunter, and was about to plunge down on him, but the hunter once more drew out his sword, and again cut off three of his heads. The monster became faint and sank down, nevertheless it was just able to rush upon the hunter, but with his last strength he slashed its tail off, and as he could fight no longer, called up his animals who tore it in pieces. When the struggle was over, the hunter unlocked the church, and found the King's daughter lying on the floor, as she had lost her senses with anguish and terror during the contest. He carried her out, and when she came to herself once more, and opened her eyes, he showed her the dragon all cut to pieces, and told her that she was now safe.

She rejoiced and said, "Now you will be my dearest husband, for my father has promised me to whoever kills the dragon." Thereupon she took off her necklace of coral, and divided it amongst the animals in order to reward them, and the lion received the golden clasp. Her pocket handkerchief, which bore her name, she gave to the hunter, who went and cut the tongues out of the dragon's seven heads, wrapped them in the handkerchief, and preserved them carefully.

That done, as he was so faint and weary with the fire and the battle, he said to the maiden, "We are both faint and weary, we will sleep awhile." Then she said, "yes," and they lay down on the ground, and the hunter said to the lion, "You shall keep watch, that no one surprises us in our sleep," and both fell asleep.

The lion lay down beside them to watch, but he also was so weary with the fight, that he called to the bear and said, "Lie down near me, I must sleep a little: if anything comes, wake me."

Then the bear lay down beside him, but he also was tired, and called the wolf and said, "Lie down by me, I must sleep a little, but if anything comes, wake me."

Then the wolf lay down by him, but he was tired likewise, and called the fox and said, "Lie down by me, I must sleep a little; if anything comes, wake me."

Then the fox lay down beside him, but he too was weary, and called the hare and said, "Lie down near me, I must sleep a little, and if anything should come, wake me."

Then the hare sat down by him, but the poor hare was tired too, and had no one whom he could call there to keep watch, and fell asleep. And now the King's daughter, the hunter, the lion, the bear, the wolf, the fox, and the hare, were all sleeping a sound sleep. The marshal, however, who was to look on from a distance, took courage when he did not see the dragon flying away with the maiden, and finding that all the hill had become quiet, ascended it. There lay the dragon hacked and hewn to pieces on the ground, and not far from it were the King's daughter and a hunter with his animals, and all of them were sunk in a sound sleep. And as he was wicked and godless he took his sword, cut off the hunter's head, and seized the maiden in his arms, and carried her down the hill. Then she awoke and was terrified, but the marshal said, "You are in my hands, you shall say that it was I who killed the dragon."

"I cannot do that," she replied, "for it was a hunter with his animals who did it."

Then he drew his sword, and threatened to kill her if she did not obey him, and so compelled her that she promised it. Then he took her to the King, who did not know how to contain himself for joy when he once more saw his dear child alive, whom he had believed to have been torn to pieces by the monster. The marshal said to him, "I have killed the dragon, and delivered the maiden and the whole kingdom as well, therefore I demand her as my wife, as was promised."

The King said to the maiden, "Is what he says true?"

"Ah, yes," she answered, "it must indeed be true, but I will not consent to have the wedding celebrated until after a year and a day," for she thought in that time she should hear something of her dear hunter.

The animals, however, were still lying sleeping beside their dead master on the dragon's hill, and there came a great bumble-bee that alighted on the hare's nose, but the hare wiped it off with his paw, and went on sleeping. The bumble-bee came a second time, but the hare again rubbed it off and slept on. Then it came for the third time, and stung his nose so that he awoke. As soon as the hare was awake, he roused the fox, and the fox, the wolf, and the wolf the bear, and the bear the lion. And when the lion awoke and saw that the maiden was gone, and his master was dead, he began to roar frightfully and cried, "Who has done that? Bear, why did you not wake me?"

The bear asked the wolf, "Why did you not wake me?" and the wolf the fox, "Why did you not wake me?" and the fox the hare, "Why did you not wake me?"

The poor hare alone did not know what answer to make, and the blame rested with him. Then they were just going to fall upon him, but he entreated them and said, "Don't kill me, I will bring our master to life again. I know a mountain on which a root grows which, when placed in the mouth of anyone, cures him of all illness and every wound. But the mountain lies two hundred miles from here."

The lion said, "You have twenty-four hours to run there and come back, and bring the root with you." Then the hare sprang away, and in twenty-four hours he was back, and brought the root with him. The lion put the hunter's head on again, and the hare placed the root in his mouth, and immediately everything united together again, and his heart beat, and life came back.

Then the hunter awoke, and was alarmed when he did not see the maiden, and thought, "She must have gone away while I was sleeping, in order to get rid of me." The lion in his great haste had put his master's head on the wrong way round, but the hunter did not observe it because of his melancholy thoughts about the King's daughter. But at noon, when he was going to eat something, he saw that his head was turned backwards and could not understand it, and asked the animals what had happened to him in his sleep. Then the lion told him that they, too, had all fallen asleep from weariness, and on awaking, had found him dead with his head cut off, that the hare had brought the life-giving root, and that he, in his haste, had laid the head the wrong way, but that he would repair his mistake. Then he tore the hunter's head off again, turned it round, and the hare healed it with the root.

The hunter, however, was sad at heart, and traveled about the world, and made his animals dance before people. It came to pass that precisely at the end of one year he came back to the same town where he had delivered the King's daughter from the dragon, and this time the town was gaily hung with red cloth. Then he said to the host, "What does this mean? Last year the town was all hung with black crape, what means the red cloth today?"

The host answered, "Last year our King's daughter was to have been delivered over to the dragon, but the marshal fought with it and killed it, and so tomorrow their wedding is to be solemnized, and that is why the town was then hung with black crape for mourning, and is today covered with red cloth for joy."

Next day when the wedding was to take place, the hunter said at midday to the innkeeper, "Do you believe, sir host, that while with you here today I shall eat bread from the King's own table?"

"Nay," said the host, "I would bet a hundred pieces of gold that that will not come true."

The hunter accepted the wager, and set against it a purse with just the same number of gold pieces. Then he called the hare and said, "Go, my dear runner, and fetch me some of the bread which the King is eating."

Now the little hare was the lowest of the animals, and could not transfer this order to any of the others, but had to go on foot himself. "Alas!" thought he, "If I bound through the streets thus alone, the butchers' dogs will all be after me." It happened as he expected, and the dogs came after him and wanted to make holes in his good skin. But he sprang away, have you never seen one running? And sheltered himself in a sentry-box without the soldier being aware of it. Then the dogs came and wanted to have him out, but the soldier did not let them pass, and struck them with the butt-end of his gun, till they ran away yelling and howling. As soon as the hare saw that the way was clear, he ran into the palace and straight to the King's daughter, sat down under her chair, and scratched at her foot.

Then she said, "Will you get away?" and thought it was her dog. The hare scratched her foot for the second time, and she again said, "Will you get away?" and thought it was her dog. But the hare did not let itself be turned from its purpose, and scratched her for the third time. Then she peeped down, and knew the hare by her necklace. She took him on her lap, carried him into her chamber, and said, "Dear hare, what do you want?"

He answered, "My master, who killed the dragon, is here, and has sent me to ask for a loaf of bread like that which the King eats." Then she was full of joy and had the baker summoned, and ordered him to bring a loaf such as that eaten by the King. The little hare said, "But the baker must likewise carry it there for me, that the butchers' dogs may do no harm to me." The baker carried if for him as far as the door of the inn, and then the hare got on his hind legs, took the loaf in his front paws, and carried it to his master.

Then said the hunter, "See, sir host, the hundred pieces of gold are mine." The host was astonished, but the hunter went on to say, "Yes, sir host, I have the bread, but now I will likewise have some of the King's roast meat."

The host said, "I should indeed like to see that," but he would make no more wagers.

The hunter called the fox and said, "My little fox, go and fetch me some roast meat, such as the King eats." The red fox knew the byways better, and went by holes and corners without any dog seeing him, seated himself under the chair of the King's daughter, and scratched her foot.

Then she looked down and recognized the fox by its necklace, took him into her chamber with her and said, "Dear fox, what do you want?"

He answered, "My master, who killed the dragon, is here, and has sent me. I am to ask for some roast meat such as the King is eating." Then she made the cook come, who was obliged to prepare a roast, the same as was eaten by the King, and to carry it for the fox as far as the door. Then the fox took the dish, and with his tail waved away the flies which had settled on the meat, and then carried it to his master.

"Look, sir host," said the hunter, "bread and meat are here but now I will also have proper vegetables with it, such as those eaten by the King." Then he called the wolf, and said, "Dear wolf, go there and fetch me vegetables such as the King eats." Then the wolf went straight to the palace, as he feared no one, and when he got to the King's daughter's chamber, he twitched at the back of her dress, so that she was forced to look round.

She recognized him by his necklace, and took him into her chamber with her, and said, "Dear wolf, what do you want?"

He answered, "My master, who killed the dragon, is here, I am to ask for some vegetables, such as the King eats." Then she made the cook come, and he had to make ready a dish of vegetables, such as the King ate, and had to carry it for the wolf as far as the door, and then the wolf took the dish from him, and carried it to his master.

"See, sir host," said the hunter, "now I have bread and meat and vegetables, but I will also have some pastry to eat like that which the King eats." He called the bear, and said, "Dear bear, you are fond of licking anything sweet; go and bring me some confectionery, such as the King eats." Then the bear trotted to the palace, and everyone got out of his way, but when he went to the guard, they presented their muskets, and would not let him go into the royal palace. But he got up on his hind legs, and gave them a few boxes on the ears, right and left, with his paws, so that the whole watch broke up, and then he went straight to the King's daughter, placed himself behind her, and growled a little.

Then she looked behind her, knew the bear, and bade him go into her room with her, and said, "Dear bear, what do you want?"

He answered, "My master, who killed the dragon, is here, and I am to ask for some confectionery, such as the King eats." Then she summoned her confectioner, who had to bake confectionery such as the King ate, and carry it to the door for the bear; then the bear first licked up the sugar drips which had rolled down, and then he stood upright, took the dish, and carried it to his master.

"Behold, sir host," said the hunter, "now I have bread, meat, vegetables and confectionery, but I will drink wine also, and such as the King drinks." He called his lion to him and said, "Dear lion, you yourself like to drink till you are intoxicated, go and fetch me some wine, such as that which is drunk by the King." Then the lion strode through the streets, and the people fled from him, and when he came to the watch, they wanted to bar the way against him, but he did but roar once, and they all ran away. Then the lion went to the royal apartment, and knocked at the door with his tail.

Then the King's daughter came forth, and was almost afraid of the lion, but she knew him by the golden clasp of her necklace, and bade him go with her into her chamber, and said, "Dear lion, what will you have?"

He answered, "My master, who killed the dragon, is here, and I am to ask for some wine such as the King drinks." Then she bade the cup-bearer be called, who was to give the lion some wine like that which was drunk by the King. The lion said, "I will go with him, and see that I get the right wine."

Then he went down with the cup-bearer, and when they were below, the cup-bearer wanted to draw him some of the common wine that was drunk by the King's servants, but the lion said, "Stop, I will taste the wine first," and he drew half a measure, and swallowed it down at one gulp. "No," said he, "that is not right." The cup-bearer glared at him, but went on, and was about to give him some out of another barrel which was for the King's marshal. The lion said, "Stop, let me taste the wine first," and drew half a measure and drank it. "That is better, but still not right," said he.

Then the cup-bearer grew angry and said, "How can a stupid animal like you understand wine?" But the lion gave him a blow behind the ears, which made him fall down by no means gently, and when he had got up again, he conducted the lion quite silently into a separate little cellar, where the King's wine lay, from which no one ever drank.

The lion first drew half a measure and tried the wine, and then he said, "That may possibly be the right sort, and bade the cup-bearer fill six bottles of it. And now they went upstairs again, but when the lion came out of the cellar into the open air, he reeled here and there, and was rather drunk, and the cup-bearer was forced to carry the wine as far as the door for him, and then the lion took the handle of the basket in his mouth, and took it to his master.

The hunter said, "Look, sir host, here have I bread, meat, vegetables, confectionery and wine such as the King has, and now I will dine with my animals," and he sat down and ate and drank, and allowed the hare, the fox, the wolf, the bear, and the lion also to eat and to drink, and was joyful, for he saw that the King's daughter still loved him. And when he had finished his dinner, he said, "Sir host, now have I eaten and drunk, as the King eats and drinks, and now I will go to the King's court and marry the King's daughter."

Said the host, "How can that be, when she already has a betrothed husband, and when the wedding is to be solemnized today?"

Then the hunter drew forth the handkerchief which the King's daughter had given him on the dragon's hill, and in which were folded the monster's seven tongues, and said, "That which I hold in my hand shall help me to do it."

Then the innkeeper looked at the handkerchief, and said, "Whatever I believe, I do not believe that, and I am willing to stake my house and courtyard on it."

The hunter, however, took a bag with a thousand gold pieces, put it on the table, and said, "I stake that on it."

Now the King said to his daughter, at the royal table, "What did all the wild animals want, which have been coming to you, and going in and out of my palace?"

She replied, "I may not tell you, but send and have the master of these animals brought, and you will know."

The King sent a servant to the inn, and invited the stranger, and the servant came just as the hunter had laid his wager with the innkeeper. Then said he, "Now, sir host, the King sends his servant and invites me, but I do not go in this way." And he said to the servant, "I request the Lord King to send me royal clothing, and a carriage with six horses, and servants to attend me."

When the King heard the answer, he said to his daughter, "What shall I do?"

She said, "Have him fetched as he desires to be, and you will do well."

Then the King sent royal apparel, a carriage with six horses, and servants to wait on him. When the hunter saw them coming, he said, "See, sir host, now I am fetched as I desired to be," and he put on the royal garments, took the handkerchief with the dragon's tongues with him, and drove off to the King.

When the King saw him coming, he said to his daughter, "How shall I receive him?"

She answered, "Go to meet him and you will do well."

Then the King went to meet him and led him in, and his animals followed. The King gave him a seat near himself and his daughter, and the marshal, as bridegroom, sat on the other side, but no longer knew the hunter. And now at this very moment, the seven heads of the dragon were brought in as a spectacle, and the King said, "The seven heads were cut off the dragon by the marshal, therefore today I give him my daughter as wife."

The hunter stood up, opened the seven mouths, and said, "Where are the seven tongues of the dragon?"

Then the marshal was terrified, and grew pale and knew not what to answer, and at length in his anguish he said, "Dragons have no tongues."

The hunter said, "Liars ought to have none, but the dragon's tongues are the tokens of the victor," and he unfolded the handkerchief, and there lay all seven inside it. And he put each tongue in the mouth to which it belonged, and it fitted exactly.

Then he took the handkerchief on which the name of the princess was embroidered, and showed it to the maiden, and asked to whom she had given it, and she replied, "To the man who killed the dragon."

And then he called his animals, and took the collar off each of them and the golden clasp from the lion, and showed them to the maiden and asked to whom they belonged. She answered, "The necklace and golden clasp were mine, but I divided them among the animals who helped to conquer the dragon."

Then the hunter said, "When I, tired with the fight, was resting and sleeping, the marshal came and cut off my head. Then he carried away the King's daughter, and pretended that it was he who had killed the dragon, but with the tongues, the handkerchief, and the necklace, I prove that he lied." And then he related how his animals had healed him by means of a wonderful root, and how he had traveled about with them for one year, and had at length again come there and had learnt the treachery of the marshal by the innkeeper's story.

Then the King asked his daughter, "Is it true that this man killed the dragon?"

And she answered, "Yes, it is true. Now I can reveal the wicked deed of the marshal, as it has come to light, for he wrung from me a promise to be silent. For this reason, however, I made the condition that the marriage should not be solemnized for a year and a day."

Then the King bade twelve councilors be summoned who were to pronounce judgment on the marshal, and they sentenced him to be torn to pieces by four bulls. The marshal was therefore executed, but the King gave his daughter to the hunter, and named him his viceroy over the whole kingdom. The wedding was celebrated with great joy, and the young King sent for his father and his foster father, and loaded them with treasures. He sent for the innkeeper too, and said, "Now, sir host, I have married the King's daughter, and your house and yard are mine."

The host said, "Yes, according to justice it is so."

But the young King said, "It shall be done according to mercy," and told him that he should keep his house and yard, and gave him the thousand pieces of gold as well.

And now the young King and Queen were thoroughly happy, and lived in gladness together. He often went out hunting because it was a delight to him, and the faithful animals had to accompany him. In the neighborhood, however, there was a forest of which it was reported that it was haunted, and that whoever entered it did not easily get out again. The young King, however, had a great inclination to hunt in it, and let the old King have no peace until he allowed him to do so. So he rode forth with a great following, and when he came to the forest, he saw a snow-white deer and said to his people, "Wait here until I return, I want to chase that beautiful creature," and he rode into the forest after it, followed only by his animals. The attendants halted and waited until evening, but he did not return, so they rode home, and told the young

Queen that the young King had followed a white deer into the enchanted forest, and had not come back again. Then she had the greatest concern about him. He, however, had still continued to ride on and on after the beautiful wild animal, and had never been able to overtake it; when he thought he was near enough to aim, he instantly saw it bound away into the far distance, and at length it vanished altogether. And now he perceived that he had penetrated deep into the forest, and blew his horn but he received no answer, for his attendants could not hear it. And as night, too, was falling, he saw that he could not get home that day, so he dismounted from his horse, lighted himself a fire near a tree, and resolved to spend the night by it. While he was sitting by the fire, and his animals were lying down beside him, it seemed to him that he heard a human voice. He looked round, but could perceive nothing. Soon afterwards, he again heard a groan as if from above, and then he looked up, and saw an old woman sitting in the tree, who wailed unceasingly, "Oh, oh, oh, how cold I am!"

Said he, "Come down, and warm yourself if you are cold."

But she said, "No, your animals will bite me."

He answered, "They will do you no harm, old mother, do come down."

She, however, was a witch, and said, "I will throw down a wand from the tree, and if you strike them on the back with it, they will do me no harm." Then she threw him a small wand, and he struck them with it, and instantly they lay still and were turned into stone. And when the witch was safe from the animals, she leapt down and touched him also with a wand, and changed him to stone. Thereupon she laughed, and dragged him and the animals into a vault, where many more such stones already lay.

As, however, the young King did not come back at all, the Queen's anguish and care grew constantly greater. And it so happened that at this very time the other brother who had turned to the east when they separated, came into the kingdom. He had sought a home, and had found none, and had then traveled about here and there, and had made his animals dance. Then it came into his mind that he would just go and look at the knife that they had thrust in the trunk of a tree at their parting, that he might learn how his brother was. When he got there his brother's side of the knife was half rusted, and half bright.

Then he was alarmed and thought, "A great misfortune must have befallen my brother, but perhaps I can still save him, for half the knife is still bright." He and his animals traveled towards the west, and when he entered the gate of the town, the guard came to meet him, and asked if he was to announce him to his consort the young Queen, who had for a couple of days been in the greatest sorrow about his staying away, and was afraid he had been killed in the enchanted forest. The sentries, indeed, thought no otherwise than that he was the young King himself, for he looked so like him, and had wild animals running behind him. Then he saw that they were speaking of his brother, and thought, "It will be better if I pass myself off as him, and then I can rescue him more easily." So he allowed himself to be escorted into the castle by the guard, and was received with the greatest joy. The young Queen indeed thought that he was her husband, and asked him why he had stayed away so long.

He answered, "I had lost myself in a forest, and could not find my way out again any sooner." At night he was taken to the royal bed, but he laid a two-edged sword between him and the young Queen; she did not know what that could mean, but did not venture to ask.

He remained in the palace a couple of days, and in the meantime inquired into everything which related to the enchanted forest, and at last he said, "I must hunt there once more." The King and the young Queen wanted to persuade him not to do it, but he held out against them, and went forth with a large following. When he had got into the forest, everything happened with him as with his brother; he saw a white deer and said to his people, "Stay here, and wait until I return, I want to chase the lovely wild beast," and then he rode into the forest and his animals ran after him. But he could not overtake the deer, and got so deep into the forest that he was forced to pass the night there. And when he had lighted a fire, he heard someone wailing above him, "Oh, oh, oh, how cold I am!"

Then he looked up, and the same witch was sitting in the tree.

Said he, "If you are cold, come down, little old mother, and warm yourself."

She answered, "No, your animals will bite me."

But he said, "They will not hurt you."

Then she cried, "I will throw down a wand to you, and if you strike them with it they will do me no harm."

When the hunter heard that, he had no confidence in the old

woman, and said, "I will not strike my animals. Come down, or I will fetch you."

Then she cried, "What do you want? You shall not touch me."

But he replied, "If you do not come, I will shoot you."

Said she, "Shoot away, I do not fear your bullets!" Then he aimed, and fired at her, but the witch was proof against all leaden bullets, and laughed, and yelled and cried, "You shall not hit me."

The hunter knew what to do, tore three silver buttons off his coat, and loaded his gun with them, for against them her arts were useless, and when he fired she fell down at once with a scream. Then he set his foot on her and said, "Old witch, if you do not instantly confess where my brother is, I will seize you with both my hands and throw you into the fire."

She was in a great fright, begged for mercy and said, "He and his animals lie in a vault, turned to stone."

Then he compelled her to go there with him, threatened her, and said, "Old witch, now you shall make my brother and all the human beings lying here, alive again, or you shall go into the fire!" She took a wand and touched the stones, and then his brother with his animals came to life again, and many others, merchants, artisans, and shepherds, arose, thanked him for their deliverance, and went to their homes. But when the twin brothers saw each other again, they kissed each other and rejoiced with all their hearts. Then they seized the witch, bound her and laid her on the fire, and when she was burnt the forest opened of its own accord, and was light and clear, and the King's palace could be seen at about the distance of a three hours walk.

After this the two brothers went home together, and on the way told each other their histories. And when the youngest said that he was ruler of the whole country in the King's stead, the other observed, "That I learned very well, for when I came to the town, and was taken for you, all royal honors were paid me; the young Queen looked at me as her husband, and I had to eat at her side, and sleep in your bed."

When the other heard that, he became so jealous and angry that he drew his sword, and struck off his brother's head. But when he saw him lying there dead, and saw his red blood flowing, he repented most violently: "My brother saved me," cried he, "and I have killed him for it," and he bewailed him aloud. Then his hare came and offered to go and bring some of the root of life, and bounded away and brought it while there was still time, and the dead man was brought to life again, and knew nothing about the wound.

After this they journeyed onwards, and the youngest said, "You look like me, have royal apparel on as I have, and the animals follow you as they do me; we will go in by opposite gates, and arrive at the same time from the two sides in the aged King's presence."

So they separated, and at the same time came the watchmen from the one door and from the other, and announced that the young King and the animals had returned from the chase. The King said, "It is not possible, the gates lie quite a mile apart." In the meantime, however, the two brothers entered the courtyard of the palace from opposite sides, and both mounted the steps. Then the King said to the daughter, "Say which is your husband. Each of them looks exactly like the other, I cannot tell."

Then she was in great distress, and could not tell; but at last she remembered the necklace which she had given to the animals, and she sought for and found her little golden clasp on the lion, and she cried in her delight, "He who is followed by this lion is my true husband."

Then the young King laughed and said, "Yes, he is the right one," and they sat down together, and ate and drank, and were merry.

At night when the young King went to bed, his wife said, "Why have you for these last nights always laid a two-edged sword in our bed? I thought you had a wish to kill me." Then he knew how true his brother had been.

61. THE LITTLE PEASANT

There was a certain village where no one lived but really rich peasants, and just one poor one, whom they called the little peasant. He had not even so much as a cow, and still less money to buy one, and yet he and his wife did so wish to have one. One day he said to her, "Say, I have a good thought, there is our friend the carpenter, he shall make us a wooden calf, and paint it brown, so that it looks like any other, and in time it will certainly get big and be a cow." The woman also liked the idea, and their friend the carpenter cut and planed the calf, and painted it as it ought to be, and made it with its head hanging down as if it were eating.

Next morning when the cows were being driven out, the little peasant called the cowherd and said, "Look, I have a little calf there, but it is still small and has to still be carried."

The cowherd said, "All right," and took it in his arms and carried it to the pasture, and set it among the grass. The little calf always remained standing and seemed to be eating all the time, and the cowherd said, "It will soon be able to run alone, just look how it eats already!"

At night when he was going to drive the herd home again, he said to the calf, "If you can stand there and eat your fill, you can also go on your four legs; I don't care to drag you home again in my arms."

But the little peasant stood at his door, and waited for his little calf, and when the cowherd drove the cows through the village, and the calf was missing, he inquired where it was. The cowherd answered, "It is still standing out there eating. It would not stop and come with us."

But the little peasant said, "Oh, but I must have my beast back again." Then they went back to the meadow together, but someone had stolen the calf, and it was gone.

The cowherd said, "It must have run away."

The peasant, however, said, "Don't tell me that," and brought the cowherd before the mayor, who for his carelessness condemned him to give the peasant a cow for the calf which had run away.

And now the little peasant and his wife had the cow for which they had so long wished, and they were heartily glad, but they had no food for it, and could give it nothing to eat, so it soon had to be killed. They salted the flesh, and the peasant went into the town and wanted to sell the skin there, so that he might buy a new calf with the proceeds. On the way he passed by a mill, and there sat a raven with broken wings, and out of pity he took him and wrapped him in the skin. As, however, the weather grew so bad and there was a storm of rain and wind, he could go no farther, and turned back to the mill and begged for shelter. The miller's wife was alone in the house, and said to the peasant, "Lay yourself on the straw there," and gave him a slice of bread with cheese on it. The peasant ate it, and lay down with his skin beside him, and the woman thought, "He is tired and has gone to sleep."

In the meantime came the parson; the miller's wife received him well, and said, "My husband is out, so we will have a feast." The peasant listened, and when he heard about feasting he was vexed that he had been forced to make do with a slice of bread with cheese on it. Then the woman served up four different things, roast meat, salad, cakes, and wine.

Just as they were about to sit down and eat, there was a knocking outside. The woman said, "Oh, heavens! It is my husband!" She quickly hid the roast meat inside the tiled stove, the wine under the pillow, the salad on the bed, the cakes under it, and the parson in the cupboard in the entrance. Then she opened the door for her husband, and said, "Thank heaven, you are back again! There is such a storm, it looks as if the world were coming to an end."

The miller saw the peasant lying on the straw, and asked, "What is that fellow doing there?"

"Ah," said the wife, "the poor knave came in the storm and rain, and begged for shelter, so I gave him a bit of bread and cheese, and showed him where the straw was."

The man said, "I have no objection, but be quick and get me something to eat."

The woman said, "But I have nothing but bread and cheese."

"I am contented with anything," replied the husband, "so far as I am concerned, bread and cheese will do," and looked at the peasant and said, "Come and eat some more with me."

The peasant did not require to be invited twice, but got up and ate. After this the miller saw the skin in which the raven was wrapped, lying on the ground, and asked, "What have you there?" The peasant answered, "I have a soothsayer inside it."

"Can he foretell anything to me?" said the miller.

"Why not?" answered the peasant, "But he only says four things, and the fifth he keeps to himself."

The miller was curious, and said, "Let him foretell something for once." Then the peasant pinched the raven's head, so that he croaked and made a noise like *krr*, *krr*. The miller said, "What did he say?"

The peasant answered, "In the first place, he says that there is some wine hidden under the pillow."

"Bless me!" cried the miller, and went there and found the wine. "Now go on," said he.

The peasant made the raven croak again, and said, "In the second place, he says that there is some roast meat in the tiled stove."

"Upon my word!" cried the miller, and went there, and found the roast meat.

The peasant made the raven prophesy still more, and said, "Thirdly, he says that there is some salad on the bed."

"That would be a fine thing!" cried the miller, and went there and found the salad.

At last the peasant pinched the raven once more till he croaked, and said, "Fourthly, he says that there are some cakes under the bed."

"That would be a fine thing!" cried the miller, and looked there, and found the cakes.

And now the two sat down to the table together, but the miller's wife was frightened to death, and went to bed and took all the keys with her. The miller would have much liked to know the fifth, but the little peasant said, "First, we will quickly eat the four things, for the fifth is something bad."

So they ate, and after that they bargained how much the miller was to give for the fifth prophesy, until they agreed on three hundred talkers. Then the peasant once more pinched the raven's head till he croaked loudly. The miller asked, "What did he say?"

The peasant replied, "He says that the Devil is hiding there in the cupboard in the entrance."

The miller said, "The Devil must go out," and opened the door; then the woman was forced to give up the keys, and the peasant unlocked the cupboard. The parson ran out as fast as he could, and the miller said, "It was true; I saw the black rascal with my own eyes." The peasant made off next morning by daybreak with the three hundred talkers.

At home the small peasant gradually launched out; he built a beautiful house, and the peasants said, "The small peasant has certainly been to the place where golden snow falls, and people carry the gold home in shovels."

Then the small peasant was brought before the Mayor, and bidden to say from where his wealth came. He answered, "I sold my cow's skin in the town, for three hundred talkers."

When the peasants heard that, they too wished to enjoy this great profit, and ran home, killed all their cows, and stripped off their skins in order to sell them in the town to the greatest advantage. The Mayor, however, said, "But my servant must go first."

When she came to the merchant in the town, he did not give her more than two talkers for a skin, and when the others came, he did not give them so much, and said, "What can I do with all these skins?"

Then the peasants were vexed that the small peasant should have thus deceived them, wanted to take vengeance on him, and accused him of this treachery before the Mayor. The innocent little peasant was unanimously sentenced to death, and was to be rolled into the water, in a barrel pierced full of holes. He was led forth, and a priest was brought who was to say a mass for his soul. The others were all obliged to retire to a distance, and when the peasant looked at the priest, he recognized the man who had been with the miller's wife. He said to him, "I set you free from the cupboard, set me free from the barrel."

At this same moment up came, with a flock of sheep, the very shepherd who the peasant knew had long been wishing to be Mayor, so he cried with all his might, "No, I will not do it; if the whole world insists on it, I will not do it!"

The shepherd hearing that, came up to him, and asked, "What are you about? What is it that you will not do?"

The peasant said, "They want to make me Mayor, if I will but put myself in the barrel, but I will not do it."

The shepherd said, "If nothing more than that is needed in order to be Mayor, I would get into the barrel at once."

The peasant said, "If you will get in, you will be Mayor."

The shepherd was willing, and got in, and the peasant shut the top down on him; then he took the shepherd's flock for himself, and drove it away. The parson went to the crowd, and declared that the mass had been said. Then they came and rolled the barrel towards the water.

When the barrel began to roll, the shepherd cried, "I am quite willing to be Mayor."

They believed that it was the peasant who was saying this, and answered, "That is what we intend, but first you shall go down below and look about you a little," and they rolled the barrel down into the water.

After that the peasants went home, and as they were entering the village, the small peasant also came quietly in, driving a flock of sheep and looking quite contented. Then the peasants were astonished, and said, "Peasant, from where do you come? Have you come out of the water?"

"Yes, truly," replied the peasant, "I sank deep, deep down, until at last I got to the bottom; I pushed the bottom out of the barrel, and crept out, and there were pretty meadows on which a number of lambs were feeding, and from there I brought this flock away with me."

Said the peasants, "Are there any more there?"

"Oh, yes," said he, "more than I could do anything with."

Then the peasants made up their minds that they too would fetch some sheep for themselves, a flock apiece, but the Mayor said, "I come first." So they went to the water together, and just then there were some of the small fleecy clouds in the blue sky, which are called little lambs, and they were reflected in the water, and the peasants cried, "We already see the sheep down below!"

The Mayor pressed forward and said, "I will go down first, and look about me, and if things look promising I'll call you." So he jumped in; *splash*! went the water; he made a sound as if he were calling them, and the whole crowd plunged in after him. Then the entire village was dead, and the small peasant, as sole heir, became a rich man.

62. THE QUEEN BEE

Two kings' sons once went out in search of adventures, and fell into a wild, disorderly way of living, so that they never came home again. The youngest, who was called Simpleton, set out to seek his brothers, but when at length he found them they mocked him for thinking that he could get through the world with his simplicity, when they both could not make their way, and yet were so much cleverer. They all three traveled away together, and came to an anthill. The two eldest wanted to destroy it, to see the little ants creeping about in their terror, and carrying their eggs away, but Simpleton said, "Leave the creatures in peace; I will not allow you to disturb them."

Then they went onwards and came to a lake, on which a great number of ducks were swimming. The two brothers wanted to catch a couple and roast them, but Simpleton would not permit it, and said, "Leave the creatures in peace, I will not allow you to kill them."

At length they came to a bee's nest, in which there was so much honey that it ran out of the trunk of the tree where it was. The two wanted to make a fire beneath the tree, and suffocate the bees in order to take away the honey, but Simpleton again stopped them and said, "Leave the creatures in peace, I will not allow you to burn them."

At length the three brothers arrived at a castle where stone horses were standing in the stables, and no human being was to be seen, and they went through all the halls until, quite at the end, they came to a door in which were three locks. In the middle of the door, however, there was a little pane, through which they could see into the room. There they saw a little grey man, who was sitting at a table. They called him, once, twice, but he did not hear; at last they called him for the third time, when he got up, opened the locks, and came out. He said nothing, however, but conducted them to a handsomely-spread table, and when they had eaten and drunk, he took each of them to a bedroom. Next morning the little grey man came to the eldest, beckoned to him, and conducted him to a stone table, on which were inscribed three tasks, that when performed could deliver the castle from enchantment. The first was that in the forest, beneath the moss, lay the princess's pearls, a thousand in number, which must be picked up, and if by sunset one single pearl was wanting, he who had looked for them would be turned into stone. The eldest went there, and sought the whole day, but when it came to an end, he had only found one hundred, and what was written on the table came to pass, and he was changed into stone. Next day, the second brother undertook the adventure; it did not, however, fare much better with him than with the eldest; he did not find more than two hundred pearls, and was changed to stone. At last the turn came to Simpleton also, who sought in the moss. It was, however, so hard to find the pearls, and he got on so slowly, that he seated himself on a stone, and wept. And while he was thus sitting, the King of the ants whose life he had once saved, came with five thousand ants, and before long the little creatures had got all the pearls together, and laid them in a heap. The second task, however, was to fetch out of the lake the key of the King's daughter's bedchamber. When Simpleton came to the lake, the ducks which he had saved, swam up to him, dived down, and brought the key out of the water. But the third task was the most difficult; from amongst the three sleeping daughters of the King he was to choose the youngest and dearest. They, however, resembled each other exactly, and were only to be distinguished by their having eaten different sweetmeats before they fell asleep; the eldest a bit of sugar; the second a little syrup; and the youngest a spoonful of honey. Then the Queen of the bees, which Simpleton had protected from the fire, came and tasted the lips of all three, and at last she remained sitting on the mouth which had eaten honey, and thus the King's son recognized the right princess. Then the enchantment was at an end; everything was released from sleep, and those who had been turned to stone received once more their natural forms. Simpleton married the youngest and sweetest princess, and after her father's death became King, and his two brothers received the two other sisters.

63. THE THREE FEATHERS

There was once upon a time a King who had three sons, of whom two were clever and wise, but the third did not speak much, and was simple, and was called the Simpleton. When the King had become old and weak, and was thinking of his end, he did not know which of his sons should inherit the kingdom after him. Then he said to them, "Go forth, and he who brings me the most beautiful carpet shall be King after my death." And that there should be no dispute amongst them, he took them outside his castle, blew three feathers in the air, and said, "You shall go as they fly." One feather flew to the east, the other to the west, but the third flew straight up and did not fly far, but soon fell to the ground. And now one brother went to the right, and the other to the left, and they mocked Simpleton, who was forced to stay where the third feather had fallen.

He sat down and was sad, then all at once he saw that there was a trapdoor close by the feather. He raised it up, found some steps, and went down them, and then he came to another door, knocked at it, and heard somebody inside calling,

> "Little green maiden small,
> Hopping here and there;
> Hop to the door,
> And quickly see who is there."

The door opened, and he saw a great, fat toad sitting, and round about her a crowd of little toads. The fat toad asked what he wanted? He answered, "I should like to have the prettiest and finest carpet in the world." Then she called a young one and said,

> "Little green maiden small,
> Hopping here and there,
> Hop quickly and bring me
> The great box here."

The young toad brought the box, and the fat toad opened it, and gave Simpleton a carpet out of it, so beautiful and so fine, that on the earth above, none could have been woven like it. Then he thanked her, and ascended again.

The two others had, however, looked on their youngest brother as so stupid that they believed he would find and bring nothing at all. "Why should we give ourselves a great deal of trouble to search?" said they, and got some coarse handkerchiefs from the first shepherds' wives whom they met, and carried them home to the King.

At the same time Simpleton also came back, and brought his beautiful carpet, and when the King saw it he was astonished, and said, "If justice be done, the Kingdom belongs to the youngest." But the two others let their father have no peace, and said that it was impossible that Simpleton, who lacked understanding in everything, should be King, and entreated him to make a new agreement with them.

Then the father said, "He who brings me the most beautiful ring shall inherit the kingdom," and led the three brothers out, and blew into the air three feathers, which they were to follow. Those of the two eldest again went east and west, and Simpleton's feather flew straight up, and fell down near the door into the earth. Then he went down again to the fat toad, and told her that he wanted the most beautiful ring. She at once ordered her great box to be brought, and gave him a ring out of it, which sparkled with jewels, and was so beautiful that no goldsmith on earth would have been able to make it.

The two eldest laughed at Simpleton for going to seek a golden ring. They gave themselves no trouble, but knocked the nails out of an old ring from the harness of a carriage horse, and took it to the King; but when Simpleton produced his golden ring, his father again said, "The Kingdom belongs to him."

The two eldest did not cease from tormenting the King until he made a third condition, and declared that the one who brought the most beautiful woman home, should have the Kingdom. He again blew the three feathers into the air, and they flew as before.

Then Simpleton without more ado went down to the fat toad, and said, "I am to take home the most beautiful woman!"

"Oh," answered the toad, "the most beautiful woman! She is not at hand at the moment, but still you shall have her." She gave him a yellow turnip which had been hollowed out, to which six mice were harnessed.

Then Simpleton said quite mournfully, "What am I to do with that?"

The toad answered, "Just put one of my little toads into it." Then he seized one at random out of the circle, and put her into the yellow coach, but hardly was she seated inside it than she turned into a wonderfully beautiful maiden, and the turnip into a coach, and the six mice into horses. So he kissed her, and drove off quickly with the horses, and took her to the King.

His brothers came afterwards; they had given themselves no trouble at all to seek beautiful girls, but had brought with them the first peasant women they chanced to meet. When the King saw them he said, "After my death the kingdom belongs to my youngest son."

But the two eldest deafened the King's ears with their clamor, "We cannot consent to Simpleton's being King," and demanded that the one whose wife could leap through a ring which hung in the center of the hall should have the Kingdom. They thought, "The peasant women can do that easily; they are strong enough, but the delicate maiden will jump herself to death." The aged King agreed to this. Then the two peasant women jumped, and jumped through the ring, but were so stout that they fell, and their coarse arms and legs broke in two. And then the pretty maiden whom Simpleton had brought with him, sprang, and sprang through as lightly as a deer, and all opposition had to cease. So he received the crown, and has ruled wisely for a length of time.

64. THE GOLDEN GOOSE

There was a man who had three sons, the youngest of whom was called Dummling, and was despised, mocked, and put down on every occasion.

It happened that the eldest wanted to go into the forest to hew wood, and before he went his mother gave him a beautiful sweet cake and a bottle of wine so that he might not suffer from hunger or thirst.

When he entered the forest he met a little grey-haired old man who bade him good day, and said, "Do give me a piece of cake out of your pocket, and let me have a drink of your wine; I am so hungry and thirsty."

But the prudent youth answered, "If I give you my cake and wine, I shall have none for myself; be off with you," and he left the little man standing and went on.

But when he began to hew down a tree, it was not long before he made a false stroke, and the axe cut him in the arm, so that he had to go home and have it bound up. And this was the little grey man's doing.

After this the second son went into the forest, and his mother gave him, like the eldest, a cake and a bottle of wine. The little old grey man met him likewise, and asked him for a piece of cake and a drink of wine. But the second son, too, said with much reason, "What I give you will be taken away from myself; be off!" and he left the little man standing and went on. His punishment, however, was not delayed; when he had made a few strokes at the tree he struck himself in the leg, so that he had to be carried home.

Then Dummling said, "Father, do let me go and cut wood."

The father answered, "Your brothers have hurt themselves by it, leave it alone, you do not understand anything about it." But Dummling begged so long that at last he said, "Just go then, you will get wiser by hurting yourself." His mother gave him a cake made with water and baked in the cinders, and with it a bottle of sour beer.

When he came to the forest the little old grey man met him likewise, and greeting him, said, "Give me a piece of your cake and a drink out of your bottle; I am so hungry and thirsty."

Dummling answered, "I have only cinder-cake and sour beer; if that pleases you, we will sit down and eat."

So they sat down, and when Dummling pulled out his cinder-cake, it was a fine sweet cake, and the sour beer had become good wine. So they ate and drank, and after that the little man said, "Since you have a good heart, and are willing to divide what you have, I will give you good luck. There stands an old tree, cut it down, and you will find something at the roots." Then the little man took leave of him.

Dummling went and cut down the tree, and when it fell there was a goose sitting in the roots with feathers of pure gold. He lifted her up, and taking her with him, went to an inn where he thought he would stay the night. Now the host had three daughters, who saw the goose and were curious to know what wonderful kind of bird it might be, and would have liked to have one of its golden feathers.

The eldest thought, "I shall soon find an opportunity of pulling out a feather," and as soon as Dummling had gone out she seized the goose by the wing, but her finger and hand remained sticking fast to it.

The second came soon afterwards, thinking only of how she might get a feather for herself, but she had scarcely touched her sister than she was held fast.

At last the third also came with the same intent, and the others screamed out, "Keep away; for goodness' sake keep away!"

But she did not understand why she was to keep away. "The others are there," she thought, "I may as well be there too," and ran to them; but as soon as she had touched her sister, she remained sticking fast to her. So they had to spend the night with the goose.

The next morning Dummling took the goose under his arm and set out, without troubling himself about the three girls who were hanging onto it. They were obliged to run after him continually, now left, now right, just as he was inclined to go.

In the middle of the fields the parson met them, and when he saw the procession he said, "For shame, you good-for-nothing girls, why are you running across the fields after this young man? Is that seemly?" At the same time he seized the youngest by the hand in order to pull her away, but as soon as he touched her he likewise stuck fast, and was himself obliged to run behind.

Before long the sexton came by and saw his master, the parson, running behind three girls. He was astonished at this and called out,

"Ho, your reverence, where do you go so quickly? Do not forget that we have a christening today!" and running after him he took him by the sleeve, but was also held fast to it.

While the five were trotting one behind the other, two laborers came with their hoes from the fields; the parson called out to them and begged that they would set him and the sexton free. But they had scarcely touched the sexton when they were held fast, and now there were seven of them running behind Dummling and the goose.

Soon afterwards he came to a city, where a king ruled who had a daughter who was so serious that no one could make her laugh. So he had put forth a decree that whoever should be able to make her laugh should marry her. When Dummling heard this, he went with his goose and all her train before the King's daughter, and as soon as she saw the seven people running on and on, one behind the other, she began to laugh quite loudly, and as if she would never leave off. Upon this Dummling asked to have her for his wife, and the wedding was celebrated. After the King's death, Dummling inherited the Kingdom and lived a long time contentedly with his wife.

65. THOUSANDFURS

There was once upon a time a King who had a wife with golden hair, and she was so beautiful that her equal was not to be found on earth. It came to pass that she lay ill, and as she felt that she must soon die, she called the King and said, "If you wish to marry again after my death, she must be as beautiful as I am, and have such golden hair as I have: this you must promise me." And after the King had promised her this she closed her eyes and died.

For a long time the King could not be comforted, and had no thought of taking another wife. At length his councilors said, "There is no helping it, the King must marry again, that we may have a Queen." And now messengers were sent about far and wide, to seek a bride who equaled the late Queen in beauty. In the whole world, however, none was to be found, and even if one had been found, still there would have been no one who had such golden hair. So the messengers came home as they went.

Now the King had a daughter, who was just as beautiful as her dead mother, and had the same golden hair. When she was grown up the King looked at her one day, and saw that in every respect she was like his late wife, and suddenly felt a violent love for her. Then he said to his councilors, "I will marry my daughter, for she is the counterpart of my late wife, otherwise I can find no bride who resembles her."

When the councilors heard that, they were shocked, and said, "God has forbidden a father to marry his daughter, no good can come from such a crime, and the Kingdom will be involved in the ruin."

The daughter was still more shocked when she became aware of her father's resolution, but hoped to change his mind. Then she said to him, "Before I fulfill your wish, I must have three dresses, one as golden as the sun, one as silvery as the moon, and one as bright as the stars; besides this, I wish for a mantle of a thousand different kinds of fur and hair joined together, and one of every kind of animal in your Kingdom must give a piece of his skin for it." But she thought, "To get that will be quite impossible, and thus I shall divert my father from his wicked intentions."

The King, however, did not give it up, and the cleverest maidens in his Kingdom had to weave the three dresses, one as golden as the sun, one as silvery as the moon, and one as bright as the stars, and his hunters had to catch one of every kind of animal in the whole of his kingdom, and take from it a piece of its skin, and out of these was made a mantle of a thousand different kinds of fur. At length, when all was ready, the King had the mantle brought, spread it out before her, and said, "The wedding shall be tomorrow."

When the King's daughter saw that there was no longer any hope of turning her father's heart, she resolved to run away from him. In the night while everyone was asleep, she got up, and took three different things from her treasures, a golden ring, a golden spinning wheel, and a golden reel. The three dresses of the sun, moon, and stars she put into a nutshell, put on her mantle of all kinds of fur, and blackened her face and hands with soot. Then she commended herself to God, and went away, and walked the whole night until she reached a great forest. And as she was tired, she got into a hollow tree, and fell asleep.

The sun rose, and she slept on, and she was still sleeping when it was full day. Then it so happened that the King to whom this forest belonged, was hunting in it. When his dogs came to the tree, they sniffed, and ran barking round about it. The King said to the hunters, "Just see what kind of wild beast has hidden itself in there."

The hunters obeyed his order, and when they came back they said, "A wondrous beast is lying in the hollow tree; we have never before seen one like it. Its skin is fur of a thousand different kinds, but it is lying asleep."

Said the King, "See if you can catch it alive, and then fasten it to the carriage, and we will take it with us."

When the hunters laid hold of the maiden, she awoke full of terror, and cried to them, "I am a poor child, deserted by father and mother; have pity on me, and take me with you."

Then said they, "Thousandfurs, you will be useful in the kitchen, come with us, and you can sweep up the ashes." So they put her in the carriage, and took her home to the royal palace. There they pointed out to her a closet under the stairs, where no daylight entered, and said, "Hairy animal, there you can live and sleep." Then she was sent into the kitchen, and there she carried wood and water, swept the hearth, plucked the fowls, picked the vegetables, raked the ashes, and did all the dirty work.

Thousandfurs lived there for a long time in great wretchedness. Alas, fair princess, what is to become of you now! It happened, however, that one day a feast was held in the palace, and she said to the cook, "May I go upstairs for a while, and look on? I will place myself outside the door."

The cook answered, "Yes, go, but you must be back here in half-an-hour to sweep the hearth."

Then she took her oil lamp, went into her den, took off her fur-dress, and washed the soot off her face and hands, so that her full beauty once more came to light. And she opened the nut, and took out her dress which shone like the sun, and when she had done that she went up to the festival, and everyone made way for her, for no one knew her, and thought no otherwise than that she was a king's daughter.

The King came to meet her, gave his hand to her, and danced with her, and thought in his heart, "My eyes have never yet seen anyone so beautiful!" When the dance was over she curtsied, and when the King looked round again she had vanished, and no one knew where. The guards who stood outside the palace were called and questioned, but no one had seen her.

She had, however, run into her little den, had quickly taken off her dress, made her face and hands black again, put on the fur-mantle, and again was Thousandfurs. And now when she went into the kitchen, and was about to get to her work and sweep up the ashes, the cook said, "Leave that alone till morning, and make me the soup for the King; I, too, will go upstairs awhile, and take a look; but let no hairs fall in, or in future you shall have nothing to eat."

So the cook went away, and Thousandfurs made the soup for the king, and made the bread soup the best she could, and when it was ready she fetched her golden ring from her little den, and put it in the bowl in which the soup was served. When the dancing was over, the King had his soup brought and ate it, and he liked it so much that it seemed to him he had never tasted better. But when he came to the bottom of the bowl, he saw a golden ring, and could not conceive how it could have got there. Then he ordered the cook to appear before him. The cook was terrified when he heard the order, and said to Thousandfurs, "You have certainly let a hair fall into the soup, and if you have, you shall be beaten for it."

When he came before the King the latter asked who had made the soup? The cook replied, "I made it."

But the King said, "That is not true, for it was much better than usual, and cooked differently."

He answered, "I must acknowledge that I did not make it, it was made by the rough animal."

The King said, "Go and bid it come up here."

When Thousandfurs came, the King said, "Who are you?"

"I am a poor girl who no longer has any father or mother."

He asked further, "Of what use are you in my palace?"

She answered, "I am good for nothing but to have boots thrown at my head."

He continued, "Where did you get the ring which was in the soup?"

She answered, "I know nothing about the ring." So the King could learn nothing, and had to send her away again.

After a while, there was another festival, and then, as before, Thousandfurs begged the cook for leave to go and look on. He answered, "Yes, but come back again in half-an-hour, and make the King the bread soup which he so much likes."

Then she ran into her den, washed herself quickly, and took out of the nut the dress which was as silvery as the moon, and put it on. Then she went up and was like a princess, and the King stepped forward to meet her, and rejoiced to see her once more, and as the dance was just beginning they danced it together. But when it ended, she again disappeared so quickly that the King could not observe where she went. She, however, sprang into her den, and once more made herself a hairy animal, and went into the kitchen to prepare the bread soup. When the cook had gone upstairs, she fetched the little golden spinning wheel, and put it in the bowl so that the soup covered it. Then it was taken to the King, who ate it, and liked it as much as before, and had the cook brought, who this time likewise was forced to confess that Thousandfurs had prepared the soup. Thousandfurs again came before the King, but she answered that she was good for nothing else but to have boots thrown at her head, and that she knew nothing at all about the little golden spinning wheel.

When, for the third time, the King held a festival, all happened just as it had done before. The cook said, "Surely, rough-skin, you are a witch, and always put something in the soup which makes it so good that the King likes it better than that which I cook," but as she begged so hard, he let her go up at the appointed time. And now she put on the dress which shone like the stars, and thus entered the hall. Again the King danced with the beautiful maiden, and thought that she had never yet been so beautiful. And while she was dancing, he contrived, without her noticing it, to slip a golden ring on her finger, and he had given orders that the dance should last a very long time. When it ended, he wanted to hold her fast by her hands, but she tore herself loose, and sprang away so quickly through the crowd that she vanished from his sight. She ran as fast as she could into her den beneath the stairs, but as she had been too long, and had stayed more than half-an-hour she could not take off her pretty dress, but only threw over it her fur-mantle, and in her haste she did not make herself quite black, but one finger remained white. Then Thousandfurs ran into the kitchen, and cooked the bread soup for the King, and as the cook was away, put her golden reel into it. When the King found the reel at the bottom of it, he had Thousandfurs summoned, and then he spied the white finger, and saw the ring which he had put on it during the dance. Then he grasped her by the hand, and held her fast, and when she wanted to release herself and run away, her mantle of fur opened a little, and the star-dress shone forth. The King clutched the mantle and tore it off. Then her golden hair shone forth, and she stood there in full splendor, and could no longer hide herself. And when she had washed the soot and ashes from her face, she was more beautiful than anyone who had ever been seen on earth. The King said, "You are my dear bride, and we will never again part from each other." Thereupon the marriage was solemnized, and they lived happily until their death.

66. THE HARE'S BRIDE

There was once a woman and her daughter who lived in a pretty garden with cabbages; and a little hare came into it, and during the wintertime ate all the cabbages. Then says the mother to the daughter, "Go into the garden, and chase the hare away."

The girl says to the little hare, "Sh-sh, hare, you are still eating up all our cabbages."

Says the hare, "Come, maiden, and seat yourself on my little hare's tail, and come with me into my little hare's hut." The girl will not do it.

Next day the hare comes again and eats the cabbages, then says the mother to the daughter, "Go into the garden, and drive the hare away."

The girl says to the hare, "Sh-sh, little hare, you are still eating all the cabbages."

The little hare says, "Maiden, seat yourself on my little hare's tail, and come with me into my little hare's hut." The maiden refuses.

The third day the hare comes again, and eats the cabbages. At this the mother says to the daughter, "Go into the garden, and chase the hare away."

Says the maiden, "Sh-sh, little hare, you are still eating all our cabbages."

Says the little hare, "Come, maiden, seat yourself on my little hare's tail, and come with me into my little hare's hut."

The girl seats herself on the little hare's tail, and then the hare takes her far away to his little hut, and says, "Now cook green cabbage and millet seed, and I will invite the wedding guests." Then all the wedding guests assembled. (Who were the wedding guests? That I can tell you as another told it to me. They were all hares, and the crow was there as parson to marry the bride and bridegroom, and the fox as clerk, and the altar was under the rainbow.)

The girl, however, was sad, for she was all alone. The little hare comes and says, "Open the doors, open the doors, the wedding guests are merry." The bride says nothing, but weeps. The little hare goes away. The little hare comes back and says, "Take off the lid, take off the lid, the wedding guests are hungry." The bride again says nothing, and weeps. The little hare goes away. The little hare comes back and says, "Take off the lid, take off the lid, the wedding guests are waiting." Then the bride says nothing, and the hare goes away, but she dresses a straw-doll in her clothes, and gives her a spoon to stir with, and sets her by the pan with the millet seed, and goes back to her mother. The little hare comes once more and says, "Take off the lid, take off the lid," and gets up, and strikes the doll on the head so that her cap falls off.

Then the little hare sees that it is not his bride, and goes away and is sorrowful.

67. THE TWELVE HUNTERS

There was once a King's son who was betrothed to a maiden whom he loved very much. And when he was sitting beside her and very happy, news came that his father lay sick and dying, and desired to see him once again before his end. Then he said to his beloved, "I must go now and leave you, I give you a ring as a remembrance of me. When I am King, I will return and fetch you."

So he rode away, and when he reached his father, the latter was dangerously ill, and near his death. He said to him, "Dear son, I wished to see you once again before my end, promise me to marry as I wish," and he named a certain King's daughter who was to be his wife.

The son was so upset that he did not think what he was doing, and said, "Yes, dear father, your will shall be done," and then the King shut his eyes, and died.

When the son had been proclaimed King, and the time of mourning was over, he was forced to keep the promise which he had given his father, and sent to the King's daughter to ask her hand in marriage, and she was promised to him.

His first betrothed heard of this, and fretted so much about his faithlessness that she nearly died. Then her father said to her, "Dearest child, why are you so sad? You shall have whatever you want."

She thought for a moment and said, "Dear father, I wish for eleven girls exactly like myself in face, figure, and size."

The father said, "If it is possible, your desire shall be fulfilled," and he ordered a search to be made of his whole kingdom, until eleven young maidens were found who exactly resembled his daughter in face, figure, and size.

When they came to the King's daughter, she had twelve suits of hunters's clothes made, all alike, and the eleven maidens had to put on the hunters's clothes, and she herself put on the twelfth suit. Then she took leave of her father, and rode away with them, and rode to the court of her former betrothed, whom she loved so dearly. Then she inquired if he required any hunters, and if he would take the whole of them into his service. The King looked at her and did not know her, but as they were such handsome fellows, he said, "Yes," and that he would willingly take them, and now they were the King's twelve hunters.

The King, however, had a lion which was a wondrous animal, for he knew all concealed and secret things. It came to pass that one evening he said to the King, "You think you have twelve hunters?"

"Yes," said the King, "they are twelve hunters."

The lion continued, "You are mistaken, they are twelve girls."

The King said, "That cannot be true! How will you prove that to me?"

"Oh, just let some peas be strewn in your anteroom," answered the lion, "and then you will soon see it. Men have a firm step, and when they walk over the peas none of them stir, but girls trip and skip, and drag their feet, and the peas roll about." The King was well pleased with the counsel, and caused the peas to be strewn.

There was, however, a servant of the King's who favored the hunters, and when he heard that they were going to be put to this test he went to them and repeated everything, and said, "The lion wants to make the King believe that you are girls."

Then the King's daughter thanked him, and said to her maidens, "Have some strength, and step firmly on the peas."

So next morning when the King had the twelve hunters called before him, and they came into the anteroom where the peas were lying, they stepped so firmly on them, and had such a strong, sure walk, that not one of the peas either rolled or stirred. Then they went away again, and the King said to the lion, "You have lied to me, they walk just like men."

The lion said, "They have got to know that they were going to be put to the test, and have assumed some strength. Just let twelve spinning wheels be brought into the anteroom some day, and they will go to them and be pleased with them, and that is what no man would do." The King liked the advice, and had the spinning wheels placed in the anteroom.

But the servant, who was well disposed to the hunters, went to them, and disclosed the project. Then when they were alone the King's daughter said to her eleven girls, "Have some constraint on yourselves, and do not look round at the spinning wheels." And next morning when the King had his twelve hunters summoned, they went through the anteroom, and never once looked at the spinning wheels. Then the King again said to the lion, "You have deceived me, they are men, for they have not looked at the spinning wheels."

The lion replied, "They have learnt that they were going to be put to the test, and have restrained themselves." The King, however, would no longer believe the lion.

The twelve hunters always followed the King to the chase, and his liking for them continually increased. Now it came to pass that once when they were out hunting, news came that the King's betrothed was approaching. When the true bride heard that, it hurt her so much that her heart was almost broken, and she fell fainting to the ground. The King thought something had happened to his dear hunter, ran up to him, wanted to help him, and drew his glove off. Then he saw the ring which he had given to his first bride, and when he looked in her face he recognized her. Then his heart was so touched that he kissed her, and when she opened her eyes he said, "You are mine, and I am your's, and no one in the world can alter that."

He sent a messenger to the other bride, and entreated her to return to her own kingdom, for he had a wife already, and a man who had just found an old dish did not require a new one. Soon the wedding was celebrated, and the lion was again taken into favor, because, after all, he had told the truth.

68. *THE THIEF AND HIS MASTER*

Hans wished to send his son to learn a trade, so he went into the church and prayed to our Lord God to know which would be most advantageous for him. Then the clerk got behind the altar, and said, "Thieving, thieving."

At this Hans goes back to his son, and tells him he is to learn thieving, and that the Lord God had said so. So he goes with his son to seek a man who is acquainted with thieving. They walk a long time and come into a great forest, where stands a little house with an old woman in it. Hans says, "Do you know of a man who is acquainted with thieving?"

"You can learn that here quite well," says the woman, "my son is a master of it."

So he speaks with the son, and asks if he knows thieving really well? The master-thief says, "I will teach him well. Come back when a year is over, and then if you recognize your son, I will take no payment at all for teaching him; but if you don't know him, you must give me two hundred talkers."

The father goes home again, and the son learns witchcraft and thieving, thoroughly. When the year is over, the father is full of anxiety to know how he is to recognize his son. As he is thus going about in his trouble, he meets a little dwarf, who says, "Man, what ails you, that you are always in such trouble?"

"Oh," says Hans, "a year ago I placed my son with a master-thief who told me I was to come back when the year was over, and that if I did not know my son when I saw him, I was to pay two hundred talkers; but if I did know him I was to pay nothing, and now I am afraid of not knowing him and can't tell where I am to get the money."

Then the dwarf tells him to take a small basket of bread with him, and to stand beneath the chimney. "There on the crossbeam is a basket, out of which a little bird is peeping, and that is your son."

Hans goes there, and throws a little basket full of black bread in front of the basket with the bird in it, and the little bird comes out, and looks up. "Hello, my son, are you here?" says the father, and the son is delighted to see his father, but the master-thief says, "The devil must have prompted you, or how could you have known your son?"

"Father, let us go now," said the youth.

Then the father and son set out homeward. On the way a carriage comes driving by, and the son says to his father, "I will change myself into a large greyhound, and then you can earn a great deal of money by me."

Then the gentleman calls from the carriage, "My man, will you sell your dog?"

"Yes," says the father.

"How much do you want for it?"

"Thirty talkers."

"Eh, man, that is too much, but as it is such a very fine dog I will have it." The gentleman takes it into his carriage, but when they have driven a little farther the dog springs out of the carriage through the window, and goes back to his father, and is no longer a greyhound.

They go home together. Next day there is a fair in the neighboring town, so the youth says to his father, "I will now change myself into a beautiful horse, and you can sell me; but when you have sold me, you must take off my bridle, or I cannot become a man again."

Then the father goes with the horse to the fair, and the master-thief comes and buys the horse for a hundred talkers, but the father forgets, and does not take off the bridle. So the man goes home with the horse, and puts it in the stable.

When the maid crosses the threshold, the horse says, "Take off my bridle, take off my bridle."

Then the maid stands still, and says, "What, can you speak?"

So she goes and takes the bridle off, and the horse becomes a sparrow, and flies out at the door, and the master becomes a sparrow also, and flies after him. Then they come together and cast lots, but the master loses, and changes himself to the water and is a fish. Then the youth also becomes a fish, and they cast lots again, and the master loses. So the master changes himself into a cock, and the youth becomes a fox, and bites the master's head off, and he died and has remained dead to this day.

69. JORINDA AND JORINGEL

There was once an old castle in the middle of a large and thick forest, and in it an old woman who was a witch dwelt all alone. In the daytime she changed herself into a cat or a screech-owl, but in the evening she took her proper shape again as a human being. She could lure wild beasts and birds to her, and then she killed and boiled and roasted them. If anyone came within one hundred paces of the castle he was obliged to stand still, and could not stir from the place until she bade him be free. But whenever an innocent maiden came within this circle, she changed her into a bird, and shut her up in a wickerwork cage, and carried the cage into a room in the castle. She had about seven thousand cages of rare birds in the castle.

Now, there was once a maiden who was called Jorinda, who was fairer than all other girls. She and a handsome youth named Joringel had promised to marry each other. They were still in the days of betrothal, and their greatest happiness was being together. One day in order that they might be able to talk together in quiet they went for a walk in the forest. "Take care," said Joringel, "that you do not go too near the castle."

It was a beautiful evening; the sun shone brightly between the trunks of the trees into the dark green of the forest, and the turtledoves sang mournfully upon the young boughs of the birch trees.

Jorinda wept now and then. She sat down in the sunshine and was sorrowful. Joringel was sorrowful too; they were as sad as if they were about to die. Then they looked around them, and were quite at a loss, for they did not know by which way they should go home. The sun was still half above the mountain and half set.

Joringel looked through the bushes, and saw the old walls of the castle close at hand. He was horror-stricken and filled with deadly fear. Jorinda was singing—

> "My little bird, with the necklace red,
> Sings sorrow, sorrow, sorrow,
> He sings that the dove must soon be dead,
> Sings sorrow, sor—jug, jug, jug."

Joringel looked for Jorinda. She was changed into a nightingale, and sang, "jug, jug, jug." A screech owl with glowing eyes flew three times round about her, and three times cried, "to-whoo, to-whoo, to-whoo!"

Joringel could not move: he stood there like a stone, and could neither weep nor speak, nor move hand or foot.

The sun had now set. The owl flew into the thicket, and directly afterwards there came out of it a crooked old woman, yellow and lean, with large red eyes and a hooked nose, the point of which reached to her chin. She muttered to herself, caught the nightingale, and took it away in her hand.

Joringel could neither speak nor move from the spot; the nightingale was gone. At last the woman came back, and said in a hollow voice, "Greetings, Zachiel. If the moon shines on the cage, Zachiel, let him loose at once."

Then Joringel was freed. He fell on his knees before the woman and begged that she would give him back his Jorinda, but she said that he should never have her again, and went away. He called, he wept, he lamented, but all in vain, "Ah, what is to become of me?"

Joringel went away, and at last came to a strange village; there he kept sheep for a long time. He often walked round and round the castle, but not too near it. At last he dreamt one night that he found a blood-red flower, in the middle of which was a beautiful large pearl; that he picked the flower and went with it to the castle, and that everything he touched with the flower was freed from enchantment; he also dreamt that by means of it he recovered his Jorinda.

In the morning, when he awoke, he began to seek over hill and dale if he could find such a flower. He sought until the ninth day, and then, early in the morning, he found the blood-red flower. In the middle of it there was a large dewdrop, as big as the finest pearl.

Day and night he journeyed with this flower to the castle. When he was within a hundred paces of it he was not held fast, but walked on to the door. Joringel was full of joy; he touched the door with the flower, and it sprang open. He walked in through the courtyard, and listened for the sound of the birds. At last he heard it. He went on and found the room from which it came, and there the witch was feeding the birds in the seven thousand cages.

When she saw Joringel she was angry, very angry, and scolded and spat poison and gall at him, but she could not come within two paces of him. He did not take any notice of her, but went and looked at the cages with the birds; but there were many hundred nightingales, how was he to find his Jorinda again?

Just then he saw the old woman quietly take away a cage with a bird in it, and go towards the door.

Swiftly he sprang towards her, touched the cage with the flower, and also the old woman. She could now no longer bewitch anyone; and Jorinda was standing there, clasping him round the neck, and she was as beautiful as ever!

70. THE THREE SONS OF FORTUNE

A father once called his three sons before him, and he gave to the first a cock, to the second a scythe, and to the third a cat. "I am already aged," said he, "my death is near, and I have wished to take thought for you before my end; money I have not, and what I now give you seems of little worth, but all depends on your making a sensible use of it. Seek out a country where such things are still unknown, and your fortune is made."

After the father's death the eldest went away with his cock, but wherever he came the cock was already known; in every town he saw from a long distance a cock, sitting upon the steeples and turning round with the wind, and in the villages he heard more than one crowing; no one would show any wonder at the creature, so that it did not look as if he would make his fortune by it.

At last, however, it happened that he came to an island where the people knew nothing about cocks, and did not even understand how to divide their time. They certainly knew when it was morning or evening, but at night, if they did not sleep through it, not one of them knew how to find out the time.

"Look!" said he, "What a proud creature! It has a ruby-red crown upon its head, and wears spurs like a knight; it calls you three times during the night, at fixed hours, and when it calls for the last time, the sun soon rises. But if it crows by broad daylight, then take notice, for there will certainly be a change of weather."

The people were well pleased; for a whole night they did not sleep, and listened with great delight as the cock at two, four, and six o'clock, loudly and clearly proclaimed the time. They asked if the creature were for sale, and how much he wanted for it? "About as much gold as an ass can carry," answered he. "A ridiculously small price for such a precious creature!" they cried unanimously, and willingly gave him what he had asked.

When he came home with his wealth his brothers were astonished, and the second said, "Well, I will go forth and see whether I cannot get rid of my scythe as profitably." But it did not look as if he would, for laborers met him everywhere, and they had scythes upon their shoulders as well as he.

At last, however, he chanced upon an island where the people knew nothing of scythes. When the corn was ripe there, they took cannon out to the fields and shot it down. Now this was rather an uncertain affair; many shot right over it, others hit the ears instead of the stems, and shot them away, whereby much was lost, and besides all this, it made a terrible noise. So the man set to work and mowed it down so quietly and quickly that the people opened their mouths with astonishment. They agreed to give him what he wanted for the scythe, and he received a horse laden with as much gold as it could carry.

And now the third brother wanted to take his cat to the right man. He fared just like the others; so long as he stayed on the mainland there was nothing to be done. Every place had cats, and there were so many of them that newborn kittens were generally drowned in the ponds.

At last he sailed over to an island, and it luckily happened that no cats had ever yet been seen there, and that the mice had got the upper hand so much that they danced upon the tables and benches whether the master were at home or not. The people complained bitterly of the plague; the King himself in his palace did not know how to secure himself against them; mice squeaked in every corner, and gnawed whatever they could lay hold of with their teeth. But now the cat began her chase, and soon cleared a couple of rooms, and the people begged the King to buy the wonderful beast for the country. The King willingly gave what was asked, which was a mule laden with gold and jewels, and the third brother came home with the greatest treasure of all.

The cat made herself merry with the mice in the royal palace, and killed so many that they could not be counted. At last she grew warm with the work and thirsty, so she stood still, lifted up her head and cried, "Mew! Mew!"

When they heard this strange cry, the King and all his people were frightened, and in their terror ran all at once out of the palace. Then the King took counsel what was best to be done; at last it was determined to send a herald to the cat, and demand that she should leave the palace, or if not, she was to expect that force would be used against her. The councilors said, "We would rather let ourselves be plagued with the mice, for to that misfortune we are accustomed, than give up our lives to such a monster as this."

A noble youth, therefore, was sent to ask the cat "whether she would peaceably quit the castle?" But the cat, whose thirst had become still greater, merely answered, "Mew! Mew!"

The youth understood her to say, "Most certainly not! Most certainly not!" and took this answer to the King.

"Then," said the councilors, "she shall yield to force." Cannon were brought out, and the palace was soon in flames. When the fire reached the room where the cat was sitting, she sprang safely out of the window; but the besiegers did not leave off until the whole palace was shot down to the ground.

71. HOW SIX MEN GOT ON IN THE WORLD

There was once a man who understood all kinds of arts; he served in war, and behaved well and bravely, but when the war was over he received his dismissal, and three farthings for his expenses on the way. "Stop," said he, "I shall not be content with this. If I can only meet with the right people, the King will have yet to give me all the treasure of the country."

Then full of anger he went into the forest, and saw a man standing there who had plucked up six trees as if they were blades of corn. He said to him, "Will you be my servant and go with me?"

"Yes," he answered, "but, first, I will take this little bundle of sticks home to my mother," and he took one of the trees, and wrapped it round the five others, lifted the bundle on his back, and carried it away.

Then he returned and went with his master, who said, "We two ought to be able to get through the world very well," and when they had walked on for a short while they found a hunter who was kneeling, had shouldered his gun, and was about to fire. The master said to him, "Hunter, what are you going to shoot?"

He answered, "Two miles from here a fly is sitting on the branch of an oak tree, and I want to shoot its left eye out."

"Oh, come with me," said the man, "if we three are together, we certainly ought to be able to get on in the world!"

The hunter was ready, and went with him, and they came to seven windmills whose sails were turning round with great speed, and yet no wind was blowing either on the right or the left, and no leaf was stirring. Then said the man, "I know not what is driving the windmills, not a breath of air is stirring," and he went onwards with his servants, and when they had walked two miles they saw a man sitting on a tree who was shutting one nostril, and blowing out of the other.

"Good gracious! what are you doing up there?"

He answered, "Two miles from here are seven windmills; look, I am blowing them till they turn round."

"Oh, come with me," said the man. "If we four are together, we shall carry the whole world before us!"

Then the blower came down and went with him, and after a while they saw a man who was standing on one leg and had taken off the other, and laid it beside him. Then the master said, "You have arranged things very comfortably to have a rest."

"I am a runner," he replied, "and to stop myself running far too fast, I have taken off one of my legs, for if I run with both, I go quicker than any bird can fly."

"Oh, go with me. If we five are together, we shall carry the whole world before us."

So he went with them, and it was not long before they met a man who wore a cap, but had put it over just one ear. Then the master said to him, "Gracefully, gracefully, don't stick your cap on one ear, you look just like a tom-fool!"

"I must not wear it otherwise," said he, "for if I set my hat straight, a terrible frost comes on, and all the birds in the air are frozen, and drop dead on the ground."

"Oh, come with me," said the master. "If we six are together, we can carry the whole world before us."

Now the six came to a town where the King had proclaimed that whoever ran a race with his daughter and won the victory, should be her husband, but whoever lost it, must lose his head. Then the man presented himself and said, "I will, however, let my servant run for me."

The King replied, "Then his life also must be staked, so that his head and yours are both set on the victory."

When that was settled and made secure, the man buckled the other leg on the runner, and said to him, "Now be nimble, and help us to win." It was fixed that the one who was first to bring some water from a far distant well was to be the victor. The runner received a pitcher, and the King's daughter one too, and they began to run at the same time, but in an instant, when the King's daughter had got a very little way, the people who were looking on could see no more of the runner, and it was just as if the wind had whistled by. In a short time he reached the well, filled his pitcher with water, and turned back. Halfway home, however, he was overcome with fatigue, and set down his pitcher, lay down, and fell asleep. He had, however, made a pillow of a horse's skull which was lying on the ground, in order that he might lie uncomfortably, and soon wake up again.

In the meantime the King's daughter, who could also run very well, quite as well as any ordinary mortal can, had reached the well, and was hurrying back with her pitcher full of water, and when she saw the runner lying there asleep, she was glad and said, "My rival is delivered over into my hands," emptied his pitcher, and ran on. And now all would have been lost if by good luck the hunter had not been standing at the top of the castle, and had not seen everything with his sharp eyes.

Then said he, "The King's daughter shall still not prevail against us," and he loaded his gun, and shot so cleverly, that he shot the horse's skull away from under the runner's head without hurting him. Then the runner awoke, leapt up, and saw that his pitcher was empty, and that the King's daughter was already far in advance. He did not lose heart, however, but ran back to the well with his pitcher, again drew some water, and was at home again, ten minutes before the King's daughter. "Look!" said he, "I have barely stretched my legs till now, it did not deserve to be called running before."

But it pained the King, and still more his daughter, that she should be carried off by a common disbanded soldier like that; so they took counsel with each other how to get rid of him and his companions. Then said the King to her, "I have thought of a way; don't be afraid, they shall not come back again." And he said to them, "You shall now make merry together, and eat and drink," and he conducted them to a room which had a floor of iron, and the doors also were of iron, and the windows were guarded with iron bars. There was a table in the room covered with delicious food, and the King said to them, "Go in, and enjoy yourselves."

And when they were inside, he ordered the doors to be shut and bolted. Then he sent for the cook, and commanded him to make a fire under the room until the iron became red-hot. This the cook did, and the six who were sitting at the table began to feel quite warm, and they thought the heat was caused by the food; but as it became still greater, and they wanted to get out, and found that the doors and windows were bolted, they became aware that the King must have an evil intention, and wanted to suffocate them.

"He shall not succeed, however," said the one with the cap. "I will cause a frost to come, that shall make the fire feel ashamed, and creep away." Then he put his cap on straight, and immediately there came such a frost that all heat disappeared, and the food on the dishes began to freeze. When an hour or two had passed by, and the King believed that they had perished in the heat, he had the doors opened to see them himself. But when the doors were opened, all six were standing there, alive and well, and said that they should very much like to get out to warm themselves, for the very food was fast frozen to the dishes with the cold.

Then, full of anger, the King went down to the cook, scolded him, and asked why he had not done what he had been ordered to do. But the cook replied, "There is heat enough there, just look yourself." Then the King saw that a fierce fire was burning under the iron room, and perceived that there was no getting the better of the six in this way.

Again the King considered how to get rid of his unpleasant guests, and had their chief brought and said, "If you will take gold and renounce my daughter, you shall have as much as you will."

"Oh, yes, Lord King," he answered, "give me as much as my servant can carry, and I will not ask for your daughter."

At this the King was satisfied, and the other continued, "In fourteen days, I will come and fetch it." Then he summoned together all the tailors in the whole kingdom, and they were to sit for fourteen days and sew a sack. And when it was ready, the strong one who could tear up trees had to take it on his back, and go with it to the King.

Then said the King, "Who can that strong fellow be who is carrying a bundle of linen on his back that is as big as a house?" and he was alarmed and said, "What a lot of gold he can carry away!"

Then he commanded a ton of gold to be brought; it took sixteen of his strongest men to carry it, but the strong one snatched it up in one hand, put it in his sack, and said, "Why don't you bring more at the same time? That hardly covers the bottom!" Then, little by little, the King had all his treasure brought there, and the strong one pushed it into the sack, and still the sack was not half full with it.

"Bring more," cried he, "these few crumbs don't fill it." Then seven thousand carts with gold had to be gathered together in the whole kingdom, and the strong one thrust them into his sack with the oxen still harnessed to them. "I will not look too closely," said he, "but will just take what comes, so long as the sack is full." When all that was inside, there was still room for a great deal more; then he said, "I will just make an end of this; I will tie up the sack even though it is not full." So he took it on his back, and went away with his comrades.

When the King now saw how one single man was carrying away the entire wealth of the country, he became enraged, and bade his horsemen mount and pursue the six, and ordered them to take the sack away from the strong one. Two regiments speedily overtook the six, and called out, "You are prisoners, put down the sack with the gold, or you will all be cut to pieces!"

"What say you?" cried the blower, "That we are prisoners! Rather than that should happen, all of you shall dance about in the air." And he closed one nostril, and with the other blew on the two regiments. Then they were driven away from each other, and carried into the blue sky over all the mountains, one here, the other there.

One sergeant cried for mercy; he had nine wounds, and was a brave fellow who did not deserve ill treatment. The blower stopped a little so that he came down without injury, and then the blower said to him, "Now go home to your King, and tell him he had better send some more horsemen, and I will blow them all into the air."

When the King was informed of this he said, "Let the rascals go. They have the best of it." Then the six carried the riches home, divided it amongst them, and lived in content until their death.

72. THE WOLF AND THE MAN

Once on a time the fox was talking to the wolf about the strength of man; how no animal could withstand him, and how all were obliged to employ cunning in order to preserve themselves from him. Then the wolf answered, "If I had but the chance of seeing a man for once, I would set on him all the same."

"I can help you to do that," said the fox. "Come to me early tomorrow morning, and I will show you one."

The wolf presented himself early, and the fox took him out on the road by which the hunters went daily. First came an old discharged soldier. "Is that a man?" inquired the wolf.

"No," answered the fox, "that *was* one."

Afterwards came a little boy who was going to school. "Is that a man?"

"No, that is going to be one."

At length came a hunter with his double-barreled gun at his back, and knife by his side. Said the fox to the wolf, "Look, there comes a man, you must attack him, but I will take myself off to my hole."

The wolf then rushed on the man. When the hunter saw him he said, "It is a pity that I have not loaded with a bullet," aimed, and fired his small shot in his face. The wolf made a very wry face, but did not let himself be frightened, and attacked him again, on which the hunter gave him the second barrel. The wolf swallowed his pain, and rushed on the hunter, but he drew out his bright knife, and gave him a few cuts with it right and left, so that, bleeding everywhere, he ran howling back to the fox.

"Well, brother wolf," said the fox, "how have you got on with man?"

"Ah!" replied the wolf, "I never imagined the strength of man to be what it is! First, he took a stick from his shoulder, and blew into it, and then something flew into my face which tickled me terribly; then he breathed once more into the stick, and it flew into my nose like lightning and hail; when I was quite close, he drew a white rib out of his side, and he beat me with it till I was all but left lying dead."

"See what a braggart you are!" said the fox. "You have overreached yourself. You throw your hatchet so far that you cannot fetch it back again!"

73. THE WOLF AND THE FOX

The wolf had the fox with him, and whatever the wolf wished, that the fox was compelled to do, for he was weaker, and he would gladly have been rid of his master. It chanced that once as they were going through the forest, the wolf said, "Red fox, get me something to eat, or else I will eat you yourself."

Then the fox answered, "I know a farmyard where there are two young lambs; if you are inclined, we will fetch one of them."

That suited the wolf, and they went there, and the fox stole the little lamb, took it to the wolf, and went away. The wolf devoured it, but was not satisfied with one; he wanted the other as well, and went to get it. Since, however, he did it so awkwardly, the mother of the little lamb heard him, and began to cry out terribly, and to bleat so that the farmer came running there. They found the wolf, and beat him so mercilessly, that he went to the fox limping and howling. "You have misled me finely," said he, "I wanted to fetch the other lamb, and the country folks surprised me, and have beaten me to a jelly."

The fox replied, "Why are you such a glutton?"

Next day they again went into the country, and the greedy wolf once more said, "Red fox, get me something to eat, or I will eat you yourself."

Then answered the fox, "I know a farmhouse where the wife is baking pancakes tonight; we will get some of them for ourselves." They went there, and the fox slipped round the house, and peeped and sniffed about until he discovered where the dish was, and then drew down six pancakes and carried them to the wolf. "There is something for you to eat," said he to him, and then went his way.

The wolf swallowed down the pancakes in an instant, and said, "They make one want more," and went back and tore the whole dish down so that it broke in pieces. This made such a great noise that the woman came out, and when she saw the wolf she called the people, who hurried there, and beat him as long as their sticks would hold together, till with two lame legs, and howling loudly, he got back to the fox in the forest. "How abominably you have misled me!" cried he, "The peasants caught me, and tanned my skin for me."

But the fox replied, "Why are you such a glutton?"

On the third day, when they were out together, and the wolf could only limp along painfully, he again said, "Red fox, get me something to eat, or I will eat you yourself."

The fox answered, "I know a man who has been killing, and the salted meat is lying in a barrel in the cellar; we will get that."

Said the wolf, "I will go when you do, that you may help me if I am not able to get away."

"I am willing," said the fox, and showed him the bypaths and ways by which at length they reached the cellar.

There was meat in abundance, and the wolf attacked it instantly and thought, "There is plenty of time before I need leave off!" The fox liked it also, but looked about everywhere, and often ran to the hole by which they had come in, and tried if his body was still thin enough to slip through it. The wolf said, "Dear fox, tell me why you are running here and there so much, and jumping in and out?"

"I must see that no one is coming," replied the crafty fellow. "Don't eat too much!"

Then said the wolf, "I shall not leave until the barrel is empty." In the meantime the farmer, who had heard the noise of the fox's jumping, came into the cellar. When the fox saw him he was out of the hole in one bound. The wolf wanted to follow him, but he had made himself so fat with eating that he could no longer get through, but stuck fast. Then came the farmer with a cudgel and struck him dead, but the fox bounded into the forest, glad to be rid of the old glutton.

74. *THE FOX AND HIS COUSIN*

The wolf gave birth to a cub and invited the fox to be godfather. "After all, he is a near relative of ours," said she, "he has a good understanding, and much talent; he can instruct my little son, and help him forward in the world."

The fox, too, appeared quite honest, and said, "Dear cousin, I thank you for the honor which you are doing me; I will, however, conduct myself in such a way that you shall be repaid for it." He enjoyed himself at the feast, and made merry; afterwards he said, "Dear cousin wolf, it is our duty to take care of the child, it must have good food that it may be strong. I know a farm from which we might fetch a nice morsel."

The wolf was pleased with the ditty, and she went out with the fox to the farmyard. He pointed out the barn from afar, and said, "You will be able to creep in there without being seen, and in the meantime I will look about on the other side to see if I can pick up a chicken."

He, however, did not go there, but sat down at the entrance to the forest, stretched his legs and rested. The wolf crept into the stable. A dog was lying there, and it made such a noise that the peasants came running out, caught cousin wolf, and poured a strong burning mixture, which had been prepared for washing, over her skin. At last she escaped, and dragged herself outside. There lay the fox, who pretended to be full of complaints, and said, "Ah, dear cousin wolf, how ill I have fared, the peasants have fallen on me, and have broken every limb I have; if you do not want me to lie where I am and perish, you must carry me away." The wolf herself was only able to go away slowly, but she was in such concern about the fox that she took him on her back, and slowly carried him perfectly safe and sound to her house.

Then the fox cried to her, "Farewell, dear cousin, may the roasting you have had do you good," laughed heartily at her, and bounded off.

75. *THE FOX AND THE CAT*

It happened that the cat met the fox in a forest, and as she thought to herself, "He is clever and full of experience, and much esteemed in the world," she spoke to him in a friendly way. "Good day, dear Mr. Fox, how are you? How is all with you? How are you getting through this dear season?"

The fox, full of all kinds of arrogance, looked at the cat from head to foot, and for a long time did not know whether he would give any answer or not. At last he said, "Oh, you wretched whisker-cleaner, you piebald fool, you hungry mouse-hunter, what can you be thinking of? Do you venture to ask how I am getting on? What have you learnt? How many arts do you understand?"

"I understand but one," replied the cat, modestly.

"What art is that?" asked the fox.

"When the hounds are following me, I can spring into a tree and save myself."

"Is that all?" said the fox. "I am master of a hundred arts, and also have a sackful of cunning. You make me sorry for you; come with me, I will teach you how people get away from the hounds."

Just then came a hunter with four dogs. The cat sprang nimbly up a tree, and sat down on top of it, where the branches and foliage quite concealed her. "Open your sack of cunning, Mr. Fox, open your sack," cried the cat to him, but the dogs had already seized him, and were holding him fast. "Ah, Mr. Fox," cried the cat. "You with your hundred arts are left in the lurch! Had you been able to climb like me, you would not have lost your life."

76. *THE PINK*

There was once on a time a Queen to whom God had given no children. Every morning she went into the garden and prayed to God in heaven to bestow on her a son or a daughter. Then an angel from heaven came to her and said, "Be at rest, you shall have a son with the power of wishing, so that whatever in the world he wishes for, that shall he have."

Then she went to the King, and told him the joyful tidings, and when the time came she gave birth to a son, and the King was filled with gladness. Every morning she went with the child to the garden where the wild beasts were kept, and washed herself there in a clear stream. It happened one day when the child was a little older, that it was lying in her arms and she fell asleep. Then came the old cook, who knew that the child had the power of wishing, and stole it away, and he took a hen, and cut it in pieces, and dropped some of its blood on the Queen's apron and on her dress. Then he carried the child away to a secret place, where a nurse was obliged to suckle it, and he ran to the King and accused the Queen of having allowed her child to be taken from her by the wild beasts. When the King saw the blood on her apron, he believed this, fell into such a passion that he ordered a high tower to be built, in which neither sun nor moon could be seen, and had his wife put into it, and walled up. Here she was to stay for seven years without meat or drink, and die of hunger. But God sent two angels from heaven in the shape of white doves, which flew to her twice a day, and carried her food until the seven years were over.

The cook, however, thought to himself, "If the child has the power of wishing, and I am here, he might very easily get me into trouble." So he left the palace and went to the boy, who was already big enough to speak, and said to him, "Wish for a beautiful palace for yourself with a garden, and all else that pertains to it." Scarcely were the words out of the boy's mouth, when everything was there that he had wished for. After a while the cook said to him, "It is not good for you to be so alone, wish for a pretty girl as a companion." Then the King's son wished for one, and she immediately stood before him, and was more beautiful than any painter could have painted her. The two played together, and loved each other with all their hearts, and the old cook went out hunting like a nobleman.

The thought, however, occurred to him that the King's son might someday wish to be with his father, and thus bring him into great peril. So he went out and took the maiden aside, and said, "Tonight when the boy is asleep, go to his bed and plunge this knife into his heart, and bring me his heart and tongue, and if you do not do it, you shall lose your life."

Thereupon he went away, and when he returned next day she had not done it, and said, "Why should I shed the blood of an innocent boy who has never harmed anyone?"

The cook once more said, "If you do not do it, it shall cost you your own life."

When he had gone away, she had a little deer brought to her, and ordered her to be killed, and took her heart and tongue, and laid them on a plate, and when she saw the old man coming, she said to the boy, "Lie down in your bed, and draw the covers over you."

Then the wicked wretch came in and said, "Where are the boy's heart and tongue?"

The girl reached the plate to him, but the King's son threw off the quilt, and said, "You old sinner, why did you want to kill me? Now I will pronounce your sentence. You shall become a black poodle and have a gold collar round your neck, and shall eat burning coals, till the flames burst forth from your throat." And when he had spoken these words, the old man was changed into a poodle dog, and had a gold collar round his neck, and the cooks were ordered to bring up some live coals, and these he ate, until the flames broke forth from his throat.

The King's son remained there a short while longer, and he thought of his mother, and wondered if she were still alive. At length he said to the maiden, "I will go home to my own country; if you will go with me, I will provide for you."

"Ah," she replied, "the way is so long, and what shall I do in a strange land where I am unknown?" As she did not seem quite willing, and as they could not be parted from each other, he wished that she might be changed into a beautiful pink, and took her with him.

Then he went away to his own country, and the poodle had to run after him. He went to the tower in which his mother was confined, and as it was so high, he wished for a ladder which would reach up to the very top. Then he mounted up and looked inside, and cried, "Beloved mother, Lady Queen, are you still alive, or are you dead?"

She answered, "I have just eaten, and am still satisfied," for she thought the angels were there.

Said he, "I am your dear son, whom the wild beasts were said to have torn from your arms; but I am alive still, and will speedily rescue you."

Then he descended again, and went to his father, and had himself announced as a strange hunter, and asked if he could enter his service. The King said yes, if he was skillful and could get game for him, he should come join him, but that deer had never taken up their quarters in any part of the district or country. Then the hunter promised to procure as much game for him as he could possibly use at the royal table. So he summoned all the hunters together, and bade them go out into the forest with him. And he went with them and made them form a great circle, open at one end where he stationed himself, and began to wish. Two hundred deer and more came running inside the circle at once, and the hunters shot them. Then they were all placed on sixty country wagons, and driven home to the King, and for once he was able to deck his table with game, after having had none at all for years.

Now the King felt great joy at this, and commanded that his entire household should eat with him next day, and made a great feast. When they were all assembled together, he said to the hunter, "As you are so clever, you shall sit by me."

He replied, "Lord King, your majesty must excuse me, I am a poor hunter."

But the King insisted on it, and said, "You shall sit by me," until he did it.

While he was sitting there, he thought of his dearest mother, and wished that one of the King's principal servants would begin to speak of her, and would ask how it was faring with the Queen in the tower, and if she were alive still, or had perished. Hardly had he formed the wish than the marshal began, and said, "Your majesty, we live joyously here, but how is the Queen living in the tower? Is she still alive, or has she died?"

But the King replied, "She let my dear son be torn to pieces by wild beasts; I will not have her named."

Then the hunter arose and said, "Gracious lord father, she is alive still, and I am her son, and I was not carried away by wild beasts, but by that wretch the old cook, who tore me from her arms when she was asleep, and sprinkled her apron with the blood of a chicken." Thereupon he took the dog with the golden collar, and said, "That is the wretch!" and caused live coals to be brought, and these the dog was compelled to devour before the sight of all, until flames burst forth from its throat. At this the hunter asked the King if he would like to see the dog in his true shape, and wished him back into the form of the cook, in which he stood immediately, with his white apron, and his knife by his side. When the King saw him he fell into a passion, and ordered him to be cast into the deepest dungeon.

Then the hunter spoke further and said, "Father, will you see the maiden who brought me up so tenderly and who was afterwards to murder me, but did not do it, though her own life depended on it?"

The King replied, "Yes, I would like to see her."

The son said, "Most gracious father, I will show her to you in the form of a beautiful flower," and he thrust his hand into his pocket and brought forth the pink, and placed it on the royal table, and it was so beautiful that the King had never seen one to equal it. Then the son said, "Now I will show her to you in her own form," and wished that she might become a maiden, and she stood there looking so beautiful that no painter could have made her look more so.

And the King sent two waiting-maids and two attendants into the tower, to fetch the Queen and bring her to the royal table. But when she was led in she ate nothing, and said, "The gracious and merciful God who has supported me in the tower, will speedily release me." She lived three days more, and then died happily, and when she was buried, the two white doves which had brought her food to the tower, and were angels of heaven, followed her body and seated themselves on her grave. The aged King ordered the cook to be torn in four pieces, but grief consumed the King's own heart, and he soon died. His son married the beautiful maiden whom he had brought with him as a flower in his pocket, and whether they are still alive or not, is known to God.

77. CLEVER GRETEL

There was once a cook named Gretel, who wore shoes with red heels, and when she walked out with them on, she turned herself this way and that, and thought, "You certainly are a pretty girl!" And when she came home she drank, in her gladness of heart, a gulp of wine, and as wine excites a desire to eat, she tasted the best of whatever she was cooking until she was satisfied, and said, "The cook must know what the food is like."

It came to pass that the master one day said to her, "Gretel, there is a guest coming this evening; prepare me two fowls very daintily."

"I will see to it, master," answered Gretel. She killed two fowls, scalded them, plucked them, put them on the spit, and towards evening set them before the fire, that they might roast. The fowls began to turn brown, and were nearly ready, but the guest had not yet arrived.

Then Gretel called out to her master, "If the guest does not come, I must take the fowls away from the fire, but it will be a sin and a shame if they are not eaten directly, when they are juiciest."

The master said, "I will run myself, and fetch the guest."

When the master had turned his back, Gretel laid the spit with the fowls on one side, and thought, "Standing so long by the fire there, makes one hot and thirsty; who knows when they will come? Meanwhile, I will run into the cellar, and take a drink." She ran down, took a jug, said, "God bless it to your use, Gretel," and took a good drink, and took yet another hearty drink.

Then she went and put the fowls down again to the fire, basted them, and drove the spit merrily round. But as the roast meat smelled so good, Gretel thought, "Something might be wrong, it ought to be tasted!" She touched it with her finger, and said, "Ah! How good fowls are! It certainly is a sin and a shame that they are not eaten directly!" She ran to the window, to see if the master was not coming with his guest, but she saw no one, and went back to the fowls and thought, "One of the wings is burning! I had better take it off and eat it." So she cut it off, ate it, and enjoyed it, and once she had, she thought, "The other must go down too, or else master will observe that something is missing." When the two wings were eaten, she went and looked for her master, and did not see him.

It suddenly occurred to her, "Who knows? They are perhaps not coming at all, and have turned in somewhere." Then she said, "Hallo, Gretel, enjoy yourself, one fowl has been cut into, take another drink, and eat it up entirely; when it is eaten you will have some peace, why should God's good gifts be spoiled?" So she ran into the cellar again, took an enormous drink and ate up the one chicken in great glee. When one of the chickens was swallowed down, and still her master did not come, Gretel looked at the other and said, "Where one is, the other should be likewise, the two go together; what's right for the one is right for the other; I think if I were to take another drink it would do me no harm." So she took another hearty drink, and let the second chicken rejoin the first.

While she was just in the best of the eating, her master came and cried, "Hurry up, Gretel, the guest is coming directly after me!"

"Yes, sir, I will soon serve up," answered Gretel. Meantime the master looked to see that the table was properly laid, and took the great knife, with which he was going to carve the chickens, and sharpened it on the steps. Presently the guest came, and knocked politely and courteously at the door. Gretel ran, and looked to see who was there, and when she saw the guest, she put her finger to her lips and said, "Hush! Hush! Get away as quickly as you can, if my master catches you it will be bad for you; he certainly did ask you to supper, but his intention is to cut off your two ears. Just listen how he is sharpening the knife for it!"

The guest heard the sharpening, and hurried down the steps again as fast as he could. Gretel was not idle; she ran screaming to her master, and cried, "You have invited a fine guest!"

"Eh, why, Gretel? What do you mean by that?"

"Yes," said she, "he has taken the chickens which I was just going to serve up, off the dish, and has run away with them!"

"That's a nice trick!" said her master, and lamented the fine chickens. "If he had but left me one, so that something remained for me to eat." He called to him to stop, but the guest pretended not to hear. Then he ran after him with the knife still in his hand, crying, "Just one, just one," meaning that the guest should leave him just one chicken, and not take both. The guest, however, thought no otherwise than that he was to give up one of his ears, and ran as if fire were burning under him, in order to take them both home with him.

78. THE OLD MAN AND HIS GRANDSON

There was once a very old man, whose eyes had become dim, his ears dull of hearing, his knees trembled, and when he sat at dinner he could hardly hold the spoon, and spilled the broth upon the tablecloth or let it run out of his mouth. His son and his son's wife were disgusted at this, so the old grandfather at last had to sit in the corner behind the stove, and they gave him his food in an earthenware bowl, and not even enough of it. And he used to look towards the table with his eyes full of tears. Once, too, his trembling hands could not hold the bowl, and it fell to the ground and broke. The young wife scolded him, but he said nothing and only sighed. Then they bought him a wooden bowl for a few half-pence, out of which he had to eat.

They were once sitting thus when the little grandson of four years old began to gather together some bits of wood upon the ground. "What are you doing there?" asked the father.

"I am making a little trough," answered the child, "for father and mother to eat out of when I am big."

The man and his wife looked at each other for a while, and presently began to cry. Then they took the old grandfather to the table, and from then on always let him eat with them, and likewise said nothing if he did spill a little of anything.

79. *THE WATER NIXIE*

A little brother and sister were once playing by a well, and while they were thus playing, they both fell in. A water nixie lived down below, who said, "Now I have got you, now you shall work hard for me!" and carried them off with her. She gave the girl dirty tangled flax to spin, and she had to fetch water in a bucket with a hole in it, and the boy had to hew down a tree with a blunt axe, and they got nothing to eat but dumplings as hard as stones. Then at last the children became so impatient, that they waited until one Sunday, when the nixie was at church, and ran away. But when church was over, the nixie saw that the birds had flown, and followed them with great strides. The children saw her from afar, and the girl threw a brush behind her which formed an immense hill of bristles, with thousands and thousands of spikes, over which the nixie was forced to scramble with great difficulty; at last, however, she got over. When the children saw this, the boy threw behind him a comb which made a great hill of combs with a thousand times a thousand teeth, but the nixie managed to keep herself steady on them, and at last crossed over that. Then the girl threw behind her a looking-glass which formed a hill of mirrors, and was so slippery that it was impossible for the nixie to cross it. Then she thought, "I will go home quickly and fetch my axe, and cut the hill of glass in half." Long before she returned, however, and had hewn through the glass, the children had escaped to a great distance, and the water nixie was obliged to retreat to her well again.

80. THE DEATH OF THE
LITTLE HEN

Once upon a time the little hen went with the little cock to the nuthill, and they agreed together that whoever of them found a kernel of a nut should share it with the other. Then the hen found a large, large nut, but said nothing about it, intending to eat the kernel herself. The kernel, however, was so large that she could not swallow it, and it remained sticking in her throat, so that she was alarmed lest she should be choked. Then she cried, "Cock, I entreat you to run as fast you can, and fetch me some water, or I shall choke."

The little cock did run as fast as he could to the spring, and said, "Stream, you are to give me some water; the little hen is lying on the nuthill, and she has swallowed a large nut, and is choking."

The well answered, "First run to the bride, and get her to give you some red silk."

The little cock ran to the bride and said, "Bride, you are to give me some red silk; I want to give red silk to the well, the well is to give me some water, I am to take the water to the little hen who is lying on the nuthill and has swallowed a great kernel, and is choking on it."

The bride answered, "First run and bring me my little wreath which is hanging to a willow." So the little cock ran to the willow, and drew the wreath from the branch and took it to the bride, and the bride gave him some water for it. Then the little cock took the water to the hen, but when he got there the hen had choked in the meantime, and lay there dead and motionless. Then the cock was so distressed that he cried aloud, and every animal came to lament the little hen, and six mice built a little carriage to carry her to her grave, and when the carriage was ready they harnessed themselves to it, and the cock drove.

On the way, however, they met the fox, who said, "Where are you going, little cock?"

"I am going to bury my little hen."

"May I drive with you?"

"Yes, but seat yourself at the back of the carriage, for in the front my little horses could not drag you." Then the fox seated himself at the back, and after that the wolf, the bear, the stag, the lion, and all the beasts of the forest did the same. Then the procession went onwards, and they reached the stream.

"How are we to get over?" said the little cock.

A straw was lying by the stream, and it said, "I will lay myself across, and you shall drive over me." But when the six mice came to the bridge, the straw slipped and fell into the water, and the six mice all fell in and were drowned.

Then they were again in difficulty, and a coal came and said, "I am large enough, I will lay myself across and you shall drive over me." So the coal also laid itself across the water, but unfortunately just touched it a little, on which the coal hissed, was extinguished and died.

When a stone saw that, it took pity on the little cock, wished to help him, and laid itself over the water. Then the cock drew the carriage himself, but when he got it over and reached the other shore with the dead hen, and was about to draw over the others who were sitting behind as well, there were too many of them, the carriage ran back, and they all fell into the water together, and were drowned. Then the little cock was left alone with the dead hen, and dug a grave for her and laid her in it, and made a mound above it, on which he sat down and fretted until he died too, and then everyone was dead.

81. BROTHER LUSTIG

There was once a great war, and when it came to an end, many soldiers were discharged. Then Brother Lustig also received his dismissal, and besides that, nothing but a small loaf of bread, and four kreuzers in money, with which he departed. St. Peter had, however, placed himself in his way in the shape of a poor beggar, and when Brother Lustig came up, he begged alms of him. Brother Lustig replied, "Dear beggar, what am I to give you? I have been a soldier, and have received my dismissal, and have nothing but this little loaf of bread, and four kreuzers of money; when that is gone, I shall have to beg as well as you. Still I will give you something." Thereupon he divided the loaf into four parts, and gave the apostle one of them, and a kreuzer likewise. St. Peter thanked him, went onwards, and threw himself again in the soldier's way as a beggar, but in another shape; and when he came up begged a gift of him as before. Brother Lustig spoke as he had done before, and again gave him a quarter of the loaf and one kreuzer. St. Peter thanked him, and went onwards, but for the third time placed himself in another shape as a beggar on the road, and spoke to Brother Lustig. Brother Lustig gave him also the third quarter of bread and the third kreuzer. St. Peter thanked him, and Brother Lustig went onwards, and had but a quarter of the loaf, and one kreuzer. With that he went into an inn, ate the bread, and ordered one kreuzer's worth of beer. When he had had it, he journeyed onwards, and then St. Peter, who had assumed the appearance of a discharged soldier, met and spoke to him thus: "Good day, comrade, can you not give me a bit of bread, and a kreuzer to get a drink?"

"Where am I to procure it?" answered Brother Lustig; "I have been discharged, and I got nothing but a loaf of bread and four kreuzers in money. I met three beggars on the road, and I gave each of them a quarter of my bread, and one kreuzer. The last quarter I ate in the inn, and had a drink with the last kreuzer. Now my pockets are empty, and if you also have nothing we can go a-begging together."

"No," answered St. Peter, "we need not do that. I know a little about medicine, and I will soon earn as much as I require by that."

"Indeed," said Brother Lustig, "I know nothing of that, so I must go and beg alone."

"Just come with me," said St. Peter, "and if I earn anything, you shall have half of it."

"All right," said Brother Lustig, so they went away together.

Then they came to a peasant's house inside which they heard loud lamentations and cries; so they went in, and there the husband was lying sick unto death, and very near his end, and his wife was crying and weeping quite loudly. "Stop that howling and crying," said St. Peter, "I will make the man well again," and he took a salve out of his pocket, and healed the sick man in a moment, so that he could get up, and was in perfect health. In great delight the man and his wife said, "How can we reward you? What shall we give you?"

But St. Peter would take nothing, and the more the peasant folks offered him, the more he refused. Brother Lustig, however, nudged St. Peter, and said, "Take something; sure enough we are in need of it."

At length the woman brought a lamb and said to St. Peter that he really must take that, but he would not. Then Brother Lustig gave him a poke in the side, and said, "Do take it, you stupid fool; we are in great want of it!"

Then St. Peter said at last, "Well, I will take the lamb, but I won't carry it; if you will insist on having it, you must carry it."

"That is nothing," said Brother Lustig. "I will easily carry it," and took it on his shoulder. Then they departed and came to a wood, but Brother Lustig had begun to feel the lamb heavy, and he was hungry, so he said to St. Peter, "Look, that's a good place, we might cook the lamb there, and eat it."

"As you like," answered St. Peter, "but I can't have anything to do with the cooking; if you will cook, there is a kettle for you, and in the meantime I will walk about a little until it is ready. You must, however, not begin to eat until I have come back, I will come at the right time."

"Well, go, then," said Brother Lustig, "I understand cookery, I will manage it." Then St. Peter went away, and Brother Lustig killed the lamb, lighted a fire, threw the meat into the kettle, and boiled it. The lamb was, however, quite ready, and the apostle Peter had not come back, so Brother Lustig took it out of the kettle, cut it up, and found the heart.

"That is said to be the best part," said he, and tasted it, but at last he ate it all up.

At length St. Peter returned and said, "You may eat the whole of the lamb yourself, I will only have the heart, give me that."

Then Brother Lustig took a knife and fork, and pretended to look anxiously about amongst the lamb's flesh, but not to be able to find the heart, and at last he said abruptly, "There is none here."

"But where can it be?" said the apostle.

"I don't know," replied Brother Lustig, "but look, what fools we both are, to seek for the lamb's heart, and neither of us to remember that a lamb has no heart!"

"Oh," said St. Peter, "that is something quite new! Every animal has a heart, why is a lamb to have none?"

"No, be assured, my brother," said Brother Lustig, "that a lamb has no heart; just consider it seriously, and then you will see that it really has none."

"Well, it is all right," said St. Peter, "if there is no heart, then I want none of the lamb; you may eat it alone."

"What I can't eat now, I will carry away in my knapsack," said Brother Lustig, and he ate half the lamb, and put the rest in his knapsack.

They went farther, and then St. Peter caused a great stream of water to flow right across their path, and they were obliged to pass through it. Said St. Peter, "You go first."

"No," answered Brother Lustig, "you must go first," and he thought, "if the water is too deep I will stay behind." Then St. Peter strode through it, and the water just reached to his knee. So Brother Lustig began to go through also, but the water grew deeper and reached to his throat. Then he cried, "Brother, help me!"

St. Peter said, "Then will you confess that you have eaten the lamb's heart?"

"No," said he, "I have not eaten it." Then the water grew deeper still and rose to his mouth. "Help me, brother," cried the soldier.

St. Peter said, "Then will you confess that you have eaten the lamb's heart?"

"No," he replied, "I have not eaten it." St. Peter, however, would not let him be drowned, but made the water sink and helped him through it.

Then they journeyed onwards, and came to a kingdom where they heard that the King's daughter lay sick and dying. "Hollo, brother!" said the soldier to St. Peter, "this is a chance for us; if we can heal her we shall be provided for, for life!" But St. Peter was not half quick enough for him, "Come, lift your legs, my dear brother," said he, "that we may get there in time." But St. Peter walked slower and slower, though Brother Lustig did all he could to drive and push him on, and at last they heard that the princess was dead. "Now we are done for!" said Brother Lustig; "that is what comes of your sleepy way of walking!"

"Just be quiet," answered St. Peter, "I can do more than cure sick people; I can bring dead ones to life again."

"Well, if you can do that," said Brother Lustig, "it's all right, but you should earn at least half the Kingdom for us by doing that." Then they went to the royal palace, where everyone was in great grief, but St. Peter told the King that he would restore his daughter to life.

He was taken to her, and said, "Bring me a kettle and some water," and when that was brought, he bade everyone go out, and allowed no one to remain with him but Brother Lustig. Then he cut off all the dead girl's limbs, and threw them in the water, lighted a fire beneath the kettle, and boiled them. And when the flesh had fallen away from the bones, he took out the beautiful white bones, and laid them on a table, and arranged them together in their natural order. When he had done that, he stepped forward and said three times, "In the name of the holy Trinity, dead woman, arise." And at the third time, the princess arose, living, healthy and beautiful. Then the King was in the greatest joy, and said to St. Peter, "Ask for your reward; even if it were half my kingdom, I would give it you."

But St. Peter said, "I want nothing for it."

"Oh, you tomfool!" thought Brother Lustig to himself, and nudged his comrade's side, and said, "Don't be so stupid! If you have no need of anything, I have." St. Peter, however, would have nothing, but as the King saw that the other would very much like to have something, he ordered his treasurer to fill Brother Lustig's knapsack with gold.

Then they went on their way, and when they came to a forest, St. Peter said to Brother Lustig, "Now, we will divide the gold."

"Yes," he replied, "we will." So St. Peter divided the gold, and divided it into three heaps. Brother Lustig thought to himself, "What craze has he got in his head now? He is making three shares, and there are only two of us!"

But St. Peter said, "I have divided it exactly; there is one share for me, one for you, and one for whoever ate the lamb's heart."

"Oh, I ate that!" replied Brother Lustig, and hastily swept up the gold. "You may trust what I say."

"But how can that be true," said St. Peter, "when a lamb has no heart?"

"Nonsense, brother, what can you be thinking of? Lambs have hearts like other animals, why should only they have none?"

"Well, so be it," said St. Peter, "keep the gold to yourself, but I will stay with you no longer; I will go my way alone."

"As you like, dear brother," answered Brother Lustig. "Farewell."

Then St. Peter went a different road, but Brother Lustig thought, "It is a good thing that he has taken himself off, he is certainly a strange saint, after all." Then he had money enough, but did not know how to manage it, squandered it, gave it away, and when some time had gone by, once more had nothing. Then he arrived in a certain country where he heard that a King's daughter was dead. "Oh, ho!" thought he, "That may be a good thing for me; I will bring her to life again, and see that I am paid as I ought to be."

So he went to the King, and offered to raise the dead girl to life again. Now the King had heard that a discharged soldier was traveling about and bringing dead persons to life again, and thought that Brother Lustig was the man; but as he had no confidence in him, he consulted his councilors first, who said that he might give it a trial as his daughter was already dead. Then Brother Lustig ordered water to be brought to him in a kettle, bade everyone go out, cut the limbs off, threw them in the water and lighted a fire beneath, just as he had seen St. Peter do. The water began to boil, the flesh fell off, and then he took the bones out and laid them on the table, but he did not know the order in which to lay them, and placed them all wrong and in confusion. Then he stood before them and said, "In the name of the most holy Trinity, dead maiden, I bid you arise," and he said this thrice, but the bones did not stir. So he said it thrice more, but also in vain: "Confounded girl that you are, get up!" cried he, "Get up, or it shall be even worse for you!"

When he had said that, St. Peter suddenly appeared in his former shape as a discharged soldier; he entered by the window and said, "Godless man, what are you doing? How can the dead maiden arise, when you have thrown about her bones in such confusion?"

"Dear brother, I have done everything to the best of my ability," he answered.

"This once, I will help you out of your difficulty, but one thing I tell you, and that is that if you ever undertake anything of the kind again, it will be the worse for you, and also that you must neither demand nor accept the smallest thing from the King for this!" Thereupon St. Peter laid the bones in their right order, said to the maiden three times, "In the name of the most holy Trinity, dead maiden, arise," and the King's daughter arose, healthy and beautiful as before.

Then St. Peter went away again by the window, and Brother Lustig was rejoiced to find that all had passed off so well, but was very much vexed to think that after all he was not to take anything for it. "I should just like to know," thought he, "what fancy that fellow has got in his head, for what he gives with one hand he takes away with the other. There is no sense whatsoever in it!" Then the King offered Brother Lustig whatever he wished to have, but he did not dare to take anything; however, by hints and cunning, he contrived to make the King order his knapsack to be filled with gold for him, and with that he departed.

When he got out, St. Peter was standing by the door, and said, "Just look what a man you are; did I not forbid you to take anything, and there you have your knapsack full of gold!"

"How can I help that," answered Brother Lustig, "if people will put it in for me?"

"Well, I tell you this, that if you ever set about anything of this kind again you shall suffer for it!"

"Eh, brother, have no fear, now I have money, why should I trouble myself with washing bones?"

"Faith," said St. Peter, "the gold will not last a long time! In order that after this you may never tread in unlawful paths, I will bestow on your knapsack this property, namely, that whatever you wish to have inside it, shall be there. Farewell, you will now never see me again."

"Good-bye," said Brother Lustig, and thought to himself, "I am very glad that you have taken yourself off, you strange fellow; I shall certainly not follow you." But of the magical power which had been bestowed on his knapsack, he thought no more.

Brother Lustig traveled about with his money, and squandered and wasted what he had as before. When at last he had no more than four kreuzers, he passed by an inn and thought, "The money must go," and ordered three kreuzers' worth of wine and one kreuzer's worth of bread for himself. As he was sitting there drinking, the smell of roast goose made its way to his nose. Brother Lustig looked about and peeped, and saw that the host had two geese standing in the oven. Then he remembered that his comrade had said that whatever he wished to have in his knapsack should be there, so he said, "Oh, ho! I must try that with the geese." So he went out, and when he was outside the door, he said, "I wish those two roasted geese out of the oven and in my knapsack," and when he had said that, he unbuckled it and looked in, and there they were inside it. "Ah, that's right!" said he, "Now I am a made man!" and went away to a meadow and took out the roast meat.

When he was in the middle of his meal, two journeymen came up and looked at the second goose, which was not yet touched, with hungry eyes. Brother Lustig thought to himself, "One is enough for me," and called the two men up and said, "Take the goose, and eat it to my health." They thanked him, and went with it to the inn, ordered themselves a half bottle of wine and a loaf, took out the goose which had been given them, and began to eat. The hostess saw them and said to her husband, "Those two are eating a goose; just look and see if it is not one of ours, out of the oven."

The landlord ran over, and behold the oven was empty! "What!" cried he, "You thievish crew, you want to eat goose as cheap as that? Pay for it this moment; or I will wash you well with green hazel-sap."

The two said, "We are no thieves, a discharged soldier gave us the goose, outside there in the meadow."

"You shall not throw dust in my eyes that way! The soldier was here but he went out by the door, like an honest fellow. I looked after him myself; you are the thieves and shall pay!" But as they could not pay, he took a stick, and cudgeled them out of the house.

Brother Lustig went his way and came to a place where there was a magnificent castle, and not far from it a wretched inn. He went to the inn and asked for a night's lodging, but the landlord turned him away, and said, "There is no more room here, the house is full of noble guests."

"It surprises me that they should come to you and not go to that splendid castle," said Brother Lustig.

"Ah, indeed," replied the host, "but it is no slight matter to sleep there for a night; no one who has tried it so far, has ever come out of it alive."

"If others have tried it," said Brother Lustig, "I will try it too."

"Leave it alone," said the host, "it will cost you your neck."

"It won't kill me at once," said Brother Lustig, "just give me the key, and some good food and wine." So the host gave him the key, and food and wine, and with this Brother Lustig went into the castle, enjoyed his supper, and at length, as he was sleepy, he lay down on the ground, for there was no bed. He soon fell asleep, but during the night was disturbed by a great noise, and when he awoke, he saw nine ugly devils in the room, who had made a circle, and were dancing around him. Brother Lustig said, "Well, dance as long as you like, but none of you must come too close." But the devils pressed continually nearer to him, and almost stepped on his face with their hideous feet.

"Stop, you devils' ghosts," said he, but they behaved still worse. Then Brother Lustig grew angry, and cried, "Ho! But I will soon make it quiet," and got the leg of a chair and struck out into the midst of them with it. But nine devils against one soldier were still too many, and when he struck those in front of him, the others seized him behind by the hair, and tore it unmercifully. "Devils' crew," cried he, "it is getting too bad, but just you wait. Into my knapsack, all nine of you!" In an instant they were in it, and then he buckled it up and threw it into a corner.

After this all was suddenly quiet, and Brother Lustig lay down again, and slept till it was bright day. Then came the innkeeper, and the nobleman to whom the castle belonged, to see how he had fared; but when they perceived that he was merry and well they were astonished, and asked, "Have the spirits done you no harm, then?"

"The reason why they have not," answered Brother Lustig, "is because I have got the whole nine of them in my knapsack! You may once more inhabit your castle quite tranquilly, none of them will ever haunt it again." The nobleman thanked him, gave him rich presents, and begged him to remain in his service, and he would provide for him as long as he lived.

"No," replied Brother Lustig, "I am used to wandering about, I will travel farther." Then he went away, and entered into a smithy, laid the knapsack, which contained the nine devils on the anvil, and asked the smith and his apprentices to strike it. So they struck with their great hammers with all their strength, and the devils uttered howls which were quite pitiable. When he opened the knapsack after this, eight of them were dead, but one which had been lying in a fold of it, was still alive, slipped out, and went back again to hell. Thereupon Brother Lustig traveled a long time about the world, and those who know them can tell many a story about him, but at last he grew old, and thought of his end, so he went to a hermit who was known to be a pious man, and said to him, "I am tired of wandering about, and want to now behave in such a manner that I shall enter into the kingdom of Heaven."

The hermit replied, "There are two roads, one is broad and pleasant, and leads to hell, the other is narrow and rough, and leads to heaven."

"I should be a fool," thought Brother Lustig, "if I were to take the narrow, rough road." So he set out and took the broad and pleasant road, and at length came to a great black door, which was the door of Hell. Brother Lustig knocked, and the gatekeeper peeped out to see who was there. But when he saw Brother Lustig, he was terrified, for he was the very same ninth devil who had been shut up in the knapsack, and had escaped from it with a black eye. So he pushed the bolt in again as quickly as he could, ran to the devil's lieutenant, and said, "There is a fellow outside with a knapsack, who wants to come in, but as you value your lives don't allow him to enter, or he will wish the whole of hell into his knapsack. He once gave me a frightful hammering when I was inside it." So they called out to Brother Lustig that he was to go away, for he should not get in there!

"If they won't have me here," thought he, "I will see if I can find a place for myself in heaven, for I must be somewhere." So he turned about and went onwards until he came to the door of Heaven, where he knocked.

St. Peter was sitting nearby as gatekeeper. Brother Lustig recognized him at once, and thought, "Here I find an old friend, I shall get on better."

But St. Peter said, "I really believe that you want to come into Heaven."

"Let me in, brother; I must get in somewhere; if they would have taken me into Hell, I should not have come here."

"No," said St. Peter, "you shall not enter."

"Then if you will not let me in, take your knapsack back, for I will have nothing at all from you."

"Give it here, then," said St. Peter.

Then Brother Lustig gave him the knapsack into Heaven through the bars, and St. Peter took it, and hung it beside his seat. Then said Brother Lustig, "And now I wish myself inside my knapsack," and in a second he was in it, and in Heaven, and St. Peter was forced to let him stay there.

82. *GAMBLING HANSEL*

Once upon a time there was a man who did nothing but gamble, and for that reason people never called him anything but Gambling Hansel, and as he never ceased to gamble, he played away his house and all that he had. Now the very day before his creditors were to take his house from him, came the Lord and St. Peter, and asked him to give them shelter for the night. Then Gambling Hansel said, "For my part, you may stay the night, but I cannot give you a bed or anything to eat."

So the Lord said he was just to take them in, and they themselves would buy something to eat, to which Gambling Hansel made no objection. Thereupon St. Peter gave him three groschen, and said he was to go to the baker's and fetch some bread. So Gambling Hansel went, but when he reached the house where the other gambling vagabonds were gathered together, they, although they had won all that he had, greeted him clamorously, and said, "Hansel, do come in."

"Oh," said he, "do you want to win the three groschen too?" At this they would not let him go. So he went in, and played away the three groschen also.

Meanwhile St. Peter and the Lord were waiting, and as he was so long in coming, they set out to meet him. When Gambling Hansel came, however, he pretended that the money had fallen into the gutter, and kept raking about in it all the while to find it, but our Lord already knew that he had lost it in play. St. Peter again gave him three groschen, and now he did not allow himself to be led away once more, but fetched them the loaf. Our Lord then inquired if he had no wine, and he said, "Alack, sir, the casks are all empty!" But the Lord said he was to go down into the cellar, for the best wine was still there.

For a long time he would not believe this, but at length he said, "Well, I will go down, but I know that there is none there." When he turned the tap, however, lo and behold, the best of wine ran out! So he took it to them, and the two passed the night there. Early next day our Lord told Gambling Hansel that he might beg three favors. The Lord expected that he would ask to go to Heaven; but Gambling Hansel asked for a pack of cards with which he could win everything, for dice with which he would win everything, and for a tree on which every kind of fruit would grow, and from which no one who had climbed up, could descend until he bade him do so. The Lord gave him all that he had asked, and departed with St. Peter.

And now Gambling Hansel at once set about gambling in real earnest, and before long he had gained half the world. Upon this St. Peter said to the Lord, "Lord, this thing must not go on, he will win, and you lose, the whole world. We must send Death to him."

When Death appeared, Gambling Hansel had just seated himself at the gaming table, and Death said, "Hansel, come out a while."

But Gambling Hansel said, "Just wait a little until the game is done, and in the meantime get up into that tree out there, and gather a little fruit that we may have something to munch on our way." Thereupon Death climbed up, but when he wanted to come down again, he could not, and Gambling Hansel left him up there for seven years, during which time no one died.

So St. Peter said to the Lord, "Lord, this thing must not go on. People no longer die; we must go ourselves." And they went themselves, and the Lord commanded Hansel to let Death come down. So Hansel went at once to Death and said to him, "Come down," and Death took him directly and put an end to him. They went away together and came to the next world, and then Gambling Hansel made straight for the door of Heaven, and knocked at it.

"Who is there?"

"Gambling Hansel."

"Ah, we will have nothing to do with him! Be gone!"

So he went to the door of Purgatory, and knocked once more.

"Who is there?"

"Gambling Hansel."

"Ah, there is quite enough weeping and wailing here without him. We do not want to gamble, just go away again."

Then he went to the door of Hell, and there they let him in. There was, however, no one at home but old Lucifer and the crooked devils who had just been doing their evil work in the world. And no sooner was Hansel there than he sat down to gamble again. Lucifer, however, had nothing to lose, but his misshapen devils, and Gambling Hansel won them from him, as with his cards he could not fail to do. And now he was off again with his crooked devils, and they went to Hohenfuert and pulled up a hop-pole, and with it went to Heaven and began to thrust the pole against it, and Heaven began to crack. So again St. Peter said, "Lord, this thing cannot go on, we must let him in, or he will throw us down from Heaven."

And they let him in. But Gambling Hansel instantly began to play again, and there was such a noise and confusion that there was no hearing what they themselves were saying. Therefore St. Peter once more said, "Lord, this cannot go on, we must throw him down, or he will make all Heaven rebellious." So they went to him at once, and threw him down, and his soul broke into fragments, and went into the gambling vagabonds who are living this very day.

83. HANS IN LUCK

Hans had served his master for seven years, so he said to him, "Master, my time is up; now I should be glad to go back home to my mother; give me my wages."

The master answered, "You have served me faithfully and honestly; as the service was so the reward shall be," and he gave Hans a piece of gold as big as his head. Hans pulled his handkerchief out of his pocket, wrapped up the lump in it, put it on his shoulder, and set out on the way home.

As he went on, always putting one foot before the other, he saw a horseman trotting quickly and merrily by on a lively horse. "Ah!" said Hans quite loud, "What a fine thing it is to ride! There you sit as on a chair; you stumble over no stones, you save your shoes, and get on one hardly knows how."

The rider, who had heard him, stopped and called out, "Hello! Hans, why do you go on foot, then?"

"I must," answered he, "for I have this lump to carry home; it is true that it is gold, but I cannot hold my head straight for it, and it hurts my shoulder."

"I will tell you what," said the rider, "we will exchange: I will give you my horse, and you can give me your lump."

"With all my heart," said Hans, "but I can tell you, you will have to crawl along with it."

The rider got down, took the gold, and helped Hans up; then gave him the bridle tight in his hands and said, "If you want to go at a really good pace, you must click your tongue and call out, "Jup! Jup!"

Hans was heartily delighted as he sat upon the horse and rode away so bold and free. After a little while he thought that it ought to go faster, and he began to click with his tongue and call out, "Jup! Jup!" The horse put himself into a sharp trot, and before Hans knew where he was, he was thrown off and lying in a ditch which separated the field from the highway. The horse would have gone off too if it had not been stopped by a countryman, who was coming along the road and driving a cow before him.

Hans got his limbs together and stood up on his legs again, but he was vexed, and said to the countryman, "It is a poor joke, this riding, especially when one gets hold of a mare like this, that kicks and throws one off, so that one has a chance of breaking one's neck. Never again will I mount it. Now I like your cow, for one can walk quietly behind her, and have, over and above, one's milk, butter and cheese every day without fail. What would I not give to have such a cow."

"Well," said the countryman, "if it would give you so much pleasure, I do not mind giving the cow for the horse." Hans agreed with the greatest delight; the countryman jumped upon the horse, and rode quickly away.

Hans drove his cow quietly before him, and thought over his lucky bargain. "If only I had a morsel of bread—and that can hardly fail me—I can eat butter and cheese with it as often as I like; if I am thirsty, I can milk my cow and drink the milk. Good heart, what more can I want?"

When he came to an inn he made a halt, and in his great content ate up what he had with him—his dinner and supper—and all he had, and with his last few farthings had half a glass of beer. Then he drove his cow onwards along the road to his mother's village.

As it drew nearer midday, the heat was more oppressive, and Hans found himself upon a moor which it took about an hour to cross. He felt it very hot and his tongue stuck to the roof of his mouth with thirst. "I can find a cure for this," thought Hans; "I will milk the cow now and refresh myself with the milk." He tied her to a withered tree, and as he had no pail he put his leather cap underneath; but try as he would, not a drop of milk came. And as he set himself to work in a clumsy way, the impatient beast at last gave him such a blow on his head with its hind foot, that he fell on the ground, and for a long time could not think where he was.

By good fortune a butcher just then came along the road with a wheelbarrow, in which lay a young pig. "What sort of a trick is this?" cried he, and helped the good Hans up. Hans told him what had happened. The butcher gave him his flask and said, "Take a drink and refresh yourself. The cow will certainly give no milk, it is an old beast; at the best it is only fit for the plow, or for the butcher."

"Well, well," said Hans, as he stroked his hair down on his head, "who would have thought it? Certainly it is a fine thing when one can kill a beast like that at home; what meat one has! But I do not care much for beef, it is not juicy enough for me. A young pig like that now is the thing to have, it tastes quite different; and then there are the sausages!"

"Listen, Hans," said the butcher, "out of love for you I will exchange, and will let you have the pig for the cow."

"Heaven repay you for your kindness!" said Hans as he gave up the cow, while the pig was unbound from the barrow, and the cord by which it was tied was put in his hand.

Hans went on, and thought to himself how everything was going just as he wished; if he did meet with any vexation it was immediately set right. Presently there joined him a lad who was carrying a fine white goose under his arm. They said good morning to each other, and Hans began to tell of his good luck, and how he had always made such good bargains. The boy told him that he was taking the goose to a christening feast. "Just lift her," added he, and laid hold of her by the wings; "how heavy she is—she has been fattened up for the last eight weeks. Whoever has a bit of her when she is roasted will have to wipe the fat from both sides of his mouth."

"Yes," said Hans, as he weighed her in one hand, "she is a good weight, but my pig is no bad one."

Meanwhile the lad looked suspiciously from one side to the other, and shook his head. "Look here," he said at length, "it may not be all right with your pig. In the village through which I passed, the Mayor himself had just had one stolen out of its sty. I fear—I fear that you have got hold of it there. They have sent out some people and it would be a bad business if they caught you with the pig; at the very least, you would be shut up in the dark hole."

The good Hans was terrified. "Goodness!" he said, "Help me out of this fix; you know more about this place than I do, take my pig and leave me your goose."

"I shall risk something at that game," answered the lad, "but I will not be the cause of your getting into trouble." So he took the cord in his hand, and drove away the pig quickly along a bypath.

The good Hans, free from care, went homewards with the goose under his arm. "When I think over it properly," said he to himself, "I have even gained by the exchange; first there is the good roast meat, then the quantity of fat which will drip from it, and which will give me dripping for my bread for a quarter of a year, and lastly the beautiful white feathers; I will have my pillow stuffed with them, and then indeed I shall go to sleep without rocking. How glad my mother will be!"

As he was going through the last village, there stood a scissors grinder with his barrow; as his wheel whirred he sang—

> "I sharpen scissors and quickly grind,
> My coat blows out in the wind behind."

Hans stood still and looked at him; at last he spoke to him and said, "All's well with you, as you are so merry with your grinding."

"Yes," answered the scissors grinder, "the trade has a golden foundation. A real grinder is a man who as often as he puts his hand into his pocket finds gold in it. But where did you buy that fine goose?"

"I did not buy it, but exchanged my pig for it."

"And the pig?"

"That I got for a cow."

"And the cow?"

"I took that instead of a horse."

"And the horse?"

"For that I gave a lump of gold as big as my head."

"And the gold?"

"Well, that was my wages for seven years' service."

"You have known how to look after yourself each time," said the grinder. "If you can only get on so far as to hear the money jingle in your pocket whenever you stand up, you will have made your fortune."

"How shall I manage that?" said Hans.

"You must be a grinder, as I am; nothing particular is wanted for it but a grindstone, the rest finds itself. I have one here; it is certainly a little worn, but you need not give me anything for it but your goose; will you do it?"

"How can you ask?" answered Hans. "I shall be the luckiest fellow on earth; if I have money whenever I put my hand in my pocket, what need I trouble about any longer?" and he handed him the goose and received the grindstone in exchange.

"Now," said the grinder, as he took up an ordinary heavy stone that lay by him, "here is a strong stone for you into the bargain; you can hammer well upon it, and straighten your old nails. Take it with you and keep it carefully."

Hans loaded himself with the stones, and went on with a contented heart; his eyes shone with joy. "I must have been born under a lucky star," he cried, "everything I want happens to me just as if I were a Sunday's child."

Meanwhile, as he had been on his legs since daybreak, he began to feel tired. Hunger also tormented him, for in his joy at the bargain by which he got the cow he had eaten up all his store of food at once. At last he could only go on with great trouble, and was forced to stop every minute; the stones, too, weighed him down dreadfully. Then he could not help thinking how nice it would be if he did not have to carry them just then.

He crept like a snail to a well in a field, and there he thought that he would rest and refresh himself with a cool drink of water, but in order that he might not injure the stones in sitting down, he laid them carefully by his side on the edge of the well. Then he sat down on it, and was to stoop and drink, when he made a slip, pushed against the stones, and both of them fell into the water. When Hans saw them with his own eyes sinking to the bottom, he jumped for joy, and then knelt down, and with tears in his eyes thanked God for having shown him this favor also, and released him in so good a way, and without his having any need to reproach himself, from those heavy stones which had been the only things that troubled him.

"There is no man under the sun so fortunate as I," he cried out. With a light heart and free from every burden he now ran on until he was with his mother at home.

84. HANS MARRIED

There was once upon a time a young peasant named Hans, whose uncle wanted to find him a rich wife. He therefore seated Hans behind the stove, and had it made very hot. Then he fetched a pot of milk and plenty of white bread, gave him a bright newly-coined farthing in his hand, and said, "Hans, hold that farthing fast, crumble the white bread into the milk, and stay where you are, and do not stir from that spot till I come back."

"Yes," said Hans, "I will do all that."

Then the wooer put on a pair of old patched trousers, went to a rich peasant's daughter in the next village, and said, "Won't you marry my nephew Hans? You will get an honest and sensible man who will suit you."

The covetous father asked, "How is it with regard to his means? Has he bread to break?"

"Dear friend," replied the wooer, "my young nephew has a snug berth, a nice bit of money in hand, and plenty of bread to break, besides he has quite as many patches as I have," (and as he spoke, he slapped the patches on his trousers, but in that district small pieces of land were called patches also). "If you will give yourself the trouble to go home with me, you shall see at once that all is as I have said."

Then the miser did not want to lose this good opportunity, and said, "If that is the case, I have nothing further to say against the marriage."

So the wedding was celebrated on the appointed day, and when the young wife went out of doors to see the bridegroom's property, Hans took off his Sunday coat and put on his patched smock and said, "I might spoil my good coat." Then together they went out and wherever a boundary line came in sight, or fields and meadows were divided from each other, Hans pointed with his finger and then slapped either a large or a small patch on his smock, and said, "That patch is mine, and that too, my dearest, just look at it," meaning that his wife should not stare at the broad land, but look at his garment, which was his own.

"Were you indeed at the wedding?"

"Yes, indeed I was there, and in fulldress. My headdress was of snow; then the sun came out, and it was melted. My coat was of cobwebs, and I had to pass by some thorns which tore it off me, my shoes were of glass, and I pushed against a stone and they said, "Klink," and broke in two.

85. *THE GOLD CHILDREN*

There was once a poor man and a poor woman who had nothing but a little cottage, and who earned their bread by fishing, and always lived from hand to mouth. But it came to pass one day when the man was sitting by the shore, and casting his net, that he drew out a fish entirely of gold. As he was looking at the fish, full of astonishment, it began to speak and said, "Listen, fisherman, if you will throw me back again into the water, I will change your little hut into a splendid castle."

Then the fisherman answered, "Of what use is a castle to me, if I have nothing to eat?"

The gold fish continued, "That shall be taken care of, there will be a cupboard in the castle in which, when you open it, shall be dishes of the most delicate meats, and as many of them as you can desire."

"If that be true," said the man, "then I can well do you a favor."

"Yes," said the fish, "there is, however, the condition that you shall disclose to no one in the world, whoever he may be, where you get your good luck. If you speak but one single word, all will be over."

Then the man threw the wonderful fish back again into the water, and went home. But where his hut had formerly stood, now stood a great castle. He opened wide his eyes, entered, and saw his wife dressed in beautiful clothes, sitting in a splendid room, and she was quite delighted, and said, "Husband, how has all this come to pass? It suits me very well."

"Yes," said the man, "it suits me too, but I am frightfully hungry, just give me something to eat."

Said the wife, "But I have got nothing and don't know where to find anything in this new house."

"There is no need to know," said the man, "for I see yonder a great cupboard, just unlock it." When she opened it, there stood cakes, meat, fruit, wine, quite a bright prospect.

Then the woman cried joyfully, "What more can you want, my dear?" and they sat down, and ate and drank together. When they had had enough, the woman said, "But husband, where do all these riches come from?"

"Alas," answered he, "do not question me about it, for I dare not tell you anything; if I disclose it to anyone, then all our good fortune will fly."

"Very good," said she, "if I am not to know anything, then I do not want to know anything." However, she was not in earnest; she never rested day or night, and she goaded her husband until in his impatience he revealed that all was owing to a wonderful golden fish which he had caught, and to which in return he had given its liberty. And as soon as the secret was out, the splendid castle with the cupboard immediately disappeared, they were once more in the old fisherman's hut, and the man was obliged to follow his former trade and fish. But fortune would so have it, that he once more drew out the golden fish.

"Listen," said the fish, "if you will throw me back into the water again, I will once more give you the castle with the cupboard full of roast and boiled meats; only be firm, for your life's sake don't reveal from whom you got it, or you will lose it all again!"

"I will take good care," answered the fisherman, and threw the fish back into the water. Now at home everything was once more in its former magnificence, and the wife was overjoyed at their good fortune, but curiosity left her no peace, so that after a couple of days she began to ask again how it had come to pass, and how he had managed to secure it. The man kept silence for a short time, but at last she made him so angry that he broke out, and betrayed the secret. In an instant the castle disappeared, and they were back again in their old hut.

"Now you have got what you want," said he, "and we can gnaw at a bare bone again."

"Ah," said the woman, "I had rather not have riches if I am not to know from whom they come, for then I have no peace."

The man went back to fish, and after a while he chanced to draw out the gold fish for a third time. "Listen," said the fish, "I see very well that I am fated to fall into your hands, take me home and cut me into six pieces; give your wife two of them to eat, two to your horse and bury two of them in the ground, then they will bring you a blessing."

The fisherman took the fish home with him, and did as it had bidden him. It came to pass, however, that from the two pieces that were buried in the ground two golden lilies sprang up, that the horse had two golden foals, and the fisherman's wife bore two children who were made entirely of gold. The children grew up, became tall and handsome, and the lilies and horses grew likewise. Then they said,

"Father, we want to mount our golden steeds and travel out in the world."

But he answered sorrowfully, "How shall I bear it if you go away, and I know not how it fares with you?"

Then they said, "The two golden lilies remain here. By them you can see how it is with us; if they are fresh, then we are in health; if they are withered, we are ill; if they perish, then we are dead."

So they rode forth and came to an inn, in which were many people, and when they perceived the gold children they began to laugh, and jeer. When one of them heard the mocking he felt ashamed and would not go out into the world, but turned back and went home again to his father. But the other rode forward and reached a great forest.

As he was about to enter it, the people said, "It is not safe for you to ride through, the wood is full of robbers who would treat you badly. You will fare ill, and when they see that you are all of gold, and your horse likewise, they will assuredly kill you."

But he would not allow himself to be frightened, and said, "I must and will ride through it." Then he took bearskins and covered himself and his horse with them, so that the gold was no more to be seen, and rode fearlessly into the forest.

When he had ridden onward a little he heard a rustling in the bushes, and heard voices speaking together. From one side came cries of, "There is one," but from the other, "Let him go, 'tis an idle fellow, as poor and bare as a church mouse, what should we gain from him?"

So the gold child rode joyfully through the forest, and no evil befell him. One day he entered a village where he saw a maiden, who was so beautiful that he did not believe that any more beautiful than she existed in the world. And as such a mighty love took possession of him, he went up to her and said, "I love you with my whole heart, will you be my wife?"

He, too, pleased the maiden so much that she agreed and said, "Yes, I will be your wife, and be true to you my whole life long."

Then they were married, and just as they were in the greatest happiness, home came the father of the bride, and when he saw that his daughter's wedding was being celebrated, he was astonished, and said, "Where is the bridegroom?" They showed him the gold child, who, however, still wore his bearskins. Then the father said wrathfully, "A vagabond shall never have my daughter!" and was about to kill him.

Then the bride begged as hard as she could, and said, "He is my husband, and I love him with all my heart!" until at last he allowed himself to be appeased.

Nevertheless the idea never left his thoughts, so that next morning he rose early, wishing to see whether his daughter's husband was a common ragged beggar. But when he peeped in, he saw a magnificent golden man in the bed, and the cast-off bearskins lying on the ground. Then he went back and thought, "What a good thing it was that I restrained my anger! I should have committed a great crime."

But the gold child dreamed that he rode out to hunt a splendid stag, and when he awoke in the morning, he said to his wife, "I must go out hunting."

She was uneasy, and begged him to stay there, and said, "You might easily meet with a great misfortune," but he answered, "I must and will go."

Thereupon he got up, and rode forth into the forest, and it was not long before a fine stag crossed his path exactly according to his dream. He aimed and was about to shoot it, when the stag ran away. He gave chase over hedges and ditches for the whole day without feeling tired, but in the evening the stag vanished from his sight, and when the gold child looked round him, he was standing before a little house, in which was a witch. He knocked, and a little old woman came out and asked, "What are you doing so late in the middle of the great forest?"

"Have you not seen a stag?"

"Yes," answered she, "I know the stag well," and a little dog which had come out of the house with her, barked at the man violently.

"Will you be silent, you odious toad," said he, "or I will shoot you dead."

Then the witch cried out in a passion, "What! Will you slay my little dog?" and immediately transformed him, so that he lay like a stone, and his bride awaited him in vain and thought, "That which I so greatly dreaded, which lay so heavily on my heart, has come upon him!"

But at home the other brother was standing by the gold lilies, when one of them suddenly drooped. "Good heavens!" said he, "My brother has met with some great misfortune! I must go away to see if I can possibly rescue him."

Then the father said, "Stay here, if I lose you also, what shall I do?"

But he answered, "I must and will go forth!"

Then he mounted his golden horse, and rode forth and entered the great forest, where his brother lay turned to stone. The old witch came out of her house and called him, wishing to entrap him also, but he did not go near her, and said, "I will shoot you, if you will not bring my brother to life again." She touched the stone, though very unwillingly, with her forefinger, and he was immediately restored to his human shape.

The two gold children rejoiced when they saw each other again, kissed and caressed each other, and rode away together out of the forest, the one home to his bride, and the other to his father. The father then said, "I knew well that you had rescued your brother, for the golden lily suddenly rose up and blossomed out again." Then they lived happily, and all prospered with them until their death.

86. THE FOX AND THE GEESE

The fox once came to a meadow in which was a flock of fine fat geese, at which he smiled and said, "I come in the nick of time, you are sitting together quite beautifully, so that I can eat you up one after the other." The geese cackled with terror, sprang up, and began to wail and beg piteously for their lives. But the fox would listen to nothing, and said, "There is no mercy to be had! You must die."

At length one of them took heart and said, "If we poor geese are to give up our vigorous young lives, show us the only possible favor and allow us one more prayer, that we may not die in our sins, and then we will place ourselves in a row, so that you can pick yourself out the fattest."

"Yes," said the fox, "that is reasonable, and a pious request. Pray away, I will wait till you are done."

Then the first began a good long prayer, forever saying, "Ga! Ga!" and as she would make no end, the second did not wait until her turn came, but began also, "Ga! Ga!" The third and fourth followed her, and soon they were all cackling together.

When they have done praying, the story shall be continued further, but at present they are still praying without stopping.

87. THE POOR MAN AND
THE RICH MAN

In olden times, when the Lord himself still used to walk about on this earth among men, it once happened that he was tired and overtaken by the darkness before he could reach an inn. Now there stood on the road before him two houses facing each other; the one large and beautiful, the other small and poor. The large one belonged to a rich man, and the small one to a poor man.

Then the Lord thought, "I shall be no burden to the rich man, I will stay the night with him." When the rich man heard someone knocking at his door, he opened the window and asked the stranger what he wanted. The Lord answered, "I only ask for a night's lodging."

Then the rich man looked at the traveler from head to foot, and as the Lord was wearing common clothes, and did not look like one who had much money in his pocket, he shook his head, and said, "No, I cannot take you in, my rooms are full of herbs and seeds; and if I were to lodge everyone who knocked at my door, I might very soon go begging myself. Go somewhere else for a lodging," and with this he shut down the window and left the Lord standing there.

So the Lord turned his back on the rich man, and went across to the small house and knocked. He had hardly done so when the poor man opened the little door and bade the traveler come in. "Pass the night with me, it is already dark," said he, "you cannot go any further tonight." This pleased the Lord, and he went in. The poor man's wife shook hands with him, and welcomed him, and said he was to make himself at home and put up with what they had; they had not much to offer him, but what they had they would give him with all their hearts. Then she put the potatoes on the fire, and while they were boiling, she milked the goat, that they might have a little milk with them. When the cloth was laid, the Lord sat down with the man and his wife, and he enjoyed their coarse food, for there were happy faces at the table.

When they had had supper and it was bedtime, the woman called her husband apart and said, "Dear husband, let us make up a bed of straw for ourselves tonight, and then the poor traveler can sleep in our bed and have a good rest, for he has been walking the whole day through, and that makes one weary."

"With all my heart," he answered, "I will go and offer it to him," and he went to the stranger and invited him, if he had no objection, to sleep in their bed and rest his limbs properly. But the Lord was unwilling to take the bed from the two old folks; however, they would not be satisfied, until at length he did it and lay down in the bed, while they themselves lay on some straw on the ground.

Next morning they got up before daybreak, and made as good a breakfast as they could for the guest. When the sun shone in through the little window, and the Lord had got up, he again ate with them, and then prepared to set out on his journey.

But as he was standing at the door he turned round and said, "As you are so kind and good, you may wish three things for yourselves and I will grant them."

Then the man said, "What else should I wish for but eternal happiness, and that we two, as long as we live, may be healthy and have every day our daily bread; for the third wish, I do not know what to have."

And the Lord said to him, "Will you wish for a new house instead of this old one?"

"Oh, yes," said the man; "if I can have that, too, I should like it very much." And the Lord fulfilled his wish, and changed their old house into a new one, again gave them his blessing, and went on.

The sun was high when the rich man got up and leaned out of his window and saw, on the opposite side of the way, a new clean-looking house with red tiles and bright windows where the old hut used to be. He was very much astonished, and called his wife and said to her, "Tell me, what can have happened? Last night there was a miserable little hut standing there, and today there is a beautiful new house. Run over and see how that has come to pass."

So his wife went and asked the poor man, and he said to her, "Yesterday evening a traveler came here and asked for a night's lodging, and this morning when he took leave of us he granted us three wishes—eternal happiness, health during this life and our daily bread as well, and besides this, a beautiful new house instead of our old hut."

When the rich man's wife heard this, she ran back in haste and told her husband how it had happened. The man said, "I could tear myself to pieces! If I had but known that! That traveler came to our house too, and wanted to sleep here, and I sent him away."

"Quick!" said his wife, "Get on your horse. You can still catch the man up, and then you must ask to have three wishes granted to you."

The rich man followed the good counsel and galloped away on his horse, and soon caught up with the Lord. He spoke to him softly and pleasantly, and begged him not to take it amiss that he had not let him in directly; he was looking for the front-door key, and in the meantime the stranger had gone away, if he returned the same way he must come and stay with him. "Yes," said the Lord, "if I ever come back again, I will do so." Then the rich man asked if might not wish for three things too, as his neighbor had done? "Yes," said the Lord, he might, but it would not be to his advantage, and he had better not wish for anything; but the rich man thought that he could easily ask for something which would add to his happiness, if he only knew that it would be granted. So the Lord said to him, "Ride home, then, and three wishes which you shall form, shall be fulfilled."

The rich man had now gained what he wanted, so he rode home, and began to consider what he should wish for. As he was thus thinking he let the bridle fall, and the horse began to caper about, so that he was continually disturbed in his meditations, and could not collect his thoughts at all. He patted its neck, and said, "Gently, Lisa," but the horse only began new tricks. Then at last he was angry, and cried quite impatiently, "I wish your neck was broken!"

As soon as he had said the words, down the horse fell on the ground, and there it lay dead and never moved again. And thus was his first wish fulfilled. As he was miserly by nature, he did not like to leave the harness lying there; so he cut it off, and put it on his back; and now he had to go on foot. "I still have two wishes left," said he, and comforted himself with that thought.

And now as he was walking slowly through the sand, and the sun was burning hot at midday, he grew quite hot-tempered and angry. The saddle hurt his back, and he had not yet any idea what to wish for. "If I were to wish for all the riches and treasures in the world," said he to himself, "I should still think of all kinds of other things later on, I know that, beforehand. But I will manage so that there is nothing at all left for me to wish for afterwards." Then he sighed and said, "Ah, if I were but that Bavarian peasant, who likewise had three wishes granted to him, and knew quite well what to do, and in the first place wished for a great deal of beer, and in the second for as much beer as he was able to drink, and in the third for a barrel of beer into the bargain."

Many a time he thought he had found it, but then it seemed to him to be, after all, too little. Then it came into his mind, what an easy life his wife had, for she stayed at home in a cool room and enjoyed herself. This really did vex him, and before he was aware, he said, "I just wish she was sitting there on this saddle, and could not get off it, instead of my having to drag it along on my back." And as the last word was spoken, the saddle disappeared from his back, and he saw that his second wish had been fulfilled. Then he really did feel warm.

He began to run and wanted to be quite alone in his own room at home, to think of something really large for his last wish. But when he arrived there and opened the parlor door, he saw his wife sitting in the middle of the room on the saddle, crying and complaining, and quite unable to get off it. So he said, "Do bear it, and I will wish for all the riches on earth for you, only stay where you are."

She, however, called him a fool, and said, "What good will all the riches on earth do me, if I am to sit on this saddle? You have wished me on it, so you must help me off."

So whether he liked it or not, he was forced to let his third wish be that she should be free of the saddle, and able to get off it, and immediately the wish was fulfilled. So he got nothing by it but vexation, trouble, abuse, and the loss of his horse; but the poor people lived happily, quietly, and piously until their happy death.

88. THE SINGING, SPRINGING LARK

There was once a man who was about to set out on a long journey, and on parting he asked his three daughters what he should bring back with him for them. The eldest wished for pearls, the second wished for diamonds, but the third said, "Dear father, I should like a singing, soaring lark."

The father said, "Yes, if I can get it, you shall have it," kissed all three, and set out.

Now when the time had come for him to be on his way home again, he had brought pearls and diamonds for the two eldest, but he had sought everywhere in vain for a singing, soaring lark for the youngest, and he was very unhappy about it, for she was his favorite child. Then his road lay through a forest, and in the middle of it was a splendid castle, and near the castle stood a tree, but quite on the top of the tree, he saw a singing, soaring lark.

"Aha, you come just at the right moment!" he said, quite delighted, and called to his servant to climb up and catch the little creature. But as he approached the tree, a lion leapt from beneath it, shook himself, and roared till the leaves on the trees trembled.

"He who tries to steal my singing, soaring lark," he cried, "I will devour."

Then the man said, "I did not know that the bird belonged to you. I will make amends for the wrong I have done and ransom myself with a large sum of money, only spare my life."

The lion said, "Nothing can save you, unless you will promise to give me for my own what first meets you on your return home; and if you will do that, I will grant you your life, and you shall have the bird for your daughter, into the bargain."

But the man hesitated and said, "That might be my youngest daughter, she loves me best, and always runs to meet me on my return home."

The servant, however, was terrified and said, "Why should your daughter be the very one to meet you, it might as easily be a cat, or dog?"

Then the man allowed himself to be persuaded, took the singing, soaring lark, and promised to give the lion whatever should first meet him on his return home.

When he reached home and entered his house, the first who met him was no other than his youngest and dearest daughter, who came running up, kissed and embraced him, and when she saw that he had brought with him a singing, soaring lark, she was beside herself with joy. The father, however, could not rejoice, but began to weep, and said, "My dearest child, I have bought the little bird dear. In return for it, I have been obliged to promise you to a savage lion, and when he has you he will tear you in pieces and devour you," and he told her all, just as it had happened, and begged her not to go there, come what might.

But she consoled him and said, "Dearest father, indeed your promise must be fulfilled. I will go there and soften the lion, so that I may return to you safely." Next morning she had the road pointed out to her, took leave, and went fearlessly out into the forest. The lion, however, was an enchanted prince and was by day a lion, and all his people were lions with him, but in the night they resumed their natural human shapes. On her arrival she was kindly received and led into the castle. When night came, the lion turned into a handsome man, and their wedding was celebrated with great magnificence. They lived happily together, remained awake at night, and slept in the daytime.

One day he came and said, "Tomorrow there is a feast in your father's house, because your eldest sister is to be married, and if you are inclined to go there, my lions shall take you."

She said, "Yes, I should very much like to see my father again," and went there, accompanied by the lions. There was great joy when she arrived, for they had all believed that she had been torn in pieces by the lion, and had long ceased to live. But she told them what a handsome husband she had, and how well off she was, remained with them while the wedding feast lasted, and then went back again to the forest.

When the second daughter was about to be married, and she was again invited to the wedding, she said to the lion, "This time I will not be alone, you must come with me." The lion, however, said that it was too dangerous for him, for if a ray from a burning candle fell on him, he would be changed into a dove, and for seven long years would have to fly about with the doves. She said, "Ah, but do come with me, I will take great care of you, and guard you from all light."

So they went away together, and took with them their little child as well. She had a chamber built there, so strong and thick that no ray could pierce through it; in this he was to shut himself up when the candles were lit for the wedding feast. But the door was made of green wood which warped and left a little crack which no one noticed. The wedding was celebrated with magnificence, but when the procession with all its candles and torches came back from church, and passed by this apartment, a ray about the breadth of a hair fell on the King's son, and when this ray touched him, he was transformed in an instant, and when she came in and looked for him, she did not see him, but a white dove was sitting there.

The dove said to her, "For seven years I must fly about the world, but at every seventh step that you take I will let fall a drop of red blood and a white feather, and these will show you the way, and if you follow the trace you can release me." Thereupon the dove flew out at the door, and she followed him, and at every seventh step a red drop of blood and a little white feather fell down and showed her the way.

So she went continually further and further in the wide world, never looking about her or resting, and the seven years were almost past; then she rejoiced and thought that they would soon be delivered, and yet they were so far from it! Once when they were thus moving onwards, no little feather and no drop of red blood fell, and when she raised her eyes the dove had disappeared. And as she thought to herself, "In this no man can help you," she climbed up to the sun, and said to him, "You shine into every crevice, and over every peak, have you not seen a white dove flying?"

"No," said the sun, "I have seen none, but I present you with a casket, open it when you are in sorest need."

Then she thanked the sun, and went on until evening came and the moon appeared; she then asked her, "You shine the whole night through, and on every field and forest, have you not seen a white dove flying?"

"No," said the moon, "I have seen no dove, but here I give you an egg, break it when you are in great need."

She thanked the moon, and went on until the night wind came up and blew on her, then she said to it, "You blow over every tree and under every leaf, have you not seen a white dove flying?"

"No," said the night wind, "I have seen none, but I will ask the three other winds, perhaps they have seen it."

The east wind and the west wind came, and had seen nothing, but the south wind said, "I have seen the white dove, it has flown to the

Red Sea, where it has become a lion again, for the seven years are over, and the lion is there fighting with a dragon; the dragon, however, is an enchanted princess."

The night wind then said to her, "I will advise you; go to the Red Sea, on the right bank are some tall reeds, count them, break off the eleventh, and strike the dragon with it, then the lion will be able to subdue it, and both will then regain their human form. After that, look round and you will see the griffin which is by the Red Sea; swing yourself, with your beloved, onto his back, and the bird will carry you over the sea to your own home. Here is a nut for you, when you are above the center of the sea, let the nut fall, it will immediately shoot up, and a tall nut tree will grow out of the water on which the griffin may rest; for if he cannot rest, he will not be strong enough to carry you across, and if you forget to throw down the nut, he will let you fall into the sea."

Then she went there, and found everything as the night wind had said. She counted the reeds by the sea, and cut off the eleventh, struck the dragon with it, whereupon the lion overcame it, and immediately both of them regained their human shapes. But when the princess, who had before been the dragon, was delivered from enchantment, she took the youth by the arm, seated herself on the griffin, and carried him off with her.

There stood the poor maiden who had wandered so far and was again forsaken. She sat down and cried, but at last she took courage and said, "Still I will go as far as the wind blows and as long as the cock crows, until I find him," and she went forth by long, long roads, until at last she came to the castle where both of them were living together; there she heard that soon a feast was to be held, in which they would celebrate their wedding, but she said, "God still helps me," and opened the casket that the sun had given her. A dress lay inside as brilliant as the sun itself. So she took it out and put it on, and went up into the castle, and everyone, even the bride herself, looked at her with astonishment. The dress pleased the bride so well that she thought it might do for her wedding dress, and asked if it was for sale.

"Not for money or land," answered she, "but for flesh and blood." The bride asked her what she meant by that, so she said, "Let me sleep a night in the chamber where the bridegroom sleeps." The bride would not, yet wanted very much to have the dress; at last she consented, but the page was to give the prince a sleeping-potion.

When it was night, therefore, and the youth was already asleep, she was led into the chamber; she seated herself on the bed and said, "I have followed after you for seven years. I have been to the sun and the moon, and the four winds, and have inquired for you, and have helped you against the dragon; will you, then, quite forget me?" But the prince slept so soundly that it only seemed to him as if the wind were whistling outside in the fir trees.

When day broke, she was led out again, and had to give up the golden dress. And as even that had been of no avail, she was sad, went out into a meadow, sat down there, and wept. While she was sitting there, she thought of the egg which the moon had given her; she opened it, and there came out a clucking hen with twelve chickens all of gold, and they ran about chirping, and crept again under the old hen's wings; nothing more beautiful was ever seen in the world! Then she arose, and drove them through the meadow before her, until the bride looked out of the window. The little chickens pleased her so much that she immediately came down and asked if they were for sale.

"Not for money or land, but for flesh and blood; let me sleep another night in the chamber where the bridegroom sleeps."

The bride said, "Yes," intending to cheat her as on the former evening. But when the prince went to bed he asked the page what the murmuring and rustling in the night had been. At this the page told all; that he had been forced to give him a sleeping-potion, because a poor girl had slept secretly in the chamber, and that he was to give him another that night. The prince said, "Pour out the potion by the bedside."

At night, she was again led in, and when she began to relate how ill all had fared with her, he immediately recognized his beloved wife by her voice, sprang up and cried, "Now I really am released! I have been as it were in a dream, for the strange princess has bewitched me so that I have been compelled to forget you, but God has delivered me from the spell at the right time." Then they both left the castle secretly in the night, for they feared the father of the princess, who was a sorcerer, and they seated themselves on the griffin which bore them across the Red Sea, and when they were in the middle of it, she let the nut fall. Immediately a tall nut tree grew up, on which the bird rested, and then carried them home, where they found their child, who had grown tall and beautiful, and they lived happily until their death.

89. THE GOOSE GIRL

There was once upon a time an old Queen whose husband had been dead for many years, and she had a beautiful daughter. When the princess grew up she was betrothed to a prince who lived at a great distance. When the time came for her to be married, and she had to journey forth into the distant kingdom, the aged Queen packed up for her many costly vessels of silver and gold, and trinkets also of gold and silver, and cups and jewels; in short, everything which appertained to a royal dowry, for she loved her child with all her heart. She likewise sent her maid in waiting, who was to ride with her, and hand her over to the bridegroom, and each had a horse for the journey, but the horse of the King's daughter was called Falada, and could speak. So when the hour of parting had come, the aged mother went into her bedroom, took a small knife and cut her finger with it until it bled, then she held a white handkerchief to it into which she let three drops of blood fall, gave it to her daughter and said, "Dear child, preserve this carefully, it will be of service to you on your way."

So they took a sorrowful leave of each other; the princess put the piece of cloth in her bosom, mounted her horse, and then went away to her bridegroom. After she had ridden for a while she felt a burning thirst, and said to her waiting-maid, "Dismount, and take my cup which you have brought with you for me, and get me some water from the stream, for I should like to drink."

"If you are thirsty," said the waiting-maid, "get off your horse yourself, and lie down and drink out of the water, I don't choose to be your servant."

So in her great thirst the princess alighted, bent down over the water in the stream and drank, and was not allowed to drink out of the golden cup. Then she said, "Ah, Heaven!" and the three drops of blood answered, "If your mother knew, her heart would break." But the King's daughter was humble, said nothing, and mounted her horse again.

She rode some miles further, but the day was warm, the sun scorched her, and she was thirsty once more, and when they came to a stream of water, she again cried to her waiting-maid, "Dismount, and give me some water in my golden cup," for she had long ago forgotten the girl's ill words.

But the waiting-maid said still more haughtily, "If you wish to drink, drink as you can, I don't choose to be your maid."

Then in her great thirst the King's daughter alighted, bent over the flowing stream, wept and said, "Ah, Heaven!" and the drops of blood again replied, "If your mother knew this, her heart would break." And as she was thus drinking and leaning right over the stream, the handkerchief with the three drops of blood fell out of her bosom, and floated away with the water without her observing it, so great was her trouble.

The waiting-maid, however, had seen it, and she rejoiced to think that she now had power over the bride, for since the princess had lost the drops of blood, she had become weak and powerless. So now when she wanted to mount her horse again, the one that was called Falada, the waiting-maid said, "Falada is more suitable for me, and my nag will do for you" and the princess had to be content with that. Then the waiting-maid, with many hard words, bade the princess exchange her royal apparel for her own shabby clothes; and at length she was compelled to swear by the clear sky above her, that she would not say one word of this to anyone at the royal court, and if she had not taken this oath she would have been killed on the spot. But Falada saw all this, and observed it well.

The waiting-maid now mounted Falada, and the true bride the bad horse, and thus they traveled onwards, until at length they entered the royal palace. There were great rejoicings over her arrival, and the prince sprang forward to meet her, lifted the waiting-maid from her horse, and thought she was his consort. She was conducted upstairs, but the real princess was left standing below. Then the old King looked out of the window and saw her standing in the courtyard, and how dainty and delicate and beautiful she was, and instantly went to the royal apartment, and asked the bride about the girl she had with her who was standing down below in the courtyard, and who she was? "I picked her up on my way for a companion; give the girl something to work at, that she may not stand idle."

But the old King had no work for her, and knew of none, so he said, "I have a little boy who tends the geese, she may help him." The boy was called Conrad, and the true bride had to help him to tend the geese.

Soon afterwards the false bride said to the young King, "Dearest husband, I beg you to do me a favor."

He answered, "I will do so most willingly."

"Then send for the knacker, and have the head of the horse on which I rode here cut off, for it vexed me on the way." In reality, she was afraid that the horse might tell how she had behaved to the King's daughter. Then she succeeded in making the King promise that it should be done, and the faithful Falada was to die; this came to the ears of the real princess, and she secretly promised to pay the knacker a piece of gold if he would perform a small service for her. There was a great dark-looking gateway in the town, through which morning and evening she had to pass with the geese: would he be so good as to nail up Falada's head on it, so that she might see him again, more than once. The knacker promised to do that, and cut off the head, and nailed it fast beneath the dark gateway.

Early in the morning, when she and Conrad drove out their flock beneath this gateway, she said in passing,

"Alas, Falada, hanging there!"

Then the head answered,

"Alas, young Queen, how ill you fare!
If this your tender mother knew,
Her heart would surely break in two."

Then they went still further out of the town, and drove their geese into the country. And when they had come to the meadow, she sat down and unbound her hair which was like pure gold, and Conrad saw it and delighted in its brightness, and wanted to pluck out a few hairs. Then she said,

"Blow, blow, you gentle wind, I say,
Blow Conrad's little hat away,
And make him chase it here and there,
Until I have braided all my hair,
And bound it up again."

And there came such a violent wind that it blew Conrad's hat far away across country, and he was forced to run after it. When he came back she had finished combing her hair and was putting it up again, and he could not get any of it. Then Conrad was angry, and would not speak to her, and thus they watched the geese until the evening, and then they went home.

Next day when they were driving the geese out through the dark gateway, the maiden said,

"Alas, Falada, hanging there!"

Falada answered,

"Alas, young Queen, how ill you fare!
If this your tender mother knew,
Her heart would surely break in two."

And she sat down again in the field and began to comb out her hair, and Conrad ran and tried to clutch it, so she said in haste,

"Blow, blow, you gentle wind, I say,
Blow Conrad's little hat away,
And make him chase it here and there,
Until I have braided all my hair,
And bound it up again."

Then the wind blew, and blew his little hat off his head and far away, and Conrad was forced to run after it, and when he came back, her hair had been put up a long time, and he could get none of it, and so they looked after their geese till evening came.

But in the evening after they had got home, Conrad went to the old King, and said, "I won't tend the geese with that girl any longer!"

"Why not?" inquired the aged King.

"Oh, because she vexes me the whole day long." Then the aged King commanded him to relate what it was that she did to him. And Conrad said, "In the morning when we pass beneath the dark gateway with the flock, there is a sorry horse's head on the wall, and she says to it,

"Alas, Falada, hanging there!"

And the head replies,

> "Alas, young Queen how ill you fare!
> If this your tender mother knew,
> Her heart would surely break in two."

And Conrad went on to relate what happened on the goose pasture, and how when there he had to chase his hat.

The aged King commanded him to drive his flock out again next day, and as soon as morning came, he placed himself behind the dark gateway, and heard how the maiden spoke to the head of Falada, and then he too went into the country, and hid himself in the thicket in the meadow. There he soon saw with his own eyes the goose girl and the goose boy bringing their flock, and how after a while she sat down and unplaited her hair, which shone with radiance. And soon she said,

> "Blow, blow, you gentle wind, I say,
> Blow Conrad's little hat away,
> And make him chase it here and there,
> Until I have braided all my hair,
> And bound it up again."

Then came a blast of wind and carried off Conrad's hat, so that he had to run far away, while the maiden quietly went on combing and plaiting her hair, all of which the King observed. Then, quite unseen, he went away, and when the goose girl came home in the evening, he called her aside, and asked why she did all these things.

"I may not tell you that, and I dare not lament my sorrows to any human being, for I have sworn not to do so by the heaven which is above me; if I had not done that, I should have lost my life."

He urged her and left her no peace, but he could draw nothing from her. Then said he, "If you will not tell me anything, tell your sorrows to the iron stove there," and he went away.

Then she crept into the iron stove, and began to weep and lament, and emptied her whole heart, and said, "Here I am deserted by the whole world, and yet I am a King's daughter, and a false waiting-maid has by force brought me to such a pass that I have been compelled to put off my royal apparel, and she has taken my place with my bridegroom, and I have to perform menial service as a goose girl. If my mother did but know that, her heart would break."

The aged King, however, was standing outside by the pipe of the stove, and was listening to what she said, and heard it. Then he came back again, and bade her come out of the stove. And royal garments were placed on her, and it was marvelous how beautiful she was! The aged King summoned his son, and revealed to him that he had got the false bride who was only a waiting-maid, but that the true one was standing there, who had been the goose girl. The young King rejoiced with all his heart when he saw her beauty and youth, and a great feast was made ready to which all the people and all good friends were invited. At the head of the table sat the bridegroom with the King's daughter at one side of him, and the waiting-maid on the other, but the waiting-maid was blinded, and did not recognize the princess in her dazzling array. When they had eaten and drunk, and were merry, the aged King asked the waiting-maid as a riddle, what a person deserved who had behaved in such and such a way to her master, and at the same time related the whole story, and asked what sentence such a one merited?

Then the false bride said, "She deserves no better fate than to be stripped entirely naked, and put in a barrel which is studded inside with pointed nails, and two white horses should be harnessed to it, which will drag her along through one street after another, till she is dead."

"It is you," said the aged King, "and you have pronounced your own sentence, and thus shall it be done unto you." And when the sentence had been carried out, the young King married his true bride, and both of them reigned over their kingdom in peace and happiness.

90. THE YOUNG GIANT

Once upon a time a countryman had a son who was as big as a thumb, and did not become any bigger, and during several years did not grow one hair's breadth. Once when the father was going out to plow, the little one said, "Father, I will go out with you."

"You would go out with me?" said the father. "Stay here, you will be of no use out there, besides you might get lost!" Then Thumbling began to cry, and for the sake of peace his father put him in his pocket, and took him with him. When he was outside in the field, he took him out again, and set him in a freshly-cut furrow. While he was there, a great giant came over the hill.

"Do you see that great bogie?" said the father, for he wanted to frighten the little fellow to make him good, "he is coming to fetch you." The giant, however, had scarcely taken two steps with his long legs before he was in the furrow. He took up little Thumbling carefully with two fingers, examined him, and without saying one word went away with him. His father stood by, but could not utter a sound for terror, and he thought nothing else but that his child was lost, and that as long as he lived he should never set eyes on him again.

The giant, however, carried him home, suckled him, and Thumbling grew and became tall and strong after the manner of giants. When two years had passed, the old giant took him into the forest, wanted to try him, and said, "Pull up a stick for yourself." Then the boy was already so strong that he tore up a young tree out of the earth by the roots. But the giant thought, "We must do better than that," took him back again, and suckled him two years longer.

When he tried him, his strength had increased so much that he could tear an old tree out of the ground. That was still not enough for the giant; he again suckled him for two years, and when he then went with him into the forest and said, "Now just tear up a proper stick for me," the boy tore up the strongest oak tree from the earth, so that it split, and that was a mere trifle to him. "Now that will do," said the giant, "you are perfect," and took him back to the field from where he had brought him. His father was there following the plow.

The young giant went up to him, and said, "Does my father see what a fine man his son has grown into?"

The farmer was alarmed, and said, "No, you are not my son; I don't want you—leave me!"

"Truly I am your son; allow me to do your work, I can plow as well as you, nay better."

"No, no, you are not my son; and you cannot plow—go away!" However, as he was afraid of this great man, he let go of the plow, stepped back and stood at one side of the piece of land. Then the youth took the plow, and just pressed it with one hand, but his grasp was so strong that the plow went deep into the earth. The farmer could not bear to see that, and called to him, "If you are determined to plow, you must not press so hard on it, that makes bad work."

The youth, however, unharnessed the horses, and drew the plow himself, saying, "Just go home, father, and bid my mother make ready a large dish of food, and in the meantime I will go over the field." Then the farmer went home, and ordered his wife to prepare the food; but the youth plowed the field which was two acres large, quite alone, and then he harnessed himself to the harrow, and harrowed the whole of the land, using two harrows at once. When he had done it, he went into the forest, and pulled up two oak trees, laid them across his shoulders, and hung on them one harrow behind and one before, and also one horse behind and one before, and carried all as if it had been a bundle of straw, to his parents' house.

When he entered the yard, his mother did not recognize him, and asked, "Who is that horrible tall man?"

The farmer said, "That is our son."

She said, "No that cannot be our son, we never had such a tall one, ours was a little thing." She called to him, "Go away, we do not want you!"

The youth was silent, but led his horses to the stable, gave them some oats and hay, and all that they wanted. When he had done this, he went into the parlor, sat down on the bench and said, "Mother, now I should like something to eat, will it soon be ready?"

Then she said, "Yes," and brought in two immense dishes full of food, which would have been enough to satisfy herself and her husband for a week. The youth, however, ate the whole of it himself, and asked if she had nothing more to set before him. "No," she replied, "that is all we have."

"But that was only a taste, I must have more." She did not dare to oppose him, and went and put a huge caldron full of food on the fire, and when it was ready, carried it in. "At length come a few crumbs," said he, and ate all there was, but it was still not sufficient to appease his hunger. Then said he, "Father, I see well that with you I shall never have food enough; if you will get me an iron staff which is strong, and which I cannot break against my knees, I will go out into the world."

The farmer was glad, put his two horses in his cart, and fetched from the smith a staff so large and thick, that the two horses could only just bring it away. The youth laid it across his knees, and snap! he broke it in two in the middle like a beanstalk, and threw it away. The father then harnessed four horses, and brought a bar which was so long and thick, that the four horses could only just drag it. The son snapped this also in two against his knees, threw it away, and said, "Father, this can be of no use to me, you must harness more horses, and bring a stronger staff." So the father harnessed eight horses, and brought one which was so long and thick, that the eight horses could only just carry it. When the son took it in his hand, he broke off a bit from the top of it also, and said, "Father, I see that you will not be able to procure me any such staff as I want, I will remain no longer with you."

So he went away, and gave out that he was a smith's apprentice. He arrived at a village, where a smith lived who was a greedy fellow, who never did a kindness to anyone, but wanted everything for himself. The youth went into the smithy and asked if he needed a journeyman. "Yes," said the smith, and looked at him, and thought, "That is a strong fellow who will strike out well, and earn his bread." So he asked, "How much wages do you want?"

"I don't want any at all," he replied, "only every fortnight, when the other journeymen are paid, I will give you two blows, and you must bear them." The miser was heartily satisfied, and thought he would thus save much money.

Next morning, the strange journeyman was to begin to work, but when the master brought the glowing bar, and the youth struck his first blow, the iron flew asunder, and the anvil sank so deep into the earth, that there was no bringing it out again. Then the miser grew angry, and said, "Oh, but I can't make any use of you, you strike far too powerfully; what will you have for the one blow?"

Then said he, "I will only give you quite a small blow, that's all."

And he raised his foot, and gave him such a kick that he flew away over four loads of hay. Then he sought out the thickest iron bar in the smithy for himself, took it as a stick in his hand and went onwards.

When he had walked for some time, he came to a small farm, and asked the bailiff if he did not require a head-servant. "Yes," said the bailiff, "I can make use of one; you look a strong fellow who can do something, how much a year do you want as wages?" He again replied that he wanted no wages at all, but that every year he would give him three blows, which he must bear. Then the bailiff was satisfied, for he, too, was a covetous fellow.

Next morning all the servants were to go into the wood, and the others were already up, but the head-servant was still in bed. Then one of them called to him, "Get up, it is time; we are going into the wood, and you must go with us."

"Ah," said he in a rough and surly tone, "you may just go, then; I shall be back again before any of you." Then the others went to the bailiff, and told him that the head-man was still lying in bed, and would not go into the wood with them. The bailiff said they were to awaken him again, and tell him to harness the horses. The head-man, however, said as before, "Just go there, I shall be back again before any of you." And then he stayed in bed two hours longer.

At length he arose from the feathers, but first he got himself two bushels of peas from the loft, made himself some broth with them, ate it at his leisure, and when that was done, went and harnessed the horses, and drove into the wood. Not far from the wood was a ravine through which he had to pass, so he first drove the horses on, and then stopped them, and went behind the cart, took trees and brushwood, and made a great barricade, so that no horse could get through. When he was entering the wood, the others were just driving out of it with their loaded carts to go home; then said he to them, "Drive on, I will still get home before you do." He did not drive far into the wood, but at once tore two of the very largest trees of all out of the earth, threw them on his cart, and turned round. When he came to the barricade, the others were still standing there, not able to get through. "Don't you see," said he, "that if you had stayed with me, you would have got home just as quickly, and would have had another hour's sleep?"

He now wanted to drive on, but his horses could not work their way through, so he unharnessed them, laid them on the top of the cart, took the shafts in his own hands, and pulled it all through, and he did this just as easily as if it had been laden with feathers. When he was over, he said to the others, "There, you see, I have got over quicker than you," and drove on, and the others had to stay where they were.

In the yard, he took a tree in his hand, showed it to the bailiff, and said, "Isn't that a fine bundle of wood?"

Then said the bailiff to his wife, "The servant is a good one, if he does sleep long, he is still home before the others."

So he served the bailiff for a year, and when that was over, and the other servants were getting their wages, he said it was time for him to take his too. The bailiff, however, was afraid of the blows which he was to receive, and earnestly entreated him to excuse him from having them; for rather than that, he himself would be head-servant, and the youth should be bailiff. "No," said he, "I will not be a bailiff, I am head-servant, and will remain so, but I will administer that which we agreed on."

The bailiff was willing to give him whatever he demanded, but it was of no use, the head-servant said no to everything. Then the bailiff did not know what to do, and begged for a fortnight's delay, for he wanted to find some way of escape. The head-servant consented to this delay. The bailiff summoned all his clerks together, and they were to think the matter over, and give him advice. The clerks pondered for a long time, but at last they said that no one was sure of his life with the head-servant, for he could kill a man as easily as a midge, and that the bailiff ought to make him get into the well and clean it, and when he was down below, they would roll up one of the millstones which was lying there, and throw it on his head; and then he would never return to daylight.

The advice pleased the bailiff, and the head-servant was quite willing to go down the well. When he was standing down below at the bottom, they rolled down the largest millstone and thought they had broken his skull, but he cried, "Chase away those hens from the well, they are scratching in the sand up there, and throwing the grains into my eyes, so that I can't see."

So the bailiff cried, "Sh-sh," and pretended to frighten the hens away.

When the head-servant had finished his work, he climbed up and said, "Just look what a beautiful necktie I have on," and behold it was the millstone which he was wearing round his neck. The head-servant now wanted to take his reward, but the bailiff again begged for a fortnight's delay. The clerks met together and advised him to send the head-servant to the haunted mill to grind corn by night, for as yet no man had ever returned from there in the morning alive.

The proposal pleased the bailiff, he called the head-servant that very evening, and ordered him to take eight bushels of corn to the mill, and grind it that night, for it was wanted. So the head-servant went to the loft, and put two bushels in his right pocket, and two in his left, and took four in a wallet, half on his back, and half on his breast, and thus laden went to the haunted mill. The miller told him that he could grind there very well by day, but not by night, for the mill was haunted, and that up to the present time whoever had gone into it at night had been found in the morning lying dead inside. He said, "I will manage it, just you go away to bed." Then he went into the mill, and poured out the corn.

About eleven o'clock he went into the miller's room, and sat down on the bench. When he had sat there a while, a door suddenly opened, and a large table came in, and on the table, wine and roasted meats placed themselves, and much good food besides, but everything came of itself, for no one was there to carry it. After this the chairs pushed themselves up, but no people came, until all at once he saw fingers, which handled knives and forks, and laid food on the plates, but with this exception he saw nothing. As he was hungry, and saw the food, he, too, place himself at the table, ate with those who were eating and enjoyed it. When he had had enough, and the others also had quite emptied their dishes, he distinctly heard all the candles being suddenly snuffed out, and as it was now pitch dark, he felt something like a box on the ear. Then he said, "If anything of that kind comes again, I shall strike out in return." And when he had received a second box on the ear, he, too struck out. And so it continued the whole night. He took nothing without returning it, but repaid everything with interest, and did not lay about him in vain.

At daybreak, however, everything ceased. When the miller had got up, he wanted to look after him, and wondered if he were still alive. Then the youth said, "I have eaten my fill, have received some boxes on the ears, but I have given some in return." The miller rejoiced, and said that the mill was now released from the spell, and wanted to give him much money as a reward. But he said, "Money, I will not have, I have enough of it." So he took his meal on his back, went home, and told the bailiff that he had done what he had been told to do, and would now have the reward agreed on.

When the bailiff heard that, he was seriously alarmed and quite beside himself; he walked backwards and forwards in the room, and drops of perspiration ran down from his forehead. Then he opened the window to get some fresh air, but before he was aware, the head-servant had given him such a kick that he flew through the window out into the air, and so far away that no one ever saw him again. Then said the head-servant to the bailiff's wife, "If he does not come back, you must take the other blow."

She cried, "No, no I cannot bear it," and opened the other window, because drops of perspiration were running down her forehead. Then he gave her such a kick that she, too, flew out, and as she was lighter she went much higher than her husband.

Her husband cried, "Do come to me," but she replied, "Come you to me, I cannot come to you." And they hovered about there in the air, and could not get to each other, and whether they are still hovering about, or not, I do not know, but the young giant took up his iron bar, and went on his way.

91. THE GNOME

There was once upon a time a rich King who had three daughters, who daily went to walk in the palace garden, and the King was a great lover of all kinds of fine trees, but there was one for which he had such an affection, that if anyone gathered an apple from it he wished him a hundred fathoms underground. And when harvest time came, the apples on this tree were all as red as blood. The three daughters went every day beneath the tree, and looked to see if the wind had not blown down an apple, but they never by any chance found one, and the tree was so loaded with them that it was almost breaking, and the branches hung down to the ground. Then the King's youngest child had a great desire for an apple, and said to her sisters, "Our father loves us far too much to wish us underground, it is my belief that he would only do that to people who were strangers." And while she was speaking, the child plucked off quite a large apple, and ran to her sisters, saying, "Just taste, my dear little sisters, for never in my life have I tasted anything so delightful." Then the two other sisters also ate some of the apple, after which all three sank deep down into the earth, where they could hear no cock crow.

When midday came, the King wished to call them to come to dinner, but they were nowhere to be found. He sought them everywhere in the palace and garden, but could not find them. Then he was much troubled, and made known to the whole land that whoever brought his daughters back again should have one of them to wed. Hereupon so many young men went about the country in search, that there was no counting them, for everyone loved the three children because they were so kind to all, and so fair of face. Three young hunters also went out, and when they had traveled about for eight days, they arrived at a great castle, in which were beautiful apartments, and in one room a table was laid on which were delicate dishes which were still so warm that they were smoking, but in the whole of the castle no human being was either to be seen or heard. They waited there for half a day, and the food still remained warm and smoking, and at length they were so hungry that they sat down and ate, and agreed with each other that they would stay and live in that castle, and that one of them, who should be chosen by casting lots, should remain in the house, and the two others seek the King's daughters. They cast lots, and the lot fell on the eldest; so next day the two younger went out to seek, and the eldest had to stay home. At midday came a small, small manikin and begged for a piece of bread, then the hunter took the bread which he had found there, and cut a round off the loaf and was about to give it to him, but while he was giving it to the manikin, the latter let it fall, and asked the hunter to be so good as to give him that piece again. The hunter was about to do so and stooped, on which the manikin took a stick, seized him by the hair, and gave him a good beating. Next day, the second stayed at home, and he fared no better. When the two others returned in the evening, the eldest said, "Well, how have you got on?"

"Oh, very badly," said he, and then they lamented their misfortune together, but they said nothing about it to the youngest, for they did not like him at all, and always called him Stupid Hans, because he did not exactly belong to the forest. On the third day, the youngest stayed at home, and again the little manikin came and begged for a piece of bread. When the youth gave it to him, he let it fall as before, and asked him to be so good as to give him that piece again.

Then said Hans to the little manikin, "What! Can you not pick up that piece yourself? If you will not take as much trouble as that for your daily bread, you do not deserve to have it."

Then the manikin grew very angry and said he was to do it, but the hunter would not, and took my dear manikin, and gave him a thorough beating. Then the manikin screamed terribly, and cried, "Stop, stop, and let me go, and I will tell you where the King's daughters are."

When Hans heard that, he left off beating him and the manikin told him that he was a gnome, and that there were more than a thousand like him, and that if he would go with him he would show him where the King's daughters were. Then he showed him a deep well, but there was no water in it. And the little man said that he knew well that the companions Hans had with him did not intend to deal honorably with him, therefore if he wished to deliver the King's children, he must do it alone. The two other brothers would also be very glad to recover the King's daughters, but they did not want to have any trouble or danger. Hans was therefore to take a large basket, and he must seat himself in it with his knife and a bell, and be let down. Below were three rooms, and in each of them was a princess, with a many-headed dragon, whose heads she was to comb and trim, but he must cut them off. And having said all this, the manikin vanished.

When it was evening the two brothers came and asked how he had got on, and he said, "pretty well so far," and that he had seen no one except at midday when a little manikin had come and begged for a piece of bread, that he had given some to him, but that the manikin had let it fall and had asked him to pick it up again; but as he did not choose to do that, the little man had begun to lose his temper, and that he had done what he ought not, and had given the manikin a beating, after which he had told him where the King's daughters were. Then the two were so angry at this that they grew green and yellow.

Next morning they went to the well together, and drew lots who should first seat himself in the basket, and again the lot fell on the eldest, and he was to seat himself in it, and take the bell with him. Then he said, "If I ring, you must draw me up again immediately."

When he had gone down for a short distance, he rang, and they at once drew him up again. Then the second seated himself in the basket, but he did just the same as the first, and then it was the turn of the youngest, but he let himself be lowered quite to the bottom. When he had got out of the basket, he took his knife, and went and stood outside the first door and listened, and heard the dragon snoring quite loudly. He opened the door slowly, and one of the princesses was sitting there, and had nine dragon's heads lying upon her lap, and was combing them. Then he took his knife and hewed at them, and the nine fell off. The princess sprang up, threw her arms round his neck, embraced and kissed him repeatedly, and took her stomacher, which was made of pure gold, and hung it round his neck. Then he went to the second princess, who had a dragon with five heads to comb, and delivered her also, and to the youngest, who had a dragon with four heads, he went likewise. And they all rejoiced, and embraced him and kissed him without stopping. Then he rang very loud, so that those above heard him, and he placed the princesses one after the other in the basket, and had them all drawn up, but when it came to his own turn he remembered the words of the manikin, who had told him that his comrades did not mean well by him. So he took a great stone which was lying there, and placed it in the basket, and when it was about halfway up, his false brothers above cut the rope, so that the basket with the stone fell to the ground, and they thought that he was dead, and ran away with the three princesses, making them promise to tell their father that it was they who had delivered them, and then they went to the King, and each demanded a princess in marriage.

In the meantime the youngest hunter was wandering about the three chambers in great trouble, fully expecting to have to end his days there, when he saw, hanging on the wall, a flute; then said he, "Why do you hang there, no one can be merry here?" He looked at the dragons' heads likewise and said, "You too cannot help me now." He walked backwards and forwards for such a long time that he made the surface of the ground quite smooth. But at last other thoughts came to his mind, and he took the flute from the wall, and played a few notes on it, and suddenly a number of gnomes appeared, and with every note that he sounded one more came. Then he played until the room was entirely filled. They all asked what he desired, so he said he wished to get above ground back to daylight, on which they seized him by every hair that grew on his head, and thus they flew with him onto the earth again. When he was above ground, he at once went to the King's palace, just as the wedding of one princess was about to be celebrated, and he went to the room where the King and his three daughters were. When the princesses saw him they fainted. At this the King was angry, and ordered him to be put in prison at once, because he thought he must have done some injury to the children. When the princesses came to themselves, however, they entreated the King to set him free again. The King asked why, and they said that they were not allowed to tell that, but their father said that they were to tell it to the stove. And he went out, listened at the door, and heard everything. Then he sentenced the two brothers to be hanged on the gallows, and to the third he gave his youngest daughter, and on that occasion I wore a pair of glass shoes, and I struck them against a stone, and they said, "Klink," and were broken.

92. THE KING OF THE
GOLDEN MOUNTAIN

There was a certain merchant who had two children, a boy and a girl; they were both young, and could not walk. And two richly-laden ships of his sailed forth to sea with all his property on board, and just as he was expecting to win much money by them, news came that they had gone to the bottom, and now instead of being a rich man he was a poor one, and had nothing left but one field outside the town. In order to drive his misfortune a little out of his thoughts, he went out to this field, and as he was walking forwards and backwards in it, a little black manikin stood suddenly by his side, and asked why he was so sad, and what he was taking so much to heart. Then said the merchant, "If you could help me I would willingly tell you."

"Who knows?" replied the black dwarf. "Perhaps, I can help you." Then the merchant told him that all he possessed had gone to the bottom of the sea, and that he had nothing left but this field. "Do not trouble yourself," said the dwarf. "If you will promise to give me the first thing that rubs itself against your leg when you are at home again, and to bring it here to this place in twelve years' time, you shall have as much money as you will."

The merchant thought, "What can that be but my dog?" and did not remember his little boy, so he said yes, gave the black man a written and sealed promise, and went home.

When he reached home, his little boy was so delighted that he held by a bench, tottered up to him and seized him fast by the legs. The father was shocked, for he remembered his promise, and now knew what he had pledged himself to do; as however, he still found no money in his chest, he thought the dwarf had only been jesting. A month afterwards he went up to the attic, intending to gather together some old tin and to sell it, and saw a great heap of money lying. Then he was happy again, made purchases, became a greater merchant than before, and felt that this world was well-governed. In the meantime the boy grew tall, and at the same time sharp and clever. But the nearer the twelfth year approached the more anxious the merchant grew, so that his distress might be seen in his face. One day his son asked what ailed him, but the father would not say. The boy, however, persisted so long, that at last he told him that without being aware of what he was doing, he had promised him to a black dwarf, and had received much money for doing so. He said likewise that he had set his hand and seal to this, and that now when twelve years had gone by he would have to give him up.

Then said the son, "Oh, father, do not be uneasy, all will go well. The black man has no power over me." The son had himself blessed by the priest, and when the time came, father and son went together to the field, and the son made a circle and placed himself inside it with his father.

Then came the black dwarf and said to the old man, "Have you brought with you that which you have promised me?"

He was silent, but the son asked, "What do you want here?"

Then said the black dwarf, "I have to speak with your father, and not with you."

The son replied, "You have betrayed and misled my father, give back the writing."

"No," said the black dwarf, "I will not give up my rights." They spoke together for a long time after this, but at last they agreed that the son, as he did not belong to the enemy of mankind, nor did he to his father, should seat himself in a small boat, which should lie on water which was flowing away from them, and that the father should push it off with his own foot, and then the son should remain given up to the water. So he took leave of his father, placed himself in a little boat, and the father had to push it off with his own foot. The boat capsized so that the keel was uppermost, and the father believed his son was lost, and went home and mourned for him.

The boat, however, did not sink, but floated quietly away, and the boy sat safely inside it, and it floated thus for a long time, until at last it stopped by an unknown shore. Then he landed and saw a beautiful castle before him, and set out to go to it. But when he entered it, he found that it was bewitched. He went through every room, but all were empty until he reached the last, where a snake lay coiled in a ring. The snake, however, was an enchanted maiden, who rejoiced to see him, and said, "Have you come, oh, my deliverer? I have already waited twelve years for you; this kingdom is bewitched, and you must set it free."

"How can I do that?" he inquired.

"Tonight come twelve black men, covered with chains who will ask what you are doing here; keep silent; give them no answer, and let them do what they will with you; they will torment you, beat you, stab you; let everything pass, only do not speak; at twelve o'clock, they must go away again. On the second night twelve others will come; on the third, twenty-four, who will cut off your head, but at twelve o'clock their power will be over, and then if you have endured all, and have not spoken the slightest word, I shall be released. I will come to you, and will have, in a bottle, some of the water of life. I will rub you with that, and then you will come to life again, and be as healthy as before."

Then said he, "I will gladly set you free." And everything happened just as she had said; the black men could not force a single word from him, and on the third night the snake became a beautiful princess, who came with the water of life and brought him back to life again. So she threw herself into his arms and kissed him, and there was joy and gladness in the whole castle. After this their marriage was celebrated, and he was King of the Golden Mountain.

They lived very happily together, and the Queen bore a fine boy. Eight years had already gone by, when the King thought of his father; his heart was moved, and he wished to visit him. The Queen, however, would not let him go away, and said, "I know beforehand that it will cause my unhappiness;" but he suffered her to have no rest until she consented. At their parting she gave him a wishing ring, and said, "Take this ring and put it on your finger, and then you will immediately be transported wherever you would be, only you must promise me not to use it in wishing me away from this place and with your father."

That he promised her, put the ring on his finger, and wished himself at home, just outside the town where his father lived. Instantly he found himself there, and made for the town, but when he came to the gate, the sentries would not let him in, because he wore such strange and yet such rich and magnificent clothing. Then he went to a hill where a shepherd was watching his sheep, changed clothes with him, put on his old shepherd's coat, and then entered the town without hindrance. When he came to his father, he made himself known to him, but he did not at all believe that the shepherd was his son, and said he certainly had had a son, but that he was dead long ago; however, as he saw he was a poor, needy shepherd, he would give him something to eat. Then the shepherd said to his parents, "I am verily your son. Do you know of no mark on my body by which you could recognize me?"

"Yes," said his mother, "our son had a raspberry mark under his right arm." He slipped back his shirt, and they saw the raspberry under his right arm, and no longer doubted that he was their son. Then he told them that he was King of the Golden Mountain, and a king's daughter was his wife, and that they had a fine son of seven years old.

Then said the father, "That is certainly not true; it is a fine kind of a king who goes about in a ragged shepherd's coat."

At this the son fell in a passion, and without thinking of his promise, turned his ring round, and wished both his wife and child with him. They were there in a second, but the Queen wept, and reproached him, and said that he had broken his word, and had brought misfortune upon her. He said, "I have done it thoughtlessly, and not with evil intention," and tried to calm her, and she pretended to believe this; but she had mischief in her mind.

Then he led her out of the town into the field, and showed her the stream where the little boat had been pushed off, and then he said, "I am tired; sit down, I will sleep awhile on your lap." And he laid his head on her lap, and fell asleep. When he was asleep, she first drew the ring from his finger, then she drew away the foot which was under him, leaving only the slipper behind her, and she took her child in her arms, and wished herself back in her own kingdom.

When he awoke, there he lay quite deserted, and his wife and child were gone, and so was the ring from his finger, only the slipper was still there as a token. "Home to your parents you cannot return," thought he, "they would say that you were a wizard; you must be off, and walk on until you arrive in your own kingdom." So he went away and came at length to a hill by which three giants were standing, disputing with each other because they did not know how to divide their father's property. When they saw him passing by, they called to him and said little men had quick wits, and that he was to divide their inheritance for them. The inheritance, however, consisted of a sword, which had this property that if anyone took it in his hand, and said, "All heads off but mine," every head would lie on the ground; secondly, of a cloak which made anyone who put it on invisible; thirdly, of a pair of boots which could transport the wearer to any place he wished in a moment.

He said, "Give me the three things that I may see if they are still in good condition." They gave him the cloak, and when he had put it on, he was invisible and changed into a fly. Then he resumed his own form and said, "The cloak is a good one, now give me the sword."

They said, "No, we will not give you that; if you were to say, 'All heads off but mine,' all our heads would be off, and you alone would be left with yours." Nevertheless they gave it to him with the condition that he was only to try it against a tree. This he did, and the sword cut in two the trunk of a tree as if it had been a blade of straw.

Then he wanted to have the boots likewise, but they said, "No, we will not give them; if you had them on your feet and were to wish yourself at the top of the hill, we should be left down here with nothing."

"Oh, no," said he, "I will not do that." So they gave him the boots as well. And now when he had got all these things, he thought of nothing but his wife and his child, and said as though to himself, "Oh, if I were but on the Golden Mountain," and at the same moment he vanished from the sight of the giants, and thus their inheritance was divided.

When he was near his palace, he heard sounds of joy, and fiddles, and flutes, and the people told him that his wife was celebrating her wedding with another. Then he fell into a rage, and said, "False woman, she betrayed and deserted me while I was asleep!" So he put on his cloak, and unseen by all went into the palace. When he entered the dining hall a great table was spread with delicious food, and the guests were eating and drinking, and laughing, and jesting. She sat on a royal seat in the middle of them in splendid apparel, with a crown on her head. He placed himself behind her, and no one saw him. When she put a piece of meat on a plate for herself, he took it away and ate it, and when she poured out a glass of wine for herself, he took it away and drank it. She was always helping herself to something, and yet she never got anything, for plate and glass disappeared immediately.

Then dismayed and ashamed, she arose and went to her chamber and wept, but he followed her there. She said, "Has the devil power over me, or did my deliverer never come?"

Then he struck her in the face, and said, "Did your deliverer never come? It is he who has you in his power, you traitor. Have I deserved this from you?" Then he made himself visible, went into the hall, and cried, "The wedding is at an end, the true King has returned."

The kings, princes, and councilors who were assembled there, ridiculed and mocked him, but he did not trouble to answer them, and said, "Will you go away, or not?" At this they tried to seize him and pressed upon him, but he drew his sword and said, "All heads off but mine," and all the heads rolled on the ground, and he alone was master, and once more King of the Golden Mountain.

93. THE RAVEN

There was once upon a time a Queen who had a little daughter who was still so young that she had to be carried. One day the child was naughty, and the mother might say what she liked, but the child would not be quiet. Then she became impatient, and as the ravens were flying about the palace, she opened the window and said, "I wish you were a raven and would fly away, and then I should have some rest." Scarcely had she spoken the words, before the child was changed into a raven, and flew from her arms out of the window. It flew into a dark forest, and stayed in it a long time, and the parents heard nothing of their child. Then one day a man was on his way through this forest and heard the raven crying, and followed the voice, and when he came nearer, the bird said, "I am a king's daughter by birth, and am bewitched, but you can set me free."

"What am I to do?" asked he.

She said, "Go further into the forest, and you will find a house, wherein sits an aged woman, who will offer you meat and drink, but you must accept nothing, for if you eat and drink anything, you will fall into a sleep, and then you will not be able to deliver me. In the garden behind the house there is a great heap of tan, and on this you shall stand and wait for me. For three days I will come every afternoon at two o'clock in a carriage. On the first day four white horses will be harnessed to it, then four chestnut horses, and lastly four black ones; but if you are not awake, but sleeping, I shall not be set free." The man promised to do everything that she desired, but the raven said, alas, "I know already that you will not deliver me; you will accept something from the woman."

Then the man once more promised that he would certainly not touch anything either to eat or to drink. But when he entered the house the old woman came to him and said, "Poor man, how faint you are; come and refresh yourself; eat and drink."

"No," said the man, "I will not eat or drink."

She, however, let him have no peace, and said, "If you will not eat, take one drink out of the glass; one is nothing." Then he let himself be persuaded, and drank.

Shortly before two o'clock in the afternoon he went into the garden to the tan heap to wait for the raven. As he was standing there, his weariness all at once became so great that he could not struggle against it, and lay down for a short time, but he was determined not to go to sleep. Hardly, however, had he lain down, than his eyes closed of their own accord, and he fell asleep and slept so soundly that nothing in the world could have aroused him.

At two o'clock the raven came driving up with four white horses, but she was already in deep grief and said, "I know he is asleep." And when she came into the garden, he was indeed lying there asleep on the heap of tan. She alighted from the carriage, went to him, shook him, and called him, but he did not awake.

Next day about noon, the old woman came again and brought him food and drink, but he would not take any of it. But she let him have no rest and persuaded him until at length he again took one drink out of the glass. Towards two o'clock he went into the garden to the tan heap to wait for the raven, but all at once felt such a great weariness that his limbs would no longer support him. He could not help himself, and was forced to lie down, and fell into a heavy sleep. When the raven drove up with four brown horses, she was already full of grief, and said, "I know he is asleep." She went to him, but there he lay sleeping, and there was no waking him.

Next day the old woman asked what was the meaning of this? He was neither eating nor drinking anything; did he want to die? He replied, "I am not allowed to eat or drink, and will not do so." But she set a dish with food, and a glass with wine before him, and when he smelled it he could not resist, and swallowed a deep drink. When the time came, he went out into the garden to the heap of tan, and waited for the King's daughter; but he became still more weary than on the day before, and lay down and slept as soundly as if he had been a stone.

At two o'clock the raven came with four black horses, and the coachman and everything else was black. She was already in the deepest grief, and said, "I know that he is asleep and cannot deliver me." When she came to him, there he was lying fast asleep. She shook him and called him, but she could not wake him.

Then she laid a loaf beside him, and after that a piece of meat, and thirdly a bottle of wine, and he might consume as much of all of them as he liked, but they would never grow less. After this she took a gold ring from her finger, and put it on his, and her name was graven on it. Lastly, she laid a letter beside him wherein was written what she had given him, and that none of the things would ever grow less; and in it was also written, "I see right well that here you will never be able to deliver me, but if you are still willing to deliver me, come to the golden castle of Stromberg; it lies in your power, of that I am certain." And when she had given him all these things, she seated herself in her carriage, and drove to the golden castle of Stromberg.

When the man awoke and saw that he had slept, he was sad at heart, and said, "She has certainly driven by, and I have not set her free." Then he perceived the things which were lying beside him, and read the letter wherein was written how everything had happened. So he arose and went away, intending to go to the golden castle of Stromberg, but he did not know where it was. After he had walked about the world for a long time, he entered into a dark forest, and walked for fourteen days, and still could not find his way out. Then it was once more evening, and he was so tired that he lay down in a thicket and fell asleep. Next day he went onwards, and in the evening, as he was again about to lie down beneath some bushes, he heard such a howling and crying that he could not go to sleep. And at the time when people light the candles, he saw one glimmering, and arose and went towards it. Then he came to a house which seemed very small, for in front of it a great giant was standing. He thought to himself, "If I go in, and the giant sees me, it will very likely cost me my life."

At length he ventured it and went in. When the giant saw him, he said, "It is well that you come, for it is long since I have eaten; I will at once eat you for my supper."

"I'd rather you would leave that alone," said the man, "I do not like to be eaten; but if you have any desire to eat, I have quite enough here to satisfy you."

"If that be true," said the giant, "you may be easy, I was only going to devour you because I had nothing else." Then they went, and sat down to the table, and the man took out the bread, wine, and meat which would never come to an end. "This pleases me well," said the giant, and ate to his heart's content.

Then the man said to him, "Can you tell me where the golden castle of Stromberg is?"

The giant said, "I will look at my map; all the towns, and villages, and houses are to be found on it." He brought out the map which he had in the room and looked for the castle, but it was not to be found on it. "It's no matter!" said he, "I have some still larger maps in my cupboard upstairs, and we will look in them." But there, too, it was in vain.

The man now wanted to go onwards, but the giant begged him to wait a few days longer until his brother, who had gone out to bring some provisions, came home. When the brother came home they inquired about the golden castle of Stromberg. He replied, "When I have eaten and have had enough, I will look in the map." Then he went with them up to his chamber, and they searched in his map, but could not find it. Then he brought out still older maps, and they never rested until they found the golden castle of Stromberg, but it was many thousand miles away.

"How am I to get there?" asked the man.

The giant said, "I have two hours' time, during which I will carry you into the neighborhood, but after that I must be at home to suckle the child that we have." So the giant carried the man to about a hundred leagues from the castle, and said, "You can very well walk the rest of the way alone." And he turned back.

The man, however, went onwards day and night, until at length he came to the golden castle of Stromberg. It stood on a glass mountain, and the bewitched maiden drove in her carriage round the castle, and then went inside it. He rejoiced when he saw her and wanted to climb up to her, but when he began to do so he always slipped down the glass again. And when he saw that he could not reach her, he was filled with trouble, and said to himself, "I will stay down here below, and wait for her."

So he built himself a hut and stayed in it for a whole year, and every day saw the King's daughter driving about above, but never could go to her. Then one day he saw from his hut three robbers who were beating each other, and cried to them, "God be with you!" They stopped when they heard the cry, but as they saw no one, they once more began to beat each other, and that too most dangerously. So he again cried, "God be with you!" Again they stopped, looked round about, but as they saw no one they went on beating each other. Then he cried for the third time, "God be with you," and thought, "I must see what these three are about," and went over and asked why they were beating each other so furiously.

One of them said that he found a stick, and that when he struck a door with it, that door would spring open. The next said that he had found a mantle, and that whenever he put it on, he was invisible, but the third said he had found a horse on which a man could ride everywhere, even up the glass mountain. And now they did not know whether they ought to have these things in common, or whether they ought to divide them. Then the man said, "I will give you something in exchange for these three things. Money indeed have I not, but I have other things of more value; but first I must try yours to see if you have told the truth."

Then they put him on the horse, threw the mantle round him, and gave him the stick in his hand, and when he had all these things they were no longer able to see him. So he gave them some vigorous blows and cried, "Now, vagabonds, you have got what you deserve, are you satisfied?" And he rode up the glass mountain, but when he came in front of the castle at the top, it was shut. Then he struck the door with his stick, and it sprang open immediately. He went in and ascended the stairs until he came to the hall where the maiden was sitting with a golden cup full of wine before her. She, however, could not see him because he had the mantle on. And when he came up to her, he drew from his finger the ring which she had given him, and threw it into the cup so that it rang. Then she cried, "That is my ring, so the man who is to set me free must be here."

The courtiers searched the whole castle and did not find him, but he had gone out, and had seated himself on the horse and thrown off the mantle. When they came to the door, they saw him and cried aloud in their delight. Then he alighted and took the King's daughter in his arms, but she kissed him and said, "Now you have set me free, and tomorrow we will celebrate our wedding."

94. THE PEASANT'S WISE DAUGHTER

There was once a poor peasant who had no land, but only a small house, and one daughter. Then said the daughter, "We ought to ask our lord the King for a bit of newly-cleared land." When the King heard of their poverty, he presented them with a piece of land, which she and her father dug up, and intended to sow with a little corn and grain of that kind. When they had dug nearly the whole of the field, they found in the earth a mortar made of pure gold.

"Listen," said the father to the girl, "as our lord the King has been so gracious and presented us with the field, we ought to give him this mortar in return for it."

The daughter, however, would not consent to this, and said, "Father, if we have the mortar without having the pestle as well, we shall have to get the pestle, so you had much better say nothing about it."

He would, however, not obey her, but took the mortar and carried it to the King, said that he had found it in the cleared land, and asked if he would accept it as a present. The King took the mortar, and asked if he had found nothing besides that? "No," answered the countryman.

Then the King said that he must now bring him the pestle. The peasant said they had not found that, but he might just as well have spoken to the wind; he was put in prison, and was to stay there until he produced the pestle. The servants had daily to carry him bread and water, which is what people get in prison, and they heard how the man cried out continually, "Ah! If I had but listened to my daughter! Alas, alas, if I had but listened to my daughter!" and would neither eat nor drink. So he commanded the servants to bring the prisoner before him, and then the King asked the peasant why he was always crying, "Ah! If I had but listened to my daughter!" and what it was that his daughter had said.

"She told me that I ought not to take the mortar to you, for I should have to produce the pestle as well."

"If you have a daughter who is as wise as that, let her come here." She was therefore obliged to appear before the King, who asked her if she really was so wise, and said he would set her a riddle, and if she could guess that, he would marry her. She at once said yes, she would guess it. Then said the King, "Come to me not clothed, not naked, not riding, not walking, not in the road, and not out of the road, and if you can do that I will marry you."

So she went away, put off everything she had on, and then she was not clothed, and took a great fishing net, and seated herself in it and wrapped it entirely round and round her, so that she was not naked, and she hired an ass, and tied the fisherman's net to its tail, so that it was forced to drag her along, and that was neither riding nor walking. The ass had also to drag her in the ruts, so that she only touched the ground with her great toe, and that was neither being in the road nor out of the road. And when she arrived in that fashion, the King said she had guessed the riddle and fulfilled all the conditions. Then he ordered her father to be released from the prison, took her as wife, and gave into her care all the royal possessions.

Now when some years had passed, the King was once drawing up his troops on parade, when it happened that some peasants who had been selling wood stopped with their wagons before the palace; some of them had oxen yoked to them, and some horses. There was one peasant who had three horses, one of which delivered a young foal, and it ran away and lay down between two oxen which were in front of the wagon. When the peasants came together, they began to dispute, to beat each other and make a disturbance, and the peasant with the oxen wanted to keep the foal, and said one of the oxen had given birth to it, and the other said his horse had had it, and that it was his. The quarrel came before the King, and he give the verdict that the foal should stay where it had been found, and so the peasant with the oxen, to whom it did not belong, got it. Then the other went away, and wept and lamented over his foal.

Now he had heard how gracious his lady the Queen was because she herself had sprung from poor peasant folks, so he went to her and begged her to see if she could not help him to get his foal back again. Said she, "Yes, I will tell you what to do, if you will promise me not to betray me. Early tomorrow morning, when the King parades the guard, place yourself there in the middle of the road by which he must pass, take a great fishing net and pretend to be fishing; go on fishing, too, and empty out the net as if you had got it full"—and then she told him also what he was to say if he was questioned by the King.

The next day, therefore, the peasant stood there, and fished on dry ground. When the King passed by, and saw that, he sent his messenger to ask what the stupid man was about? He answered, "I am fishing."

The messenger asked how he could fish when there was no water there? The peasant said, "It is as easy for me to fish on dry land as it is for an ox to have a foal."

The messenger went back and took the answer to the King, who ordered the peasant to be brought to him and told him that this was not his own idea, and he wanted to know whose it was? The peasant must confess this at once. The peasant, however, would not do so, and said always, God forbid he should!—The idea was his own. They laid him, however, on a heap of straw, and beat him and tormented him so long that at last he admitted that he had got the idea from the Queen.

When the King reached home again, he said to his wife, "Why have you behaved so falsely to me? I will not have you any longer for a wife; your time is up, go back to the place from where you came, to your peasant's hut."

One favor, however, he granted her; she might take with her the one thing that was dearest and best in her eyes; and thus she was dismissed. She said, "Yes, my dear husband, if you command this, I will do it," and she embraced him and kissed him, and said she would take leave of him.

Then she ordered a powerful sleeping potion to be brought, to drink farewell to him; the King took a long drink, but she took only a little. He soon fell into a deep sleep, and when she perceived that, she called a servant and took a fair white linen cloth and wrapped the King in it, and the servant was forced to carry him into a carriage that stood before the door, and she drove with him to her own little house. She laid him in her own little bed, and he slept one day and one night without awakening, and when he awoke he looked round and said, "Good God! Where am I?" He called his attendants, but none of them were there.

At length his wife came to his bedside and said, "My dear lord and King, you told me I might bring away with me from the palace that which was dearest and most precious in my eyes. I have nothing more precious and dear than yourself, so I have brought you with me."

Tears rose to the King's eyes and he said, "Dear wife, you shall be mine and I will be yours," and he took her back with him to the royal palace and was married again to her, and at the present time they are very likely still living.

95. OLD HILDEBRAND

Once upon a time lived a peasant and his wife, and the parson of the village had a fancy for the wife, and had wished for a long while to spend a whole day happily with her. The peasant woman, too, was quite willing. One day, therefore, he said to the woman, "Listen, my dear friend, I have now thought of a way by which we can for once spend a whole day happily together. I'll tell you what; on Wednesday, you must take to your bed, and tell your husband you are ill, and if you only complain and act being ill properly, and go on doing so until Sunday when I have to preach, I will then say in my sermon that whoever has at home a sick child, a sick husband, a sick wife, a sick father, a sick mother, a sick brother or whoever else it may be, and makes a pilgrimage to the Göckerli hill in Italy, where you can get a peck of laurel leaves for a kreuzer, the sick child, the sick husband, the sick wife, the sick father, the sick mother, the sick sister, or whoever else it may be, will be restored to health immediately."

"I will manage it," said the woman promptly. Now therefore on the Wednesday, the peasant woman took to her bed, and complained and lamented as agreed on, and her husband did everything for her that he could think of, but nothing did her any good, and when Sunday came the woman said, "I feel as ill as if I were going to die at once, but there is one thing I should like to do before my end. I should like to hear the parson's sermon that he is going to preach today."

At that the peasant said, "Ah, my child, do not do it—you might make yourself worse if you were to get up. Look, I will go to the sermon, and will attend to it very carefully, and will tell you everything the parson says."

"Well," said the woman, "go, then, and pay great attention, and repeat to me all that you hear." So the peasant went to the sermon, and the parson began to preach and said, if anyone had at home a sick child, a sick husband, a sick wife, a sick father a sick mother, a sick sister, brother or anyone else, and would make a pilgrimage to the Göckerli hill in Italy, where a peck of laurel leaves costs a kreuzer, the sick child, sick husband, sick wife, sick father, sick mother, sick sister, brother, or whoever else it might be, would be restored to health instantly, and whoever wished to undertake the journey was to go to him after the service was over, and he would give him the sack for the laurel leaves and the kreuzer.

Then no one was more rejoiced than the peasant, and after the service was over, he went at once to the parson, who gave him the bag for the laurel leaves and the kreuzer. After that he went home, and even at the house door he cried, "Hurrah! Dear wife, it is now almost the same thing as if you were well! The parson has preached today that whoever had at home a sick child, a sick husband, a sick wife, a sick father, a sick mother, a sick sister, brother or whoever it might be, and would make a pilgrimage to the Göckerli hill in Italy, where a peck of laurel leaves costs a kreuzer, the sick child, sick husband, sick wife, sick father, sick mother, sick sister, brother, or whoever else it was, would be cured immediately, and now I have already got the bag and the kreuzer from the parson, and will at once begin my journey so that you may get well the faster," and thereupon he went away. He was, however, hardly gone before the woman got up, and the parson was there directly.

But now we will leave these two for a while, and follow the peasant, who walked on quickly without stopping, in order to get the sooner to the Göckerli hill, and on his way he met his gossip. His gossip was an egg merchant, and was just coming from the market, where he had sold his eggs. "May you be blessed," said the gossip, "where are you off to so fast?"

"To all eternity, my friend," said the peasant, "my wife is ill, and I have been today to hear the parson's sermon, and he preached that if anyone had in his house a sick child, a sick husband, a sick wife, a sick father, a sick mother, a sick sister, brother or anyone else, and made a pilgrimage to the Göckerli hill in Italy, where a peck of laurel leaves costs a kreuzer, the sick child, the sick husband, the sick wife, the sick father, the sick mother, the sick sister, brother or whoever else it was, would be cured immediately, and so I have got the bag for the laurel leaves and the kreuzer from the parson, and now I am beginning my pilgrimage."

"But listen, gossip," said the egg merchant to the peasant, "are you, then, stupid enough to believe such a thing as that? Don't you know what it means? The parson wants to spend a whole day alone with your wife in peace, so he has given you this job to do to get you out of the way."

"My word!" said the peasant. "How I'd like to know if that's true!"

"Come, then," said the gossip, "I'll tell you what to do. Get into my egg basket and I will carry you home, and then you will see for yourself." So that was settled, and the gossip put the peasant into his egg basket and carried him home.

When they got to the house, hurrah! But all was going merry there! The woman had already had nearly everything killed that was in the farmyard, and had made pancakes, and the parson was there, and had brought his fiddle with him. The gossip knocked at the door, and the woman asked who was there. "It is I, gossip," said the egg merchant, "give me shelter this night; I have not sold my eggs at the market, so now I have to carry them home again, and they are so heavy that I shall never be able to do it, for it is dark already."

"Indeed, my friend," said the woman, "you come at a very inconvenient time for me, but as you are here it can't be helped, come in, and take a seat there on the bench by the stove." Then she placed the gossip and the basket which he carried on his back on the bench by the stove. The parson, however, and the woman, were as merry as possible.

At length the parson said, "Listen, my dear friend, you can sing beautifully; sing something to me."

"Oh," said the woman, "I cannot sing now, in my young days indeed I could sing well enough, but that's all over now."

"Come," said the parson once more, "do sing some little song."

At that the woman began and sang,

> "I've sent my husband away from me
> To the Göckerli hill in Italy."

Thereupon the parson sang,

> "I wish 'twas a year before he came back,
> I'd never ask him for the laurel leaf sack.
> > Hallelujah."

Then the gossip who was in the background began to sing (but I ought to tell you the peasant was called Hildebrand), so the gossip sang,

"What are you doing, my Hildebrand dear,
There on the bench by the stove so near?
                                Hallelujah."

And then the peasant sang from his basket,

"All singing I ever shall hate from this day,
And here in this basket no longer I'll stay.
                                Hallelujah."

And he got out of the basket, and cudgeled the parson out of the house.

96. THE THREE LITTLE BIRDS

About a thousand or more years ago, there were in this country nothing but small kings, and one of them who lived on the Keuterberg was very fond of hunting. Once on a time when he was riding forth from his castle with his hunters, three girls were watching their cows upon the mountain, and when they saw the King with all his followers, the eldest girl pointed to him, and called to the two other girls, "If I do not get that one, I will have none."

Then the second girl answered from the other side of the hill, and pointed to the one who was on the King's right hand, "Hello! Hello! If I do not get him, I will have no one."

These, however, were the two ministers. The King heard all this, and when he had come back from the chase, he had the three girls brought to him, and asked them what they had said yesterday on the mountain. This they would not tell him, so the King asked the eldest if she really would take him for her husband? Then she said, "Yes," and the two ministers married her two sisters, for they were all three fair and beautiful of face, especially the Queen, who had hair like flax.

But the two sisters had no children, and once when the King was obliged to go from home he invited them to come to the Queen in order to cheer her, for she was about to bear a child. She had a little boy who brought a bright red star into the world with him. Then the two sisters said to each other that they would throw the beautiful boy into the water. When they had thrown him in (I believe it was into the Weser) a little bird flew up into the air, which sang,

> "To your death are you sped,
> Until God's word be said.
> In the white lily bloom,
> Brave boy, is your tomb."

When the two heard that, they were frightened to death, and ran away in great haste. When the King came home they told him that the Queen had birthed a dog. Then the King said, "What God does, is well done!" But a fisherman who dwelt near the water fished the little boy out again while he was still alive, and as his wife had no children, they reared him. When a year had gone by, the King again went away, and the Queen had another little boy, whom the false sisters likewise took and threw into the water. Then up flew a little bird again and sang,

> "To your death are you sped,
> Until God's word be said.
> In the white lily bloom,
> Brave boy, is your tomb."

And when the King came back, they told him that the Queen had once more given birth to a dog, and he again said, "What God does, is well done." The fisherman, however, fished this one also out of the water, and reared him.

Then the King again journeyed forth, and the Queen had a little girl, whom also the false sisters threw into the water. Then again a little bird flew up on high and sang,

> "To your death are you sped
> Until God's word be said.
> In the white lily bloom,
> Bonny girl, is your tomb."

And when the King came home they told him that the Queen had delivered a cat. Then the King grew angry, and ordered his wife to be cast into prison, and there she was shut up for many long years.

In the meantime the children had grown up. The eldest once went out with some other boys to fish, but the other boys would not have him with them, and said, "Go your way, foundling."

Hereupon he was much troubled, and asked the old fisherman if that was true? The fisherman told him that once when he was fishing he had drawn him out of the water. So the boy said he would go forth and seek his father. The fisherman, however, entreated him to stay, but he would not let himself be hindered, and at last the fisherman consented. Then the boy went on his way and walked for many days, and at last he came to a great body of water by the side of which stood an old woman fishing. "Good day, mother," said the boy.

"Many thanks," said she.

"You will fish long enough before you catch anything."

"And you will seek long enough before you find your father. How will you get over the water?" said the woman.

"God knows."

Then the old woman took him up on her back and carried him through it, and he sought for a long time, but could not find his father.

When a year had gone by, the second boy set out to seek his brother. He came to the water, and all fared with him just as with his brother. And now there was no one at home but the daughter, and she mourned for her brothers so much that at last she also begged the fisherman to let her set forth, for she wished to go in search of her brothers. Then she likewise came to the great body of water, and she said to the old woman, "Good day, mother."

"Many thanks," replied the old woman.

"May God help you with your fishing," said the maiden. When the old woman heard that, she became quite friendly, and carried her over the water, gave her a wand, and said to her, "Go, my daughter, ever onwards by this road, and when you come to a great black dog, you must pass it silently and boldly, without either laughing or looking at it. Then you will come to a great high castle, on the threshold of which you must let the wand fall, and go straight through the castle, and out again on the other side. There you will see an old fountain out of which a large tree has grown, whereon hangs a bird in a cage which you must take down. Take likewise a glass of water out of the fountain, and with these two things go back by the same way. Pick up the wand again from the threshold and take it with you, and when you again pass by the dog, strike him in the face with it, but be sure that you hit him, and then just come back here to me." The maiden found everything exactly as the old woman had said, and on her way back she found her two brothers who had sought each other over half the world. They went together to the place where the black dog was lying on the road; she struck it in the face, and it turned into a handsome prince who went with them to the river. There the old woman was still standing. She rejoiced much to see them again, and carried them all over the water, and then she too went away, for now she was freed. The others, however, went to the old fisherman, and all were glad that they had found each other again, but they hung the bird on the wall.

But the second son could not settle at home, and took his crossbow and went hunting. When he was tired he took his flute, and made music.

The King was hunting too, and heard that and went there, and when he met the youth, he said, "Who has given you leave to hunt here?"

"Oh, no one."

"To whom do you belong, then?"

"I am the fisherman's son."

"But he has no children."

"If you will not believe, come with me."

That the King did, and questioned the fisherman, who told everything to him, and the little bird on the wall began to sing,

> "The mother sits alone
> There in the prison small,
> O King of royal blood,
> These are your children all.
> The sisters both so false,
> They wrought the children woe,
> There in the waters deep
> Where the fishermen come and go."

Then they were all terrified, and the King took the bird, the fisherman and the three children back with him to the castle, and ordered the prison to be opened and brought his wife out again. She had, however, grown quite ill and weak. Then the daughter gave her some of the water of the fountain to drink, and she became strong and healthy. But the two false sisters were burned, and the daughter married the prince.

97. THE WATER OF LIFE

There was once a King who had an illness, and no one believed that he would come out of it with his life. He had three sons who were much distressed about it, and went down into the palace garden and wept. There they met an old man who inquired as to the cause of their grief. They told him that their father was so ill that he would most certainly die, for nothing seemed to cure him. Then the old man said, "I know of one more remedy, and that is the water of life; if he drinks of it he will become well again; but it is hard to find."

The eldest said, "I will manage to find it," and went to the sick King, and begged to be allowed to go forth in search of the water of life, for that alone could save him.

"No," said the King, "the danger of it is too great. I would rather die." But he begged so long that the King consented.

The prince thought in his heart, "If I bring the water, then I shall be best beloved of my father, and shall inherit the Kingdom."

So he set out, and when he had ridden forth a little distance, a dwarf stood there in the road who called to him and said, "Where away so fast?"

"Silly shrimp," said the prince, very haughtily, "it is nothing to do with you," and rode on. But the little dwarf had grown angry, and had wished an evil wish. Soon after this the prince entered a ravine, and the further he rode the closer the mountains drew together, and at last the road became so narrow that he could not advance a step further; it was impossible either to turn his horse or to dismount from the saddle, and he was shut in there as if in prison. The sick King waited long for him, but he did not come.

Then the second son said, "Father, let me go forth to seek the water," and thought to himself, "If my brother is dead, then the Kingdom will fall to me."

At first the King would not allow him to go either, but at last he yielded, so the prince set out on the same road that his brother had taken, and he too met the dwarf, who stopped him to ask, where was he going in such haste? "Little shrimp," said the prince, "that is nothing to you," and rode on without giving him another look. But the dwarf bewitched him, and he, like the other, rode into a ravine, and could neither go forwards nor backwards. So fare haughty people.

As the second son also remained away, the youngest begged to be allowed to go forth to fetch the water, and at last the King was obliged to let him go. When he met the dwarf and the latter asked him where he was going in such haste, he stopped, gave him an explanation, and said, "I am seeking the water of life, for my father is sick unto death."

"Do you know, then, where that is to be found?"

"No," said the prince.

"As you have borne yourself kindly, and not haughtily like your false brothers, I will give you the information and tell you how you may obtain the water of life. It springs from a fountain in the courtyard of an enchanted castle, but you will not be able to make your way to it, if I do not give you an iron wand and two small loaves of bread. Strike thrice with the wand on the iron door of the castle and it will spring open: inside lie two lions with gaping jaws, but if you throw a loaf to each of them, they will be quieted. Then hasten to fetch some of the water of life before the clock strikes twelve, else the door will shut again, and you will be imprisoned."

The prince thanked him, took the wand and the bread, and set out on his way. When he arrived, everything was as the dwarf had said. The door sprang open at the third stroke of the wand, and when he had appeased the lions with the bread, he entered the castle, and came to a large and splendid hall, wherein sat some enchanted princes whose rings he drew off their fingers. A sword and a loaf of bread were lying there, which he carried away. After this, he entered a chamber, in which was a beautiful maiden who rejoiced when she saw him, kissed him, and told him that he had delivered her, and should have the whole of her kingdom, and that if he would return in a year their wedding should be celebrated; likewise she told him where the spring of the water of life was, and that he was to hasten and draw some of it before the clock struck twelve. Then he went onwards, and at last entered a room where there was a beautiful newly-made bed, and as he was very weary, he felt inclined to rest a little. So he lay down and fell asleep.

When he awoke, it was striking a quarter to twelve. He sprang up in a fright, ran to the spring, drew some water in a cup which stood near, and hastened away. But just as he was passing through the iron door, the clock struck twelve, and the door fell to with such violence that it carried away a piece of his heel. He, however, rejoiced at having obtained the water of life, went homewards, and again passed the dwarf.

When the latter saw the sword and the loaf, he said, "With these you have won great wealth; with the sword you can slay whole armies, and the bread will never come to an end."

But the prince would not go home to his father without his brothers, and said, "Dear dwarf, can you not tell me where my two brothers are? They went out before I did in search of the water of life, and have not returned."

"They are imprisoned between two mountains," said the dwarf. "I have condemned them to stay there, because they were so haughty." Then the prince begged until the dwarf released them; but he warned him, however, and said, "Beware of them, for they have bad hearts."

When his brothers came, he rejoiced, and told them how things had gone with him, that he had found the water of life and had brought a cupful away with him, and had rescued a beautiful princess, who was willing to wait a year for him, and then their wedding was to be celebrated and he would obtain a great kingdom. After that they rode on together, and chanced upon a land where war and famine reigned, and the King already thought he must perish, for the scarcity was so great. Then the prince went to him and gave him the loaf, with which he fed and satisfied the whole of his Kingdom, and then the prince gave him the sword too with which he slew the hosts of his enemies, and could now live in rest and peace. The prince then took back his loaf and his sword, and the three brothers rode on. But after this they entered two more countries where war and famine reigned and each time the prince gave his loaf and his sword to the Kings, and had now delivered three kingdoms, and after that they went on board a ship and sailed over the sea.

During the passage, the two eldest conversed apart and said, "The youngest has found the water of life and not we, for that our father will give him the Kingdom the Kingdom which belongs to us, and he will rob us of all our fortune." They then began to seek revenge, and plotted with each other to destroy him. They waited until they found him fast asleep, then they poured the water of life out of the cup, and took it for themselves, but into the cup they poured salt seawater. Now therefore, when they arrived home, the youngest took his cup to the sick King in order that he might drink out of it, and be cured. But scarcely had he drunk a very little of the salt seawater than he became still worse than before. And as he was lamenting over this, the two eldest brothers came, and accused the youngest of having intended to poison him, and said that they had brought him the true water of life, and handed it to him. He had scarcely tasted it, when he felt his sickness departing, and became strong and healthy as in the days of his youth.

After that they both went to the youngest, mocked him, and said, "You certainly found the water of life, but you have had the pain, and we the gain; you should have been sharper, and should have kept your eyes open. We took it from you while you were asleep at sea, and when a year is over, one of us will go and fetch the beautiful princess. But beware that you do not disclose any of this to our father; indeed he does not trust you, and if you say a single word, you shall lose your life into the bargain, but if you keep silent, you shall have it as a gift."

The old King was angry with his youngest son, and thought he had plotted against his life. So he summoned the court together and had sentence pronounced upon his son, that he should be secretly shot. And once when the prince was riding forth to the chase, suspecting no evil, the King's hunter had to go with him, and when they were quite alone in the forest, the hunter looked so sorrowful that the prince said to him, "Dear hunter, what ails you?"

The hunter said, "I cannot tell you, and yet I ought."

Then the prince said, "Say openly what it is, I will pardon you."

"Alas!" said the hunter, "I am to shoot you dead, the King has ordered me to do it."

Then the prince was shocked, and said, "Dear hunter, let me live; there, I give you my royal garments; give me your common ones in their stead."

The hunter said, "I will willingly do that, indeed I should not have been able to shoot you." Then they exchanged clothes, and the hunter returned home; the prince, however, went further into the forest.

After a time three wagons of gold and precious stones came to the King for his youngest son, which were sent by the three Kings who had slain their enemies with the prince's sword, and maintained their people with his bread, and who wished to show their gratitude for it. The old King then thought, "Can my son have been innocent?" and said to his people, "Would that he were still alive, how it grieves me that I have suffered him to be killed!"

"He still lives," said the hunter, "I could not find it in my heart to carry out your command," and told the King how it had happened. Then a stone fell from the King's heart, and he had it proclaimed in every country that his son might return and be taken into favor again.

The princess, however, had a road made up to her palace which was quite bright and golden, and told her people that whoever came riding straight along it to her, would be the right wooer and was to be admitted, and whoever rode by the side of it, was not the right one, and was not to be admitted. As the time was now close at hand, the eldest thought he would hasten to go to the King's daughter, and give himself out as her deliverer, and thus win her for his bride, and the Kingdom to boot. Therefore he rode forth, and when he arrived in front of the palace, and saw the splendid golden road, he thought, it would be a sin and a shame if he were to ride over that, and turned aside, and rode on the right side of it. But when he came to the door, the servants told him that he was not the right man, and was to go away again. Soon after this the second prince set out, and when he came to the golden road, and his horse had put one foot on it, he thought, it would be a sin and a shame to tread a piece of it off, and he turned aside and rode on the left side of it, and when he reached the door, the attendants told him he was not the right one, and he was to go away again. When at last the year had entirely expired, the third son likewise wished to ride out of the forest to his beloved, and with her forget his sorrows. So he set out and thought of her so incessantly, and wished to be with her so much, that he never noticed the golden road at all. So his horse rode onwards up the middle of it, and when he came to the door, it was opened and the princess received him with joy, and said he was her deliverer, and lord of the kingdom, and their wedding was celebrated with great rejoicing. When it was over she told him that his father invited him to come to him, and had forgiven him. So he rode there, and told him everything; how his brothers had betrayed him, and how he had nevertheless kept silence. The old King wished to punish them, but they had gone to sea, and never came back as long as they lived.

98. DOCTOR KNOWALL

There was once on a time a poor peasant called Crabb, who drove with two oxen a load of wood to the town, and sold it to a doctor for two talkers. When the money was being counted out to him, it so happened that the doctor was sitting at table, and when the peasant saw how daintily he ate and drank, his heart desired what he saw, and he would willingly have been a doctor too. So he remained standing a while, and at length inquired if he too could not be a doctor. "Oh, yes," said the doctor, "that is soon managed."

"What must I do?" asked the peasant.

"In the first place buy yourself an ABC book of the kind which has a cock on the frontispiece: in the second, turn your cart and your two oxen into money, and get yourself some clothes, and whatever else pertains to medicine; thirdly, have a sign painted for yourself with the words, "I am Doctor Knowall," and have that nailed up above your door."

The peasant did everything that he had been told to do. When he had doctored people awhile, but not long, a rich and great lord had some money stolen. Then he was told about Doctor Knowall who lived in such and such a village, and must know what had become of the money. So the lord had the horses put in his carriage, drove out to the village, and asked Crabb if he were Doctor Knowall? Yes, he was, he said. Then he was to go with him and bring back the stolen money. "Oh, yes, but Grethe, my wife, must go too." The lord was willing and let both of them have a seat in the carriage, and they all drove away together.

When they came to the nobleman's castle, the table was spread, and Crabb was told to sit down and eat. "Yes, but my wife, Grethe, too," said he, and he seated himself with her at the table. And when the first servant came with a dish of delicate fare, the peasant nudged his wife, and said, "Grethe, that was the first," meaning that was the servant who brought the first dish.

The servant, however, thought he intended by that to say, "That is the first thief," and as he actually was so, he was terrified, and said to his comrade outside, "The doctor knows all: we shall fare ill, he said I was the first."

The second did not want to go in at all, but was forced. So when he went in with his dish, the peasant nudged his wife, and said, "Grethe, that is the second." This servant was just as much alarmed, and he got out. The third did not fare better, for the peasant again said, "Grethe, that is the third." The fourth had to carry in a dish that was covered, and the lord told the doctor that he was to show his skill, and guess what was beneath the cover. The doctor looked at the dish, had no idea what it was, and cried, "Ah, poor Crabb."

When the lord heard that, he cried, "There! He knows it, he knows who has the money!"

On this the servants looked terribly uneasy, and made a sign to the doctor that they wished him to step outside for a moment. When therefore he went out, all four of them confessed to him that they had stolen the money, and said that they would willingly restore it and give him a heavy sum into the bargain, if he would not denounce them, for if he did they would be hanged. They led him to the spot where the money was concealed. With this the doctor was satisfied, and returned to the hall, sat down to the table, and said, "My lord, now I will search in my book where the gold is hidden." The fifth servant, however, crept into the stove to hear if the doctor knew still more. The Doctor, however, sat still and opened his ABC book, turned the pages backwards and forwards, and looked for the cock. As he could not find it immediately he said, "I know you are there, so you had better show yourself."

Then the fellow in the stove thought that the doctor meant him, and full of terror, sprang out, crying, "That man knows everything!" Then Dr. Knowall showed the count where the money was, but did not say who had stolen it, and received from both sides much money in reward, and became a renowned man.

99. *THE SPIRIT IN THE BOTTLE*

There was once a poor woodcutter who toiled from early morning till late night. When at last he had laid by some money he said to his boy, "You are my only child, I will spend the money which I have earned with the sweat of my brow on your education; if you learn some honest trade you can support me in my old age, when my limbs have grown stiff and I am obliged to stay at home." Then the boy went to a high school and learned diligently so that his masters praised him, and he remained there a long time. When he had worked through two classes, but was still not yet perfect in everything, the little pittance which the father had earned was all spent, and the boy was obliged to return home to him.

"Ah," said the father, sorrowfully, "I can give you no more, and in these hard times I cannot earn a farthing more than will suffice for our daily bread."

"Dear father," answered the son, "don't trouble yourself about it, if it is God's will, it will turn to my advantage I shall soon accustom myself to it." When the father wanted to go into the forest to earn money by helping to pile and stack wood and also chop it, the son said, "I will go with you and help you."

"Nay, my son," said the father, "that would be hard for you; you are not accustomed to rough work, and will not be able to bear it, besides I have only one axe and no money left to buy another."

"Just go to the neighbor," answered the son, "he will lend you his axe until I have earned one for myself."

The father then borrowed an axe of the neighbor, and next morning at break of day they went out into the forest together. The son helped his father and was quite merry and brisk about it. But when the sun was right over their heads, the father said, "We will rest, and have our dinner, and then we shall work as well again."

The son took his bread in his hands, and said, "Just you rest, father, I am not tired; I will walk up and down a little in the forest, and look for birds' nests."

"Oh, you fool," said the father, "why should you want to run about there? Afterwards you will be tired, and no longer able to raise your arm; stay here, and sit down beside me."

The son, however, went into the forest, ate his bread, was very merry and peered in among the green branches to see if he could discover a bird's nest anywhere. So he went up and down to see if he could find a bird's nest until at last he came to a great dangerous-looking oak, which certainly was already many hundred years old, and which five men could not have spanned. He stood still and looked at it, and thought, "Many a bird must have built its nest in that."

Then all at once it seemed to him that he heard a voice. He listened and became aware that someone was crying in a very smothered voice, "Let me out, let me out!"

He looked around, but could discover nothing; nevertheless, he fancied that the voice came out of the ground. Then he cried, "Where are you?"

The voice answered, "I am down here among the roots of the oak tree. Let me out! Let me out!"

The scholar began to loosen the earth under the tree, and search among the roots, until at last he found a glass bottle in a little hollow. He lifted it up and held it against the light, and then saw a creature shaped like a frog, springing up and down in it. "Let me out! Let me out!" it cried anew, and the scholar thinking no evil, drew the cork out of the bottle. Immediately a spirit ascended from it, and began to grow, and grew so fast that in a very few moments he stood before the scholar, a terrible fellow as big as half the tree by which he was standing.

"Do you know," he cried in an awful voice, "what your wages are for having let me out?"

"No," replied the scholar fearlessly, "how should I know that?"

"Then I will tell you," cried the spirit; "I must strangle you for it."

"You should have told me that sooner," said the scholar, "for I should then have left you shut up, but my head shall stand fast for all you can do; more persons than one must be consulted about that."

"More persons here, more persons there," said the spirit. "You shall have the wages you have earned. Do you think that I was shut up there for such a long time as a favor? No, it was a punishment for me. I am the mighty Mercurius. Whoever releases me, I must strangle."

"Softly," answered the scholar, "not so fast. I must first know that you really were shut up in that little bottle, and that you are the right spirit. If, indeed, you can get in again, I will believe and then you may do as you will with me."

The spirit said haughtily, "That is a very trifling feat," drew himself together, and made himself as small and slender as he had been at first, so that he crept through the same opening, and right through the neck of the bottle in again. Scarcely was he inside than the scholar thrust the cork he had drawn back into the bottle, and threw it among the roots of the oak into its old place, and the spirit was betrayed.

And now the scholar was about to return to his father, but the spirit cried very piteously, "Ah, do let me out! Ah, do let me out!"

"No," answered the scholar, "not a second time! He who has once tried to take my life shall not be set free by me, now that I have caught him again."

"If you will set me free," said the spirit, "I will give you so much that you will have plenty all the days of your life."

"No," answered the boy, "you would cheat me as you did the first time."

"You are playing away with your own good luck," said the spirit; "I will do you no harm but will reward you richly."

The scholar thought, "I will venture it, perhaps he will keep his word, and anyhow he shall not get the better of me." Then he took out the cork, and the spirit rose up from the bottle as he had done before, stretched himself out and became as big as a giant.

"Now you shall have your reward," said he, and handed the scholar a little bag just like a plaster, and said, "If you spread one end of this over a wound it will heal, and if you rub steel or iron with the other end it will be changed into silver."

"I must just try that," said the scholar, and went to a tree, tore off the bark with his axe, and rubbed it with one end of the plaster. It immediately closed together and was healed. "Now, it is all right," he said to the spirit, "and we can part." The spirit thanked him for his release, and the boy thanked the spirit for his present, and went back to his father.

"Where have you been racing about?" said the father, "Why have you forgotten your work? I said at once that you would never get on with anything."

"Be easy, father, I will make it up."

"Make it up indeed," said the father angrily, "there's no art in that."

"Take care, father, I will soon hew that tree there, so that it will split." Then he took his plaster, rubbed the axe with it, and dealt a mighty blow, but as the iron had changed into silver, the edge turned;

"Hollo, father, just look what a bad axe you've given me, it has become quite crooked."

The father was shocked and said, "Ah, what have you done? Now I shall have to pay for that, and have not the wherewithal, and that is all the good I have got by your work."

"Don't get angry," said the son, "I will soon pay for the axe."

"Oh, you blockhead," cried the father, "with what will you pay for it? You have nothing but what I give you. These are students' tricks that are sticking in your head, but you have no idea of woodcutting."

After a while the scholar said, "Father, I can really work no more, we had better take a holiday."

"Eh, what!" answered he, "Do you think I will sit with my hands lying in my lap like you? I must go on working, but you may take yourself off home."

"Father, I am here in this wood for the first time, I don't know my way alone. Do go with me."

As his anger had now abated, the father at last let himself be persuaded and went home with him. Then he said to the son, "Go and sell your damaged axe, and see what you can get for it, and I must earn the difference, in order to pay the neighbor."

The son took the axe, and carried it into town to a goldsmith, who tested it, laid it in the scales, and said, "It is worth four hundred thalers, I have not so much as that with me."

The son said, "Give me what you have, I will lend you the rest." The goldsmith gave him three hundred thalers, and remained a hundred in his debt. The son thereupon went home and said, "Father, I have got the money, go and ask the neighbor what he wants for the axe."

"I know that already," answered the old man, "one thaler, six groschen."

"Then give him two thalers, twelve groschen, that is double and enough; see, I have money in plenty," and he gave the father a hundred thalers, and said, "You shall never know want, live as comfortably as you like."

"Good heavens!" said the father, "How have you come by these riches?" The scholar then told how all had come to pass, and how he, trusting in his luck, had made such a good hit. But with the money that was left, he went back to the high school and went on learning more, and as he could heal all wounds with his plaster, he became the most famous doctor in the whole world.

100. THE DEVIL'S SOOTY BROTHER

A disbanded soldier had nothing to live on, and did not know how to get on. So he went out into the forest and when he had walked for a short time, he met a little man who was, however, the Devil. The little man said to him, "What ails you, you seem so very sorrowful?"

Then the soldier said, "I am hungry, but have no money."

The Devil said, "If you will hire yourself to me, and be my serving-man, you shall have enough for all your life. You shall serve me for seven years, and after that you shall again be free. But one thing I must tell you, and that is, you must not wash, comb, or trim yourself, or cut your hair or nails, or wipe the water from your eyes."

The soldier said, "All right, if there is no help for it," and went off with the little man, who straightway led him down into hell. Then he told him what he had to do. He was to poke the fire under the kettles wherein the hell-broth was stewing, keep the house clean, drive all the sweepings behind the doors, and see that everything was in order, but if he once peeped into the kettles, it would go ill with him. The soldier said, "Good, I will take care."

And then the old Devil went out again on his wanderings, and the soldier entered upon his new duties, made the fire, and swept the dirt well behind the doors, just as he had been bidden. When the old Devil came back again, he looked to see if all had been done, appeared satisfied, and went forth a second time.

The soldier now took a good look on every side; the kettles were standing all round hell with a mighty fire below them, and inside they were boiling and sputtering. He would have given anything to look inside them, if the Devil had not so particularly forbidden him: at last, he could no longer restrain himself, slightly raised the lid of the first kettle, and peeped in, and there he saw his former corporal shut in. "Aha, old bird!" said he, "Do I meet you here? You once had me in your power, now I have you," and he quickly let the lid fall, poked the fire, and added a fresh log.

After that, he went to the second kettle, raised its lid also a little, and peeped in; his former ensign was in that. "Aha, old bird, so I find you here! You once had me in your power, now I have you." He closed the lid again, and fetched yet another log to make it really hot.

Then he wanted to see who might be sitting up in the third kettle—it was actually a general. "Aha, old bird, do I meet you here? Once you had me in your power, now I have you." And he fetched the bellows and made hell-fire blaze right under him.

So he did his work seven years in hell, did not wash, comb, or trim himself, or cut his hair or nails, or wash the water out of his eyes, and the seven years seemed so short to him that he thought he had only been half a year. Now when the time had fully gone by, the Devil came and said, "Well Hans, what have you done?"

"I poked the fire under the kettles, and I have swept all the dirt well behind the doors."

"But you have peeped into the kettles as well; it is lucky for you that you added fresh logs to them, or else your life would have been forfeited; now that your time is up, will you go home again?"

"Yes," said the soldier, "I should very much like to see what my father is doing at home."

The Devil said, "In order that you may receive the wages you have earned, go and fill your knapsack full of the sweepings, and take it home with you. You must also go unwashed and uncombed, with long hair on your head and beard, and with uncut nails and dim eyes, and when you are asked where you are from, you must say, "From hell," and when you are asked who you are, you are to say, "The Devil's sooty brother, and my King as well."

The soldier held his peace, and did as the Devil bade him, but he was not at all satisfied with his wages. Then as soon as he was up in the forest again, he took his knapsack from his back, to empty it, but on opening it, the sweepings had become pure gold. "I should never have expected that," said he, and was well pleased, and entered the town.

The landlord was standing in front of the inn, and when he saw the soldier approaching, he was terrified, because Hans looked so horrible, worse than a scarecrow. He called to him and asked, "Where do you come from?"

"From hell."

"Who are you?"

"The Devil's sooty brother, and my King as well."

Then the host would not let him enter, but when Hans showed him the gold, he came and unlatched the door himself. Hans then ordered the best room and attendance, ate, and drank his fill, but neither washed nor combed himself as the Devil had bidden him, and at last lay down to sleep. But the knapsack full of gold remained before the eyes of the landlord, and left him no peace, and during the night he crept in and stole it away.

Next morning, however, when Hans got up and wanted to pay the landlord and travel further, his knapsack was gone! But he soon composed himself and thought, "You have been unfortunate from no fault of your own," and straightway went back again to hell, complained of his misfortune to the old Devil, and begged for his help.

The Devil said, "Seat yourself, I will wash, comb, and trim you, cut your hair and nails, and wash your eyes for you," and when he had done with him, he gave him the knapsack back again full of sweepings, and said, "Go and tell the landlord that he must return you your money, or else I will come and fetch him, and he shall poke the fire in your place."

· Hans went up and said to the landlord, "You have stolen my money; if you do not return it, you shall go down to hell in my place, and will look as horrible as I." Then the landlord gave him the money, and more besides, only begging him to keep it secret, and Hans was now a rich man.

He set out on his way home to his father, bought himself a shabby smock-frock to wear, and strolled about making music, for he had learned to do that while he was with the Devil in hell. There was however, an old King in that country, before whom he had to play, and the King was so delighted with his playing, that he promised him his eldest daughter in marriage. But when she heard that she was to be married to a common fellow in a smock-frock, she said, "Rather than do that, I would go into the deepest water."

Then the King gave him the youngest, who was quite willing to do it to please her father, and thus the Devil's sooty brother got the King's daughter, and when the aged King died, the whole Kingdom likewise.

101. BEARSKIN

There was once a young fellow who enlisted as a soldier, conducted himself bravely, and was always the foremost when it rained bullets. So long as the war lasted, all went well, but when peace was made, he received his dismissal, and the captain said he might go where he liked. His parents were dead, and he had no longer a home, so he went to his brothers and begged them to take him in, and keep him until war broke out again. The brothers, however, were hardhearted and said, "What can we do with you? You are of no use to us; go and make a living for yourself."

The soldier had nothing left but his gun; he took that on his shoulder, and went forth into the world. He came to a wide heath, on which nothing was to be seen but a circle of trees; under these he sat sorrowfully down, and began to think over his fate. "I have no money," thought he, "I have learned no trade but that of fighting, and now that they have made peace they don't want me any longer; so I see beforehand that I shall have to starve."

All at once he heard a rustling, and when he looked round, a strange man stood before him, who wore a green coat and looked right stately, but had a hideous cloven foot. "I know already what you are in need of," said the man; "gold and possessions you shall have, as much as you can make away with, do what you will, but first I must know if you are fearless, that I may not bestow my money in vain."

"A soldier and fear—how can those two things go together?" he answered; "You can put me to the proof."

"Very well, then," answered the man, "look behind you." The soldier turned round, and saw a large bear, which came growling towards him.

"Oho!" cried the soldier, "I will tickle your nose for you, so that you shall soon lose your fancy for growling," and he aimed at the bear and shot it through the muzzle; it fell down and never stirred again.

"I see quite well," said the stranger, "that you are not wanting in courage, but there is still another condition which you will have to fulfill."

"If it does not endanger my salvation," replied the soldier, who knew very well who was standing by him. "If it does, I'll have nothing to do with it."

"You will look to that for yourself," answered Greencoat; "you shall for the next seven years neither wash yourself, nor comb your beard, nor your hair, nor cut your nails, nor say one paternoster. I will give you a coat and a cloak, which during this time you must wear. If you die during these seven years, you are mine; if you remain alive, you are free, and rich to boot, for all the rest of your life." The soldier thought of the great extremity in which he now found himself, and as he so often had gone to meet death, he resolved to risk it now also, and agreed to the terms. The Devil took off his green coat, gave it to the soldier, and said, "If you have this coat on your back and put your hand into the pocket, you will always find it full of money." Then he pulled the skin off the bear and said, "This shall be your cloak, and your bed also, for on this you shall sleep, and in no other bed shall you lie, and because of this apparel you shall be called Bearskin." After this the Devil vanished.

The soldier put the coat on, felt at once in the pocket, and found that the thing was really true. Then he put on the bearskin and went forth into the world, and enjoyed himself, refraining from nothing that did him good and his money harm. During the first year his appearance was passable, but during the second he began to look like a monster. His hair covered nearly the whole of his face, his beard was like a piece of coarse felt, his fingers had claws, and his face was so covered with dirt that if cress had been sown on it, it would have grown. Whoever saw him, ran away, but as he always gave the poor money to pray that he might not die during the seven years, and as he paid well for everything he still always found shelter. In the fourth year, he entered an inn where the landlord would not receive him, and would not even let him have a place in the stable, because he was afraid the horses would be scared. But as Bearskin thrust his hand into his pocket and pulled out a handful of ducats, the host let himself be persuaded and gave him a room in an outhouse. Bearskin was, however, obliged to promise not to let himself be seen, lest the inn should get a bad name.

As Bearskin was sitting alone in the evening, and wishing from the bottom of his heart that the seven years were over, he heard a loud lamenting in a neighboring room. He had a compassionate heart, so he opened the door, and saw an old man weeping bitterly, and wringing his hands. Bearskin went nearer, but the man sprang to his feet and tried to escape from him. At last when the man perceived that Bearskin's voice was human he let himself be prevailed on, and by kind words bearskin succeeded so far that the old man revealed the cause of his grief. His property had dwindled away by degrees, he and his daughters would have to starve, and he was so poor that he could not pay the innkeeper, and was to be put in prison. "If that is your only trouble," said Bearskin, "I have plenty of money." He had the innkeeper brought there, paid him and put a purse full of gold into the poor old man's pocket besides.

When the old man saw himself set free from all his troubles he did not know how to be grateful enough. "Come with me," said he to Bearskin; "my daughters are all miracles of beauty, choose one of them for yourself as a wife. When she hears what you have done for me, she will not refuse you. You do in truth look a little strange, but she will soon put you to rights again." This pleased Bearskin well, and he went.

When the eldest saw him she was so terribly alarmed at his face that she screamed and ran away. The second stood still and looked at him from head to foot, but then she said, "How can I accept a husband who no longer has a human form? The shaven bear that once was here and passed itself off for a man pleased me far better, for at any rate it wore a hussar's dress and white gloves. If it were nothing but ugliness, I might get used to that."

The youngest, however, said, "Dear father, that must be a good man to have helped you out of your trouble, so if you have promised him a bride for doing it, your promise must be kept."

It was a pity that Bearskin's face was covered with dirt and with hair, for if not they might have seen how delighted he was when he heard these words. He took a ring from his finger, broke it in two, and gave her one half, the other he kept for himself. He wrote his name, however, on her half, and hers on his, and begged her to keep her piece carefully, and then he took his leave and said, "I must still wander about for three years, and if I do not return then, you are free, for I shall be dead. But pray to God to preserve my life."

The poor betrothed bride dressed herself entirely in black, and when she thought of her future bridegroom, tears came into her eyes. Nothing but contempt and mockery fell to her lot from her sisters. "Take care," said the eldest, "if you give him your hand, he will strike his claws into it."

"Beware!" said the second. "Bears like sweet things, and if he takes a fancy to you, he will eat you up."

"You must always do as he likes," began the elder again, "or else he will growl."

And the second continued, "But the wedding will be a merry one, for bears dance well."

The bride was silent, and did not let them vex her. Bearskin, however, traveled about the world from one place to another, did good where he was able, and gave generously to the poor that they might pray for him.

At length, as the last day of the seven years dawned, he went once more out onto the heath, and seated himself beneath the circle of trees. It was not long before the wind whistled, and the Devil stood before him and looked angrily at him; then he threw Bearskin his old coat, and asked for his own green one back. "We have not got so far as that yet," answered Bearskin, "you must first make me clean." Whether the Devil liked it or not, he was forced to fetch water, and wash Bearskin, comb his hair, and cut his nails. After this, he looked like a brave soldier, and was much handsomer than he had ever been before.

When the Devil had gone away, Bearskin was quite lighthearted. He went into the town, put on a magnificent velvet coat, seated himself in a carriage drawn by four white horses, and drove to his bride's house. No one recognized him, the father took him for a distinguished general, and led him into the room where his daughters were sitting. He was forced to place himself between the two eldest, they helped him to wine, gave him the best pieces of meat, and thought that in all the world they had never seen a handsomer man. The bride, however, sat opposite to him in her black dress, and never raised her eyes, nor spoke a word. When at length he asked the father if he would give him one of his daughters to wed, the two eldest jumped up, and ran into their bedrooms to put on splendid dresses, for each of them fancied she was the chosen one. The stranger, as soon as he was alone with his bride, brought out his half of the ring, and threw it in a glass of wine which he reached across the table to her. She took the wine, but when she had drunk it, and found the half ring lying at the bottom, her heart began to beat. She got the other half, which she wore on a ribbon round her neck, joined them, and saw that the two pieces fitted exactly together. Then said he, "I am your betrothed bridegroom, whom you saw as Bearskin, but through God's grace I have again received my human form, and have once more become clean." He went up to her, embraced her, and gave her a kiss.

In the meantime the two sisters came back in full dress, and when they saw that the handsome man had fallen to the share of the youngest, and heard that he was Bearskin, they ran out full of anger and rage. One of them drowned herself in the well, the other hanged herself on a tree. In the evening, someone knocked at the door, and when the bridegroom opened it, it was the Devil in his green coat, who said, "You see, I have now got two souls in the place of your one!"